Shhhh...

Murder!

Edited by
Andrew MacRae

DARKHOUSE
BOOKS

Anthology copyright © 2018 by Darkhouse Books
ISBN 978-1-945467-14-1
Published September, 2018
Published in the United States of America

Darkhouse Books
160 J Street, #2223
Niles, California 94539

Shhhh... *Murder!*
Table of Contents

Continued on following page.

Shhhh... *Murder!*
Table of Contents

Continued on following page.

Shhhh... *Murder!*
Table of Contents

Introduction

by Andrew MacRae

Nothing sickens me more than the closed door of a library.
   –Barbara Tuchman

Something many writers share is a love for libraries, and had we any doubts, they were easily dispatched by the subsequent overflowing of our submissions hopper after we put out a call for crime stories featuring libraries and librarians.

How many of our readers, and writers, can recall the finger technique for riffling fast through a tray of the cards? Or the serendipitous discovery of a book or author, totally unrelated to your search, whose card just happened to be adjacent to the book you sought?

I freely admit to a fondness for the libraries of old. When young, I spent so much time at our public library that our mother would regularly have to telephone and ask that I be sent home for supper. And then there was the thrill of finally receiving a card that allowed me to check out books from the grownup stacks upstairs, no longer restricted to the children's section.

Yet, I also enjoy the amenities of modern libraries. I sit at a table in one now, as this is written. In only a minute's time I was able to hop onto the Internet and look up the Barbara Tuchman quotation at the start of this introduction. Thirty years ago, that search would have required combing through massive tomes of collected quotations.

Some of the stories selected for our anthology are set in present day, replete with Internet workstations and racks of DVDs. Others are set firmly in the era of elegant card catalogs, polished like fine furniture. Settings for our stories include public libraries, private libraries, research libraries, and even the Vatican Library. Our book offers up a smorgasbord of librarians, as well, and you will be hard-pressed to find even one who takes after the popular public image of those who work in that profession.

So, settle yourself in your favorite chair, make yourself comfortable, and dive into the world of Shhhh… *Murder!*

Andrew MacRae
September, 2018
Niles, California

We open our anthology with a boisterous tale that begins when a librarian discovers a body in her library. But Bronte will brook no bad behavior, and sets out to bag the bad guy.

Longtime friends, authors Deborah Lacy and Pat Hernas relate the first of a series relating the rollicking adventures of Bronte Williams: Librarian & Crime Solver.

Wuthering Stacks

by Deborah Lacy and Pat Hernas

The last thing Brontë Williams expected when she asked the shelving team to arrive early to work that day was to find one of them dead. Now, she didn't quite know what to do.

When she first saw all of the torn pages on the floor, she thought a goat had been let loose in the library again. A favorite nighttime prank of Agriculture majors, it happened every quarter, right about the time the students got bored with cow tipping. Piermont College could brag of many advantages, but being located two hours outside of Sacramento, California, a rich and varied social life was not one of them.

Someone or something had attacked these poor books with gusto and, today was the worst possible day that a mess like this could happen. Her concern about the mess vanished when she saw Greg buried under a pile of torn books, passed out with his mouth open and his tongue hanging at a weird angle.

Books went flying as she pulled them off him, so she could take his pulse. When she saw the white iPhone cord wrapped around his neck and the thick red mark it had left, it occurred to her that there might not be a pulse. His neck felt clammy. She hoped if she starred at his chest that it would rise and fall proving her wrong, but it stayed as still and silent. She fought panic, telling herself to be calm for Greg, but he didn't have a pulse. He didn't need anyone to be calm for him any more.

9-1-1. She had to call 9-1-1, but she'd dropped her phone among the torn books and had no idea where it landed. She didn't want to leave him alone to walk all the way to the Circulation Desk to use the landline.

Greg loved to tease her with quotes from the Brontë sisters' books, just yesterday he'd quoted Jane Eyre, "Life appears to me too short to be spent in nursing animosity or registering wrongs," after he snagged the last chicken salad sandwich from the catering truck, knowing full well that she wanted it.

Yes, Greg. Life appears too short. She closed his glassy eyes and said a quick prayer.

The library would, of course, have to be closed at least for the day, probably longer. The police would need to see the scene exactly as she'd found it, or exactly as she'd left it once she stopped trying to help him. She'd have to call Janet Myers and cancel the presentation. After months and months of delivering on Mrs. Myers' every request, she had no doubt the woman would take her million dollar donation elsewhere. Which meant, now she would have to lay off half the staff.

The torn books were from the art collection that had recently been left to the little college library by Mr. Reynolds, a local man who loved art and loved books. The dear old man had left the library more than a thousand art books, some famous, some signed, most of them with amazing illustrations, spanning from the late 1800s to the early 1900s. At least twenty of them were ruined, strewn about the floor. If this collection was the cause of Greg's death, she wished they'd never accepted it.

She heard the front door to the library open. "Who's there?"

"It's Agnes and Shirley," Agnes called, "We're here to help prepare for presentation, as if there is a question Mrs. Myers could possibly ask that she hasn't already," she said, in her Irish accent.

"Stay there," Bronte said as firmly as she could. Brontë could tell from the footsteps that they weren't listening. She removed her blue cardigan sweater and put it over Greg's face. The least she could was spare both of them the sight of a dead colleague.

"Is that Greg lying on the floor under your sweater?," Shirley said. "Are you sleeping with my boyfriend? *on the library floor!*"

"Let's discuss this in my office," Bronte held her hand up and walked towards them.

"I told you he was having an affair. I knew it!"

"Sleeping he's not," Agnes said and she didn't look surprised, or shocked or sad. "She's covered him up like my Ma covered up my dog when he accidentally drank anti-freeze. Sweater over the face. You don't do that if someone is still alive."

Shirley screamed.

The sound echoed through the library.

"You killed him!" she screeched. "For stealing books?"

Brontë stood there stunned. "What? No."

"Just because he sold our oldest copy of Anne Brontë's *The Tenant of Wildfell Hall.*"

"I wondered where that went," Brontë said forgetting herself for a moment. The books of Anne Bronte were often overlooked because they aren't as well known as those of Emily and Charlottte. In fact, Agnes herself shared the same name as the first novel written by Anne Brontë, but she seemed unaware of that fact.

"She didn't kill him," Agnes said, putting her arm around her friend who had started to cry softly. "Not the killing type. And certainly not for stealing a book worth less than a hundred dollars."

"So then who did then?" she said through her tears.

Brontë wanted to know too, and she also wanted to know how Agnes knew the precise value of that book. That was a remarkable piece of information for a new hire to have.

"We need to call the police. Do either of you have your cell phones?"

"My phone battery is dead, but I can go to the desk and do it."

The library door opened, the sound echoing through the stacks. Clearly the girls had forgotten to lock the door behind them.

"Um, we're not open yet," Brontë called.

"No worries," a male voice said, the footsteps getting closer. "I'm here to see Greg."

All three of them froze and looked at one another.

"Greg's indisposed at the moment, maybe you could come back later."

Agnes picked up a one of the old, sturdy wooden chairs and when the man walked from behind a shelf she whacked him over the head with it. He fell to the ground unconscious.

"What did you do that for?" Brontë found herself kneeling down to check for a pulse the second time that morning.

"He killed Greg," Shirley said, "Calls himself, The Professor. He bought the stolen library books and Greg wouldn't get him more expensive ones, so he killed him."

"He's alive, that's something. Do you know his real name?"

Shirley shook her head "I think we should tie him up with duck tape," Shirley suggested.

"He's already unconscious. It's not necessary."

"Why would he kill his source for books and then come back to the library as if he had an appointment with Greg?" Agnes asked. "It doesn't make sense."

"He did it to trick us," Shirley said.

"We really need to call 9-1-1," Brontë said. "Agnes, call them now."

Finally, Agnes did as she was told and headed for the Circulation Desk.

"Greg only stole entire books that weren't being checked out, never cut pages out to sell the illustrations and he never took anything that was actively in circulation," Shirley said.

"But the torn pages on the floor," Brontë said. "If he didn't cut books, why are there torn pages on the floor?"

Shirley continued defending Greg as if she hadn't heard the question, "And he never took a book that was worth more than one hundred dollars. The Professor wanted him to steal books from Mr. Reynolds collection, but Greg wouldn't do it. He said you have to have boundaries. He was only trying to get by. Since the pay cuts. Our rent is the same but our salaries aren't."

"You get paid about the same as he did, and you don't steal books," she said.

Shirley shrugged her shoulders, "It's harder for a man to economize."

Brontë wondered if Shirley was telling the truth. Now that she thought about it, there had been a lot of books missing lately, and many of the books were worth considerably more than one hundred dollars. Brontë thought it was a glitch in the new checkout software, but now she wondered if someone else was stealing books, too. No one on staff deserved the cuts, but the dean wanted to spend the money on some kind of new technology for the science lab, said we needed it for enrollment. At the time, she reasoned it would be better to cut everyone's pay than lay anyone off. Now she wondered if she had made the right choice.

She thought about the iPhone cord around Greg's neck. One shouldn't think ill of the dead. Then she realized that Greg didn't have an iPhone. He'd been saving for one, but had to be content with an old Samsung his Mom gave him. She'd have to tell the police that the killer probably had an iPhone.

She wished she knew where she'd dropped her own cell phone among the books.

Agnes returned from the desk, "Paramedics are on their way."

"And the police?"

She nodded, "I'm hope'n they get here fast."

"I need to call Mrs. Myers, and tell her not to come today."

"All those months of works, pulling books and books from the stacks for her, all for nothing," Agnes said. "That woman must have touched every book in the entire place."

Shirley pulled her cell phone and handed it to Brontë to make the call. It was an iPhone.

"If you had your phone on you, why did you make me go to the desk?" Agnes asked her.

Shirley shrugged her shoulders. It was a little odd.

The library door squeaked open again. She'd forgotten to ask Agnes to lock it, or perhaps she'd mistakenly thought that Agnes could think for herself.

Shirley picked up another chair.

Brontë reached for the leg and gently pulled it out of Shirley's hands before she could knock someone else out and quietly put it on the floor. She shook her head at Shirley.

"Helllllloooo!" called a women's voice Janet Myers, the woman that she hoped could save the library. "This is so exciting that I came early! Couldn't help myself. I hope that's okay."

She looked at the two men lying prone on the library floor. Nothing was okay.

Brontë looked up at her favorite quotation. She'd painted it on the wall this past summer.

"Silence is of different kinds, and breathes different meanings."
—Charlotte Brontë, *Villette*

She wished she could be silent on a great many subjects, but today she would have to tell Janet Myers the truth.

"Stay here," she instructed Agnes and Shirley. "I mean it."

Brontë walked to the front of the library. "Hello, Janet," she said, "We've had a little accident here in the library and I'm afraid we're going have to postpone the presentation. I'm so sorry for the inconvenience."

"An accident?" she asked, visibly upset. "What kind of accident?

The library door opened yet again, and two male paramedics rushed in. "Where's the unconscious male?" A tall blond man asked.

"Unconscious male?" Janet asked.

"Janet, we're going to have to reschedule."

Brontë led the paramedics back to the stacks where "The Professor" still lay on the floor.

Shirley picked up another chair, "Shirley!" Brontë yelled. It was enough of a warning for the tall paramedic to catch one of the chair legs on the way down.

"What the hell?" the tall one said, setting the chair down and grabbed both of her wrists. Shirley didn't fight as the paramedic wrapped her hands together with white medical tape.

"Why did you do that?"

"How do we know they're really paramedics? They could be imposters here to steal Greg's body."

"Agnes, take Shirley to my office."

"She's going to have to wait right here, ma'am," said the tall paramedic as he took The Professor's vital signs. "Where we can see her. The police will want to talk to her."

"Greg's body?" The voice belonged to Janet Myers. "He's been murdered?"

Brontë studied Janet. No one had said that Greg was murdered. Maybe she guessed that from Shirley's remark. Her imagination was going into overdrive. The police would be here soon. They would figure out what happened.

But still.

"Janet, can I borrow your iPhone?"

The woman pulled her phone out of her purse and handed it to Brontë. This didn't prove anything. Millions of people have iPhones. She twirled the phone in her hand while she was thinking.

"Aren't you going to make a call?"

She nodded and dialed the Dean's office number. Voice mail picked up. She wasn't about to tell him a library employee was dead in a voice mail, so she asked him to come to the library as soon as he got the message. She handed the phone back to Janet, and saw Shirley pushing her chair back away from the paramedics. Was she guilty and trying to get away? She'd been behaving really strangely all week.

"Shirley," she said, hoping that calling her name out would stop her from pushing the chair back further. Out of the corner of her eye she saw Mrs. Myers handle one of the illustrations torn from the library books. Then the woman stuck it in her purse.

"What are you doing, Janet?"

"This illustration is so lovely and the book was already ruined, I thought I'd take it home and get it framed."

Brontë reached for the illustration and Janet pulled it away from her. Even from this distance, she could see that it had blood on it, and that there was a rather large scrape on Janet's hand. "One little drawing isn't too much to ask, is it? After all, I am donating millions."

"But is she?" asked Shirley. "Months, and months, and months of making us pull out book after book, after book. What else could you possibly need to know before you donate the money? You have the entire staff at your beck and call."

Agnes walked up to the woman and tugged at her hair. The red hair came away, revealing a short blonde haircut.

The Professor, revived by the efforts of the emergency team, sat up and looked at her, "That's Barbara Cardiff, The Book Ripper. I'd know her anywhere, book rippers are the worst in the world, destroying beautiful old volumes, with no respect for books, only money."

"Greg must have caught her in the act, and she killed him," Shirley exclaimed.

"That's ridiculous," Janet said, stepping back. "I'll come back later when you people have calmed down and we can reschedule the presentation."

"Besides, you don't need her money," The Professor said, "Twenty of these pages on the floor, and a few of Mr. Reynolds books, and that would set this library up for decades. That's why The Book Ripper has been mining the place."

Brontë didn't even think about it. She just picked up the closest wooden chair and whacked Janet Myers over the head.

Michael Bracken tells us the source of his story is in his childhood, when bookmobiles played a major role. It's set in Quarryville, Texas, the small town setting of many of his stories. While we always welcome stories by Michael, this particular story touched us greatly.

Mr. Bracken has received numerous awards for his writing, including the Edward D. Hoch Memorial Golden Derringer Award. His work has been published in every major mystery and crime publication, as well as most of the minor ones.

Mr. Sugarman Visits the Bookmobile

by Michael Bracken

When the bookmobile pulled to the curb outside the boarded-up Woolworth in Quarryville, Texas, Tuesday morning, Graham Sugarman was the only patron awaiting its nine a.m. arrival. As the librarian—a wide-hipped brunette in her mid-forties who doubled as the bookmobile's driver—opened the door and saw Graham standing there, she adjusted her scarf and said, "Good morning, Mr. Sugarman."

Graham thrust five books into her hands and followed her inside. Because the library imposed a five-book limit and the book-mobile visited Quarryville only once each week, Graham's returned books were thick as bricks, chosen for their heft rather than their subject matter because there was little else for him to do but read.

Quarryville, a dried-out scab of a town in West Texas, had once shipped granite east to Dallas. After the quarry closed in the early 1950s, the town began a long, slow slide into oblivion that only recently reversed course. Though many of the storefronts along Main Street were still boarded up, a pawnshop, a Texaco, and the ubiquitous Dairy Queen showed signs of life. At the far end of Main Street, a converted Conoco Station transformed into the Quarryville Smokehouse drew a steady stream of visitors after being named one of the best barbecue joints in Texas. This had sparked a rebirth on Main Street, and an antiques shop and an art gallery were scheduled to open within the month. For the previous several weeks, workmen had been in and out of the two buildings that shared the block with the boarded-up Woolworth.

"I have *Infinite Jest*," the librarian said, "and I found a copy of *Sironia, Texas*, through inter-library loan. I also thought you might like *The Stand* and—"

She stopped abruptly and backed away from the open door. Graham barely noticed that the librarian was staring over his shoulder at someone or something outside the bookmobile. More concerned with selecting his reading material for the coming week, he thumbed through the top book in the stack of books she had selected for him.

"I—I'm sorry," she said. "Where was I?"

Graham held up a copy of *Gone with the Wind*. "I've already read this."

"You have?" she asked. She glanced toward the windshield and then refocused her attention on Graham. "I'm sorry. You're such a voracious reader, I can't remember everything you've checked out."

"If I was allowed more books—"

"I wish I could let you check out more books, Mr. Sugarman, but the rules are the rules," she said. "Maybe there's something on the shelf?"

"I'll look."

While Graham searched every shelf for a book to replace *Gone with the Wind*, the librarian kept glancing out the windshield. He finally returned with a short story anthology titled *By Hook or by Crook*.

She had already removed *Gone with the Wind* from his stack, and he replaced it with his new selection before shoving the books across the tiny counter to her.

"Have any plans for the day?" the librarian asked.

Graham stared at her for a moment before answering. "Same as always," he said. "I plan to read."

"Oh, yes, of course," she replied as she processed each of the books. "Seems a shame, though, to spend the day inside. I hear the weather's supposed to be quite pleasant."

Graham just grunted in response. He didn't understand why the librarian was talking so much. When she finished checking out his books, he scooped them into his arms, exited the bookmobile, and walked home.

He lived in a two-bedroom bungalow on the other side of the railroad tracks that paralleled the state highway bisecting Quarryville, in a neighborhood of single-family homes constructed for quarry employees during the town's heyday. The streets lacked curbs and the chip seal roads fought a losing battle against encroaching lawns. During his walk, Graham realized the librarian was right about the weather. As soon as he returned home, he opened all the windows so he could enjoy the cross-breeze while he read.

Then he opened a Dr Pepper, settled into his favorite chair, and opened *The Stand.*

Three hours later, a pot-bellied deputy sheriff parked his cruiser on the street in front of Graham's house, hitched up his pants, and moseyed up to the porch where his insistent knock interrupted Graham halfway through page 127.

Graham marked his place with a finger between the pages before answering the door. "Yes?"

The deputy introduced himself and then said, "I'm sorry to be the one to tell you this, but Alice Boyette's been killed."

Graham stared at the deputy without comprehension. "Do I know her?"

"That book in your hand," the deputy said, "you get it from the bookmobile this morning?"

Graham glanced down at *The Stand* and then looked back at the deputy. "Yes."

"Miss Boyette's the one who drove the bookmobile."

"She was always nice."

"I'm sure she was," the deputy said. "How did she seem this morning when you visited her?"

"She tried to give me a book I had already read."

"Did that upset you?"

"No. I found another." Graham abruptly disappeared inside the house and returned a moment later holding *By Hook or by Crook*. "This one."

"So, Miss Boyette seemed all right to you?"

"She talked too much."

"Talked too much?" the deputy asked. "What do you mean?"

"She asked about my day," Graham said. "She talked about the weather."

"That wasn't like her?"

"I needed to come home."

The deputy asked a few more questions, realized Graham's answers provided no usable information, and thanked Graham for his time. As the deputy returned to his cruiser, Graham returned to his favorite chair and resumed reading.

The following Tuesday, Graham stood at the curb in front of the boarded-up Woolworth and waited thirty minutes for the bookmobile to arrive. Finally, a recent high-school graduate who worked the morning shift left the Dairy Queen and joined him.

"The bookmobile ain't coming today, Mr. Sugarman," she said. "It might never come back."

"But—"

"Why don't you come on inside and I can get you a dip cone."

Graham stared up the highway for a moment before he turned and followed the young woman.

"We're not open yet," said the new assistant manager, a young man who had moved from Chicken Junction after he accepted the job a week earlier.

"We are for Mr. Sugarman."

She made Graham a small dip cone and didn't charge him for it. He sat in a booth by the window watching the highway as he ate, careful not to drip vanilla ice cream on the five library books he had intended to return that morning.

Graham could hear their conversation but paid no attention to it.

The new assistant manager lowered his voice. "What's special about him?"

"Mr. Sugarman ain't been the same since the accident."

"What accident?"

"He was the one driving the school bus during that big storm a couple of years ago, the one that went off the bridge into Devil's Canyon Creek," she explained. "He saved the two kids that was on the bus with him, but he was under the water a long time before they pulled him out."

"So, he was some kind of hero," the new assistant manager said. "That don't mean you can hand out free food."

"You better talk to the owner about that. He said Mr. Sugarman can have a dip cone anytime he likes," she said. "One of them kids was his."

Graham finished his dip cone, wiped his lips and fingers with a tiny napkin, gathered up his library books, and walked home. Once there, he was at a loss for what to do. He had read all five books and he never read the same book twice.

After pacing his living room several times, he examined his library card. He located the phone number for the county library's main branch and used the phone mounted on the kitchen wall to call the number.

A young woman answered. "Arroyo County Library. How may I direct your call?"

"Where's the bookmobile?"

"I'll connect you to the library director."

Innocuous hold music filled his ear, interrupted a moment later by another woman's voice.

The library director introduced herself and said, "I understand you have a question about the bookmobile."

"Where is it?"

"This is Tuesday," she said, "so you must be in Quarryville, Mr.—" When Graham did not provide his last name, the library director cleared her throat and continued. "We've been at a loss since the untimely death of Alice Boyette. We've all been struggling to—"

"The bookmobile. Where's the bookmobile?"

"We've had to put the community outreach program on hold," the library director explained. "The sheriff has impounded the bookmobile as a crime scene and, even if he were to release it, none of our employees have a Commercial Driver's License."

"No bookmobile."

"I'm sorry sir."

"How will I get my books?"

"Can you drive?"

He could, but he didn't.

"If you'll provide me with your name," the library director said, "I'll see if there's some way we can accommodate your needs."

"Graham Sugarman."

He heard, but did comprehend her sharp intake of breath. After moment of silence, she said, "You were the last person to see Alice alive."

That evening, a knock roused Graham from a lethargic state and he opened the front door to find a gray-haired woman near his own age standing on his porch holding five thick paperbacks. He said, "Yes?"

"Mr. Sugarman?" the woman said. "I'm Beth Wilson, from the county library."

"You want your books back?"

"Well, actually, I brought these for you." She held out the five paperbacks. "We can trade."

He took them from her hand and looked at the titles. "I haven't read these."

"Oh, good," Beth said, seeming relieved. "Alice told me you didn't like to reread books, so when I found these I reviewed your history to ensure that you hadn't ever checked them out."

"I'll get your books."

As he turned away, she stopped him. "Mr. Sugarman? May I come in?"

"Why?"

"Well, this is embarrassing, but I drank a large Dr Pepper on the drive down from Chicken Junction and I need to use the bathroom."

Graham examined her for a moment and then stepped out of the doorway to let her pass. "End of the hall."

When Beth returned to the living room a few minutes later, Graham was sitting in his favorite chair, one of the new books open in his hand and the other four on the coffee table next to the five he had tried to return that morning. He pointed to them and said, "I'm done with those. You can take them."

Instead of picking up the stack of library books, Beth surprised him by settling onto the couch. He closed the paperback he was reading and stared at her.

"Alice talked about you all the time," Beth said. "She told us how much you enjoyed reading and how you were always the first in line for the bookmobile when she came to Quarryville."

Graham didn't respond.

"When the director told us you'd phoned this morning, I volunteered to select some books for you and bring them down."

"Why?"

"Why?" Beth repeated. "Good customer service, I suppose, and because I wouldn't want a regular library patron like yourself to think we don't care. We do. More than you might think. You see, if we lose too many more of our outlying patrons, we'll lose funding for the bookmobile and won't be able to service patrons like you."

"You already lost the bookmobile."

"Because it's been impounded? That's only temporary. The sheriff will catch Alice's killer and then we'll get the bookmobile back."

"When?"

"When what?"

"When will he catch Alice's killer and when will you get the bookmobile back?"

"Oh, soon," Beth said. "Real soon."

Even though Beth told him not to expect the bookmobile the following Tuesday, Graham arrived in front of the boarded-up Woolworth at nine a.m., five thick paperbacks in hand, and waited. He did not stare up the highway as he had the previous Tuesday. Instead, he stood with his back to the road and stared first at the boarded-up Woolworth and then at the other two buildings on the block. The artist's studio opened the previous day but renovations to the building that would house the antiques shop had not yet been completed. Graham watched two men clamber out of a pick-up truck parked at the end of the block. He had seen them several times before, including the morning of the librarian's murder.

"Hey, Dumbo," one of the men called to him. "Your girl-friend's not coming today."

"That isn't nice."

Graham turned to see the young woman from the Dairy Queen addressing the men.

She insisted, "You take that back."

The two men laughed at her and went inside.

When they were gone, she turned to Graham and said, "The bookmobile isn't coming today."

"I know," Graham said.

"Then why are you standing here?"

"I do this every Tuesday."

"Come on inside," she said. "I'll get you a dip cone."

Graham followed her into the Dairy Queen and waited at the counter while she prepared his dip cone under the watchful eye of the new assistant manager. When she handed him the cone, Graham said, "He doesn't like me."

"He doesn't like to give food away."

"I can pay."

"I know," she said, "but you don't have to. You know that."

Graham took his dip cone and his library books to the table by the window and watched the workmen going in and out of the antiques store. When he turned just so, he saw a reflection of the interior of the Dairy Queen and he caught sight of the assistant manager glaring at him.

He finished his cone, wiped his fingers and lips, and headed home.

Beth's knuckles had barely touched Graham's front door before he snatched it open, surprising her. She dropped three of the five novels she held in her arms, and she quickly stooped to retrieve the books.

"Have you read any of these, Mr. Sugarman?" she asked as she rose and handed the books to Graham.

He examined each in turn. "No."

"Good," she said.

He stepped out of the doorway. "End of the hall."

She stared at him for a moment, and then said, "I don't need to use the bathroom this evening, Mr. Sugarman. I'm fine. Thank you."

"Graham," he said. "My friends call me Graham."

He turned and walked away, leaving Beth on the porch. After hesitating a moment, she followed. He sat in his favorite chair with the five books in his lap and she settled onto the couch. The five paperbacks she'd brought the previous week were stacked on the coffee table.

"I waited for the bookmobile today," he said.

"I'm sorry," she said. "It's still in the impound lot."

"You said it would be released soon."

"Oh, I'm certain it will be. That's what the sheriff told us."

"But no one can drive it."

"None of us has a Commercial Driver's License," Beth said. "Only Alice had one."

"I have one."

"One what?"

"A Commercial Driver's License."

"Really?" Beth said. "The director told us you don't drive."

"I don't."

Beth stared at him for a moment. "I hate to mention this, Mr.—" She stopped to correct herself. "Graham, but I'm feeling a bit parched. Do you have anything to drink?"

"Sweet tea," he said. "In the kitchen. I'll get it."

He placed the new library books on the end table, stood, and headed into the kitchen.

Beth followed him. "You have a nice house."

"Yes."

"Very clean," she said. "I've not met many single men who keep a house this neat."

Graham retrieved two glasses from the cabinet above the sink and a jug of store-bought sweet tea from the refrigerator. He filled two glasses and returned the jug to the refrigerator.

"The sheriff came to the library yesterday," Beth said. "He told us there were no witnesses. He told us—he told us you were the last person to see her, Graham."

He was about to correct her, but stopped himself.

As tears pooled in the corners of her eyes, Beth continued, "Alice was my best friend. She didn't deserve to die like that. No one deserves to die like that."

"How did she die?"

"You don't know?" she asked. "It was all over the news."

Graham had been in the news for several days following the accident at Devil's Canyon Creek. After returning home, he had given away his television and cancelled his subscription to the newspaper. "I don't follow the news."

Beth contemplated his answer and then said, "Alice was strangled with her own scarf, right there in the bookmobile. Why would someone do that? Why?"

Graham reached out to touch Beth's hand, to soothe her, to quiet her, and was surprised when she collapsed into his arms and cried on his shoulder. He patted her back and let her cry.

After several minutes, Beth drew away, wiped at her eyes with the backs of her hands, and apologized for dampening Graham's shirt.

"Here." He handed her a paper towel. Then he carried the two tea glasses to the kitchen table and suggested they sit.

Beth joined him at the table and took a sip from her glass. "I'm sorry. I don't know why I did that. I didn't even cry at Alice's funeral. I just—I just have been holding it all inside and it finally came out."

Graham let her talk.

"The sheriff spoke to everyone who knew Alice. He wanted to know if anyone had a reason to kill her, but no one could think of a reason. Everyone loved Alice. She was everybody's friend."

"Was she—?" Graham didn't complete his question, unable to say the words that had come to mind.

Beth's eyes widened when she realized what Graham was asking. She shook her head. "No, nothing like that. She wasn't violated. Thank God. And the killer didn't take anything, either. Her money and her credit cards were still in her purse."

Beth reached across the table and took Graham's hand in hers. "I—I haven't been honest with you, Graham. I didn't bring you books last week because I thought it would be good customer service. I came to see you because you were the last person so see Alice. I came to ask you what she was like that morning, what she said and what you talked about, and—and last week I just couldn't bring myself to ask."

"A deputy already asked me those questions."

"Yes," Beth said. She dabbed at the corners of her eyes with a paper towel. "Yes, I'm sure he did, but I wanted to hear it from you."

Graham saw the longing in Beth's eyes, so he told her everything he told the deputy that day. He told her about Alice offering him a book he'd already read and how she had been more talkative than usual. "She asked about my day. She talked about the weather."

"Why do you think she was so eager to talk?"

"I don't think she wanted me to leave, but I had to. I had to come home."

Beth pressed. "Why didn't she want you to leave?"

Graham hesitated as he thought back to that morning. "She saw something outside that disturbed her."

"Some*thing* or some*one*?"

"I don't know," Graham said. "There were workmen going in and out of the building down the street, but she wasn't looking in that direction."

"Where was she looking?"

"Out the windshield, mostly."

"And when you left, what did you see?"

Graham shrugged. "The workmen at the end of the block."

"And in the other direction?"

"Dairy Queen. They were getting ready to open," Graham said. "And there was a car getting gas at the Texaco."

"What kid of car?"

"An SUV. A green one."

"Anything else unusual?"

Graham thought hard and then shook his head.

"Nothing?"

Beth sounded disappointed, so Graham thought even harder. Then he shook his head again.

Beth finally released his hand, and Graham immediately felt a sense of loss. Holding Beth while she cried and holding her hand while they talked were the kind of physical intimacies he had avoided since his release from the hospital. He had not realized how much he missed the touch of others.

She interrupted his thoughts with a question. "Why don't you drive?"

"I was in an accident."

"We've all been in accidents," Beth said. "That doesn't stop us from driving."

Graham hesitated a moment. Then he stood and left the room. A moment later he returned with a scrapbook filled with newspaper reports about the accident at Devil's Canyon Creek.

She opened the scrapbook, saw the photograph of a school bus submerged in Devil's Canyon Creek and read the headline "Hero Driver Saves Children." Then she looked up. "That was you?"

He nodded.

"What you did was very brave."

Graham shook his head. "I wasn't brave. I was afraid."

She took his hand again. "Afraid of what?"

"Afraid I couldn't save the children."

"But you did," she said.

He nodded.

"You weren't afraid for yourself, afraid you might—?"

She didn't complete her question but he knew the missing piece. The reporters had all asked the same question, and his answer had always been the same. "I was never afraid for me," Graham had told them. For Beth, he added, "I thought it was my time to go and I was ready."

"You don't really believe that?" she asked.

He shrugged, almost imperceptibly.

She started to ask another question, but he deflected it by asking, "Have you had dinner? I have leftover brisket."

Graham did not stop in front of the Woolworth the next Tuesday, and he did not carry any library books. He walked directly to the Dairy Queen and rapped on the glass door.

The assistant manager called from the other side. "We're not open yet."

Graham rapped again.

The assistant manager unlocked the door and held it open just far enough that he could talk through the gap.

Graham said, "I want a dip cone."

"I told you, we're not open."

"Where's the girl?"

"She isn't in yet."

"I want a dip cone."

"Go away, old man. You're no hero to me."

The two stared at one another for a moment. Then the assistant manager closed and relocked the door, leaving Graham standing outside without a dip cone. After several minutes, Graham turned away.

He walked to the spot in front of the boarded-up Woolworth where he usually waited for the bookmobile and stood looking in every direction until he found himself staring at the Dairy Queen and discovered the assistant manager staring back at him.

Then he slowly walked home.

Once there, he took his Commercial Driver's License from his wallet, laid it on the kitchen table, and checked the expiration date. Though he had not driven since the accident, he had taken his annual physical three months earlier and had been cleared to return to the road.

He thought long and hard about the things missing from his life, about the things he could not find in the books he devoured, and about how he had felt when Beth held his hand. He called the Arroyo Country Library and asked to speak to her.

Beth was surprised to hear Graham's voice when he asked, "If the bookmobile had a driver, who would be the librarian?"

"I suppose I would be," she said.

"Are you bringing me books tonight?"

"If you'd like me to."

"Will you stay for dinner?"

"I would like that very much," she said, "very much indeed."

Graham spent the rest of the day preparing for Beth's visit that evening. He cleaned his already spotless house, set the kitchen table with his best dinnerware, and put a small roast in the oven. Then, sweaty from all the activity, he filled the bathtub with warm water, hoping to soak for a while before dressing for the evening.

He was about to step into the tub when the doorbell rang. He pulled on his robe, walked through the house, and opened the door to find the Dairy Queen's assistant manager standing on his front porch.

"You've been spying on me, old man." The young man pushed into his house. "I know you have. You know something, don't you?"

Confused, Graham had no idea how to respond except by stepping backward each time the young man jabbed his finger into his chest. He asked, "What do you want?"

"Who else knows about me? Have you told anyone? Anyone at all?"

"No, I—"

"You knew she recognized me that day, didn't you? *Didn't you!*"

Graham shuffled backward as he realized what the young man was telling him. Then he turned and ran for the bathroom, the only room with a door that locked.

He didn't make it. The young man propelled himself into the bathroom with Graham and bounced him against the wall. They scuffled, but Graham was no match for the young man, and soon he was on his knees, bent over the bathtub, exhausted, battered, and bruised.

The killer shoved Graham's head into the tub and held it beneath the water. At first Graham struggled, but then he resigned himself to his fate. He had been here before, trapped in the school bus in Devil's Creek Canyon as the water rose. He relaxed, knowing what would come when he could no longer hold his breath, and drew in lungsful of water.

He regained consciousness to find himself in the hallway with Beth giving him the kiss of life.

When she saw the spark in his eyes, she drew back. "I thought I'd lost you."

He smiled up at her before he faded away again.

Later, in the hospital, he learned the rest of the story from Beth. She had arrived early for dinner and found his front door standing open. When she heard the sounds of a struggle in the bathroom, she used her cellphone to call the sheriff. Then she stormed down the hall, barged into the bathroom, and began beating Graham's assailant about the head with a hardcover edition of *A Game of Thrones*.

A sheriff's deputy dining nearby at the Quarryville Smokehouse caught the call and arrived moments later to corral the librarian's killer while Beth dragged Graham from the tub and resuscitated him.

"You're in the news again," she said. "Looks like you caught Alice's killer."

"I didn't do anything."

"That's not what he says. He says you were watching him, and he knew that you knew and he had to eliminate you before you told anyone."

Later, the sheriff visited and provided the missing piece to the story when Graham asked why Alice had been killed.

"The same reason he tried to kill you," the sheriff said, "only she really did see him kill someone. A few months ago, there was a hit-and-run just down the road from the Dew Drop Inn. We didn't figure we'd ever find the drunk who mowed down Mavis Mayweather, but it turns out Alice Boyette saw the whole thing. She phoned it in from the pay phone outside the IGA but didn't leave her name or any contact information, and we wouldn't have even known it was her until this nimrod confessed to everything. He said he saw her plain as day and she saw him."

The sheriff released the bookmobile from the impound lot two weeks later. Library staff cleaned it and restocked it, and Graham accepted a temporary job with the Arroyo County Library driving the bookmobile while Beth studied for her Commercial Diver's License.

Until that day arrived, though, he was quite content to spend his weekdays in Beth's company, surrounded by more books than he could ever hope to read.

Our next story, by Warren Bull, combines libraries, mysteries, and Shakespeare to create a droll story certain to interest, and perhaps confound, fans of the Bard.

Mr. Bull is a prolific author and familiar to readers of our anthologies. He is a lifetime professional member of Sisters in Crime and is an active member of Mystery Writers of America.

Elsinore Noir

by Warren Bull

Maybe I should have just bitten my tongue, but the patron was getting on my nerves and at the Multnomah County Public Library we do our best to help people find what they want.

I said, "You say you've read our entire collection of Brass Knuckles, Goldenbaum's Ghost and Debbie Holt, Psychic Kitten novels. I'm sorry we don't have any more books in those three series. I'm not sure what else to recommend."

The patron, a small pale man dressed in a long black coat and an enormous bowtie over a ruffled shirt spoke with a soft southern accent.

"I want to read about a man who tries to stay true to himself in a corrupt world, but never gets a break. He's in despair as those in power plot against him, but he persists, knowing he will probably lose or even die at the end."

I looked into his burning eyes as dark as three midnights in a jug.

"That sounds like something noir, or for that matter, *Hamlet.*"

"You mean Dashiell Hamlet? I've read all his books," the man said.

"Um, no," I said. "I mean Shakespeare."

He shrugged. "Does it have a dame in it?"

"Yes but the relationship ends badly."

"Does the hero crack wise?"

"Some of his lines are downright famous."

"Do tell."

"You should know it's a play, not a novel," I said. "It was written so long ago that the language can be quite hard to understand."

"And it's still in print?"

"A lot of people consider it a classic," I explained. "It starts with Hamlet, Prince of Denmark, suspecting that his father has been murdered. He comes to the royal court to investigate. The murderer plots against him, and Hamlet doesn't know who he can trust. At the end the stage is knee deep in bodies."

"Didn't Raymond Chandler use a similar plot?"

"I'm sure he did, but *Hamlet* was written first."

"Sounds interesting, I'll check it out."

I hoped for a respite from the patron, but he caught me coming back from a break the very next day. I steeled myself for a complaint, but he surprised me.

"You were right about the language," he said. "It took a while, but once I caught on it was really moving, almost poetic."

"I agree."

"So who do you think the ghost was?" he asked.

"Pardon me."

"You know, the ghost. Do you believe in ghosts?"

"Well, no."

"Neither do I. So somebody has to be pretending to be the ghost."

I was speechless for moment. "I've never considered that, but Hamlet thinks it's his father. I suppose it has to be someone who resembles the dead king."

He nodded. He said, "Exactly. It couldn't have been the king. I thought it might be at first but I don't think he could have faked his own death. Too bad. I like that. It's subtle."

He turned and left. I was not surprised when he showed up the next day.

"I'm sure the traveling players are a clue," he said. "But I haven't yet figured out what they're a clue to. Also, I can't see it working out between Hamlet and Ophelia. Something bad is bound to happen."

He paused and then continued.

"Do you think Gertrude was in on the hit?"

"As I remember, at that point in the play, it hard to know," I said. "A doll in heat is not the most logical person on earth, if you know what I mean. Neither is a guy in heat for that matter. Apparently Gertrude was a stone fox. You can see why Claudius was tempted."

"I liked the part where Hamlet thought Claudius was praying and spared his life," he said. "But Claudius could not repent and could not pray."

"Yes, I liked that too," I said. "I've always thought that scene gives Claudius a conscience and makes him a much more interesting killer. It seems to me if Hamlet had killed him right then, in the eyes of the people Hamlet would become the mad assassin and Claudius would become the martyred king. I think Hamlet wants the world to know what Claudius did."

I turned to help an elderly but spritely woman who wanted a book on poisonous plants. When I turned back the man was gone.

When the library opened after the weekend, the man was among the first to enter. He dodged a fellow with a very stiff military mustache and almost ran to my desk.

"Hamlet's in the soup now," he exclaimed. "He stabbed through a curtain, not knowing who was on the other side and killed an innocent man. You can understand it with all the pressure he's been under, but you can't forgive him."

"And Hamlet can't forgive himself," I said.

"Betrayal, madness, drowning and pirates. This scribbler Shakespeare doesn't miss a trick. Hamlet has to know that the so-called 'playing' with foils with the son of a man he murdered is a trap."

"But he's going to do it anyway," I said.

"I almost have the identity of the man playing the ghost worked out. For a while I thought it was Horatio."

I thought about it for a moment and then shook my head. "I know he's the least likely candidate, but I never really doubted his loyalty."

"At one point I thought he might be boffing Gertrude too, but that didn't work as a motive. It was just a passing thought. It's nicely written; so many characters have secret agendas, but Horatio is just what he appears to be. Then I thought the ghost was one of the school chums, but they're just red herrings. I've eliminated almost everyone. There's one character I've almost settled on. I'll let you know if I'm right."

"I can hardly wait," I said. I honestly couldn't.

He strutted in the next day and gave me thumbs up.

"So." He said. "Who do you think pretended to be the ghost?"

"I really don't have a clue." I said.

"I admit there aren't a lot of clues. But think this Shakespeare dude was fair to his readers. Who is the most dangerous man in the play?"

"Claudius?"

"No. He kills only one man. And the man he kills is asleep."

I rubbed my chin as I thought. "Hamlet?"

"You're getting closer. I wouldn't want to cross swords with that mug. What do Claudius and Hamlet have in common?"

"Family, royalty, a claim to the throne."

"Precisely. One other person has all three." He smirked at me. "That character ends up with the whole ball of wax."

I bit my lip and frowned.

"Fortinbra."

"What?" I asked. "The guy from Norway? He was such a minor character. He was hardly ever on stage."

"Ah, so. Number one librarian, check this out. Think back. In the beginning of the play we learn Hamlet's father, also named Hamlet, and Fortinbra's father, also named Fortinbra. met in single combat. The Dane won. Denmark got territory that would otherwise belong to Norway."

"Okay."

"We learn that the younger Fortinbra was raising an army and might be trying to get land back for Norway. Well, he was. All royal families were related. With a little makeup, Fortinbra could easily pass for the dead king. He sent the younger Hamlet on a dangerous path."

"Yes. But still—"

"If Fortinbra could pretend to be the dead king, he could also pretend to be one of the players. He enacted the murder with such detail that Claudius could not stand to see it. That confirmed Hamlet's suspicions. He resolved to kill Claudius."

"I'm not sure about that," I said.

"Consider what remains when we eliminate the impossible. Poisoned foils? Fortinbra had weapons for his army. He showed up at the end and waltzed away with the Danish throne. Happenstance? I don't think so."

"Wait, Fortinbra could not have expected the entire royal family to end up at room temperature," I said.

"No, but either Claudius would kill Hamlet or Hamlet would kill Claudius. Either way Denmark would be weakened. Her people would be divided and dispirited. The country would be ripe for plucking. He'd only have to eliminate whoever remains. Femme fatale, Gertrude, has already hopped from one bed to another. She could be persuaded to try bed number three. As it happened, she died too. Fortinbra won the whole shebang without a single battle."

I shook my head. "As many times as I've read Hamlet, that never occurred to me."

The man smiled. "I like this Shakespeare guy. Do you have anything else by him?"

"There is one play actors consider cursed. They don't refer to it by name. They call it the Scottish play."

His eyes lit up, "Cursed?"

"It has everything Hamlet has, plus witches."

"I want to read it," he said.

As he walked by holding a copy of *Macbeth,* I motioned him over to my desk. He leaned toward me. I whispered, "In the third scene of the third act, watch out for the third murderer.

Sharon Marchisello tells us that just such a happenstance as occurs in the following story provided the genesis of her tale. For all who have searched for a writing critique group, this one is for you.

Ms Marchisello is the author of Going Home (Sunbury Press, 2014) a murder mystery inspired by her mother's battle with Alzheimer's disease. She is an active member of Atlanta Sisters in Crime.

The Wrong Coffee Shop

by Sharon Marchisello

Shelley was late. She slid her S.U.V. into a narrow parking spot and killed the engine, wiper blades frozen in the middle of the windshield, like watch hands at the moment of a disaster. Her spot was close to the entrance, so she didn't bother to search for the broken, cheap umbrella that lay somewhere in the back seat among boxes of unsold books and empty cloth grocery bags. The coffee shop's awning would protect her from most of the downpour if she made a dash for it. She did.

She pulled open the heavy glass door and inhaled the aroma of rich, brewed coffee and freshly baked pastries. Raindrops splotched her waist-length corduroy jacket. She pushed a moist strand of brown hair behind her ear. Which cluster of chatting customers was her group?

No one looked familiar. Julie and Denny were the only members she knew, and it had been so long since the group last met in person—at the DeKalb Public Library that time— she wasn't sure she'd even recognize them. Maybe everyone had canceled at the last minute because of the rain, or maybe they were all stuck in traffic. People in Atlanta forgot how to drive when it rained.

She looked down at her smartphone. She had forgotten to add Julie's number to her contacts. Maybe it was on the email.

Should she order a coffee? Or should she first make sure the meeting was still on? This wasn't Starbucks, but the prices were just as high.

A clean-shaven young man wearing glasses looked up from his laptop, made eye contact, and waved her over.

Gratefully, Shelley slid into the seat across from him at the small wooden table. She set her black leather handbag on the tile floor beside her chair. The chair made a scraping sound against the tile as she scooted it closer to the table and adjusted her position.

"Sheila?" He extended a hand.

"Shelley." She shook his hand. "Where is—?"

He withdrew his hand and pointed to the cell phone he was holding. With an apologetic smile, he returned to his conversation.

"I'll make sure she knows—" He nodded, cast a glance at Shelley, gave an eye roll.

"I wrote it all out." The expression on his face grew impatient. "Of course, we can ensure discretion." He sighed. "Okay. I'll remind her to get out of there as soon as it's done."

He looked at Shelley again. She averted her eyes so he wouldn't think she'd been eavesdropping.

Two more wet patrons came through the door. One man scraped his boots against an invisible doormat as he folded up his dripping umbrella. Shelley didn't recognize them, either, and they didn't seem to be looking for anyone.

The man on the phone appeared to be on hold.

Shelley took advantage of the lull. "Have you seen Julie yet? She's still coming, isn't she?"

His brow furrowed. Then the person on the other end of the line came back to the conversation and regained his attention. "Of course. I understand. Leave nothing behind." He reached into a leather portfolio, retrieved a sheet of paper, and pushed it across the table to Shelley.

"You wrote this?" she mouthed.

He nodded and focused back on his phone call.

Shelley had thought today's meeting would be strictly social, but hey, when you have the opportunity to get together with a group of other experienced writers, why not share a work-in-progress and get some feedback? She picked up the paper and started to read.

"Okay. Got it." Finally, he disconnected the call. He looked at Shelley. "Sorry." As she lifted her eyes from the paper, he asked, "Well, what do you think?"

She shrugged. "Is this your whole synopsis?"

"Synopsis? What do you mean?"

"As written, it looks like the plot has a few holes. I mean, no one would actually—"

"What are you talking about?"

Oh dear, he's getting defensive. He must be new. Shelley took a deep breath. "It's good and all. Great concept. Is this going to be your first novel?"

"Novel?" He studied her face. "What did you say your name was?"

"Shelley."

"You're not Sheila."

"No, I'm still Shelley."

"I was supposed to meet *Sheila* here." He snatched the paper away from Shelley and placed it back in his portfolio.

Shelley touched her hand to her mouth. "You're not with the Midtown Atlanta Writers Circle?"

He shook his head. An amused smile tickled his lips. "So, you're a writer? Not—"

"Not Sheila." She smiled. "I make my living as a librarian, but yes, I'm a writer."

"What do you write?"

"Murder mysteries."

He stifled a chuckle. "Murder mysteries." He looked around the room. "Where's your group? Your partners in crime?"

"I don't know." Shelley glanced at her phone. She had found Julie's email and verified that she had the date and time correct.

"We were supposed to meet at ten o'clock this morning. The San Francisco Coffee House on Highland Avenue."

"Which one?"

"The San Francisco Coffee House on Highland Avenue," Shelley repeated.

"This one?"

"Isn't this the San Francisco Coffee House on Highland Avenue?" Shelley had just typed "San Francisco Coffee House" into her GPS, and the directions had taken here.

"It is, but there's another one about two miles north of here."

Shelley re-read the email. Julie had not given the address of the coffee shop where they were to meet, but she had mentioned a cross street Shelley did not remember passing. "There are two San Francisco Coffee Houses on Highland Avenue?" *In a city where half the streets are named Peachtree, why should I be surprised?*

He nodded. "I bet your friends went to the other one. It's bigger. More room to spread out and have a meeting."

Blushing, she picked up her handbag and rose from her chair. Again, its wooden legs scraped the tile as she extricated herself. "Sorry."

"You found some holes in my plot?" He still wore that half-smile as his eyes assessed her head to toe. "Are you sure you don't want to be Sheila? We could make it better."

Shelley headed for the door. "Nice meeting you," she called over her shoulder. *Whatever your name is.*

Before she could reach the handle, the door swung open, admitting a willowy redhead in a tight, black leather skirt, dark fishnet stockings, and a wide-brimmed hat.

The air outside felt cool; the rain had stopped. Shelley held the door to let the woman pass. "Sheila," she addressed the newcomer, and Shelley could have sworn there was a flicker of recognition at the sound of the name. "Someone's waiting for you."

Ever wonder what really goes on behind the circulation desk at your library? Have you ever wondered at what forbidden knowledge might be stored back there? Here's a story that explores what might be stashed behind the stacks of popular books, safe from the innocent public's inquiring gaze.

Jacqueline Seewald brings her professional experience as a librarian to this story. Ms Seewald is the author of the popular Kim Reynolds mystery novels, and her short stories, poetry, and other writing has appeared in The Writer, L.A. Times, and Library Journal, and a wealth of other publications. This story was previously published in slightly different form in Over My Dead Body! in 2016.

Ask a Librarian

by Jacqueline Seewald

His first day on the job, Harold Stevens gazed with interest at his surroundings. He'd been hired to work in the information services area of the city's small but prestigious special library, the Gainsworth. According to the director, the library was dedicated to the noble pursuit of scholarly learning in the humanities. From Harold's viewpoint, the Gainsworth was an anachronism, a stuffy, elitist club with admission available only to a well-heeled few.

Harold stood in the director's oak-paneled office in front of an elegant marble Louis the Fourteenth fireplace, surrounded by portraits of Shakespeare, Dryden and Shaw, and he thought of his pop. How the old man would have laughed to see him here. Pop didn't suffer fools or snobs without hurling a few epithets.

"Becoming accustomed to us?" Wolf Renning, Supervisor of Information Services, smiled through nicotine-stained teeth. He was a gaunt, unaesthetic figure, but his eyes betrayed a sharp intelligence.

"Quite a place," Harold acknowledged.

"We like to think so." Renning's tone was patronizing. He cleared his throat in a ponderous manner. "The public is just beginning to understand that information is a very valuable commodity that can be bought and sold. Knowledge is power, young man. Never forget that." Renning turned his attention to an attractive woman. "Ms. Manus, you'll be working with Mr. Stevens. You're also now in charge of the Genesis Collection, since Robert is no longer with us. Do not let anyone who isn't authorized near it. Is that clear?"

There was a severity to Renning's tone of voice that caused Harold to raise an eyebrow. Ms. Manus gave a quick nod. Harold thought she looked nervous. Now what was that all about?

Renning moved onward with measured strides. Harold glanced over at Lara Manus. She was a striking honey-blonde, but her mouth was set in a deep frown as if something were troubling her. Good time to ask a few relevant questions? He'd find out.

"How long you been working here?"

"What? Oh, long enough." She definitely appeared distracted.

A good reference librarian being something of a detective, Harold reasoned no one would think anything of it if he attempted to ferret out what lay behind Lara Manus's manner. There was something going on here; he trusted his instincts.

"So am I taking this fellow Robert's place?"

"As a matter of fact, you are." She snapped like a turtle.

"Well, I hope you won't hold that against me." He gave her his most charming smile hoping to disarm her antipathy.

"Robert Weber was excellent at information services. If you're half as good a librarian as he was, we'll get along just fine." With that, she walked quickly away, heels clicking on marble flooring. So much for charm.

He observed an assistant bringing out a requested manuscript on a red velvet cushion and recalled what the Director had told him. Because the library was privately endowed, patrons had to make an appointment to use the collection. If their requests were accepted, they were treated in kingly fashion--but not everyone was accepted.

When Lara Manus returned to the desk, she was still uncommunicative.

"So why did Robert Weber leave the library?"

"What?" Her eyelids fluttered like butterfly wings.

"Should I repeat the question?"

"I don't think that's any of your business."

He'd hit a nerve. Now what was that about? "Au contraire. I think it is my business. I'm his replacement, aren't I?"

Ms. Manus pursed her lips. "Mr. Weber disappeared. Nobody knows where he is or what became of him. End of story." Her sky blue eyes met his squarely. But he saw a shadow in them, as if she were scared of something or someone.

Harold decided to do a little more fishing. "Maybe Robert Weber got a better offer and didn't want to tell anyone."

Her eyes became frosty as a lake in winter. "No, he would have told me."

That was an interesting comment. "Are you sure?"

"No one's heard from him, not even his sister. It's as though he walked off the face of the earth."

"Have you talked to the cops?"

She twisted the watch on her wrist. "There was a detective around. He promised to investigate."

Wolf Renning returned and Lara stopped talking. She seemed uneasy, not that Harold blamed her. There was something sinister about the man. Renning's fine, black hair fringed a face that nearly came to a point. Bright eyes moved about restlessly under beetle brows. A scent of Turkish pipe tobacco clung to his Harris Tweed jacket.

"Ms. Manus, there will be someone asking for the Genesis Collection later in the day. Make it available."

Did Harold imagine her shiver? He didn't think so.

Harold watched Renning disappear into the murky depths of the room that served as his office. He tried to shake off the eerie sensation of menace that Renning left in his wake.

"What could be in a library collection that would require a closed stack?"

"This is a special library, not like any other. Have you looked around? Really looked?"

Lara Manus swept her hand toward the glass display cases. "See those Medieval illuminated manuscripts? Their pages gleam as if new. Did you notice the rare books with jewel-encrusted covers, and those with ancient Near Eastern seals carved from serpentine and chalcedony?"

"Right, but anyone can see them. They're in plain sight. What kind of volumes would be under lock and key?"

Lara didn't answer. She bit down on her lower lip, a shadow crossing her face. "I have things to do," she said, "and so do you."

What could this Genesis Collection hold? The library itself was full of valuable manuscripts worth a king's ransom. Certain unscrupulous people might pay a fortune and ask no questions if such artifacts showed up for sale. Was Renning stealing from the library?

Later that afternoon, a man came to the reference desk and asked to see the Genesis Collection.

"I would be glad to show it to you," Harold assured the patron.

He studied the small, nondescript individual. The man's eyes looked at him askance from an egg-shaped head with a bald spot reminiscent of a medieval monk's pate. Was the Genesis Collection a group of books of a religious nature, possibly documents stolen from a monastery somewhere?

"Do you happen to know where the key is kept?" Harold asked the diminutive man.

"I have it," Lara Manus said, approaching hurriedly. "Why don't you take care of the client over there? Remember, we never keep our patrons waiting." She handed Harold a form, dismissing him the way a teacher would a pupil.

But Harold didn't leave, instead he watched and waited. With a set of keys she drew from her skirt pocket, Lara Manus opened a desk drawer and removed yet another key that she used to open the door of a small room separated from the reference area.

"Call when you finish," she told the patron as he entered the room. She discreetly shut the door, and then turned her attention back to Harold. "Why are you still here?" She seemed nervous, almost frightened.

"I'm supposed to be learning the routines."

"The Genesis Collection is my responsibility."

"We could share it," Harold suggested. "I could close up after he finishes. Maybe take some of the pressure off you. Give you a chance to relax. You seem tense."

Her lower lip set in granite. "I have to do this, now that Robert is…" her voice trailed off.

"What do you think happened to him?"

She shook her head but didn't answer.

"Did Robert Weber know what was in the Genesis Collection? Was he a curious kind of guy?"

Lara Manus steepled her fingers and then looked down at them. "The day Robert disappeared, he was staying late. He said something wasn't quite right."

"About the Collection?"

Her eyes still did not meet his.

"You think the Collection had something to do with his disappearance?"

"It's possible," she said in a barely audible voice. "You see why I don't think you should have any involvement with it?"

Actually, he saw all the more reason to find out what was contained in the collection, but he didn't say that to her.

"What about that policeman? Have you told him what you suspect?"

"I didn't see the need." She seemed alarmed. "Why do you want to know?"

"Just as one detective to another."

She suddenly laughed. "You're a librarian, not a detective."

"People are always asking librarians to solve mysteries for them, aren't they?"

She shrugged. "That's just a matter of finding information."

"Good reference librarians fit pieces of a puzzle together until all the information makes a complete answer on a quest for truth. It's detective work, kind of like what a P.I. does."

"All right, I won't argue with your logic."

Harold knew then that he would help her, and she'd help him; he felt it in his bones. His instincts were kicking in again.

Later, he made certain to walk Lara Manus out as they left work and headed toward the street. "Can we have dinner together?"

She tried to refuse, but he knew how to be persistent. He hailed a cab and offered to take her wherever she chose.

She smiled at him for the first time. "I know exactly what you earn. If you don't mind something simple like an omelet, we can have dinner at my apartment."

He accepted with a wide grin.

She left him in her small living room after they arrived at her apartment. He quickly saw that it was a tastefully furnished place, although he barely glanced around before following her into the kitchen.

Dinner went well, just as he hoped it would. Lara was a good cook. Harold impressed her, in turn, by doing an adequate job cutting and tossing the salad.

"You're a handy man with a knife."

"I'm just loaded with killer skills," he responded with an insinuating smile.

She didn't say anything but her face flushed with color.

After they'd eaten, he turned to her. "So were you and Robert a couple?"

"Just friends," she said.

"I can't imagine any man willing to just be friends with you," he said.

"Well, actually, Robert was gay, which I must say you obviously are not. In fact, you don't remind me very much of a librarian at all. You seem kind of dangerous, a bad boy. You have a formidable aura." Her head turned to one side in a gesture of appraisal.

He smiled but didn't respond to her observation. Time to change the subject. "Don't you want to know what's in that collection?"

"Not that again!" She rolled her eyes.

"If you were Robert Weber's friend, you should want to find out if there really is a connection."

"It could mean my job," she said.

He saw the fear clouding her eyes but did not relent. "Shouldn't we find out what happened to your friend?"

"Just tell me why you care," she countered, her eyes narrowing with suspicion.

"Professional curiosity."

He decided not to tell her that he was certain she was in danger as long as she was in charge of the Genesis Collection. It was time to take action, and the sooner the better.

At eleven o'clock, the library was dark and deserted. Harold lurked in the shadows, shivering in the chill night air as Lara stealthily opened the doors with her keys. She had trouble with the lock because her hands were shaking. He joined her as they silently entered the building.

Lara removed the special keys from the reference desk as he held a small flashlight for her. A light flickered along the walls as she unlocked the door to the chamber that housed the Genesis Collection, and a voice called out, "Anyone there?"

Harold pulled Lara down beside him as the beam of the night watchman's flashlight flickered over the desk. He wondered if the man could hear the hammer pounding in his chest. The watchman's footsteps receded down the corridor and to the staircase. Harold took Lara's cold, trembling hand and held it reassuringly in his own. Unlike Lara he loved the danger, thrived on it.

Lara led Harold into a small room. A collection of books filled a shelf behind a small desk. But these weren't ancient religious books as he'd expected. That was a surprise. In fact, all the books had something to do with codes. Lara unlocked a large drawer in the desk. It held equipment, state of the art technology. Harold sat down at the desk, removed a notebook computer, and booted it up. His attempt to by-pass the access code was instantly denied. He glanced around, found a crumpled paper in the trash, and studied it. The partially shredded e-mail message was in some sort of mathematical code. Who would use encryption? Spies maybe? The lights came on, momentarily blinding him.

"What are you doing here?" The voice resonated ominously.

Wolf Renning viewed him through hooded eyes. "I like to be able to trust the people who work here. I had a feeling there was something not quite right about you, Stevens."

"We'll be leaving."

"Yes, you will indeed be leaving. You're both fired," Renning said. "Hand me your keys, Ms. Manus."

"It's my fault, not hers," Harold said quickly. "I talked her into it." He wondered if Renning had caught Weber here. Had he been fired too? Or was the punishment more serious—and more permanent?

"I don't understand the need for secrecy," Lara said in a tremulous voice. "If you have scholars who require privacy, that's hardly reason to..."

"Kill someone?"

Lara lifted her head, eyes blazing blue light. "You killed Robert, didn't you? You actually murdered him because he found out what your stupid collection was about." Her anger went beyond indignation. "How senseless and obscene!"

"It wasn't quite that simple. The man had the audacity to suggest that he was going to report me. I would have been arrested for treason. The government doesn't approve of abetting spies who transmit classified information to foreign powers."

"How narrow-minded of them," Harold said sarcastically. "So, just out of curiosity, what exactly is in the Genesis Collection?"

"Only some useful books on coding plus this special computer notebook that's untraceable. And naturally as a professional librarian I did keep thorough records on those who used it. I've found that list to be most profitable."

"Let me guess: Robert happened to see those records. Did he threaten to blackmail you?"

"I don't think that's any of your business." Renning really was an ugly character, especially when he sneered. "And now that you know, I regret that you will have to disappear like Mr. Weber."

Renning held up a shiny revolver and pointed it directly at them. Light careened crazily off the black, snub-nosed barrel.

"You really don't think we'd come here without telling the police first, do you?" he said to Renning in a calm but strong voice.

Renning laughed loudly, shaking his head in a contemptuous manner. "Of course, you told the police that you were going to break into the library tonight, Mr. Stevens."

"No, I said that we would be in search of evidence that would disclose how and why Weber disappeared. They're outside by now. I phoned before we left and suggested they be here 11:30."

Renning motioned with the weapon. "We're leaving," he said. "If you try to alert the guard, I'll shoot you dead on the spot. I'll explain I was threatened by intruders."

Harold took Lara's hand and led her out ahead of him. He would protect her somehow.

He hoped Renning would lock the door to the collection as a reflex action. He did, and as the older man turned, Harold lunged, throwing him off-balance, and knocking him to the floor. As they wrestled, the revolver discharged toward the ceiling. The sound brought the watchman, followed by two police detectives with drawn guns. Harold yanked the weapon from Renning's hand.

Harold straightened up and placed the pistol on the desk in front of the two cops. "I'm here to serve. My job is providing information." He spoke with a straight face.

In spite of the gravity of the situation, both policemen laughed. The older and heavier of the two slapped Harold on the back.

"You got your old man's sense of humor, Harry. If I didn't know you were a detective, I'd swear you really were a librarian. You fit the part perfectly."

Lara Manus stared at him in open-mouthed surprise. "Is it true? You're a detective?"

"The private kind. Your friend's sister came to me after filing a missing person's report with these guys. She told me Weber said he was frightened for his life because of something he'd found out at his job. I used to work undercover for the department until I got blown."

He wouldn't tell her the rest until he knew her better. Near fatal gunshot wounds that ended his career as a police detective weren't meant for casual conversation. "I figured I could find out more by working here. Robert's family has some influence here. They have been long-time donors to the library, and the director was willing to go along with my plan. So I became a librarian."

"Actually, a rather good one," Ms. Manus said with a smile.

"Well, thank you, Ma'am. We are definitely going to have to discuss that at length some later time. Right now, these two police detectives are going to insist we provide them with a statement."

"Take your hands off me!" Wolf Renning tried to shove the officers away from him as they handcuffed him.

Unperturbed, the older of the two detectives, Al Jenkins, read Wolf Renning his Miranda Rights.

"I refuse to speak until I've consulted an attorney."

"That's your right, sir. For now, we're taking you to the precinct. You're under arrest for attempted murder."

"I think those charges are soon going to include the murder of one Robert Weber," Harold said.

He and Lara watched as the two detectives led Renning from the library. Lara let out a deep sigh of relief. Harold took her hand in a gesture of support.

"It's going to be fine," he told her.

She smiled and nodded.

"Shall we go?"

Harold offered his arm and Lara accepted. He decided that if he ever stopped being a P.I., reference work at a library might not be half bad.

Our next story provides an interesting puzzle in the form of a traditional who-dun-it. As an impoverished library considers selling its most prized possession, there is at least one person who intends to stop the sale, even if it takes murder to do it.

Anne-Marie Sutton is another frequent author within our anthologies. She is the author of the Newport Mysteries, including the just-released Invest In Death, the fourth in the series. Although the following story was informed by her association with Redwood Library and Athenaeum (chartered 1847), Ms Sutton assures us there is no similarity to actual people or events.

The Adams Miniatures

by Anne-Marie Sutton

"And here comes the library's director, Dr. Solari."

The tour group of eleven people stared obediently at the tall, well-dressed man striding toward them.

In the quiet that heralded his arrival, Nicholas Solari let his eyes move from one to another of the group, both the women and the men, savoring their undisguised appreciation of his own handsome features. His sleek black hair greying at the temples, the deep blue color of his eyes, his square jaw and perfect Roman nose of his ancestors.

"Welcome to the Pembroke Library," Nick said after he was sure everyone had locked him into their memories of the day. "I'm sure that Liz—" and here he waved a hand at the plain, middle-aged woman who was leading the tour "—has told you that our library is the oldest private library in the country still actively lending books. Quite a distinction, don't you think?"

The tour group nodded as one.

"Our library is named after its founder George C. Pembroke," Dr. Solari continued. "There are only a few of these treasured institutions left in the United States. They date to the eighteenth century, a time in America's history when there were no public libraries. Private libraries, similar to ours, provided a space for members to meet and have access to a collection of books they could not afford to have as individuals. The members paid a subscription fee—as ours still do today. But it was well worth the money as these libraries grew to house, as the Pembroke does, not only treasured volumes, but also art galleries and museums to which prominent people of the community made generous donations from their collections."

Nick paused for a breath. He'd had a busy morning breakfasting with the library's banker and had not planned to stop to lecture this tour group on the history of the Pembroke Library. But it was hard for him to pass up a captive audience.

He turned to Liz McNamara to indicate that she should resume her commentary.

"Thank you, Dr. Solari," she said, grateful that he was finished interrupting her tour as he often did. Really, the man should have gone into show business.

"Now, if you will all follow me into the next room," Liz instructed, "I will show you the pride of the Pembroke's collection, the famous Adams Miniatures, which I know you've been waiting to see." She moved quickly and hoped everyone was following her. But as she glanced back she saw two of the women hanging back to hear something Dr. Solari was saying. She didn't need to listen. It was the same thing he said to every visitor headed for the miniatures.

"Ah, the Adams Miniatures, depicting the small, painted portraits on ivory of John and Abigail Adams. A gift to John Quincy Adams from his wife Louisa early in their marriage." And then the pregnant pause followed by a wink. "Before Louisa understood how much her husband disliked his overbearing mother."

Really, thought Liz. With that sense of timing the man *should* be on the stage.

Anna White was working at her desk when Nick Solari entered her small office situated outside the spacious and well-appointed one that housed the director. She was constructing the agenda for the next day's Board of Trustees meeting. Items on the agenda had to be carefully worded, and she was in the throes of deciding whether *Sale of Items in the Collection* could be changed to *Discussion of the Endowment*.

The former language had come in an email she had received that morning from the board's chair, Claire Peeling, setting the meeting's agenda. The chair's description was sure to spark an immediate argument among the board members, and Anna would prefer to change the wording to something less controversial. Part of her job was to take the secretary's notes at the meetings and she dreaded having to summarize the heated discussion that was certain to follow.

"Good morning, Dr. Solari," she said cheerfully. Like her co-worker Liz, Anna was a middle-aged woman, but she took great pride in her grooming and appearance. "How are you this morning?"

"I was just chatting with the 10 a.m. tour. I saw them on their way to see the Adams Miniatures." His eyes met hers with a forceful gaze that always turned his administrative assistant's insides warm. Nick was near enough to Anna for her to smell his cologne. She would recognize it if she were blindfolded in a cave.

"We must never let them leave the Pembroke, Anna," he said. "We can't let the trustees vote tomorrow to sell the miniatures."

"Of course not, Doctor. You know I'll do whatever I can to help." She was conscious of his right hand, which he had placed on her desk. She slid her hand closer to his, hoping to brush against the long tanned fingers with their curly dark hair and manicured nails.

"I've just had an idea," Solari said, pulling his hand away from hers. Anna sighed.

"What is it?"

"We ought to have some attendance figures for tomorrow's trustees' meeting, to prove the miniatures' popularity to that damned Peeling woman."

"What would we compare them to? We don't have attendance figures from when we didn't own them. They've been here since 1889."

Nick looked flustered for a second. "Well, I mean, the numbers must go up every year, don't you think? We've had lots of recent publicity about them. Last year there was that column in *Antiques Today*. And all the New England guide books and web sites point out that they are the centerpiece of our collection when they list the Pembroke Library as a must-see tourist attraction in Massachusetts."

Anna gazed at him in unmistaken admiration. "I'll see what I can do," she said.

Anna finished the agenda while Nick was out to lunch, and then tracked down the attendance figures he had wanted. Finally, she ate her lunch at her desk, her usual salad brought from home.

Liz McNamara came in with her sandwich and coffee and made herself comfortable on a corner of Anna's desk.

"Tomorrow's board of trustees meeting is bound to be a brouhaha, don't you think?" Liz asked, not bothering to hide her pleasure at the prospect. "Mrs. Peeling is determined to sell those miniatures, and she will bully the other trustees into doing it."

"Don't be so sure," Anna said. "Doctor Solari has been on the phone all week to the board asking for their support."

"Nobody listens to him. You're the only one around here who thinks he walks on water. Don't underestimate the power of the Peeling." Again Liz was positively gleeful. "If she wants to sell the Adams Miniatures to finance the new roof and the heating and air conditioning system, you can bet that's what the board will do."

"Doctor Solari can be very persuasive," Anna said stubbornly.

"With you, maybe… since you're in love with him."

"I am not!"

"He's married. He wears a wedding ring."

"His wife can't mean much to him. He doesn't even have a photograph of her in his office."

"I give up," Liz said, rolling her eyes. "Fantasize all you want."

"I don't fantisize."

"Whatever. But you have to admit that this place is falling apart and needs repairs. The Adams Miniatures are worth a small fortune. It's the only practical decision the trustees can make."

"Doctor Solari was at the bank this morning to see about a loan so we don't have to sell the miniatures.

"And how did that go?"

"He didn't say. But he won't let the board sell the miniatures. Doctor Solari will do what it takes to keep them here." Her eyes flashed with anger. "Mrs. Peeling is not getting her way this time!"

The next morning, fifteen minutes before the trustees were expected to convene their meeting, Anna put copies of the agenda in front of each member's place around the massive antique mahogany table in the board room.

The room was paneled in a rich brown wood that glowed with the polish regularly administered by the building's caretaker. Several oil paintings of unsmiling colonial personages hung on two of the walls, the women in bonnets looking tired of life, while the men seemed proud and prosperous. And between the room's two windows with their heavy gold damask draperies stood a locked glass case, housing the prize of the Pembroke's collection: the precious Adams Miniatures.

Anna called through the open doorway. "Liz! Can you bring in those two ice water carafes and glasses now? We'll wait until the trustees arrive to serve the coffee. And don't forget to make enough decaf for Mrs. Peeling. And please make sure you use her special red cup, the one with the seal of the state on it. She obsesses that she will get caffeinated coffee by mistake, and I've told her that is her cup, only to be used for her decaf."

"Yes, yes," Liz answered. "I know all that. Don't worry. But how about this? She gets the caffeine, drops dead, and problem solved."

"She wouldn't drop dead. Only have some kind of nervous fit that will make things even more difficult. Please do what I ask, and hurry up with it."

Claire Peeling did get her red cup of decaf coffee, and she finished it before calling the meeting to order.

"After we approve the minutes, I'd like to take up the most important item on our agenda, the sale of items from our collection." There being no objections, the minutes of the previous meeting were duly approved.

That formality concluded, Claire continued. "Everyone knows how I feel about this. Our job as trustees is to run the Pembroke Library on a business-like basis. Our present small endowment cannot begin to cover the cost of repairs needed now and in the future to this old building. If we sell the Adams Miniatures and invest the proceeds wisely, we will give the Pembroke a large enough endowment to ensure its sound financial future for decades to come."

"Madame Chair," Nick said, "I couldn't disagree more. What will the Pembroke Library be without the signature holding in our collection, entrusted to us over a hundred years ago by members of the Adams family? The miniatures *are* the Pembroke. They are our identity, and we have a moral obligation to the Adams family to be their steward."

"The trustees surely realize, Doctor Solari," Claire rejoined, glaring down the table at the director, "that just because we are a non-profit organization, it doesn't mean that we should not care about making sound financial decisions." She paused to clear her throat and tried to swallow. Suddenly her small grey eyes bulged, and she appeared to be having trouble focusing.

"I feel so dizzy," she said.

"Oh no," Anna said. "Someone has given her the caffeinated coffee." She grabbed for the offending red cup as if that could rectify the mistake.

Claire Peeling clutched at her throat. Nick reached her chair as she slumped forward, her forehead sounding a nasty thump as it met the table's top.

Nick bent over the stricken woman. He found her hands and began to rub them.

"This doesn't look good," he said trying to contain a nervous laugh. He looked up at the startled faces around the table.

"I think she might be dead."

———

Nick remained next to Claire Peeling's body, watching her with an expression of uneasiness, while the others huddled in the far end of the room,. Anna's face was unreadable as she stared woodenly at the delicate images of John and Abigail, safe in their case.

"The ambulance is coming and also the police," Liz announced as she came into the room. She was carrying a large serving tray to clear the white porcelain coffee service from the table.

"Don't touch anything, Liz," Nick ordered. "Leave everything as it is for the police to see when they arrive."

"Whatever, Doctor. I was just trying to help."

He frowned. "I suppose we should close the library. Can you get the rest of the staff to ask everyone to leave? Say there is a gas leak or something. Would you mind taking care of that?" He looked at Anna, who seemed in a trance. "I don't think Anna is up to it."

"The police are coming!" Anna said in a shrill voice. "They'll think I did this. They'll say it was me." She was wild-eyed as she spoke. "But you know I didn't kill her, Doctor Solari. It wasn't me."

"Get hold of yourself, Anna," Nick said. "You're becoming hysterical."

"I didn't do it, I didn't kill her. It wasn't me."

"Let's get you out of here. I don't know what's come over you. You can rest on the sofa in my office until you can get hold of yourself."

Anna collapsed into Nick's grip and allowed herself to be led from the room.

Nick settled the still limp Anna on the yellow down sofa in his office, easing a pillow under her head. She grabbed his arm.

"Don't leave me."

"Anna, I have to go to talk to the police when they come. I have to go."

"No."

"They'll expect to see the director."

"I didn't kill her," Anna repeated.

"Why do you keep saying that she was killed and that you didn't kill her? When the ambulance comes, we'll find out that this tragedy is all due to some health condition Claire had. A weak heart, or maybe even an aneurysm. You must have heard of people dropping dead and no one knew they had one of those aneurysms." He began rubbing Anna's hands in much the same way he had massaged the dead woman's.

"If she died of a heart attack, why are the police coming?"

"It's procedure in the case of an unexplained death like this. The authorities need to examine the scene, ask questions. You've seen this a hundred times on TV shows."

"Yes, and it all ends up being murder."

"Don't be silly. Murder doesn't happen at the Pembroke."

"Are you doing better?" Liz asked as she poked her head around the door to the director's office. Anna was still lying down. She had been gazing at the photograph of Nick taken at the helm of a sailboat that was on the credenza behind the sofa. Next to him in the picture stood a dark-haired man, a younger version of himself. She wondered if it could be his brother. He never spoke of his family.

"Anna, are you okay? I hope so. Listen. I can't find Mrs. Peeling's red cup. It's not on the table with the other cups. I'll have to tell the police about that when they come."

Anna straightened up on the sofa. "Why?"

"Don't you see that's suspicious?"

Anna shook her head.

"She was poisoned," Liz said triumphantly, "and I know who did it, and so do you if you think about it."

"I can't imagine what you are talking about."

"It could only be Doctor Solari who killed her. He had the motive."

"No! It isn't true."

"He has what he wants now. The miniatures won't be sold."

"You made the decaf," Anna said accusingly. "So you're the one who could have put poison in it."

Liz had no answer to her outrageous suggestion, and left the room shaking her head.

Nick Solari watched closely as the paramedics from the ambulance crew examined the body. Two uniformed police officers from the Aylesbury Police Department waited for them to finish.

"Have they told you anything about what happened, Doctor Solari?" Liz asked. She had left Anna contemplating things in his office.

Solari shook his head. They both stared as the medics conferred with the police. After a few minutes, the older of the officers, a black male in his forties with sergeant stripes on his uniform and a nametag which read *Ellis*, approached Nick.

"We'd like to know what information you can give us on what Mrs. Peeling had to eat or drink while she was here."

"Um," Nick began. "I'm sure I don't know."

"I can help you, Sergeant," Liz offered. "She drank her first, and only cup of coffee right before the meeting started at ten.

She usually asked for a second during the meeting and sometimes a third if things went on too long."

"No food?"

"We never serve food at the board meetings. Mrs. Peeling's orders"

"I see. Do you know which cup was hers?" Sgt. Ellis pointed to the cups and saucers scattered about the mahogany table.

"It's missing," Liz said, matter of factly.

"Missing? Are you sure?"

"Of course I'm sure. All these cups are white. Mrs. P. had a special red cup."

"Red?"

"Yes, for her decaf. Anna bought it at the antiques consignment shop in town, special for her. It's dark red and has the state seal on it. Anna thought it was part of an old service used at the governor's mansion. We always put Mrs. Peeling's coffee in it. Nobody else drinks decaf. That way we couldn't mix hers up with the caffeinated stuff. She was always worried she'd get the wrong coffee."

Sgt. Ellis motioned to the other officer to join them.

"We've got to search for a red coffee cup. Be careful if you find it. We'll need to check for fingerprints."

"Mine will be on it," Liz said. "I made the coffee and poured hers."

"Where?"

"In the small kitchen through there." She pointed to a doorway.

"Did you serve it to her immediately?"

Liz thought for a few seconds. "No. I filled the sugar bowl and creamer and brought everything in here on the tray."

"Who else was in the kitchen?"

Liz looked at Nick. "Didn't you come through that way from the hallway by your office?"

The two police officers remained to continue their investigation after the body was removed by the ambulance crew. It was the young patrolman who found the red cup wedged behind the case containing the Adams Miniatures. With its discovery the questioning began.

First to be interrogated was Nick, who insisted he did not hide the cup, reminding Sgt. Ellis of his statement that he didn't even know of its existence. Next Liz was asked what she knew about the hiding place, and her response was an angry disavowal of having anything to do with the concealment of the cup.

"Who was sitting next to Mrs. Peeling?" Sgt. Ellis asked Nick.

"Anna," Liz answered for him. "She takes notes at the meeting for the minutes."

"Where is Anna? What's Anna's full name?"

"Anna White is my administrative assistant. She is in my office," Nick said. "She's quite upset about all this, and I told her to lie down."

"Take me to see her. She needs to be questioned."

"Of course," Nick said, and he led Sgt. Ellis through the kitchen to his office.

When the two men reached the director's office they found that Anna had fallen asleep.

"Do you have to wake her?" Nick asked.

"I'm afraid so. She could have valuable information."

Nick went over to Anna and touched her gently on the shoulder. She opened her eyes, staring up at him with a surprised expression that quickly turned to joy.

"The police want to talk to you, Anna," he said. "Try to sit up. Sgt. Ellis is going to ask you some questions." He let her grab hold of his hand while she pulled herself up and swung her feet onto the floor. She blinked her eyes at the sergeant's figure.

"Ms. White, I understand you were sitting next to Mrs. Peeling at the meeting." Anna nodded. "Did you see her drink the coffee? From a red cup, I understand."

"Yes," Anna said. "It was her cup."

"Why did she have her own cup? Everyone else's was white."

"Oh, it was because of the decaf," Anna said. "She couldn't have caffeine, and with the different color cup we always made sure she got the decaf."

"Did you serve her that decaf coffee this morning?"

"Me? No. That was Liz's job. Liz McNamara."

"Yes. I've already talked to her."

"Then you know all this." Irritation had crept into Anna's voice.

"What I don't know is how the cup then came to be found behind the glass case in the board room. What can you tell me about that?"

She looked across at Nick. "Does he mean the case with the miniatures?"

"Yes," Nick answered. "The police found this red cup hidden between the wall and the case."

"Did you put it there, Ms. White?"

"Of course not. Why would I do that?"

"Somebody did. Who do you think it was?"

"I don't like to say."

"This is a police investigation. You *have* to say."

"Liz made the coffee," she said reluctantly.

"But you were sitting next to the victim. You had the perfect opportunity to add a foreign substance to the dead woman's coffee."

"Why would Anna murder the chair of the library's board of trustees, Sgt. Ellis?" Nick asked.

Ellis shrugged. "I haven't the faintest idea, sir. I'm only trying to make sense of what happened here this morning."

At that moment, the door flung open and a man burst into the room. He rushed to Nick and grabbed hold of him in a bear hug.

Anna recognized him immediately as the man in the photograph on the credenza.

"I came as soon as you called, Nicolo. This is so terrible."

"Massimo," Nick said, extricating himself from their embrace, "I didn't mean for you to leave work."

"But I was so worried about you." He looked at Sgt. Ellis. "The police. An investigation."

"It's going to be fine, Massimo. Really, you shouldn't have come."

"May I ask who you are, sir?" Sgt. Ellis asked.

"It's Dr. Solalri's brother," Anna said.

"Brother!" Massimo said in a shocked voice. "I am no brother. I am Nicolo's husband."

"Husband!" Anna cried out. "What about your wife, Doctor Solari?"

"Nicolo has no wife, Signora," Massimo said. "*We* are married."

"No," Anna said, "you can't be." She looked at Nick for a denial.

"I don't have a wife, Anna. I don't know why you thought I did."

"But your ring."

Massimo extended his left hand. Anna saw that he was wearing the identical ring to Nick's.

She slumped back on the sofa, grabbing her chest.

"Oh, I've been such a fool," she said, tears welling in her eyes. "Such a stupid, stupid fool."

"It's all right, Anna," Nick said. "I've never said much about my private life. You couldn't have known."

"But if I had known…" Anna's voice trailed off and she buried her head in her hands.

"I hope who I was married to won't make any difference to you."

"Don't you see, Doctor Solari," she said in a whisper. "I knew how important keeping the Adams Miniatures here at the Pembroke was to you."

"If I knew I could never have your love, I wouldn't have poisoned Mrs. Peeling's coffee with nicotine to stop her from selling them."

We head Down Under for our next story, set in the copper-clad Fisher Library of the University of Sydney, where a philosophy professor seeks to find the truth behind a murder.

Aislinn Batstone is an Australian writer, who like her protagonist, taught philosophy to undergraduates. Today she writes across genres, including crime, romance, speculative and contemporary fiction.

Case Study on the Principles of Morals and Legislation

by Aislinn Batstone

"Help!"

Kate Moseby's shout echoed through the metal stacks of Sydney University's Fisher Library, and then a second of pure silence followed, during which dust in a shaft of sunlight danced over the prostate man. Kate dropped her stack of books and stumbled towards the bloody figure.

"Somebody, help!"

Kate touched the man's shoulder, rolling him slightly towards her. A pallid face, brown hair, a satyric goatee neatly framing the slack mouth. Blood soaked the front of his white shirt, darkest crimson near a rip in the fabric to the left of his chest. Staring eyes told Kate her first aid would be of no use. She drew her hand away sharply and stood.

Her mouth felt papery and dry. She could smell the man's blood, almost taste it, metallic over the familiar and beloved scent of books. Who was he?

The sound of footsteps came from between the stacks. Shadows fell over the body. Two wide-eyed students stood in the gap. They were passive, wordless, clutching their books.

"Call the police," Kate ordered in her lecture theatre voice, "and tell a librarian that there's a body in the library."

***

Someone had wrapped a blanket around her shoulders; probably one of the paramedics, finding little to offer the corpse inside. Fisher Library was locked down and through her own reflection in the front doors Kate watched as the police took names and contact details of those still inside. Her face seemed paler in the glass, hair dark and wild above it. The blanket obscured her figure, shrouding her with a suggestion not of death but of a holy order. How long had she been standing here? Half an hour? An hour?

As Kate contemplated her reflection it split and re-formed. Two uniformed officers walked to an idling police car. One of them leaned through the front passenger window and spoke to the driver. Kate swayed.

An officer by the doors stepped closer towards her. "You right?"

Sun-damaged skin placed her in her fifties. Red hair pulled back tight under her uniform cap. Ice-blue eyes with a glint of compassion. "PC Judith Friend."

Kate pulled the blanket more tightly around her. "Just in shock, I guess. I mean, on campus. A student."

"No." PC Friend turned back to the doors. "A dealer."

"What?" Kate noticed the books she'd dropped in the library, now piled in a green shopping bag near her feet. "Hey, did you bring me my books?" She had a reading group that afternoon and a class to prepare in the morning. Could it all go ahead after this? Would she be expected to teach? Over towards her office, the sky above the sandstone quadrangle was immense, porcelain blue, and a warm spring wind brought scented drifts of wattle and eucalyptus. It had become a beautiful day.

PC Friend's thin mouth twitched at one corner. "You might want to give the books a wipe down."

Shuddering, Kate said, "Blood! I don't want them. They'll have to get rid of them."

"Cocaine. Baggy popped open when he fell—spilled all over the scene."

Kate gasped, threw off the blanket and brushed at her clothes.

"You'll be right, love." The PC shook her head. "Just have a nice long shower when you get home."

"What—what was he doing in the library?"

"What do you think?"

Kate narrowed her eyes to the glare off the golden stone, the walls of the building imbued with a hundred and fifty years of education and the essence of people who came here to better themselves. "Who was he?"

"A guy named Silas Brown, don't mention that to the press yet though, love."

Glass doors clunked and whirred and Kate whipped around, half-expecting to see the goateed man swagger out with his hands in his pockets. A stream of students emerged. Some looked shaken and pale, others chatted and smiled. There were a few familiar faces including two of the enthusiastic second-years from her Philosophy of Law reading group, Gabriel Wu and Stebby Rodriguez. Gabriel gave his broad smile and Kate felt her cheeks flush. Sometimes the age gap between herself and her students seemed all too narrow and she wished she'd taken the long way around to her doctorate.

Beside his handsome friend, Stebby Rodriguez was diminutive and badly dressed. He'd grown his dark hair very long and it looked wet, as if he'd had a shower and pulled it into the ponytail at the nape of his neck. His flannel shirt was wrongly buttoned and hung lower on one side of his jeans than the other. He must have sensed Kate staring at him; he looked in her direction but, seeing her, turned his face away.

Kate reached for her bag of books. "Am I allowed to go?"

"Yeah. We've got your details."

Kate stepped from the library's shade into the sunshine. Her steps loosened and she sucked warm fresh air deep into her lungs. Her cosy office beckoned. Head in a book was her preferred way of dealing with life's difficulties, which now included a cocaine dealer's dead body.

⸻ ♦ ⸻

The bells of the Sydney University Carillon chimed one o'clock as Kate took a narrow staircase to her corridor. Two hours until her reading group. She closed herself in her room with a sigh. The shelves filled with books, the honey-coloured desk by the leaded-glass window looking out on the lone jacaranda in the quadrangle.

Kate slumped into her swivel chair and dragged the green shopping bag alongside. She'd assigned a comparison of James Bentham and John Stuart Mill for this afternoon's special reading group. Though she knew the views of both thinkers almost by heart, she'd snagged a volume of Bentham's correspondence from the library on the suggestion of a colleague. It paid to stay one step ahead of the brighter students and she hoped to find a subtlety in Bentham's views on the nature of human good to add to her understanding of his *Introduction to the Principles of Morals and Legislation*.

Gabriel Wu was one of her brighter students. Sometimes she felt he understood the material as well as she did herself, but he was unfailingly courteous in class, listening intently, asking intelligent questions and responding carefully to those who were slower to grasp the concepts. His written work was neatly argued and impeccably referenced. High Distinction material.

The biggest problem she'd encountered in her first year of teaching, both in the Philosophy of Law lectures and the optional reading group, was Stebby Rodriguez. He constantly asked questions that seemed to Kate quite irrelevant, in a pointed manner edging on rude, in a way that seemed to suggest he knew something she didn't. He had confidence in spades but his thoughts on paper were disorganised and he'd be lucky to get a Distinction, in spite of his combative brand of enthusiasm and his evident intelligence.

Kate sighed and pulled out the library books. Bentham's correspondence came first, a thick hardcover, followed by two extra reference books for the coming weeks of Law lectures. At the bottom was a copy of the 1948 edition of Bentham's *Introduction to the Principles of Morals and Legislation*. Kate studied the inside cover. The copy was marked with Fisher Library's stamp, but she hadn't checked it out. How had it come into her bag?

Kate closed her eyes. Weariness washed over her as she tried to recall the details of that hazy time between discovering the body and finding herself outside Fisher Library. She had stood in the foyer talking to detectives, and someone had asked for her library card. She'd thought the police were checking her identity, but now it seemed a librarian had thought to check out her books.

Her electronic library record would tell her if the Bentham had been among them. Kate pulled herself closer to the desk and woke her computer. She logged on to the library system. Yes, the list of books assigned to her card included the Bentham as well as the others she'd brought back in the bag. Someone had gathered her books from the aisle near the dealer's body and somehow, the Bentham had been among them.

It was a small thing, but it niggled at her. By what coincidence had the Bentham come to be among her books on the floor in the stacks where the dead man lay? Who had dropped it there? Gabriel and Stebby had both been in the library when the murder took place, two of her students who were required to read selections from Bentham's *Introduction* for the reading group this afternoon. She'd seen them leaving the library, and what's more, Stebby had seemed anxious not to meet her gaze.

He might have been in the stacks at the same time as Silas Brown, might have grappled with Brown, stabbed him, dropped the book, dashed away. Kate shook her head. This was ridiculous. What reason would Stebby Rodriguez have for murdering a drug dealer in the Fisher Library stacks? Her imagination was running away with her, and she really should focus on work.

Kate had just typed 'Silas Brown' into her computer's search engine when someone tapped on her office door.

"Come in," she called, minimising the browser with a click. She swivelled on her chair towards the door.

The third member of her reading group, Sarah Dickinson, stood in the doorway, shifting from foot to foot like a stick insect. So tall that she'd developed a habitual stoop, the teenager had short blonde hair and inconspicuous brows and lashes. Her features seemed too large for her face, especially her enormous blue eyes and what Kate uncharitably thought of as her sad goldfish lips. She was the kind of girl who hid herself in formless sweaters and shredded jeans. Kate was relieved that she had made some good friends at the University—she had formed an alliance this year with Stebby and Gabriel, and the three had come to Kate with the idea of the reading group.

Sarah stepped into the office with a waft of Dove soap. "Hey, um, I just got here and the library's closed. Police cars everywhere."

"Mmm."

"Um, I haven't had a chance to read that chapter of Jeremy Bentham yet. It's in Fisher." The girl hooked her thumbs through her backpack straps. "Could I maybe photocopy yours?"

"Of course." Kate eyed the library copy of the *Principles*. It might be tainted with cocaine. She stood and pulled her own copy off the shelf. "I'll give you my code for the staff photocopier if you like." She scribbled it on a piece of paper.

"Oh, thanks, that's great." Sarah set off down the hallway.

Kate turned back to her computer. Her internet search revealed that Silas Brown had been the owner of a seedy club in Darlinghurst. Peripheral in numerous drug investigations, he had somehow avoided prosecution. She clicked on 'images' and the satyric face from the library floor beamed out at her from a page of photographs. His hair was slightly receding at the temples, but apart from that he'd been attractive and physically well-built. His dress sense leaned towards designer suits and flashy ties, and he often appeared with his arm around a beautiful girl.

Someone in the doorway coughed. Kate minimised the browser again and turned.

Sarah held out the book, saying, "Thanks for that."

"You're welcome, Sarah. I'll see you at three?"

The girl nodded. When she'd left, Kate shut and locked the door. She returned to her desk to see if the Internet could tell her anything more about the dead man, Silas Brown.

Kate dragged herself away from the computer forty-five minutes later. Her vision was blurred from staring at the screen, and her notepad was full of scribbles. Most disturbingly, Kate had discovered that Stebby Rodriguez's brother, Charles, had died of a heroin overdose outside Silas Brown's Darlinghurst club just after his eighteenth birthday.

Kate found herself chilled to read of the connection. It confirmed her suspicion of Stebby. She checked the time. It was nearly time for the reading group. She was about to come face-to-face with Stebby. She needed to talk to someone, but who could she trust with her suspicions that her student was guilty of murder? Who could talk some sense into her, and get her to leave this stupid mess alone?

Her colleague, Phillip Turner, might know Stebby; he taught into the first year program. He was sympathetic, too. She didn't need to tell him exactly what she was thinking… she could just sound out the ideas.

Kate's cheeks were so hot, she felt almost feverish. She locked her office carefully when she left. Phillip's office was along the other side of the corridor, looking out towards Fisher Library. His door was open and she tapped to get his attention.

"Hiya, Kate. How's it going?"

"Phillip, have you ever taught Stebby Rodriguez?"

He raised an eyebrow. He was a tall, angular man in his fifties, all elbows and knees, but his grey eyes betrayed a smoothly-functioning intelligence at odds with his awkward physique. He stood up and walked around Kate, closed the office door, and turned to her "I'm teaching him this semester in Logic."

"How does he strike you?"

Phillip frowned. "He's fine. A little arrogant, perhaps…You've had problems?"

"Some." Kate sat down. "I… I just found out about his brother."

Phillip shook his head. "I don't know anything about him."

"He died. Heroin."

"That's sad. These kids that come to us… We don't always know much about them, do we? What they might've been through."

Kate stared at the diamond-shaped panels in Phillip's casement window. "Do you think there's any way I can find out more about Stebby?"

"Short of asking, no… well, you could have a look in student records. That would tell you about any period of exclusion, any difficulties in his academic history. Not that I remember anything to speak of. Try not to worry, Kate. I'm sure you've treated him fairly, no matter how difficult he's been."

Kate nodded. "Thanks." She stood and went to the door. "See you, then." She couldn't bring herself to ask anything more of Phillip. It all seemed so crazy when she imagined herself saying it out loud. Perhaps Phillip would tell her to go home, that she was in shock, that she should take the afternoon off.

Her hands were slick with sweat. She gripped her key tightly and turned it in the lock. It was twenty-five minutes to three, twenty-five minutes until Stebby, Gabriel and Sarah were due to arrive for the reading group. She pulled out a manila folder from her filing cabinet. It contained a print-out of her Philosophy of Law students' names and student IDs. She logged into Student Records and keyed in Stebby's student ID.

Kate flicked through the database. Usually there was very little need for her to enter the general database. When marking, she used a separate grading sheet that mysteriously fed into that database through the Philosophy administrators. She was unfamiliar with the system and dreaded what she might do by accident, but finally she came upon a summary of Stebby's student record. She scanned it and saw nothing untoward. He'd started at the University the previous year in a straight Bachelor of Arts. Since then, he'd achieved consistent Credits and Distinctions in all units of study, except first year Logic, in which he'd managed a High Distinction.

It was a quarter to three. Kate's stomach knotted with anxiety. She clicked back to the search page and typed in Sarah Dickinson's student ID and navigated straight through to the student record. Sarah's record was patchier, with numerous bare passes and a repeat of a History unit she'd failed in her first year of study. Something caught Kate's eye. Halfway through her first year at University, the administration had recorded a change of legal name. Sarah's previous surname was listed as St George. Why would an eighteen year-old change her name?

Kate flicked her browser open again, and searched the names 'Silas Brown' and 'Sarah St George' together. A full screen of results appeared. Kate clicked on one and found herself in Sydney's social pages with the search terms highlighted under one of the images of Brown with his arm around a beautiful girl.

Kate stared at the beautiful girl. Understanding clicked into place like a jigsaw piece. While the mane of blonde hair had been chopped and the lashes and brows left untinted, the lips now unpainted, the features were Sarah Dickinson's. Kate clicked onto 'images' again, and the page filled with Silas and Sarah. In every photo, Sarah's body and face were displayed to devastating effect in glittering dresses and professional make-up. The big blue eyes huge, rimmed with liner. Those lips, those goldfish lips, pillowy-soft, painted pink. But Sarah looked so young; she couldn't have been more than seventeen in most of those photos.

Hearing footsteps in the corridor, Kate quickly shut down the browser. The footsteps went past and she breathed deeply. Picking up a notepad and pen, she set to work for her reading group, waiting for the knock at the door that would indicate the students had arrived.

Kate saw Sarah's beauty now, not up front, but tucked away and ignored by its host like an unwelcome guest. And once she'd seen it nothing could erase it from her awareness. Not the stoop, not the girl's pallor or her self-inflicted haircut, and not her deliberately shapeless clothes.

The three students had filed in and made themselves comfortable, Gabriel and Stebby elbow-to-elbow on the small sofa, Sarah apart from them in the wooden-armed chair. The room seemed stuffy all of a sudden and Kate moved to open the window that looked out over the quadrangle.

"Right, let's get started." The pitch of her voice sounded high, too high. She gathered her teaching materials from the desk and sat opposite Sarah with her papers piled on her lap, a shield. She glanced at her notes, at the questions she'd written but didn't know if she would have the courage to ask.

"So, today we're discussing utilitarianism and its relation to the law. Bentham's view is that *the good* amounts to pleasure. In terms of a utilitarian ethical theory, that would mean that individual actions should aim to maximise pleasure and minimise pain." Kate looked around at her students' faces. "What do you think of that?"

Gabriel, ever-willing to contribute, smiled and shrugged. "I think it sounds okay. It justifies us caring about animal welfare. Rules out a lot of cruelty."

"Will it work in all instances, though? Let's try to think of counter-examples." Kate took a deep breath, hoping they didn't notice how it hitched. "Drug addiction. Addicts experience pleasure from a high—perhaps an intense pleasure, perhaps relief from emotional problems. Would a… drug dealer be doing good, on Bentham's theory? Providing a great deal of pleasure?" Kate looked at Sarah's wide, blue eyes.

But the response came from Stebby, who had leaned forwards to catch Kate's attention. His eyes were narrowed, eyebrows drawn down. "Of course it's not the right thing to do. Most of an addict's suffering is withdrawal. Whenever they're not high, they're suffering—something they'd never experience if it wasn't for the dealer."

Kate continued to play devil's advocate. "But surely, if a person starts using—heroin, ice, cocaine—it's a symptom of an inner struggle, unhappiness…"

"Not necessarily," Sarah said, quietly. "They might just be young. Curious. Easily led."

Stebby nodded vigorously.

Gabriel, clasping his hands together, seemingly unaware of any tension, said, "In any case, if they were unhappy, wouldn't they be better off trying to fix that? Not, like, taking a drug that'll make it worse in the end."

Kate nodded. Their responses might have been the same, on any other day. "All right, so we seem to have agreed that a drug dealer is actually a *cause* of great unhappiness." She shot a glance at Sarah, who seemed to have grown paler. "Well, let's continue with that example. A drug dealer is someone who inflicts pain, spreads unhappiness. Both Bentham and J.S. Mill argue that the right action is the one which maximises overall happiness, and both thinkers agreed that the law can separate from morality—one of our major discussion points today. So, for instance, the law might allow an action that is, on the utilitarian approach, taken to be immoral, or even forbid an act which is morally necessary." Kate paused, looking at each of her students in turn. She swallowed. "If, say, one had the opportunity to remove a great source of unhappiness, one might judge that something illegal is the morally right thing to do."

Kate held her gaze on Sarah. Long moments passed as the two stared at one another. Finally, Sarah looked down, and Kate knew that she had found the truth, and that Sarah knew she had too.

Sarah's lip trembled, and she whispered, "It wasn't because of Bentham. It wasn't because it was the right thing to do. I didn't think of it that way at all."

"Why, then?" Kate's concentration on the girl was so intense that she had forgotten about the boys. Their faces swam in her peripheral vision, fixed on Sarah, who spoke again.

"He wouldn't leave me alone. Wouldn't give me a chance… I've turned everything around since I came to Uni, I have a new life, I'm learning so much—I feel strong, except when I'm with him, and he follows me…" A pink flush spread around the rims of Sarah's eyes and her lips, while her cheeks grew even paler. "He finds me wherever I am, I never know when he's going to show up… I started to carry a little knife in my bag, I didn't even really know why…"

"Shhh." Kate put her finger to her lips and turned to the boys. Both stared at Sarah, and Kate tried to read their expressions. Stebby had known some of this—had he been there in the stacks as well?—and his gaze was angry—anger at Silas Brown, though, not at Sarah. Gabriel, on the other hand, showed signs of shock.

"He was scum," Stebby said quietly.

Kate sighed and looked down at her papers. What would she do? There was no sense of triumph at having learned the truth. It was a mess.

"Why don't you tell us what you really believe? About the ethics, I mean." It was Gabriel who spoke. He had recovered his equilibrium, and his face invited her to share the burden that had come to rest on her shoulders.

Yes, it would help to tell them what she really believed. But what was that, precisely? She searched for some kind of understanding that would cut through the chaos of real events. Kant, Hume, Bentham, Mill. Never before had she been called on to test their theories in a matter of life and death.

She put her hands flat down over her notes. "I believe that it is wrong to kill." Kant, for whom principles were everything. Certainty was clearer in her voice than she felt. The students watched anxiously, as if she was deciding something for all of them, which she supposed, she was. "But I do not believe that much good will come of telling anyone what we have learned here today." Hume, the humanist. Kate turned to Sarah and, fighting a trembling that threatened to take over her face, neck and arms, spoke. "Unless you decide it will be better for you to turn yourself in to the police. I leave it to you. I don't believe you would find yourself in a situation like this again." Bentham, Mill, powerful minds seeking and weighing every viewpoint.

Sarah shook her head, but it was Stebby who spoke, fiercely. "Of *course* she won't."

The words echoed into silence in the small room. The four of them sat without speaking, and after a moment, through the window came a tumble of voices from a class released into the quadrangle below. Laughter drifted up from the sandstone cloisters and a gust of warm spring air brought aromas of grass and earth, and the promise of all that was good.

We turn next to a classic tale of detection, first published in 1988. This story is a blending of characters from the authors' independent crime stories, and serves as a near word-perfect example of a dying clue mystery.

Fast friends, John Lutz and Josh Pachter have been writing, editing, and best of all, selling entertaining tales to every major publication in existence since the late Pleistocene age.

Previously published in An Eye for Justice, the third Private Eye Writers of America anthology, edited by Bob Randisi and published by Mysterious Press in 1988, and Detectives (AMSCO, 2000)

DDS 10752 LIBRA

by John Lutz and Josh Pachter

Dwight Stone hunched over the telephone in the yellow glow from the antique lamp atop his desk. His voice was pitched low and excited. The huge oak roll top was the dominant feature of Stone's cluttered living room, also serving as his office. Most of the furniture scattered around was ancient, because he couldn't afford anything newer; the desk and lamp, legacies from a long-dead aunt, were the only pieces of value in the apartment.

A mischievous smile flickered briefly across his lips as he cradled the receiver, but his clear brown eyes were troubled. He crossed to the tiny cubicle his landlord called a kitchenette, made coffee on a hot plate, and carried a steaming mug back to his desk. He pulled a blank expense-account form from one of the drawers and laboriously began to fill it in, now and then darting out a hand for coffee or to work the cantankerous old adding machine at his side. He was a large man, with too much upholstery straining the material of his clothes; he and his overstuffed furniture were perfectly compatible.

In a silence between ratchety growls of the adding machine, Stone suddenly sat up straight. A slight noise from behind had alerted him. He turned, and saw the tarnished brass knob of the front door slowly rotating, heard a floorboard creak outside in the hall. Fear lanced through his bowels like a shaft of ice as he realized that he *had* been followed home, after all.

Fright momentarily numbed him. Like most small-town private investigators, he never carried a gun, didn't even own one. He regretted that now, because he had no illusions about who it was who stood outside his door. Or about what it was the man had come for.

True, the door was locked, but the lock was a joke and would offer little resistance. It would slow down the man outside for a moment, but it wouldn't stop him.

There wasn't much time. Within the next few minutes, Stone knew, he would be out of time forever.

Swallowing his terror, he scribbled hastily at the bottom of the paper he was working on. There was an ominous *click* from the doorway, and he dropped his pen and reached for one of the desk's many cubbyholes.

Seconds later, the apartment door swung open behind him.

<hr>

Nudger watched the two detectives nosing around the ransacked apartment. The place was a mess. Stone hadn't been much of a housekeeper to begin with, and whoever had killed him had taken the time to toss the four small rooms with frantic thoroughness.

The policemen were both in their fifties and they moved with the studied nonchalance typical of small-town cops. They were a team: one was named Byrnes (the plodder, Nudger soon decided), the other was Allen (the brains of the operation). Nudger resisted making the obvious crack about George and Gracie. He didn't figure this pair for a comedy act.

"Go through it again," said Byrnes, standing in the light from the front window. The lamp on the big old roll top where Stone had died was still on. Nudger had found it on when he'd arrived, an hour earlier, and had left it that way. He hadn't touched the body, either; it lay slumped across the surface of the desk, as he had discovered it. The expression on the half of Stone's face he could see was twisted, terrorized. There was no blood on the desk or the floor because the small-caliber bullet that had left a neat little hole in the back of Stone's head on entry hadn't come out the other side. Nudger was glad about that; he hated the sight of blood. Murder scared him all by itself, without the accompanying gore.

"Stone had been hired to recover a set of drawings stolen from the office of a fashion designer here in town," he said tiredly, starting in on the story for the third time. "He phoned me in the city last night and told me about the case. He'd only been brought in a couple of days ago, but he'd already managed to get his hands on the drawings. He was worried that the thief would try to get them back, though, so he'd hidden them someplace where he was sure they'd be safe. He wouldn't tell me where they were, but he seemed pretty clear the thief would never be able to find them. He was going to work up an expense account, he said, then catch some sleep. He wanted me to meet him here this morning and go with him to pick up the drawings and deliver them to his client. Just in case the thief tried to get them back."

Byrnes and Allen listened impassively.

"When I showed up here," Nudger went on, "he didn't answer my knock. I slipped the lock with a credit card and came in to wait for him."

Byrnes stirred. "That's breaking and entering," he said.

Actually, it was trespassing, but Nudger decided not to quibble. Somehow the time seemed wrong for a discussion of legal niceties. "Bull," he said. "Dwight Stone and I have been friends for years. I let myself in whenever I come calling and find him out. He doesn't mind; he does the same thing at my place. *Did.*" He motioned toward the body at the desk. "Anyway, I found him like that and phoned the police immediately."

Allen's pale blue eyes were unreadable. If he held any particular opinion about Nudger's story, he wasn't letting it show. Byrnes, on the other hand, had a more provincial personality; he was making no effort to conceal his disdain for the hotshot city-slicker PI.

"You didn't touch anything?" Allen asked.

"Of course not."

"Just like on TV," said Byrnes. Nudger couldn't tell if he was kidding.

"Tell us more about this case Stone was working on," Allen suggested.

"There's not much to tell. Geoffrey Devane's got a small but very successful fashion house here in your town. He does all the designing himself and employs about two dozen people to manufacture and market the clothing. When he opened his safe on Monday morning, the drawings for his spring line were missing. Four of his employees know the combination, and Devane figured one of those four must have swiped the designs, planning on selling them to a competitor."

"Industrial espionage," Allen murmured.

"Exactly. Devane reported the theft, but your department didn't seem very encouraging, so he decided to bring in a private investigator. He got Stone's number out of the Yellow Pages, and it took Dwight three days to pin down the thief's identity and recover the stolen drawings."

"Only the thief wanted them back"—Allen picked up the narrative—"so he followed Stone home and killed him and turned the place upside down looking for them."

"That's the way I figure it," Nudger agreed.

Allen trudged to the window and gazed outside. He was framed by sunlight, so Nudger had to squint to look at him. That was the sort of technique cops used on suspects, not fellow professionals. Nudger's stomach twitched out a warning. He thumbed back the foil on a roll of antacid tablets and popped two of the chalky disks into his mouth.

"Nervous?" Allen asked.

"My stomach is."

"Ulcer?"

"Don't know. Afraid to find out."

"Dumb."

"I guess."

"You say you used a credit card to slip the lock?"

Nudger nodded. "The killer must have locked the door behind him when he left last night."

"Why last night? Why not this morning, sometime before you got here?"

"The lamp on the desk," said Nudger. "It must have been dark outside when Stone was shot, that's why he had it switched on."

"You look good for this, you know," Byrnes scowled, "in spite of your pretty story." He seemed to relish the opportunity to speak in Hollywood clichés.

"You mean I'm a suspect?" asked Nudger, as if the thought had just now occurred to him. It was uncomfortable, standing there in a room with two homicide detectives as they plied their trade. It was uncomfortable standing there in a room with a dead body in it. The combination of cops and corpse was lousy. "Don't forget," he said to Allen, who seemed the more open-minded of the two, "I'm the one who called it in in the first place."

"Subterfuge," Allen suggested. "You and Stone were pals. You figured we'd get around to you sooner or later, so you called in the murder to convince us you had nothing to do with it."

Now they were ganging up on him. It didn't seem fair. "I'm not that devious," Nudger said. "And what about the murder weapon? I'm not carrying a gun, and you haven't found one in the apartment. And the door was locked when I got here."

"That's *your* story," said Byrnes doggedly. He shot a glance at the corpse. "What's *his* story?"

"What about my motive?" Nudger tried.

"We might just find one."

Or invent one, Nudger thought. He popped another antacid tablet into his mouth. Small-town murder, small-town cops, small-town judge and jury. Put it all together, and it might spell big-time trouble.

"Mind if I look at the desk for a minute?" he asked.

"Be our guest," Allen told him.

Nudger crossed the room, riffled through the papers on the roll top's surface, explored its cubbyholes carefully.

"The expense account," he said at last, straightening and looking over at Allen. "Stone told me he was going to work it up for Devane after he got through talking with me, but there's no sign of the form on his desk."

"*You* say he told you," Byrnes reminded Nudger. "What *I* say is you and Stone were together last night. You had an argument, or you've got some other motive we haven't tumbled to yet. You shot him, then realized we'd tie you to him eventually. So you went away and ditched the gun, then came back this morning so you could 'find' the body and call us in and feed us your carefully rehearsed version of the facts."

Nudger thought back over the last fifteen hours and realized he'd been completely alone between the time he'd hung up the phone after talking with Stone and his discovery of the body this morning. *Alone on the phone with Stone;* the words ran through his mind and kept him from thinking clearly. The law couldn't prove he was here when Stone was murdered, that was certain—but Nudger couldn't prove he *wasn't* here, either. His stomach dived and did a few tight loops.

"The fingerprint man and photographer ought to be here soon," Byrnes announced. "Then we'll be leaving."

"I know," Nudger said. "You're going to take me downtown for another little chat."

"This *is* downtown," Allen told him. "You can call your lawyer from headquarters."

"I'll wait until I'm charged before I do that," Nudger muttered. He wasn't at all sure Byrnes and Allen had enough evidence to hold him on a murder rap.

Allen shrugged. Byrnes smiled. Nudger figured they probably thought they had enough.

Staring at the big roll top desk and the position of the body, he had an idea. Or maybe it was just a final straw to clutch at before drowning in a sea of lawyers, judges, and jurors. And then jailers.

"Maybe he hid it," he said.

"Hid what?" That was Allen, of course. Byrnes had better things to do than pay attention to anything Nudger might have to offer.

"The expense account form. Stone was sitting at his desk when he was shot. What if he heard somebody at the door behind him? He might have had enough time to scrawl a message on the form and hide it from his killer."

"That's right," said Byrnes, deadpan, "he was working on his expenses when he bought it."

"Which would explain how come there's no expense account form in plain sight on the desk now," Nudger continued. "He wrote a message on it and hid it before the killer entered the apartment."

That line of reasoning seemed to sway Allen slightly. He gave Nudger an encouraging smile. Byrnes looked like he was wishing they could wind this whole thing up, so he could file his report and head for home. Police work, this minor matter of the rest of Nudger's life, was apparently annoying him.

Nudger walked back to the desk, and neither officer moved to stop him.

"We looked and you looked," Byrnes said.

"Can I look again?"

"Why not?" Allen shrugged. "With a minimum of touching, please."

Nudger stood back from the desk and scanned it carefully. Nothing he could see even remotely resembled an expense account form.

"We already checked under the body," said Byrnes, hoping to hurry things along. "We did everything but take the damn desk apart."

"You didn't look where you couldn't see, though, did you?"

"What do you mean?" Allen's forehead wrinkled with puzzlement.

Ignoring him, Nudger stepped to the desk and eased the roll top down as far as possible, almost to the point where it would have touched Stone's body.

A printed form was attached to the accordion S-roll of the retractable top with a bit of cellophane tape. Stone must have had just enough time to use the tape, and then push the roll top up and out of sight before his murderer came into the room.

Nudger tore the form away from the wooden roll top triumphantly. Byrnes and Allen had already moved to flank him, and the three of them read the combination of letters and numbers scribbled across the bottom of the sheet:

DDS 10752 LIBRA

"Libra," said Byrnes, with a disgusted look at his partner. "Don't tell me this turns out to be another one of your damn Zodiac cases."

"Zodiac cases?" Nudger repeated, turning the words into a question.

Allen frowned. "Couple years back," he explained, "I solved a case where a dying man's last word was 'Gemini,' and Byrnes here thinks that makes me some kind of astrology expert."

"Libra," Byrnes grumbled. "And DDS. And 10752. What the hell's that all supposed to mean?"

Nudger fumbled with his roll of antacid tablets, then changed his mind and slipped the roll back into his pocket. "The DDS part I understand," he said. "Stone once told me he was born during Eisenhower's first presidential campaign. His parents were staunch Republicans, so they named him Dwight David. Which made his initials DDS."

"And," Allen mused, "he was born during Ike's campaign." He bent over the body and slid a thin billfold from the dead man's hip pocket. Unfolding it, he leafed through its half-dozen plastic windows until he located Stone's driver's license. "Uh-huh. He was born on October seventh, 1952; that's 10/7/52."

"Which makes him a Libra, all right," Byrnes contributed, "same as my wife." Suddenly he faced Nudger and snapped, "What's *your* sign?"

"No Smoking," Nudger told him.

"Get serious, tough guy."

"I'm not tough and I am serious. I don't have any idea what my sign is. My birthday's September thirteenth, does that help?"

"Virgo," said Byrnes, as if a lot of things had just been explained.

"So the letters are his initials, the numbers are his birth date, and Libra is his astrological sign," Allen nodded. "But, I mean, so *what?*"

"Maybe the killer was a Libra, too," Byrnes suggested feebly.

"Or a dentist," said Nudger, glad to see that the focus of the investigation had shifted away from him for a change. "DDS could stand for Doctor of Dental Surgery, you know, instead of Dwight David Stone."

Before Byrnes could formulate an appropriately snide comeback, the fingerprint man and photographer arrived. They turned out to be the same man, a wiry scarecrow with bristly gray hair and a genuine Speed Graphic camera, like the press used to rely on in the Thirties and Forties. Then a second man turned up, the county's medical examiner and town's mortician. There was a lot of versatility in this backwater. Stone hadn't had any family, and the M.E. was sizing up the furniture to see how big a funeral the estate might be expected to cover.

While the experts went about their tasks, Nudger, Byrnes, and Allen turned back to Dwight Stone's last desperate message.

"We oughta check his horoscope for today," Byrnes proposed.

Nudger thought that was about as logical an idea as anything else he'd heard so far.

"Never mind that," Allen said, snapping his fingers. There was a hunter's gleam in his eye. "Let's go."

"Go?" Byrnes asked gruffly. "Go where?"

"You'll see," said Allen. "And you're not going to like it when I tell you Nudger here gave me the idea."

"Me?" Nudger looked around blankly, making sure there was no one else by that name in the apartment. "What'd I say?"

"You said maybe the killer was a dentist." Allen smiled mysteriously, and they couldn't get another word out of him.

They left Stone's apartment and crossed the street to a dusty unmarked car parked illegally next to a fire hydrant. Halfway to their destination, Nudger realized where they were going, and why. He was impressed. Maybe there was something to be said for small-town detective work, after all.

If Allen turned out to be right, that is.

The building was suitably quiet. There were people there—old ladies in padded armchairs devouring Barbara Cartland romances, college types copying term papers from assorted encyclopedias, a prim woman with her hair in a bun pulling outdated Periodicals out of plastic covers and replacing them with more recent issues—but all of them went about their business in silence.

It took only a few minutes for Allen to find the shelf he was looking for. He ran his index finger along the spines of the books lined up there until he reached the one whose white gummed label read 107.52 and, beneath that, *Mol.* He eased the book from the shelf and pronounced its title aloud: "*Teaching Philosophy,* by Vincent Molloy. Should make fascinating reading, if that's the sort of reading that fascinates you. Me, I like the 87th Precinct."

There were several sheets of paper sandwiched between the book's removable dust jacket and permanent hard cover. Allen slid them free and unfolded them. Each page displayed a sketch of a woman dressed in delicate pastel clothing, and each drawing had been signed by Geoffrey Devane in the lower right corner.

On the top sheet, in Dwight Stone's handwriting, the name of Devane's comptroller had been penciled in.

"I'm still not sure I understand it all," Byrnes complained, as Nudger and the two detectives sat over coffee in a closet-sized office at headquarters. Luther Higham, Devane's comptroller, had confessed to the theft of the drawings and the killing of Dwight Stone, and was in a holding cell awaiting arraignment on charges of industrial espionage and murder.

Nudger was glad to explain. "Higham opened the safe and stole his boss' drawings, planning to sell them to a competitor. But unfortunately—for the thief, that is — Stone was able to recover the sketches. He was afraid to keep them in his apartment, though, figuring — correctly, as it turned out—that the thief might know who he was, where he lived, and come after them. So he stashed them at the local library, figuring he and I would pick them up this morning and deliver them to Devane."

Byrnes finished his coffee and set down his styrofoam cup, still looking perplexed. "That much I get," he said. "And to make sure he wouldn't forget which book he'd hidden the drawings in, he used the volume whose call number matched his birthdate. But why did he put his initials on the note he left you? And why the *hell* did he bother writing down his sign?"

"They weren't his initials," said Allen, "and it wasn't his sign. It was Nudger who tipped me off to that, when he pointed out that DDS didn't *have* to stand for Dwight David Stone. Well, it didn't stand for a dentist, either: it stood for Dewey Decimal System, the cataloguing system used for classifying nonfiction books by subject. Stone was telling Nudger that he'd hidden the drawings in the book shelved under number 107.52 according to the Dewey Decimal System."

"But why Libra?" Byrnes demanded.

Allen grinned. "Stone didn't have time to finish his message *and* hide it away before Devane's comptroller broke into his apartment. It was more important to hide it than to finish it, so he stopped writing, two letters before what he'd intended to be the end of the message, and counted on Nudger to realize what he meant."

"*Library*," Byrnes sighed. "Dewey Decimal System number 107.52, in the public library."

"Only I managed to miss it," said Nudger. "I guess I'm not as bright as Stone thought. Good thing for me your partner worked it out."

Byrnes washed a hand across his face. "Yeah, sure is. Listen, Nudger, looks like I owe you an apology. I jump to conclusions sometimes. It's a lousy habit, I know, but I do it anyway. Like with that astrology business—"

Nudger stood up from his straight-backed chair, feeling his stomach begin to react to the acidic coffee he'd only half finished. He smiled and waved a hand negligently and said, "Forget the apology. Let's just say you owe me a decent cup of coffee. The stuff you guys drink is awful."

"Point of fact," Byrnes grinned, "we usually drink tea. So the Zodiac Detective here can read the leaves."

An article about nineteenth century wallpaper samples inadvertently laced with arsenic was the impetus for our next story, from Jennie MacDonald, while her experience shelving books and staging public events for the Denver Public Library provided the fodder.

Jennie MacDonald, PhD, is a prize-winning author of stories and plays. She also pens academic articles concerning eighteenth and nineteenth century Gothic literature, theatre, and material culture.

Clean Cup

by Jennie MacDonald

A Thimbleful of Poison hurled through the book drop flap just as I was retrieving the last returns of the day from the bin. It was the evening of the Wonderland Tea Party fundraiser. The decorators were already setting up lights and paperboard scenery. The caterers were putting a bar in order and draping cabaret tables. Our Head Librarian Mrs. Moody—Mrs. M. to us—was overseeing the silent auction tables. The rest of us staff were clearing things away, fretting over whether our transitional work clothes were dressy enough, and bracing for the arrival of the guests.

I didn't know, of course, what *A Thimbleful of Poison* was, other than a book, and what it meant at that moment because it struck my knuckles quite hard. I mean, really, who throws books into drop boxes like that? Especially old books? Even if they were considered pretty lowbrow when they first came out.

I fished it up with the rest, the picture books, the new bestsellers that immediately went out again because they had such long waiting lists, and the videos that are the bane of the books-only crowd. It was a slight book, the sunned red cloth cover fraying at the ends of the spine. The title was barely legible. More visible was a gilt image of a thimble on the front. This rang a bell. I left the other returns on a cart and carried this one to the circulation desk.

There was no scanning label--it was that old. I had to manually check the shelving location number on the checkout card pocket pasted in the front of the book. The computer system did not recognize any of the details, so with a little thrill of curiosity I looked up the library's *Have You Seen Me?* list. Started in 1953 by the legendary Head Librarian Isabella Sharp, the *Have You Seen Me?* list catalogued every book gone missing, not only from the shelf but evidently from the library's online database, as well.

And there it was. *A Thimbleful of Poison* by Ruth Hays, published by Doubleday in 1950. Last checked out: 1952.

I admit it. My heart leapt up just as Wordsworth's did when he beheld the rainbow in the sky. Such are the thrills of a library shelver's life. I leafed through the book for errant items. Dollar bills sometimes turn up, or old recipes and grocery lists, things people tuck into library books to hold their place (thank God for anything resembling a bookmark, or our books would be dog-earred to death). How often do library books take the place of purses and briefcases? Once I found a declaration of love on a Valentine from the 1950s, and I wondered, but would never know, *what happened next?*

All of those found objects went into a tabletop display we call *Between the Covers: Found in Returned Books,* except for very recent dollars. Those went into the Children's Literacy Fund. Eric Doyle (no relation to Arthur Conan, sadly), the other part-time shelver at the Mary Chase Library branch of the Denver Public Library, held the record for the most dollar bills found in books. He also found the largest amount, a twenty that turned up in a copy of *Casino Royale.* We contacted the patron who had checked out the book, but he, to our great surprise, denied having any relationship with the money at all. He didn't even pretend it was his but instead was happy to hear it was going into the fund. One by one, people may be able to shore up my faith in humanity.

A shelver's life, however, is not just one restorative after another. I had this long-lost copy of *A Thimbleful of Poison* in my hands and no clue as to where it had been all this time. The checkout card had surely been consigned to oblivion at some point over the decades. I couldn't even begin to think where to look for it. Renovations to not only the Mary Chase but also the many other libraries in the system had obliterated many hard copy records from the early years. No doubt some patron had blithely wandered by the drop box, and, relieved of the burden, trundled on to a future of carefree days.

But wait. Whoever had returned the book had done so quite violently. It hadn't been casually slipped through the metal flap. It had been thrown in as if the patron (if indeed it was a patron) had wanted to get rid of it, to *be* rid of it. *Why?*

"What have you got there?" Eric appeared, really *appeared* out of thin air so unexpectedly it did make me wonder if he had graduated to a new level of the magic tricks he liked to do for the kids at Storytime.

"*A Thimbleful of Poison*," I said, showing him the cover. "It's a 'Have You Seen Me?' book."

"No way!" He reached for it. "I've been looking for a copy of that forever. For my dissertation."

"You actually know this book?" Once again tentacles of envy crept up to wrap around me. Eric's dissertation had to do with the use and imagery of poison in 20th-century American fiction. My dissertation, on the other hand, had yet to be determined. I was trying to work Agatha Christie into something on family curses. It was not going well.

"It's kind of a mash-up," he said, snatching it with a quick move. Add *ninja* to his list of talents. "A bit of *Trifles*--you know, that play about the wife who kills her husband with a leg of lamb--"

"And disposes of it in a very clever way," I injected.

"Yes, and one by your Agatha Christie, *Sparkling Cyanide*. Multi-generational murder. Listen to this opening line of *Thim-*

bleful: 'Dorothy Sherman didn't take offense lightly.' Real poison *and* poison by insinuation. I've got to read it."

"But not now. Sorry to remind you, but we're supposed to be helping out at this party, not indulging in murder mysteries, even if they are dissertation-worthy. Give that to me. I'll put it in the basket under the counter. Go on, someone's got to corral the caterers before they start using books for coasters." I'd actually seen that happening at a Central Library gala once--before the librarians swept in like the Valkyrie. That was a fundraising moment for the ages.

The reluctance with which he gave *A Thimbleful of Poison* back to me dragged through time. But off he went, almost with a skip, almost as though letting go of the book itself returned him to his usual effervescence.

I understood how much it meant to him, though I hadn't yet found the key to my own dissertation research. I couldn't say why the stupid book slipped from my fingers and struck the edge of the counter before falling to the floor. Maybe, like Tolkien's one ring, the thing inside the book wanted to be found; it wanted to be *found out*.

"What's this?" A cloud of Mrs. M.'s Chantilly perfume wafted over me as she bent to retrieve the book.

"It'll make you happy," I said. "It's a 'Have You Seen Me?' book."

"Oh, good!" She was a fluff-ball of book advocacy. Date stamp ink ran in her veins, and everybody loved her. On the rare occasions when I'd witnessed her Paddington-like hard stare, I'd blinked and thought I'd just imagined it. But it did happen. She reserved it for extremely late returns and parents who pulled their kids out of Storytime. I thought I saw it when Marilyn Van Horten, the Children's Literacy Foundation president, first visited to scrutinize the suitability of the Mary Chase for the fundraising party. "And what's this? Your eyesight's much younger than mine."

The fall had shaken loose a bookmark that both Eric and I had missed when we flipped through the pages. Mrs. M. held it out.

It wasn't the sort of bookmark people buy these days at places like bookstores and museums. It was just a narrow rectangle, hand-cut from a thick paper that reminded me of something. There was a pretty design on one side: a delicate bouquet of mixed flowers tied with a ribbon like a nosegay on a pale green background. I brushed it with one finger that came away with a bit of dust. The reverse was blank and surprisingly rough. I realized what it was.

"Wallpaper," I said, looking at the design again and guessing at how old it might be. A shudder ran through me. I fished a plastic bag out from the shelf below the computer. "Mrs. M., I think we'd better put the book in here. The bookmark, too. Right now."

She did so, and I put the bag inside another at the back of the shelf. "Why?"

"Because that bookmark looks *exactly* like one of the samples in *Shadows from the Walls of Death*. That was the collection of poisonous wallpaper samples we read about in the ALA newsletter last fall. Remember? The Michigan State Board of Health sent a hundred sets to state libraries in order to educate the public. All but four of them have been destroyed."

Her genial expression crumpled. "You mean we have a poisonous book just because of a bookmark?"

"I think so. The article had a bunch of illustrations of the samples. I'm positive this is the same as one of them. I have a very accurate visual memory."

"Photographic, I'd say. You never forget a book cover."

"That faded green, the dust—don't panic—but, it's probably arsenic. In fact, we should both go scrub our hands."

"We should lock up that book."

I shoved some things in front of the bag. "No one will be looking for it. We'd better hurry."

When we came out of the restroom, other people were starting to arrive. I spotted the actors I was supposed to supervise for the evening's entertainment. The Foundation members made a group entrance. As the official hosts, they launched into action organizing guest lists, gift bags, and generally taking over from our staff.

Mrs. Van Horten greeted Mrs. M. in a giddy embrace. "It's going to be a great success!" She nodded at me, her pink Glinda the Good crown dipping in a hazardous fashion.

I collected the actors and handed out their costumes. They had to change in the public restrooms, transforming into characters from *Alice in Wonderland*. The plan, devised by members of the Children's Literacy Fund Foundation, was to have the characters mingle with the invitees as they arrived and during passed hors d'oeurvres and cocktails. Then they would vanish into the downstairs auditorium to be discovered in a *tableau vivant*, the tea-party scene. They were to act the scene in an improvised fashion. It would end with the surprise arrival of the Queen of Hearts. Strawberry tarts would then be liberally dispensed among the guests to nibble during short readings from classic children's books, and a fundraising plea by the foundation's president. Throughout the evening the silent auction would entice the public with fanciful gift baskets described as having been created by well-known literary characters. I felt especially partial to the one designed by 'Miss Marple,' patron saint of knitting detectives everywhere.

The attendees were soon upon us. They paused at the main entrance to check in and relinquish their coats, before making for the bar, and then exploring the Wonderland the decorators had created. Swaths of pastel-colored tulle disguised (and protected) the library's original wooden bookcases. Fanciful trees and animals were stationed in the corners to amuse. A flock of pink flamingoes clustered before the cathedral window where Storytime was usually held. A string quartet played "A Very Merry Unbirthday" as everyone paraded in. The Foundation knew how to put on a good show, I'll say that for them.

The invitations had encouraged wearing costumes inspired by children's literature. The guests took that directive to every possible iteration. A clutch of Special Collections librarians turned up as Nancy Drew and her two detecting chums, Bess and George, along with Frank and Joe Hardy. Several local authors came as a set of *The Phantom Tollbooth* characters. I couldn't name members of Denver society, but you could tell who they were: lots of fairy tale characters and classics like *Little Women* and *Treasure Island* that enabled them to dress up in elegant costumes that made the wearers glamorous.

"What do you think?" The voice cut through my thoughts. It was Maureen, one of the actors, dressed as Alice, and looking remarkably two-dimensional. I suspect she would have taken that as a compliment.

"Perfect," I said without hesitation. The few people I knew in the theatre insisted I only say positive things to the actors and keep it clean and simple so as not to agitate them.

She fairly bounced with glee. "Where should I go?"

"Why don't you hang out by the silent auction? Encourage people to bid. You know, say things like 'Curiouser and curiouser that this basket only has five bids.' That sort of thing."

"Fun!" she said and started off. "Oh, did you get that book I turned in? An old, reddish thing, with a gold thing on the cover?"

"You mean a thimble? You turned that in?"

"Yeah. We're cleaning out my Gran's house. She was, like, a hoarder, you know? I thought about just throwing it away. I mean, it was so old probably no one would want to check it out anymore. But it had that Denver Public Library pocket in the front, so I figured I'd better put it in the book drop, just in case."

"But why did you throw it in? I mean, you really chucked it in, like you wanted to get rid of it."

"Oh, Gran said it was dangerous. Like toxic, you know. I didn't want to touch it any longer than I had to."

"Toxic? What do you mean?"

"Well, it's about poison, isn't it?"

"Maureen, did your Gran put a bookmark in it? Did she ever live in Michigan?"

"Oh, yeah. She kept that piece of wallpaper as a bookmark. It reminded her of home, she said, and Granddad. He died a long time ago, but she never remarried. She liked living on her own, right up to the end. But that old book --I should have thrown it away, huh?"

Then the White Rabbit was there, offering his faux-furry arm to Alice. I waved them both off to the silent auction. The White Rabbit is a bit of an in-joke at the Mary Chase. Her famous play, of course, was *Harvey*, the one about the six feet three and a half inch tall invisible white rabbit. At the Mary Chase we say that Alice's White Rabbit is what Harvey would look like if he were visible.

Rather than watch them make their animated way through the happy crowd, I glanced at Mrs. M. standing nearby. A Paddington hard stare was etched on her face. She wouldn't have liked hearing Maureen suggest that old books should just be thrown away. I wanted to say something to snap her out of it. At that moment, though, the party reached a point of visual and audible saturation, a table got knocked over, and I went running to save a New Fiction display from toppling into the mess.

Staff, of course, weren't supposed to drink at a library-sponsored function, but I didn't say no when Eric brought me some merlot in a paper cup. We strolled along the silent auction, bidding up the low numbers. The money was going to children's literacy, after all. I showed him where I'd put the book. The things I'd put in front of the bag had been disturbed. The book was still there, but the wallpaper sample bookmark was gone.

"Mrs. M.'s the only one who knew it was here." My voice shook.

"What would she want with it?"

"She got so mad when Maureen was talking about throwing away the book, just because it was old. I saw that look on her face."

"The hard stare?" He laughed.

"I mean it. She was furious." I grabbed his arm. "She seems so mild-mannered, but what if she's capable of doing something?"

"What could she do with a little old piece of wallpaper?"

"If you soaked it in liquid and made someone drink it, they could get sick. They might even die!"

"Maureen's never going to have a minute to drink something. She's too busy acting."

The thought came to us at the same minute.

"The tea party!" I said. "There's supposed to be tea in the cups, in the teapot, on the stage."

We jumped up. The crowd filled the stairs to the auditorium. Eric pushed me toward the elevator. It was slow and creaky, but no one else was waiting for it. When the bell dinged and the door started closing a group still at the top of the stairs started toward us like zombies hunting for brains. I pounded the "Close" button, and the old elevator sank to the lower depths.

The auditorium was half-full already. On the stage, the actors sat frozen in poses straight out of John Tenniel's tea party illustration. All but Alice, who stood halfway between the curtain and the tea table, just arriving for the scene.

"I'll go backstage and try to tell Maureen not to drink the tea," I whispered to Eric.

Mrs. Van Horten's enormous pink tulle-skirted form intercepted my flight. "Everything is going splendidly, um, Carol?"

It was her moment to *thank the staff individually*. I could just see it as an item on her To Do list. "Carolyn," I corrected her.

"Oh, yes, of course. Like, ah, Carolyn Keene? Nancy Drew?"

" Actually, yes. My mother loved the originals." *Was I really sharing this with Mrs. Van Horten-Hears-a-Who, as the children called her when she graced them with a Storytime reading one time?*. Please excuse me!"

I got around her skirt and navigated the meandering guests as fast as I could. At last I was backstage.

"Maureen!" I whispered from the wings. "Can you hear me?"

"I can't talk to you now," she said through gritted teeth. "I'm supposed to be frozen."

"Don't drink the tea," I said.

"What?"

At that moment the string quartet struck a chord and began a brief overture to get the crowd to quiet down and pay attention.

Maureen broke from her pose and ran toward the table, hands fluttering, voice quavering with excitement. "Why, it's a tea party!"

I could never get her attention now unless I ran out there myself. Clutching the dusty velvet curtain I debated.

"Move down! Move down!" shouted the Hatter.

"Pour the tea! Pour the tea!" cried the March Hare.

"Clean cup! Clean cup!" snuffled the Dormouse.

If I ran out now and grabbed the teapot, I could put an end to it. But that would put an end to everything. The evening would be ruined. Mrs. Van Horten would hunt me down and skewer me with Glinda's pink-glitter staff. The children would never learn to read.

I didn't know for sure that the tea was poisoned.

I didn't know that it wasn't.

"Here, Carolyn." Mrs. M. emerged from the shadows behind the props table. She set a teacup on the table. The wallpaper sample was in it, now in a sealed Ziploc bag. "No one's going to drink any arsenic on my account."

"But you took the bookmark."

"I was worried about it just sitting there for anyone to find. I admit that girl made me very angry, but you didn't really think I would poison someone for saying things like that, did you? Librarians are made of sterner stuff than that. We have to be. Someone has to stand up for books, after all. They can't stand up for themselves."

"What are you doing back here?"

"I confess, I got stuck here when the audience started coming in. I didn't want to spoil the illusion by an awkward entrance."

"I don't entirely believe you," I said.

"Poisoning the teapot did occur to me, is that what you think?"

My face went hot as it does when I'm about to cry. "Yes. I do."

"That's almost a compliment," she said. "It crossed my mind. And kept going."

———•◦•———

At last the crowd was gone. The Foundation members were adding up the money and congratulating each other. Mrs. M. waited with me for the actors to turn in their costumes. The rental shop had given us a wheeled cart and a box for the accessories. The White Rabbit, the Hatter, the March Hare, the Dormouse, and the Queen of Hearts all were piled in a heap. Maureen had neatly folded her Alice ensemble and set it on top of the rest. She looked at us, smiling.

"This was really great," she said. "And you know what totally just came to me? I shouldn't have said what I did about that old book. I mean, yeah, it was old. But *Alice in Wonderland* is an old book--and people still love it. *I* love it. At least, I love the movie. But everyone always says the book is better than the movie. So I'm going to read the book after this, and I'll love it. I just know it. So I shouldn't have been so mean about that old book. Just because something is *old* doesn't mean it's not *loved*--or import-ant--or valuable."

She bounded down the stairs. At the bottom she flung her arms out to announce to the world, "Just look at Shakespeare, you know!"

I helped Mrs. M. on with her coat. "So epiphanies come to us all. We'll have to dispose of that book though, I'm afraid," she sighed. "We can't have arsenic in the library." She was sorry, the sort of librarian who feels deeply wounded when a book has to be taken out of circulation. She glanced at me.

"Don't worry at all," I said. "I'll take care of it."

Eric and I had to stay to the bitter end, to see the party detri-tus cleaned up, to collect the costumes, to set the alarm and lock up. I gave him the bookmark and the book, which he promised to copy and then destroy in some responsible fashion. By the time we were walking down the front steps to our separate cars the full moon was up, caught in a tangle of iridescent clouds.

I was so tired.

At my car Eric waited while I fumbled with the key and then the door. I almost tripped getting in. He opened the passenger door and set a large basket festooned with yarn on the seat beside me. "Miss Marple's" contribution to the silent auction. I pulled free a pair of shiny lavender knitting needles from a ball of knobby lamb's wool.

"How did you know?" I asked, pointing a knitting needle at him.

"Are you kidding? It was obvious from the start."

"Well, you know what *I* think?"

"What?"

"That you are the one who 'finds' dollars in returned books. That's why you have the record."

"Okay, it's true, but I never put a twenty in a book."

I saluted him with the knitting needle. "One day."

He grinned. "One day."

Next up, a story for those for whom life is a constant search for more books and space for more books, for those whose shelves are boards and bricks, and those blessed with floor-to-ceiling bookcases, for those with stacks of books next to beds, and for those who have learned to double-stack vintage paperbacks.

Gwenda R. Jensen has lived in the United States and New Zealand, and now lives in Canada with books, cats, coffee, and her husband.

Different Lights

By Gwenda R. Jensen

Lindsay is looking at her own reflection in one of the library's floor-to-ceiling windows when the lights go off. Her reflection disappears. No longer does she see a white oval framed by short brown hair. No grey rectangle pullover. No black-clad legs. The reflected image of the room behind her disappears. No multi-colored ranks of mixed-sized books (thousands). No chestnut brown leather chairs (eight), matching settees (three), polished oak desks (two), small tables (seven), silk shaded lamps (six), Japanese bird and bamboo-painted rice paper floor lamps (five).

Before her eyes adjust to the unexpected change Lindsay sees only the darkness of a winter night. Eyes adjusting, she sees city lights (yellow and orange) far away where the highway runs east west beside the lake. She sees glittering (white) from the moonlit ripples on Grenadier Pond, which lies below *La Residence Thibaux-Marshall*, the huge, book-filled mansion within which she stands. Lindsay knows that the Pond's edge is approximately 20 meters below and 45 meters away horizontally from where she stands. She is separated from the Pond by two panes of glass, one vacuum between, and one garden filled with paths, steps, trees and shrubbery. And a boatshed, Lindsay remembers. Martin had said that there was a boatshed with a small jetty.

Lindsay looks up, searching for the moon, which reason tells her should be visible. To her left, she sees a bright semi-circle, its geometric simplicity spoiled by irregular black branches. Black fingers reaching upwards towards the heavens, she thinks. A fanciful thought—not hers.

Was the thought from one of Martin's poems, she wonders. Her own thoughts are about numbers and geometry, straight lines, primary colors, clear-cut categories, everything clean and tidy and functional. Nothing rough-edged or ambiguous. Things that are so straight-forward that they can be packed up quickly into boxes and taped shut. She always has boxes and tape on hand, ready for the next move.

Lindsay sighs. We will need those boxes, she thinks, when I stop work in another month. Martin wants to throw them away. We're together and settled, he said. Trust me. Lindsay had protested, but not strongly. She wanted to believe him.

Lindsay straightens her shoulders, takes a deep breath, exhales slowly. I will find more boxes, if I must, she decides. Large boxes for clothes and shoes and crockery. Small boxes for books. His collection of jazz. Her romances. His abandoned but not quite buried dissertation. Her management textbooks. Their stuff.

She pulls a white handkerchief from her jacket pocket, wipes away her tears, blows her nose. All better now, she thinks, and imagines a kind, maternal hand patting her shoulder.

There is a small bookcase off to her right, beside a stretch of leather-covered window seat. She walks over, steps on the floor switch for the nearby lamp, which switches on and shines a soft light through its rice paper painting of pond, cranes, water lilies and bamboo. Lindsay guesses that the main lights were turned off automatically from a central switch. The smaller lights can still be switched on independently. The automatic lighting would be one way to protect *La Residence* and its treasures from burglars. Martin had told her that Delphine Thibaux and Tom Marshall travelled frequently. They were away for weeks, sometimes months at a time. This house needed good security even before their deaths the previous month.

Lindsay grimaces. Martin has the lawyer's documents that give him the right to be there. But he is upstairs, checking the rooms on levels three and four: Bedrooms (six), dens (two), bathrooms (four), artist's studio (one), living area (one). If security guards arrive I can explain, she thinks.

Lindsay sits down on the window seat and pushes a tapestry cushion behind her back. She is tired. Her back hurts. She is there to support Martin, who is panicking about what the lawyer wants him to do. Once Martin returns with a more complete inventory of *La Residence*'s book holdings, she will help him to decide what to do next.

———————

Three hours before, Lindsay is in their one bedroom apartment, heating up tomato soup for dinner.

Martin arrives home late. He is upset. Martin is a book dealer with a reputation for helping families to dispose of private libraries when an elderly parent dies. He had met a lawyer, Stephanie White, who had contacted him over disposal of a large private library. The library's owners were recently deceased.

"The Beneficiary is pressuring me," Stephanie White had explained. "He'll inherit the bulk of the estate. A sizeable inheritance. We're talking hundreds of millions." Martin had seen the lawyer's eyes glow as she said these words. "But the will requires me to settle the books first." The lawyer had explained that she would pay Martin above-market rates if he could expedite the job.

Martin had gone with Stephanie White to view the library. It was in a modern style, many-storied mansion of honey-colored stone in horizontal lines near High Park. The library took up one whole floor of the huge house. There were more books throughout the rest of the house, the lawyer had said. She had given him the security card and code so that he could begin work immediately.

"What this lawyer wants is impossible," Martin tells Lindsay over dinner. "Impossible." He shakes his head. "To find homes for so many books, so quickly. It can't be done. Even if the will allowed me to simply dump the books," Martin says. "Packing and moving that many books would take time."

Lindsay hears his voice crack on the word "dump."

"But the will doesn't allow that." Martin says. His voice raised, his hands clenched.

"Lindsay, I have to find places that will take the books. Second-hand bookshops are closing down everywhere. They don't want truckloads of books. Prisons, schools, libraries—they only have so much room. And they're choosy about what they'll take. This could take months, *months*. And the lawyer insists that all the books, the whole library must be cleared out of there in three weeks. Impossible. *Impossible!*"

The books, Lindsay thinks. This is about the books. This lawyer, this *bitch*, wants Martin to destroy the library, separate the books, place them any old where. They'll be neglected and unloved. Martin would take the books himself, if he could. Lindsay knows that. But their apartment is too small for their own books. Soon there will be even less room.

Lindsay promises to help. "I'll come up with a proposal," she says. "I'll talk to this lawyer. I can take a few days off work, and help out as your project manager. We're in a lull right now, with the annual financial statements signed off. I'll convince the lawyer that you need more time."

Martin asks Lindsay to come with him right away to see the library. "We'll be out late," he says. "But tomorrow is Saturday. We can sleep in." He smiles. "I'll make you breakfast in bed," Martin promises.

Lindsay agrees. She understands. Her promise has slowed, but not stopped, Martin's momentum into despair. Martin needs more reassurance. He wants her to see the library and love it as much as he does.

You're the one that I love, Lindsay thinks. I will care for this library, because you care for it.

Lindsay thinks about the task, the lawyer's insistence on urgency, her offer to pay Martin more than market if he disposes of the books, no questions asked. Her eyes narrow. The library is a problem for her to solve; a problem that could be an opportunity. They finish the washing up, leave the dishes to dry, pull on jackets and scarves and winter boots, and go out.

In *La Residence* Lindsay has placed the cushion to her satisfaction. The winter cold is still on the other side of two panes of glass with one vacuum between. The semi-circle moon has moved slightly further upwards and westwards. Martin is still upstairs.

Lindsay looks at the small bookcase. It contains poetry. She picks up an anthology of modern verse and flicks through it, looking for poems about moonlight or ponds or birds. There is a bookmark at page 24. She reads the first verse of the poem on page 24: "*The tiger's world is circumscribed/ by concrete bedded metal bars/ the iron sky above his head / is pierced by bolts instead of stars.*"

She looks at the bookmark. It has a picture of blue and green on one side, and the word MoMA. On the other side black-lettered words say *Composition Green Background, Henri Matisse (French, 1869-1954)*. Lindsay does the calculation in her head. Thirty-one plus fifty-four. Matisse lived for 85 years. Twenty-six years longer than Delphine Thibaux. Twenty-four years longer than Tom Marshall.

Lindsay returns the bookmark to page 24 and returns the book to its place in the small bookcase. She works her way systematically through the 31 other books on that shelf. All poetry. All with small items inside of them. She finds bookmarks (seven), photographs (two), and packets of stamps (three). There is a letter in French, which seems to be very old. She handles the letter carefully, holds it close to the lamp, reading with incredulity the scrawled signature at the bottom of the yellow-brown sheet of paper.

In an anthology of Scottish love poems Lindsay finds a post-card with a sketch of two swallows at page 37. Under the swallows the postcard asks: *Qué pasa con las golondrinas que llegan tarde al colegio??*

There is a subscript that says *Extracto del Libro de Las Preguntas de Pablo Neruda.* Spanish, she thinks. She doesn't know any Spanish.

She uses her iPhone to photograph the stamps and the letter. Before she moves on to the next shelf she does a quick internet search. Lindsay shakes her head in disbelief. Her heartbeat is loud in her ears. Her hands are clammy. She wipes her hands against her pants, and picks up the first book on the next shelf.

The last book in the small bookcase is *The Complete Poems of Emily Dickinson.* Lindsay finds a photograph of a child at page 157; a girl about three years old, with short blond hair, dark eyes and pink cheeks, wearing a button-up red winter coat and a knitted white toque.

She reads the first line of the poem on page 157: *He is alive, this morning—*

The photograph of the little girl looks old, although it is in good condition. Perhaps a new print of a picture from the 1960s or 70s? Martin has told her that the Thibaux-Marshalls had no children. Was this girl a niece, a cousin, or was she perhaps Delphine Thibaux herself as a child?

Lindsay puts the photograph back in the book and the book back on the shelf. She turns off the lamp. She sits on the window seat, looking out onto darkness and moonlight and water. She has a plan. The plan requires boxes and bookshops and documents to establish ownership. In her imagination everything is simple. There are arrows between different-colored rectangles. There is a timetable. The critical path is clear.

———————

Martin's sock-clad feet are quiet on the library's wool carpet, as he threads his way between the tables and chairs and rice paper floor lamps to reach Lindsay. He has brought a pocket torch and uses it to light his way through the dark room.

Lindsay doesn't turn around. She is gazing out into the moonlit night. She sees the reflection of the torchlight as Martin comes to her. He slides his arms around her. She leans back into his hug. She feels his warmth, his strength. If I'm lost you will find me, she thinks. If you fall I will catch you. Foolish, love-song thoughts. Hers.

"What did you find in the other rooms?" She asks Martin.

"More books," he says. "Of course." Martin swallows. "I can't do this, Lindsay. This library should be preserved, not destroyed." He shakes his head. "Stephanie White, the lawyer, I'll talk to her on Monday. Ask her for more time. Or tell her no, I can't help her."

Lindsay feels his breathing, uneven against her back. Martin's anguish hurts her. "Tell me about the books upstairs," she says. "Are they fiction or non-fiction?"

Martin takes a deep breath. "The studio at the top," he says, "where Delphine Thibaux used to paint, has the most amazing collection of books about art and artists; biographies, histories, and how-to books. One of the bedrooms has children's books, the other has science fiction They have two complete sets of Tintin, in French and English, and all my favorites—Maurice Sendak, Robert Munsch, Joan Aiken, Margaret Mahy—alongside first editions of Hillaire Belloc, George MacDonald and E. Nesbit."

Martin laughs. "I think that room has all the books that Tom and Delphine loved most to read when they were kids, and books that their parents loved, and their grandparents. All their favorites—well-worn, with inscriptions."

Lindsay feels the rumble of his voice, a warm vibration against her back.

Martin's voice rises with excitement: "I looked at their set of *The Lord of the Rings*, and the first book in the trilogy, *The Fellowship of the Ring*, is signed by Tolkien. Above his signature, Tolkien has written something in Elvish. Can you imagine?"

Lindsay thinks of the letter she discovered. Anything is possible here, she decides.

"How many books?" Lindsay asks. Martin's arms leave her. She turns and sees him pull his Notebook from his satchel. She narrows her eyes against its bright light.

Martin touches the screen. A spreadsheet appears. Lindsay sees that the rows are rooms, the columns bookcases. Each cell has a number. "Somewhere between 27,000 and 30,000," Martin replies.

Martin sucks in a deep breath. "Lindsay, I think this lawyer, Stephanie White, knows what she's really asking me to do. She's not stupid. She wants me to ignore the will and dump the books. That's all that anyone could do in just three weeks." Martin's fingers, seen by the light of the screen, are trembling. "Stephanie White can claim to have fulfilled the will's requirement to find homes for the books, through her instructions to me." Martin shakes his head. "It's wrong."

"We can save the library," Lindsay tells Martin. "I have a plan."

Later that night, lying awake in their bed, Martin breathing quietly beside her, Lindsay asks herself: "Am I Eve tempting Adam with an apple? Or am I Judith using subterfuge to kill Holofernes and save my people?" I'm me, she decides. Me, just me. No one else. Me.

Monday, they visit the lawyer at her office on the 27th floor of a downtown, Bay Street building. The building's street level entrance has mirrors and marble. Far above the street the entrance to Stephanie White's offices has mahogany and wool. Gilt-framed Group of Seven prints decorate its grey walls. The lawyer's receptionist asks them to wait. Martin and Lindsay sit down in a dimly lit square of fake leather couches.

Lindsay places her briefcase on the floor beside her. She picks up a magazine about golf, flicks through it, puts it down. She picks up a magazine about cottages for sale, flicks through it, puts it down.

The receptionist gestures. Martin and Lindsay follow her into the lawyer's office. Lindsay squints at the morning light pouring through the long windows. Stephanie White presses the remote she holds, and the harbor view dims as the window darkens. Nice trick, thinks Lindsay.

Stephanie White looks over the papers Lindsay has brought with her and agrees to her proposal. The proposal includes a consultancy fee that will earn Lindsay her annual salary in just four weeks. The lawyer accepts that, for a speedy transfer, the three bookshops that Lindsay has identified will need to be paid to take the books off their hands. The lawyer approves generous hourly rates for a team of book packers (eight), truck drivers (three) and off-loaders (six).

As Executor of The Will, acting on The Beneficiary's instructions, Stephanie White signs the ownership transfers (three) for the library; sets of books (three, as listed) and contents of those books (all) transferred to bookshops (three).

"We want everything to be clear-cut," Lindsay explains. "If we start to find things in the books as we sort them—photographs, papers, mementos, etc.—and need to remove them and refer them to you, then that will slow down the transfer significantly."

Stephanie White smiles her understanding. She has a reassuringly ordinary appearance; average height, professional woman's standard jacket and skirt outfit, high heels (but not too high), gold at her neck and rings (gold and diamonds) on the fourth finger of her left hand. On her desk there is a picture of a younger her, with a man and three teenage children. At some time towards the end of the hour they spend with her, Martin leaves the room for a few minutes. The lawyer's face changes subtly. Later Lindsay can't explain the specifics. "She relaxed with me," she tells Martin. "While you were out of the room, she relaxed and confided, as if we were friends. Women together, with a shared secret."

"Mrs. Avery," the lawyer says. "I am so relieved at your involvement with this matter. On Friday, when I showed your husband the library and explained to him what needs to be done I sensed a problem. Really this should be very simple. The Beneficiary is in urgent—very urgent—need of funds." The lawyer's right eye flickers in a blink that isn't quite a wink. She smiles, shrugs. "It could happen to anyone," she says.

What, wondered Lindsay. What could happen to anyone?

"But my instructions are clear. The will requires disposal of the books before the investments can be released. The investments are the main event. The books are a mere trifle by comparison." The lawyer shrugs again. She lifts her short-nailed, manicured hands in a gesture of helpless resignation. "Your intervention—for him, for me—it is priceless. The answer to my prayers. You, my dear, are a godsend."

For a moment Lindsay fears the woman means to reach out and touch her. Lindsay's face tightens. She readies her body to jump backwards.

A slight noise heralds Martin's return. The lawyer quickly murmurs, "After all, my dear, they're only books." Lindsay nods silently. Stephanie White moves back behind her desk as Martin rejoins them. For Lindsay the room is going dark. I'm going to faint, she thinks. The lawyer turns to smile at Martin. Lindsay opens her mouth and sucks in air.

At the end of their meeting the lawyer hands Lindsay a prepaid money card. "It has $50,000 on it," she says, "for incidental expenses." Again, her right eye flickers in a blink that isn't quite a wink. Lindsay smiles a smile of managerial competence, which softens very slightly into a smile that is almost, but not quite, conspiratorial. She turns to go, then swings back.

"The house," Lindsay says. "Did you say that the house will be for sale, once the library is gone?"

The lawyer's face hardens for a moment. She calculates. Then her face softens into another smile. "Yes," she says. "The house." Now there is a gleam in her eye. "In the circumstances," she says. "A quick sale is imperative. It might not go onto the market, if we can find a buyer willing to pay something like the market price, with no financing to delay matters. If you know anyone who might be interested, please refer them to me."

<hr>

Lindsay uses the prepaid card to rent warehouses (three). She calls the warehouses "shell bookshops" and names them after companies (three) that she owns; Maid in Toronto, Transparent Accountability, and Saydi's Line. Stephanie White's signature on the three ownership transfers means that Lindsay owns the books and all their incidental contents, through her ownership of these three companies.

One third of the books are packed into cardboard boxes, loaded into trucks, and moved into the warehouse named "Maid in Toronto." One third of the books are moved into the warehouse named "Transparent Accountability." One third of the books are moved into the warehouse named "Saydi's Line." At the end of the month *La Residence* is empty of books, and ready for a quick, private sale.

Lindsay has the poetry from the small bookcase beside the library's window seat moved in one of the first truckloads. The same truckload includes historical atlases (five) which contain more packets of rare stamps. Martin and Lindsay have found other treasures pressed between the pages of Audubon's *Birds of America*, tucked into the dust jacket of Dashiell Hammett's *The Glass Key*, in beige envelopes inside *Marc Chagall: Complete Lithographs*.

Lindsay and Martin find that the sale of just the rare stamps provides enough to purchase *La Residence*.

Lindsay does not need to sell the old letter, which she found that first night in the library. She keeps it. The letter amuses her. In the letter Napoleon Bonaparte complains to his friend, François Thibaux, that Paris stinks worse than usual. We need more sewers, Napoleon writes.

Lindsay also uses the prepaid card to pay for catered parties (two). Of course the caterer is also one of her own companies—Delicious Delights Ltd. The catered parties have champagne and good food. All the packers and drivers and unpackers are invited. They are friends and family of Martin and Lindsay.

The first party celebrates completion of the first move (out of *La Residence* and into the warehouses). The second party, a month later, celebrates completion of the second move (out of the warehouses and back into *La Residence*). The trees and shrubbery in the back garden have the green of spring growth and the chatter of spring birds. Soon the park across from Grenadier Pond will be obscured by leaves, although the Pond itself will still be visible from *La Residence*. Friends and family toast Lindsay and Martin's kindness in involving them in this lucrative endeavor. Lindsay and Martin toast the library, which has made all of this possible.

Lindsay smiles. She is drinking orange juice. Her back hurts. She is tired. Later she and Martin climb the stairs to their bedroom. In sleep Lindsay dreams of decorating the nursery. Martin dreams of the library. Together they dream of a little girl with curly brown hair. "Who are the funny people?" the little girl asks. She points at the elderly couple sitting together on the window seat, smiling at each other.

Delphine Thibaux and Tom Marshall wander through Martin and Lindsay's dreams. They wander back out into the house and into the library. Tom smiles at Delphine. "Children, he says. "Soon there will be children here."

Delphine smiles back. "Yes." she says. "The one happiness denied us."

"Should we stay longer?" Tom asks.

"A little longer," Delphine answers. "I want to see the humming birds once more, before I go."

Our next story takes us to a small city where a librarian pokes a stick into the cogs of civic corruption, and benefits the library to boot.

While author LD Masterson is a great fan of her local library, she would like readers to know that the following story is not based her local librarian. Ms. Masterson's short stories have been published in numerous anthologies and magazines and she is working on her second novel.

Drop Goes the Weasel

by LD Masterson

I've known John Wessel since he was a thoroughly unlikeable child. As a man, he is a common low life whose shady dealings drove his mother into an early grave, God rest her soul. His nickname is Johnny Weasel, very appropriate to my mind. He certainly isn't a heavy thinker, or a reader, so I'm a bit taken aback to see him at the circulation desk with three rather large books in his hands.

He lays one of our new computerized library cards on the counter along with the books. I wonder when he got it. *I* certainly didn't issue it to him.

"Good morning, Grace. Excuse me, I mean Miss Percell." His smirk robs the apology of any sincerity.

I will not lower myself to respond in kind but offer him a short nod as I take the books. *Raising Dairy Goats, The History of the New York Ballet,* and the classic *War and Peace.* I don't know about the other two but I'm quite certain Johnny Weasel will never read *War and Peace.*

Using the little handheld reader, I scan his card, then the bar code label on the back of each book. It still feels strange to me after so many years of card pockets and date stamps, but one must adjust to the times. As he waits, Johnny Weasel runs one hand over his well-greased hair and I cringe inwardly at the thought of that hand holding one of my books. He is tall and wears a shirt just tight enough to show off the muscles in his arms and shoulders. There are stories of his working as an enforcer for some of the illegal gambling establishments in town. I expect they're true.

I remember when there was no illegal gambling in this town. Before the good, God fearing people of Brookville took leave of their senses and elected Walter Soot mayor.

The computer prints out a small paper receipt, which I tuck inside the cover of *War and Peace*. "These are due back in three weeks."

Another smirk. "No problem." He dips his head in a mock bow, picks up the books and turns away. I watch him cross the worn marble floor of the main hall and feel an odd sense of relief when he passes through the large double doors.

I will admit to being a bit protective of this library. I've worked here almost fifty years, since I was a girl fresh out of school. Now I'm the head librarian. I love this building, I love the books, I love sharing the joy of reading with all the townspeople, young and old.

But the library is in trouble. Mayor Walter Soot, whose heart is as black as his name, has no interest in libraries, or parks, or any type of community service. His interests run to prostitution, gambling, drugs, and all the other criminal activities that have sprung up in Brookville over the eight years since he took office. Each year our budget is cut, along with the number of staff and the library hours. I haven't been able to buy a new release in months. If something isn't done about Mayor Soot, I fear the library will have to close its doors.

The next day Johnny Weasel is back. He goes directly to the book return drop slot, places the three books in the chute, and walks away. Well, he certainly didn't read *War and Peace* in one day, never mind the other two. I check the three back into stock and place them with the books to be re-shelved.

Two days later, I receive another surprise. Ed Witkowski, one of Mayor Soot's lackeys is approaching the desk, his shoes making a disturbing clatter against the marble floor, as though he's wearing taps. I am reasonably certain I've never seen him in the library before.

"May I help you?"

Ed Witkowski is a little man, in stature as well as bearing. He wears his mousey brown hair in a very sad comb-over and his mustache is too sparse to make up for his weak chin. He clears his throat before speaking. "Um, yes, I need to get a card or whatever…so I can check out a book."

"Of course. Are you a resident of Brookville?" I decide it's better not to admit I recognize him, or his connection to the Mayor.

He nods.

"I'll just need to see a photo ID with your address, please. A driver's license will be fine."

This draws a faint scowl. I imagine Mr. Witkowski is unused to producing his ID. He pulls his wallet from a back pocket and hands me his license. I pull the proper form up on my monitor and begin typing in his information.

"I get the card today, right? I mean, I can check out a book now?"

"Well, no and yes. Your actual card will be sent by mail in a few days but I can give you a temporary card that you can use today."

He shifts his weight from foot to foot, looking at the rows of shelves then at his watch.

"How do you find a book in the place? A certain book."

I continue typing as I answer. "Different types of books are found in different sections. Is there a particular title you're looking for?"

"Yeah. *War and Peace.*"

My fingers freeze on the keyboard. This could not be a coincidence. "I can show you where to find that." I struggle to appear disinterested and finish typing. There was a soft whirr from the printer. "Here's your temporary card."

After I had assisted Mr. Witkowski in locating and checking out *War and Peace*, I try to make sense of what is going on. Johnny Weasel checks out three books he can't possible want to read, returns them in a day, and two days later Ed Witkowski takes out a library card just to check out one of those books. My first thought is they're using my books to pass some illegal material between them; but that's not likely. I always give my books a good shake out when they're returned, to dislodge whenever might be stuck between the pages. You'd be surprised what people will use as a bookmark when they read. I've found unpaid bills, candy wrappers, coupons, even one rather explicit love note which was fortunately unsigned. No, it has to be something else, but if it involves Johnny Weasel, Ed Witkowski, and by extension, Mayor Soot, it's not something good.

I didn't see Mr. Witkowski return War and Peace. It was in the night drop box the next day. I gave it an extra good shake and flipped through the pages but found nothing.

One month to the day of his last visit, Johnny Weasel returns. He crosses the main hall toward the shelves, tossing an arrogant nod in my direction. It takes him almost ten minutes to make his selections and bring them to me. Again, three rather thick volumes. All non-fiction this time—one on birdwatching, one biography, and a book on picking up women. He sets them on the counter, then retrieves one and makes a show of blowing dust from the top edge, as though I don't dust every shelf in the building myself once a week.

"Did you enjoy *War and Peace* last month?" I can't resist asking him as I scan the first book.

"You know, it was the funniest thing. I got a couple pages into it and realized I'd read it before. Just forgot the title."

Unlikely. I scan the other two and tuck the receipt into the cover of the top book, "*How to Pick Up Women.*" Well, I hope these will be more helpful.

The next day, when Johnny Weasel brings back his books, I don't return them to their place on the shelves. I keep them on my desk for a careful, after-hours examination. Two are clean, but the third is littered with pencil marks. How dare they carry on their underhanded dealings by defacing *my* books? My hand itches to grab an eraser and remove the offending marks immediately. But first I need to know what they mean.

Some marks underline a word or number, and other numbers are written in the lower inside corner of a page. Obviously, these marks create some sort of coded message that I will have to decipher. I return to the title page and find the number *17* lightly penciled in the lower left corner. Going page by page, I search for the next mark and find it on page seventeen. The word *zoo* is underlined. In the corner is the number *268*. Could it be that simple? I turn to page 268. The underlined word is *monument*. The number is 109. I turn to page 109. The underlined word is *street*. Dear Lord. It is just that simple. I work my way through the book, following the sequence of the page numbers written in the corner of each marked page and writing down the underlined word or number. Zoo. Monument. Street. Entrance. Bench. Inside. On. Left. Under. Rose. Bushes. Four. Thirty. Not a code at all. A simple set of instructions. An address and what I believe is a time. But for what?

The following day I hear the distinctive, annoying tapping of Ed Witkowski's footsteps. I keep my head down, my eyes focused on the purchase order on my desk while he passes, heading for the shelves in the rear section. It takes him longer than I expect but after several minutes I hear the steps returning. They stop in front of the circulation desk. I look up, giving him my best professional smile, and move to the counter.

"May I help you?"

"Um, yes, I'm looking for *How to Pick Up Women*. It's not on the shelf."

He flushes crimson and I feel my lips twitch. I wonder if Johnny Weasel enjoyed making Mr. Witkowski check-out that particular title.

I make a show of checking the reserved rack. "I'm sorry, sir. That book is on reserve."

"What do you mean?"

"I mean another customer has reserved that book. It's on hold until they pick it up."

"On hold. For how long?"

"Well, we hold reserved books for ten days. Of course, once it's checked out, it won't be due back for the usual three weeks."

Mr. Witkowski begins to perspire although it is never too warm in the main hall. He stares at the reserve rack, the book he needs clearly visible. Considering his demeanor and Johnny Weasel's, I'm fairly certain Johnny Weasel has the upper hand in whatever's going on here. It surprises me. Mr. Witkowski is the mayor's man and I didn't think anyone had the upper hand on Mayor Soot. In a way, I rather enjoy the idea.

"Um, would it be possible for me to just take a quick look at the book? I mean, not to check it out, just look at it for a couple minutes."

"Well, I… we don't usually…"

"Please, I just want to look something up." He pulls out a handkerchief and dabs at his forehead.

I step over and pick up the requested volume. "You understand, you can't take it out of the library."

"Yes, of course. I just… can I take it to that table?" He motions toward one of the study tables in the reference area.

I nod, handing him the book. "All right. Bring it back to me when you're finished."

He carries the book to the table and sits with his back to me. I take the re-stock cart I prepared earlier, wheel it to a good vantage point, and go through the motions of placing books on the shelf while I watch Mr. Witkowski. He's flipping through the pages, going forward and back, pausing to write something on a note pad each time he stops. Then he takes a pencil and rubs the eraser on the page.

Seeing quite enough, I take my cart and make my way back to the circulation desk. A few moments later, Mr. Witkowski follows and hands me the mistreated book.

"Thank you."

"Did you find what you needed?"

"Yes, thank you." He flushes again and hurries toward the front door, his shoes tapping a rapid cadence.

Ten minutes later I call my single volunteer from her job re-stocking shelves to cover the desk. She is expecting this, I made arrangements yesterday to leave my post for the afternoon, claiming a dentist appointment. That's wrong of me, I know, but I do have time off accrued and the dentist excuse allows me to avoid any awkward questions. I walk to the corner bus stop, just a block away, but can't resist stopping once to lift my face to the warmth of the afternoon sun. The sunlight never reaches my area in the library's main hall and many days I'm at my post till long after the sun has gone down. Another gift from Mayor Soot. Not enough staff to cover the library during evening hours.

I arrive at the corner in time for the number three bus. It takes me to within four blocks of the zoo entrance on Monument Street. I trust that my interpretation of Johnny Weasel's instructions is correct and the *four thirty* at the end of the list of words is the appointed time for whatever is to happen here. As I walk through the lovely wrought iron gates, I see the bench on my left, flanked by rose bushes on the far side. The buds have not quite opened but the greenery is lush and dark. The path extends in a straight line well into the zoo so I am able to move a fair distance from the bench near the entrance and still have a good line of sight. I pick a bench further along and sit down. I have a book with me, to hide me face if needed, but for now I simply watch the people pass by, and keep an eye on the bench by the gate.

Mr. Witkowski is very punctual. At precisely four thirty, he enters the Monument Street gate and moves directly to the bench on the left, which fortunately is unoccupied. He sits there for a moment, looking around. I employ my book but I don't believe he would notice me either way. He opens the dark bag he is carrying and removes a small package. After glancing all around, he bends over and reaches under the nearest rose bush. I lose sight of the package but when he straightens, it's no longer in his hand. He rises quickly and walks back through the gate and disappears.

I wait a full thirty minutes before I see Johnny Weasel. He enters through the same gate, strides directly to the bench and sits on the end nearest the roses. He doesn't seem concerned that Mr. Witkowski might have waited or sent someone else to watch and see who picked up the package. After a quick look around, he reaches down and retrieves what Mr. Witkowski left for him.

I wait ten more minutes and walk back to my bus stop.

That night I consider the possibilities. The rather convoluted exchange of information would indicate that Johnny Weasel doesn't want Mr. Witkowski or, I would assume, Mayor Soot to know who is leaving the instructions. Yet Johnny Weasel hadn't seemed overly cautious at the zoo today. Then there was Mr. Witkowski's reaction earlier when the book wasn't readily available. Yes, Johnny Weasel definitely had the upper hand here. And what I saw today looked very much like a payoff. Blackmail. Or extortion, if you prefer. The corruption in the Mayor's office is well-known but unproven. Even the State Police, though they've investigated Mayor Soot several times, have found nothing they could act on.

Well, our State Police may not have been able to get something on Mayor Soot but it appeared Johnny Weasel could. His lack of concern over being seen would mean his victim knew if any harm came to the blackmailer, whatever he was using to extort the Mayor would come to light. But there are still some pieces missing. How does Mr. Witkowski know which book to check out? If Johnny Weasel is sending him the book title, couldn't he simply send him the drop instructions the same way? But then, Johnny Weasel is not, as they say, the sharpest tool in the shed. He quite possibly came up with this grand scheme so he could feel like a criminal mastermind, and for the joy of making Mr. Witkowski and Mayor Soot jump through some hoops of his ordering.

The question now is what I should do with this information. Johnny Weasel has something on Mayor Soot that the Mayor is willing to pay to keep quiet. That means it is serious. Possibly enough to put him behind bars, or at the very least, removed from office. The local police are all Mayor Soot's men so they would be no help. I could go to the State Police, but Johnny Weasel will simply deny having incriminating evidence against the Mayor, and I have nothing to offer as proof. It appears I will have to take action myself. This is the chance all the good people of Brookville have been looking for—a chance to rid ourselves of Mayor Walter Soot and take back our town. And, of course, save the Brookville Public Library.

The next month seems interminable but finally we reach the date of Johnny Weasel's regular visit. He checks out his usual three books with his usual smirk and returns them the next day. That evening, I extract the message giving the drop place and time, and I return all three books to their proper place.

When Mr. Witkowski comes to the library to receive the latest message from Johnny Weasel, I have another "dentist appointment" already scheduled. At 2:00 that afternoon, thirty minutes after the designated drop time in his instructions to Mr. Witkowski, Johnny Weasel arrives at Founder's Park to pick up his package. I'm not far away, although screened by a flowering hedge so I'm reasonably certain he can't see me. I know this park will be filled with children once school lets out, which may account for the earlier drop time than last month. The drop spot is a depression in the base of the statue of our town founder, August Brook. I watch Johnny Weasel retrieve what was left there but it's not a package this time, just a small flat envelope. He tears it open and pulls out a single piece of paper. As he looks at it, the self-satisfied smirk is replaced by an angry scowl. He crushes the paper in his hand with an oath I'm afraid I make out quite clearly even though I can't hear him. Then he turns and strides away.

At 3:30, Mr. Witkowski arrives at gardens on the grounds of the First Baptist Church - the location indicated in the book he checked out a few hours before, the book with carefully altered instructions. He finds the large concrete flower pot, leaves his package, and hurries down the walk. He has no idea that Johnny

Weasel, going to the drop spot in his original instructions, found only a typed note that read: *"I'm done. You're not getting another dime from me. Do your worst. When I catch up with you, you're a dead man."*

I wait about five minutes before scooping the little package into my bag and returning to the bus stop. On the way, I drop two letters into a sidewalk mailbox. One is a letter to the State Police explaining that John Wessel has been blackmailing Mayor Soot and probably has information they would be interested in. The other is a short note addressed to the Mayor's office that reads: "It was John Wessel." I believe even if Johnny Weasel doesn't have the courage to release whatever he has on Mayor Soot, he certainly has incentive now to cooperate with the State Police. The end result should be the same. Good-bye, Mayor Soot.

I return to the library at the end of the day before closing. I don't like to leave that to the volunteers. Once I'm alone, I retrieve Mr. Witkowski's package from my bag. My hands tremble as I tear open one end and look inside. *Oh my.* The bundle of bills is quite a bit more than I imagined. I stare at it for a very long moment, thinking of all the books I'll now be able to buy. Then I remove one twenty dollar bill and place in the library cash drawer. It will cover Johnny Weasel's and Mr. Witkowski's fines for defacing books in the Brookville Public Library.

A book reading for a newly published mystery novel at a small library on a dark and stormy night—what could go wrong?

Kate Fellowes has worked in a public library for over thirty years. She regards it as the best place on earth for a writer to work, with inspiration on every shelf. As an author, her short fiction, novels, and essays have been published in a large number of periodicals and anthologies.

Gotcha Covered

by Kate Fellowes

This is the story of how I ended up at the Silverdale Public Library one rainy November night.

After years of reading mystery novels, I decided to take the plunge and try writing one of my own. Convinced I'd absorbed story structure and plotting through literary osmosis, I opened my laptop and began.

A year later, my Great American Mystery was finished, ready to be sent forth and rejected by every publisher on both sides of the Atlantic.

Except it wasn't. A small but respectable press liked it and before you could say "Once upon a time", I was my own dream come true. I, Francie Spencer, was a published novelist, ready to hold my first-ever book signing event on an oh-so-appropriate dark and stormy night, when anyone with any sense would stay home reading.

The library director, Dale Swift, was a short, balding guy approaching retirement. He went all out for the event, as if I were Janet Evanovich. There was a big sign in the front window of the library and helium balloons with skulls and crossbones tied to the awnings.

A ten-foot oblong table stacked high with copies of my novel, (let's just say that again. My. Novel.) stood right in the middle of the library, beside a freestanding stone fireplace. On the the table sat a giant sheet cake and about a hundred paper plates. Mr. Swift thought big.

"It was that or some cartoon character," he said, gesturing at the skull and crossbones repeated in the cake's frosting. "And I certainly don't want any copyright infringement!"

"Smart thinking," I said, setting my tote bag full of promotional postcards and bookmarks on the chair closest to the cake. (I'm quite fond of cake.)

Mr. Swift took my wet coat and headed for the staff lounge to hang it up. I used the opportunity to find the restroom and check my lipstick, then looked around as I headed back to the table.

The small library was bright and tidy, lit by bronze chandeliers shaped like pinecones hung at regular intervals throughout the space. Shelves for non-fiction filled one area of the library, fiction another. One corner of the fiction section—long wall, shorter aisle—was devoted to mysteries, with its mirror image on the other side of the aisle holding mainstream fiction and romances. The children's section ran along the back wall, closest to the restroom, the Circulation desk right up front.

On either side of the big stone fireplace, glass cabinets were positively jammed with items. It didn't make for much of a display, actually, because there was just too much to see.

I bent to examine each shelf. All things Sherlockian, including a plaster bust of the great man himself, occupied the bottom shelf. Children's things—card games, puzzles and toys featuring characters from mystery fiction—filled the shelf above that. Mystery and spy films lined the next shelf up, a bit heavy on the James Bond memorabilia.

And what I saw on the top shelf took my breath away. I leaned closer, put my hands against the glass and stared.

It was a first edition of the most famous first novel in the neo-noir genre. *Three Steps From Danger*, by Walter Lake. I knew it was the first edition because of the dust jacket. Only the first edition had it and the print run had been small. For a first novel by an unknown writer, that was no surprise. But what had been a surprise was the runaway popularity of the book—and the movie, which inevitably followed. Lake wrote only one other book before retiring to the Upper Peninsula and living as a recluse. This first edition—now right in front of me—was so rare it was the Holy Grail of crime fiction. The novel had nurtured my own love for mystery so very long ago. After Nancy Drew and Trixie Belden, reading that book felt scandalous.

My breath fogged the glass. I'd read the copy owned by my public library. By the time I got to it, the binding had split and been repaired, some pages had dog-eared corners and a coffee ring marred the title page. This copy looked mint. The colors of the jacket were bright, the edges sharp as the day it was printed.

I was still oohing and aahing when Mr. Swift returned.

"See something you like there?"

"I see something I can hardly believe," I said, pointing.

"Oh, my pride and joy. I bought it new and read it every year." He shook his head. "There will never be his equal."

He walked to the back of the case, slid the glass door aside and took the book out. I held it as gently as a newborn when he handed it over.

"Don't you keep this case locked?" I asked, astonished. "Someone could steal it and it's worth a fortune!"

Mr. Swift smiled. "You," he said, "are used to life in the big city, but this is Silverdale. We're a pretty honest crowd."

My own town has a population of 25,000, not a "big city" in anyone's book, but I'd concede the point.

Running my hand over that fabulous cover—a dead guy seen only from the soles of his shoes—I said, "Wow."

"Indeed." Mr. Swift held out a hand. He didn't say, "time's up", but it was and I passed the book back to him.

Once more, he slid the door aside and moved a bit awkwardly to position the book as it had been, facing out. When he pushed the door shut, the edge of the unused lock snagged on the cuff of his sweater. He pulled free with a practiced air, as if used to the problem.

A clattering sound came from behind us as a pretty teenager appeared, pushing a trolley holding a coffee urn.

"Here's Alyssa," Mr. Swift said by way of introduction. "Right on schedule, as ever."

Alyssa, tall, blonde, and dimpled, smiled. "Where did you want this, Mr. Swift?"

"Next to the cake," he said, gesturing. "On a jaunty angle."

She positioned the cart accordingly then asked, "Should I turn on the fireplace, too? You know, to make it cozy."

"Good idea." Mr. Swift nodded his approval.

A gas fireplace, I assumed, and then was surprised to see her walk around the back of the display case. She knelt down and popped open a drawer at the bottom. Inside were two DVD players and two remote controls. She punched a few buttons on the remotes and—presto!—the back-to-back flat screen TVs which were, indeed, in the fireplace grate, burst into pre-recorded flames.

At my astonished look, Mr. Swift explained. "This is an old building. It was a lot cheaper to get TVs and DVDs of a fireplace than it would have been to actually fix the chimney and the flue and the…" he waved his hands abstractly, "whatever."

"Good idea!" I said. "And no danger of fire."

"Patrons like it. They pull chairs up here. Sit and read, as if it were the real thing."

"Especially the Professor," Alyssa said. "who's writing a book, too," she added in an excited whisper.

"Right here by of our fireplace," Mr. Swift said, with a wink.

"Do you run it all the time?"

"Not all the time. Someone wants it on, they turn it on." He shrugged. "The Book Club always wants it on, of course, for ambience. They're really looking forward to meeting you tonight."

I caught my lip between my teeth. My novel is darn good. A cozy thriller, more than a mystery. I'm proud of it—but would it pass muster with a book club?

Mr. Swift read the doubt on my face and gave my arm a reassuring squeeze. "They'll love you."

"Here's hoping!"

The door opened and a gust of cold air blew down the main aisle, announcing the arrival of the very first patron to my very first book signing.

I stood up straighter, shoulders back, smoothed my hands over my new black blouse and smiled with my teeth apart, the way I'd learned in my college pageant days not that long ago.

"Tony!" Mr. Swift greeted the newcomer with a big smile, too. "Thanks so much for coming out on a night like this."

Tony, I was pleased to see, was thirty-five or forty. Tall and lean, with chestnut colored hair just beginning to thin at the crown, he wore jeans and a sweater under a well-worn barn coat, and walked with an air of confidence.

"You're early, but that way you can meet the author first," Mr. Swift said as the man drew closer.

This had to be the Professor, I thought. He looked intelligent, competent, serious. So I was surprised when we were introduced.

"This is Tony Sheridan, Francie. He runs an eBay shop out of his farmhouse."

"Really?" I stepped forward to shake his hand.

When he smiled, creases fell into place near his eyes. They were brown, those eyes.

"I also have a thriving farm which Dale neglected to mention. Between the two, I keep busy."

"What do you farm?" I had to know.

"Organic vegetables."

"Interesting combination," I said and he shrugged, still smiling.

"I'm going to buy a dozen of your books," he told me, "and have you autograph them all. With the reviews you've been getting, it seems like first editions of your first novel might be a very good investment."

I blushed. But I really had gotten some pretty good write-ups. (No brag, just fact.) He'd clearly done his homework.

The door opened again. This time it brought plenty of chatter as well as cold air. Half a dozen women ranging from twenty-five to sixty-five scurried in at once, talking a mile a minute.

"The Book Club," Mr. Swift said.

They'd barely begun shaking off jackets and umbrellas when the door opened once more, admitting seven or eight others. Men and women, mostly middle-aged, they too were quickly identified.

"The Writers Group." Mr. Swift again.

"What a great turn-out!" Alyssa cheered from just beside me. "I hope we have enough cake." She frowned a little, her eyes sweeping over the gigantic cake and towering coffee urn.

"I think we'll be okay," I assured her.

When I looked down the main aisle again, it seemed as if the entire population of Silverdale was headed my way. Mr. Swift swept an arm around me, shepherding me to my place behind the table near the stack of books.

I gave a talk about writing and my experiences for fifteen minutes or so, as the crowd, which topped out at about twenty-five, stood around holding plates of cake and cups of coffee. I'd thought we'd do refreshments after the signing, not at the beginning, but apparently Mr. Swift did things his own way.

I still had to take questions from the audience and sign all those books before I could eat any cake. Watching one chubby member of the Writers Group make his third trip to the skull and crossbones confection, I had to wonder if Alyssa was right. Would there be enough cake? More importantly, would there be a slice left for me?

There was enthusiastic applause at the end of my program and Mr. Swift rose to direct traffic.

"Let's make a tidy line down the aisle now," he said, waving everyone into place. "We'll let Francie sign your books and then Alyssa can ring you up as you leave."

I was grateful to them for helping me with the book sale part of the evening, but again, it seemed a funny order for things. Shouldn't everyone buy their book before I wrote in it? Maybe Mr. Swift was on to something when he said I didn't know life in a small town.

The next half hour was a delight, if that doesn't sound too gushy. Some people were pleasant, some were amusing. Some were amusing without meaning to be. A few of the men were flirty, but not, I'm sad to report, Tony, who said he'd wait until the end of the line, since he was buying so many copies.

Such a considerate guy, I thought.

I met a multi-published romance writer, the leader of the Writers Group, who was absolutely charming. She gave me an open invitation to attend their meetings and an honorary lifetime membership in the group.

Another guest turned out to be—gulp!—Joe Merrill, the book reviewer for the biggest newspaper in this half of the state. Fifty years old, in a corduroy jacket with patches on the elbows, he read the back cover of my novel while standing right in front of me, holding up the line and not caring that he did.

Shaking my hand and taking the book I'd signed, he said, "Best of luck with your career, Francie," and smiled like he meant it.

Then, hot on his heels, came the Professor, who turned out to be a she not a he, wearing a gorgeous figure-hugging sweater dress done in a tapestry of rich colors. I'd assumed all wrong, based on the few sentences Alyssa and Mr. Swift had said. Filing away that fact, (it would make a great clue in my next novel—the errant assumption), I greeted her warmly and asked about the book she was writing.

Professor Belinda Birchwood explained she was working on a young adult coming-of-age novel with a sci-fi bent. It sounded ambitious and unfathomable to me.

"More power to you!" I said, signing her copy of my book.

As I mentioned, my novel is a cozy and it has a cozy cover. Two cups of coffee sit beside a plate of cookies and brownies. The coffee cups are steaming and the steam looks very vaguely like a skull. In the background is a red bicycle propped up against a brick wall. I wondered what the cover of a young adult sci-fi novel would look like.

While a few of the customers lingered, most left the library after stopping by Alyssa at the cash box. The wind had picked up outside. The awnings were flapping and the skull and crossbones balloons danced in the light from the streetlamps. Even near the back of the building I could hear rain that sounded like hail hitting the windows.

Suddenly, the lights flickered like a candle flame.

"Yikes," I said. Rising to my feet, I stretched my hands, cramped from all that writing.

Tony, packing his dozen autographed copies, (plus an extra one I'd added just for him), into two carrier bags, caught my eye. "Not to fear, Francie. We're used to the occasional outages here. Especially in a high wind. Got your flashlights, Dale?"

Mr. Swift nodded. "Always. But I don't think we'll have any trouble."

Famous last words.

Just at that instant, the lights flickered again and then died. The furnace quit running, too, and the sudden silence was shocking. The store was black as pitch, without even the flickering firelight from the fake fireplace.

No one moved at first, but there were plenty of surprised gasps. Then there came a lot of shuffling as flashlights were retrieved from the Circulation Desk. In the process, the cake table got jostled and the coffee urn nearly bit the dust, the liquid inside sloshing around ominously. A minute later, as Mr. Swift headed toward us with beaming flashlights in each hand, the power was back, furnace humming, lights blazing inside and out, everyone relieved.

"That was exciting!" I said.

"Hope the coffee's still warm," Joe, the book reviewer, commented, filling a paper cup and sipping experimentally.

Coffee seemed like a good idea. I helped myself, and glanced hopefully at the cake. Over two-thirds of the slices were history, but there was still plenty left for the half dozen of us remaining. I took the corner piece, the one with frosting on two sides.

I'd just lifted the plastic fork to my mouth when Mr. Swift let out a shout. It was a wordless shout like you might use to frighten off a bear.

We all jumped, and I looked around quickly. Had the storm broken a window? Were the awnings ripped away? Had someone made off with the cash box in the dark?

Mr. Swift had been robbed all right, but not at the cash box.

Standing by the display case with the remote control in his hand, he was staring at the top shelf of the overcrowded display. Where *Three Steps From Danger* had had pride of place there was, instead, a big empty space.

"It's gone!" he said, not pointing, just staring. "It's …"

So much for the honest people of small towns, I thought, but didn't say.

What followed next was an interesting exercise in small group behavior.

Tony stepped into the leadership role, suggesting a search. "Someone could have taken it out just to look at and set it down somewhere else," he said.

Professor Belinda snorted at the idea and Tony nodded.

"It's a long shot, I know, but we should look around before we call the police. Dale, you check History," Tony went on, assigning each of us a section of the library. Had he always been a farmer? I wondered.

I was searching every shelf in the Romance department when Alyssa shouted, "Got it!" triumphantly.

She was in the children's area, just behind the fireplace and the cozy seating. We all gathered around within seconds.

"At least, I think this is it," she said, sounding a bit less certain. She held out a clothbound hardcover to Mr. Swift. "The title is right, but…" She didn't continue for we could all see.

The gorgeous, rare, pristine, mint-condition cover was gone.

"Where was it?" Joe asked and Alyssa pointed at a run of children's series titles.

"Just there. Tucked on the end."

"Then the cover must have fallen off or something," I said. "If someone meant to steal the book, they'd take the whole thing."

"Not necessarily." Tony spoke from the other side of our little knot of people. "Seventy percent of an old book's value can be in the dust jacket," he told us. "They usually don't last. Get torn. Stained. Lost somewhere. It's rare to find a vintage title with a clean cover. Especially one as perfect as that."

"I still think we should look around more," I said and Professor Belinda backed me up, so we all spent another ten minutes searching before admitting the truth.

Someone had stolen only the cover.

Mr. Swift flopped down into a squashy chair, rubbing a hand over his face. *Three Steps From Danger* lay on his lap.

"How many people were in here tonight?" he asked. "Any one of them could be the thief. Any one of them could have come around here in the crowd." He let out a breath that quivered at the end.

It was hard to see the kindly, friendly man deal with such a devastating realization. Someone he knew and trusted had taken his precious possession. I got a lump in my throat and had to blink back the threat of tears. When I looked up, Tony was looking right at me. The corners of his mouth twitched in some sort of response, but I just looked away, embarrassed.

"Okay, let's be logical," Joe began.

"And call the cops," I said firmly.

The Professor shook her head. "In a storm like this he'll be dealing with downed trees or power lines and won't get here for hours."

"He? There's only one cop?" I couldn't believe that.

"One cop per shift. Budget cuts." Mr. Swift sounded forlorn.

Alyssa gave her boss a pat on the shoulder. "Would you like some coffee, Mr. Swift?" she offered sweetly, moving off to get it even before he nodded.

I took the opportunity to refill my own cup from the nearly-empty urn and picked up another slice of cake. (Sugar helps me think. I put on five pounds while doing revisions.)

"I see security cameras." Joe pointed up at the ceiling.

"Dummies," Mr. Swift said. "Couldn't afford real ones. Never thought we'd need them." He sighed.

"Can we rule anyone out?" Tony asked. "We need to narrow our field."

"I'd say it was an outsider," Professor Belinda said. "Not someone from Silverdale. Not a friend." She emphasized the last word.

Beside me, I felt Joe bristle. "That's a ridiculous supposition."

"Spoken like a true outsider." The Professor smiled, but it was a cold one.

"Hey, I'm not the only one," Joe said. "And I'm from the next town. She's from a hundred miles away!"

Fork to my lips, I was surprised to see everyone look at me. Me!

"Or maybe he took it for the insurance money." Now, Joe was pointing at poor Mr. Swift.

While it's certainly true librarians are underpaid, one look at his face would convince anyone Mr. Swift hadn't stolen his own book so he could sue the city for stolen property.

"Maybe you took it," I suggested. "You're a book reviewer. You love books—"

"My house is full of books I've gotten for free," Joe said defensively. "I don't need to steal them. And," he added, "I don't sell them to the highest bidder, either."

It was Tony's turn in the spotlight.

"Just what are you implying?" Tony asked in a clear, steady voice that did not bode well.

"All right. That's enough. Let's get clear heads here. Logical, remember?" Professor Belinda held up her hands. "It's true the cover could have been stolen by anyone who was in the library tonight. Where would you hide a book's dust jacket without damaging it?" she asked.

We all thought and some of us called out suggestions.

"In a tote bag?" Alyssa ventured.

"That would rule out the men," Tony said.

"Under the dust jacket of another book?" I said, making another mental note. What a great idea for my next novel!

"Spoken like a true mystery writer," Mr. Swift said, sounding normal for the first time since the discovery of the theft.

"That would rule out anybody who only bought Francie's paperback," Tony said.

"Did anybody buy hardcovers tonight?" Mr. Swift directed his question to Alyssa.

"I can check the receipts," she offered and hurried to the front of the library.

While we waited for her return, I started to tidy up, tossing paper plates and cups into the garbage can beside the coffee urn, putting the remaining slices of cake onto clean plates, scraping crumbs and frosting into the trash.

In the process, no surprise, I got frosting on my fingers. If I knew no one would see, I might have just licked it off. But….

"Be right back," I said to no one in particular and made for the restroom at the back of the library, opposite the staff workspace.

The simplest of rooms, it held only a toilet and a sink. A roll of paper towels in a simple plastic holder hung on the wall with a step-on garbage can directly beneath it.

As I washed my hands I tried to think. Where else could you hide something as big as a dust jacket? Inside an atlas? Behind a picture? And who would have had the opportunity?

I reached for a piece of paper toweling—and paused, the water trickling down my arm to my elbow.

"A roll of paper towel is nearly the same width," I said out loud, the way I plot. "And if you rolled the cover, you wouldn't damage it. And you could retrieve it later when the hullabaloo died down."

In high excitement, I popped the roll from the holder and looked inside. Then, I was out the door in a flash, brandishing the tube like a flag.

"Got it!" I called.

Even as I smiled and rushed toward Mr. Swift, I tried to see the faces of the others. Who would not be surprised at my discovery?

Mr. Swift looked at the cardboard cylinder in confusion, as did Tony. Joe and the Professor had their backs to me, still waiting for Alyssa to return.

"It's inside!" I explained. "Look!"

Mr. Swift held the tube to the light, as I'd done, and gasped. Then, carefully, he extracted the dust jacket, inch by inch.

Still clean and crisp and bright, the cover was none the worse for its adventure. It was a joy to watch Mr. Swift slip it around the book, reuniting the priceless items.

"Thank you, my dear," he said, smoothing his hand over the cover lovingly.

"Don't thank me, just start locking this cabinet," I said, standing beside it and fingering the unused lock.

"So," Tony spoke now, "whoever took the cover is a frequent visitor to the library. Someone familiar with everything from the display case to the restroom. Someone who is definitely not an outsider."

Professor Belinda shrugged. "So it seems," she agreed.

"That lets me out," Joe said. "You, too," he added, looking to me.

"It's someone who is still in this room," I said. Okay, my announcement was dramatic, but it was also the absolute truth… maybe.

"How can you be so sure?" Joe asked, crossing his arms.

"Because whoever took it and hid it away won't want to wait for their treasure," I said.

(Just between us, I was bluffing, playing a hunch. If I were the thief, waiting is exactly what I'd do. Come in the next day to check up on Mr. Swift, make a stop in the restroom and leave with the valuable dust jacket tucked into my tote bag. Yes, that's what I'd do, but I think up crimes for a living. Well, not for a living—yet. I still have my day job, but you get my point.)

"I did not steal my own book for insurance money, or to sue the city," Mr. Swift reiterated, an edge to his voice. It had been a long evening. "I love this book." He gave it a pat. "I don't care how much money its worth."

"You mean, it's like an antique?" Alyssa asked.

I guessed we could cross her off our list. She clearly had no idea of its value.

"If you check my website," Tony began, "you'll see I only sell books. With covers or without them. But I don't sell covers alone. That would be a totally different market." He dropped down into the other squashy chair opposite our host. "Can you imagine I'd steal such a well-known item and put it on my site? Or would I sell it through a fence?" he asked, smiling at the absurdity of the thought.

We all turned to look at Professor Belinda.

"What did you say you're a professor of?" Joe asked.

She shifted from one foot to the other. "Sorry to disappoint you but it's not literature. I'm a professor of art."

Mr. Swift got a funny look on his face. Puzzled, then thoughtful, then certain.

"But that would work!" he said. "I remember we had that discussion about cover art once. You were quite knowledgeable on the subject."

"Aha!" Joe said.

"Art is my field of study. Of course I'm knowledgeable." She spoke in a brisk tone.

I jumped in. "And everyone knows that cover. It's really special. The last one ever done by the most famous cover artist of all time, Owen P. MacDougall."

Of course I knew perfectly well the artist's name was not Owen P. MacDougall. It was—

"MacNamara," Professor Belinda corrected me before she could stop herself. "Owen P. MacNamara."

An electric charge swept around our group, bypassing the Professor. Or perhaps not.

"Well, it's common knowledge," she said.

No one spoke for a moment then Tony took the lead.

"Not really," he said. "Nobody but you knows the library, knows this book and knows that artist's name. The trifecta."

From my spot by the display cabinet I hurried to add, "And no one but you is wearing a sweater dress with a big snag on the cuff."

Professor Belinda looked down at her right cuff, where the material was pulled tight, puckering.

"I believe you'll find this thread—the one caught on this cabinet—is a perfect match." I pointed at a thin dark red fiber snagged on the unused lock, just where Mr. Swift's sleeve had snagged when he'd first shown me the book.

"Gotcha!" Joe summed up the situation in a word.

The door to the library opened again, startling everyone. A police officer wearing a wet rain slicker and a hat covered in plastic stepped inside.

"Somebody here reported a robbery?" he asked.

Alyssa raised her hand. "I did," she said. "I called when I was checking the receipts," she told Mr. Swift.

Professor Belinda Birchwood said a very rude word and picked absently at her cuff.

Mr. Swift got up to meet the officer and I took the opportunity to fill his vacated chair.

"Whew! What a night!" I said to Tony, sighing.

"Plenty of excitement," he agreed, leaning toward me in a way I liked.

"I mean, we solved a real mystery!"

"And then there was that," he said, brown eyes twinkling.

My cheeks warmed as I blushed. *Being a writer is the best thing ever!* I thought just as our hands stretched toward each other and touched.

Sometimes, just as might a fabled western gunslinger, a librarian has to do what a librarian has to do. After all, they are entrusted with the safeguarding of knowledge, are they not?

KM Rockwood is a familiar name to readers of crime fiction, having published many, many stories anthologies and periodicals. In this story, she draws upon her experience working in libraries, private, prison, and public. Her popular Jesse Damon crime novels draw upon a different work experience, in a steel fabrication plant, and are published by Wildside Press.

Map to Oblivion

by KM Rockwood

As she climbed the steps to the Historical Society Library, Pricilla Mummert smiled to herself. Now that she had proof, the director would have to listen to her.

She gripped the handle of her briefcase tightly. Inside were the rare antique maps she'd bought off the Internet. From one Daphne Willow-Smythe.

The Daphne Willow-Smythe, a frequent visitor to the Special Collections division of the library. She wasn't even a member of the Historical Society. Why she had been given access to its resources was a mystery to Pricilla.

How many Daphne Willow-Smythes could there be?

And how many people were on the Internet, trying to sell these specific antique maps?

Maps that were razored out of books in the Special Collections of the Historical Society Library.

Special Collections that were under Pricilla's care and management.

She clenched her jaw hard, willing herself not to scream in frustration.

All that remained now was to check the visitor's log for the entries that would show how often and when Daphne Willow-Smythe had visited the library.

People streamed into the building. Staff reported at eight in the morning; the library opened to users at nine. Only one security guard was on duty at the entrance, sitting at a raised counter and checking IDs of people entering the building. That was strange—there were usually two guards. Pricilla waited patiently for a break in the onslaught.

Finally the last person in line was admitted. Pricilla put on her nicest smile. While she was pretty sure she could get permission to look at the log if she asked her supervisor, it would be much quicker if the guard would just let her take a look.

"I wondered if there was any possibility I could check the visitor's log for the last week?" she asked.

The guard frowned. A contingent of new arrivals swept through the door into the lobby.

"I guess," he said, reaching under the counter and plopping a heavy book on the counter in front of the empty chair next to him. "I can't let you take it away. But you can sit in Jerry's place and look at it."

She slid into the seat. "Thank you. Where is Jerry, anyhow?"

"Putting up barriers in front of one of the elevators. It's not working right, and the company says they can't send anybody to fix it until tomorrow. So somebody has to go to every floor to make sure the doors to that elevator are blocked off."

Pricilla flipped through the pages of the logbook, scanning the names. "What's the matter with the elevator?"

"I'm not sure. But someone reported that the doors opened when the car wasn't there. That could be pretty dangerous."

"True." Pricilla turned another page in exasperation. "I'm looking for Daphne Willow-Smythe. I can't find her name. But I *know* she's been here recently. Yesterday, as a matter of fact. Don't all visitors have to sign in?"

"Well, they're supposed to. But that big donor, Evangeline Smythe, doesn't. She just sails right through. Ms. Herndon, the director, told us just to let her go on ahead. We recognize her, and we just put it in ourselves." He leaned over and pointed to a scribbled note in the margin. It said "E. Smythe + 3."

"Plus three? What does that mean?"

"It means she brought three other people with her, and none of them signed the log."

Pricilla sat back. "So you don't know who came in with her?"

"Not for sure. Sometimes she brings her husband or some friends. If the weather's bad, she lets her chauffeur come in and sit in the staff lounge. And then there's this girl who never looks up from her cell phone, even when you say 'Good morning' to her." He laughed. "One time she was concentrating so hard on her phone that her scarf got caught on the metal detector and she just kept going. She almost strangled herself!"

Pricilla was tempted to join his laughter at the idea of Daphne strangled by her fashionable scarf, but she just said, "Isn't that a security lapse, to have people come in without telling you who they are?"

"You'd think. But Ms. Herndon was adamant, and she's the boss. She says don't stop Ms. Smythe's party, so we don't."

"Thanks." Pricilla hefted the book back under the counter.

That was a setback. She wouldn't be able to say for sure when Daphne had been in.

Only a small setback, though. On her computer, Pricilla had her own record of who had requested what when in the Special Collections. Dates and times and materials and names of the people who looked at them. None of it was as good as having a sign-in in Daphne's own handwriting, but who would think Pricilla's own computerized records couldn't be trusted?

The lobby was crowded with people waiting for the elevator. One of the two was blocked off with two sawhorses and traffic cones. A small crowd gathered in front of the remaining functional one, and Pricilla had to wait for its second trip before she could squeeze in.

Her office was on the sixth floor, just off the elevator lobby so she could see anyone who stopped at Special Collections. She picked up the phone and punched in the number for Ruth Herndon, the director of the library.

Ms. Herndon's secretary answered. "I'm afraid that Ms. Herndon isn't available right now. May I take a message?"

"It's rather urgent, a matter concerning someone with unauthorized access to the materials. It's creating problems." Pricilla looked down at the maps she'd taken from her briefcase. "When would be a good time to call back?"

"Ms. Herndon is quite busy today. You may have noticed that we are having a problem with one of the elevators. She is attempting to deal with that right now. And later this morning, she has appointments with important fundraisers. I can't see her being free to speak with you today at all. I'll let her know that you're trying to get in touch with her, though."

Pricilla would just have to wait. She said, "Thank you" and hung up. Arguing with a secretary was never a good idea.

An entire stack of newly acquired journals and letters awaited her attention. She started to sort them, but realized she was too agitated to concentrate on the task. Rather than risk an error in judgment, she decided wait until she could evaluate them properly. She moved them to an archive box and began searching her computer records to see when Daphne had been in and what she requested.

She was in the midst of transcribing the entire list when her computer dinged, letting her know she had an email.

A message from Ruth Herndon.

Eagerly, Pricilla opened it. Perhaps there was time for a hurried meeting today after all. She wanted to talk to Ms. Herndon about all this before Daphne showed up again.

The contents of the email immediately quashed that thought. It was curt and to the point. "If you need to see me, please follow procedure and call my secretary for an appointment. I will not be available until sometime late next week."

That was bad enough. But then she added, "If this has anything to do with your improper 'investigation' of Ms. Smythe's niece's use of the facilities, please be aware that Ms. Willow-Smythe is researching sea-going routes in the fifteenth and sixteenth centuries for her thesis, and has been given special permission to have access to all the resources available at the Historical Society Library."

Someone—perhaps the security guard at the entrance—must have spoken to Ms. Herndon about Pricilla examining the logbooks.

The email went on to say, "Ms. Smythe has been a donor and supporter of the Historical Society Library for many years, and we are pleased to extend this courtesy to Ms. Willow-Smythe, although she is not herself a member of the Friends of the Historical Society."

Pricilla felt her throat close. Ruth Herndon may as well have said that Daphne could continue her thefts with impunity. Pricilla would not be able to stop her from stealing valuable pages from the irreplaceable books and selling them.

The elevator sighed to a stop in the lobby outside Pricilla's door. She looked up.

The doors opened and Daphne stepped out. She barely looked up from her cell phone as she stepped into the reading room, her filmy scarf trailing behind her. "I'd like to see that volume on sixteenth century Portuguese exploration in the New World that I was looking at yesterday." She hadn't even bothered to remember the title.

Pricilla formed her mouth into a tight smile. "Of course." She stared at the big bag Daphne carried. People who were not employees of the library were supposed to leave their bags with the security staff at the entrance. No doubt the guards had been told to disregard that regulation, too.

After Daphne left yesterday, Pricilla had kept the book in her office to scrutinize for missing pages. So far, she hadn't found any, but she'd had difficulty finding the places in the books from which Daphne had removed the maps that now sat on her desk.

Feeling helpless, Pricilla carted the huge leather-bound volume into the reading room.

As usual, Daphne had positioned herself so her back was to the security camera. Her large colorful bag was up on the table, placed to further shield her actions from view.

Would she remove some of the maps from the book today? Pricilla could hardly stand the thought. She *had* to put a stop to this.

A number of ugly ideas swirled in her head, one worse than the other. Locking the reading room and setting fire to it. But think of the possible damage to the materials! Taking an antique sword from the Historical Society's collection and chopping off her hand. Grabbing the ends of that scarf and pulling hard in opposite directions until Daphne's face turned blue. Standing behind her at the elevator shaft and giving a shove, then watching as she careened down it.

Pricilla stopped and stared at the sawhorses blocking the elevator.

Maybe that one wasn't such a far-fetched idea.

She went into the lobby and looked at the barriers blocking off the faulty elevator. It was the work of but a few minutes to move the sawhorses and traffic cones from their position and place them in front of the functional elevator. Then she went back to her office.

She tried to fix herself a cup of tea, her hands trembled and she spilled so much boiling water from the hot pot that more landed on the floor than made it into her mug. She found it hard to breathe, much less swallow, so she abandoned that effort and just sat down in her chair. She stared at the computer screen, even after it went blank.

An hour later, Daphne got up from the table and left the reading room, lugging her bag. Her eyes were glued to her cell phone. Of course, she didn't bother to return the book she'd been perusing to the reshelving cart. That's what the staff was for.

Pricilla hovered in the recessed entryway of her office and watched as Daphne stood in front of the unobstructed elevator door. The one to the elevator that wasn't working properly.

Daphne took a thumb away from her cell phone long enough to press the call button.

After a slight pause, the door to the working elevator, the one now behind the barriers, slid open. It was empty.

Daphne didn't look up from her phone, and she didn't move.

When that door shut and the working elevator continued its journey, she reached over to push the call button again.

This time, the doors in front of her slid open.

Pricilla tried to step forward, but her feet felt frozen to the floor. She stifled the cry that rose in her throat.

Without taking her eyes off the phone, Daphne stepped forward into the empty elevator shaft. When her foot failed to meet a solid floor, she looked up in surprise.

But it was too late. She tumbled forward and disappeared. Her scarf caught on the edge of the door and paused momentarily before ripping. Disengaged from Daphne's neck, it floated briefly in the air. Then it, too, disappeared, wafting after Daphne at a leisurely pace.

A muted cry resonated in the hollow shaft, followed by low gargling sound and a whiff of machine oil.

Pricilla had been expecting a piercing scream that would draw immediate attention, but it failed to materialize.

Now all she had to do was move the safety barriers back and reshelve the books Daphne had been using.

The maps and illustrations in the Special Collections were safe once again.

Living with one's genius brother can be trying, but Tom van der Grimmen makes the most of it, while writing the Great American Movie. A trip to his local library to check an errant fact, leads him to a murder, and from there…

DG Critchley is a retired librarian who lives in northern New Jersey. His stories maybe be found in The Killer Wore Cranberry #5, and Murder Among Friends. He requested that it be made clear that any resemblance between characters in this story and his former supervisors is strictly coincidental.

The Body in the Book Drop

by DG Critchley

I was ready to start production on my destined-to-be-steam-punk-classic *Dinosaur Women of Lake Erie*, but my brother Robert controlled the company checkbook and he insisted I fix geographical errors regarding train routes and travel times in 1890 upstate New York. Usually, once a script passed his algorithm for probable profitability, he calculated a budget and dumped it back on me to actually film and edit. So, normally he didn't have any further input, but something caught his eye this time. I couldn't really argue - ever since he bought half the production company to keep it afloat, we hadn't lost money on a film. Even if I didn't make money on a film, at least I broke even. *Swamp of the Spider Zombies* had actually won awards. So, if my brother the brain trust wanted to be a stickler for geography, so be it.

Unfortunately for me, that required an antique atlas or an old timetable from Buffalo's train station. But for some reason, the Internet is not awash in 100-year-old train schedules. My brother

Robert's vast personal book collection, his library took up three rooms in our house, may or may not have what I needed, but it was useless without his assistance. Robert's only card catalog was in his head, and his help would include an obligatory twenty-minute lecture on the merits of my learning the Library of Congress cataloging system. It was not worth the effort—and I don't mean just the lecture.

So, Monday morning, I wandered down to Lockhaven Public library. It opened at ten and I hoped I could slip in and out with enough time to avoid the noon book club crowd. I didn't use the library much. The librarian, Buffy Minington, had a budget so minuscule, that her idea of collection development was based on seeing what could be salvaged from donations to the annual book sale. The shelves were heavy on romances, mysteries, and self-help fads from years past, none which were really my style. But because Lockhaven was originally a train town, she kept anything with train information in the "special collection" room, which was really just an alcove full of material no one used. Hopefully, it would have the train routes I needed. A quick glance at an atlas and I would merrily be on my way back home to my office to finish revising the script.

I walked up to the building as Buffy was unlocking the door. She saw me and came running over. "Tom… Bowie … blood…" Buffy was white as death and collapsed into my arms sobbing. She was hysterical and blood is a trigger word in my life. I held her up as best I could in one hand and pulled out my phone.

The phone rang once. "Lockhaven Sheriff's Office, this is Del."

"Del, this it Tom van der Grimmen. I may have a situation."

There was a pause on the other end. EZ's voice came on. "Tommy, what do you mean by 'a situation'?" The sheriff did not sound happy to hear from me. This by itself was not an uncommon thing.

"EZ, I'm outside the library. Buffy is hysterical and all I can get out of her is something about blood."

For once, she didn't volunteer to shoot me for annoying her. "Ok, Tommy. I'll be right there."

I put my phone away and half-carried Buffy into the library and sat her down.

EZ showed up five minutes later. She stepped in the door and looked at me. Buffy was still a wreck, but she was able to point toward a side room in-between sobs.

She stepped in and closed the door. A minute passed. And then another. Buffy started looking a little less ashen so I sat down next to her.

EZ came out of the room. She motioned me over. "Bowie Richards."

Bowie was the janitor, although there are times he apparently thought he was in charge of the entire operation.

"I've already called the county medical examiner to take Bowie down to the morgue in Fort Lauderdale. Can you keep Buffy calm until Del picks up your brother and gets here?"

"Robert? Why is Robert coming? A death is bad enough without bringing Robert into it."

EZ's look became more familiar, something in the range of seething irritation. "One, because I'm the sheriff and I said so," she hissed. "Two, because this is a homicide investigation and your brother is the only local with a forensics background."

Now it made sense. I had assumed the old custodian had keeled over from a heart attack or hit his head or something. Robert had more degrees than a geometry book, including what he dismissively referred to as "just a master's degree in forensic science." EZ had actually deputized him after an attempted Thanksgiving poisoning to keep the ME in Fort Lauderdale from raising a stink about her letting civilians into crime scenes."

Del tapped on the door as EZ's phone rang. She picked it up and gestured for me to let Del and Robert in.

The two walked over as EZ was putting her phone away. "That was the county medical examiner. They're sending out the meat wagon to pick up Bowie, but the forensics team is tied up at multiple crime scenes." EZ was not happy.

"Del, as soon as the hearse shows up, we're going to have a crowd out there. Look around outside on the remote chance there's any evidence that survived the rain last night—don't use crime tape unless you spot something. No point in attracting a crowd sooner than we need to. Robert, walk me through the crime scene. Tommy, keep Buffy company, I'll need to ask her a few more questions."

Del never talked unless necessary, and Robert uncharacteristically nodded and kept silent. EZ had threatened to shoot me more than once so I certainly wasn't going to be the first one to say anything.

I sat by Buffy as she watched Del unlock the door. "Why do they keep going out the front door?"

I looked at her. "Because it's the entrance?"

Buffy shook her head. "No, it's the public entrance. It might easier to use the delivery door behind the circulation desk. That way, they're not locking and unlocking the door all the time. The staff and volunteers use it because it's a shorter walk to staff parking if it's raining. "

"I don't think any of them knew there was another door."

Buffy glared at me. "State fire codes—we're required to have at least two marked exits—we have three." She was starting to feel better. It was a good thing, I guess.

She looked around. "I can't just sit here. I'll make coffee." She stood up and walked behind the circulation desk.

I went over to the room. The door was open. It was a small room. A metal box sat in the corner beneath the slot from the outside book drop with a couple of book carts. There was a battered folding table along the wall with piles of books. EZ and Robert were conferring in the back corner near some sort of closet. Bowie was on the floor, covered with a sheet. I carefully knocked on the door. Both looked up.

"Um," I said, carefully avoiding EZ's death glare. "Buffy's feeling better and is making coffee. She also wants to know why you keep using the front door when the side door doesn't need to be relocked each time you leave."

EZ still had the death glare. She pointed her hand at me, then raised her thumb, making it look like a gun. I took the hint and backed quietly out of the room.

Buffy brought out a carafe of coffee out. "Did I miss anything?"

I shook my head. I poured coffee into a Styrofoam cup. "I don't suppose you have any scotch in the break room?"

Buffy shook her head. "Alcohol is not allowed in the building." She looked around, reached in her pocket, and pulled out a flask. "However, I make the rules, I can break rules. Bourbon?" She poured a slug in each of our cups.

About an hour later, the county ME truck arrived. By the time they wheeled the gurney out the door, word had gotten out that something was up and a crowd was gathering. EZ followed the gurney to the door. She looked at the crowd.

"Del, see if you can break up that crowd. As far as you know, there was an attempted break-in the library. That's it. You don't know anything else—got it?" He nodded and followed the gurney out. Del gets all the fun jobs.

EZ walked over to the table. "Buffy, I know you're upset, but I really need you to focus. Take a deep breath. Let's start with an easy question. What is that room used for?" EZ's eyes never left Buffy.

Buffy glanced through the glass door as the hearse pulled away. "It's officially the book drop room. Book returns go through the slot in the wall and drop into a bin, and then we load them on to carts to check in and reshelve. But the book return takes up so little room that we also sort donations in there. Donations get moved to the table, where the volunteers decide what to keep for the book sale and what to discard. Keepers are priced, packed up, and put in the closet in the back of the room. We had a big batch of donations dropped off Saturday—we had volunteers here past closing on Saturday, just trying to get ahead of it before the book sale."

Everyone knew about the book sale. It was a social event second only to the "Fall Fair Festival" and "July Julep Jubilee." Sometimes you found something interesting, but usually, you'd buy something that you ended up donating back to next book sale.

EZ pulled up a chair and sat down. She had done this countless times as a county homicide detective.

"So far, so good. Tell me about the big book donation." EZ was very good at gaining people's confidence and trust. I seem to be the exception.

"It was a normal day until the afternoon. Someone dropped off five large boxes of books. He said he was from County Brook and was cleaning out his uncle's estate. He didn't want to wait until the Weston library reopened to donate the books."

County Brook was an upscale private golf community on the far side of Weston. Weston had fought the development and lost. Since nobody in Lockhaven actually liked the uppity rich snowbirds in Weston, we had been endlessly amused by that town's attempts to keep even more rich people from building next door.

"Weston library has been shut down for about two weeks while they replace carpets. He was a nice man—said his uncle loved books and he thought it was better to donate them than toss them in the recycling. He didn't want a receipt. I had Bowie stack the boxes in the book drop room. The room is big, but not big enough for that many boxes. I called Holly Enger. She coordinates the volunteers. She got hold of a couple of people and they started sorting through the boxes about three that afternoon."

EZ shifted forward in the chair. "You're doing fine, Buffy."

"The girls worked until I closed the library at five. They wanted to finish up, so I locked everyone in. Bowie had the key. He stayed and would let them out when they decided to call it a night. That's the whole story—unless you include the false alarm Saturday night."

"Another false alarm?"

Buffy nodded. The library's fire alarm was in cahoots with the library roof. Every time there was a heavy rain, the roof leaked and water got into the wiring, setting off the alarm. There was never any fire. And in Florida, heavy rains at night are not a rare event. Each time it happened, the Lockhaven Volunteer Fire Department would drive to the library and wait for someone to let them in to reset the alarm, and then head back to their poker game. This had been going on for years—the council wouldn't pay to replace the roof, and multiple patch jobs had never stopped the leak.

Buffy nodded. "It was about 8 PM. They called me to let them in to reset the panel. They couldn't reach Bowie, so I had to…" She stopped and covered her mouth. "Could Bowie have already been dead?"

EZ glanced at me. I started to come up with a reassuring lie when there was a tapping at the door. It was Del.

I let him in while EZ and Buffy stayed at the table. He wore a rubber gloves and carried a three-foot metal bar. He set it on the table. "This was in a puddle in the parking lot. I don't know what it is, but it seemed out of place."

Buffy spoke up. "That's the wheel brace for the book drop. The bin has wheels and the floor isn't level. So we put that against the wheels so it doesn't roll around."

EZ was gauging Buffy's emotional state. "All right Buffy, ready to go take a look at some things in the other room?"

She nodded but it didn't look like she was thrilled about it. She clutched my arm, and I escorted her to the door. For once EZ didn't say anything.

Robert was peering in the closet when we came in. He stepped out and closed the door. "Mrs. Minington, your volunteers label the boxes very thoroughly—very easy to find specific genres."

"Thank you?" Buffy was not expecting that. Neither was I but I was used to Robert's tangents.

Robert walked over to the table. "Just to make sure I understand the process. Donations come in, they're sorted on this table, and then placed in boxes for the book sale."

Buffy nodded.

He pointed to the books on the table. "Are these also the donations?"

Buffy looked. "I guess so. Anything the volunteers didn't box up are judgment calls for me to look at. Looking at the pile, I'd guess they wondered if they were too old to bother trying to sell."

I glanced at the table. It appeared to be mostly books about golfing, some old spy novels, last year's bestsellers, and fad diet books.

Robert glanced at the table again. "Logical. What about old books, like antiques and collectibles?"

Buffy glanced at EZ, who nodded encouragingly. "We'd call Gibby Carols to take a look. If they were valuable, she'd take them and sell them in her antique shop for us."

Robert glanced as Del walked in the room, guarding his evidence. "Ah—that's what I was looking for—the murder weapon."

Robert took the metal bar. "Blunt force trauma to the temporal bone above the ear."

Instinctively, we all now looked down at the blood splattered on the floor. Buffy's nails dug into my arm. "Uh, we're going to go back outside if it's all the same to you." EZ nodded and we headed out, followed by all three of them. Everyone sat at the table.

EZ looked at the librarian. "Walk me through the process of shutting down the library."

"We announce we're closing 5 minutes before. I chase out stragglers and lock the door. Then I double check the stacks. Then I head out the delivery door. Bowie stays behind to vacuum, empty the trash, and shut off the lights. Then he heads out."

"Do volunteers stay after closing very often?"

Buffy shook her head. "No—they only stay late on the nights just before the book sale, or situations like Saturday, where we need to clear out boxes."

EZ nodded. "How did Bowie feel about volunteers staying after closing?"

Buffy sadly smiled. "He hated it. He understood why and didn't say anything, but he had a set routine and liked to stick to it. Plus, he was notorious for going into the book sale closet after closing and rummaging through the boxes. He'd borrow books to read—he liked whodunnits. He'd returned them, but put them in the wrong boxes. It drove Holly and Cat nuts."

EZ looked at her. "I know Holly Enger is the head of the volunteers. Who's Cat?"

Buffy looked at her. "You must know Cat Commings—she's the photographer for the *West County Gazette*." She pointed to a large framed photo on the wall. Based on the hoop skirts and guys dressed like Colonel Sanders, I assumed it was a shot from a past July Julep Jubilee.

EZ nodded, but I could tell she was not the small town newspaper subscribing type. "Okay, who was here Saturday?"

"I called Holly, she brought Carol Wiggins. Cat was also here —she left about at five as I was locking the door." Buffy thought for a moment. "And Allie stopped in briefly but she didn't stay long."

Robert, who had as few dealings with the locals as possible, looked lost, but the rest of the names were familiar, even to me. Carol was a retired teacher working on a history of Lockhaven and was involved anything even remotely civic—reenactments, festivals, town, blood drives, summer programs—whatever. She was busier in retirement than she had been working. Allie Cathaway tended to get involved in causes. She was on a couple of town boards, including the Library Board, and was very good a delegating duties, even when she wasn't the one in charge.

"Buffy, who has a key to the library?" EZ seemed to be running out of ideas.

Buffy paused. "I have one, Bowie has another. That's it."

EZ looked at her. "Are you sure? None of the volunteers have one, no one at town hall has a spare?"

Buffy shook her head. "No. Town Council has been firm about that. In fact, I've tried to get the fire department a copy, just to allow them to come in and reset the alarm without me having to come down here. Me—or Bowie." Her eyes welled up again when she said his name.

EZ noticed. "Buffy, why don't you go sit in your office. We're going to discuss some things that will just make you more upset. Tommy will come and get you if we have any questions. Buffy nodded. I noticed she checked her pocket to make sure she had her flask, then walked away. I was apparently supposed to sit still and shut up per usual.

EZ folded her hands. "All right, what do we know?"

Robert blinked. "I believe Mr. Richards's death was accidental. Another inch toward the back and it would have been a scalp wound. There would be more blood, but it would not have been fatal."

Del looked toward the door to the book drop room. "Are we sure that metal bar was the weapon?"

Robert nodded. "I am fairly certain. The county will need to run tests to see if any blood trace survived the rain. If it was blocking the wheels during the attack, there would be a void in the splatter when it was moved. There is none, so it was grabbed and used as an improvised weapon."

EZ nodded. "So we know that sometime before eight o'clock on Saturday, someone got into the library and killed Bowie in an unplanned attack. Bowie's keys are still on him. So he locked himself back in after letting the volunteers out the front. Someone magically appeared in a locked building and killed him. All we're missing is who, why, and how they got in the library. We've practically solved this case."

Robert nodded. Sarcasm was another thing Robert was oblivious to. "I have a theory as to why, and if I am correct, one of your volunteers is the culprit."

EZ didn't bother asking him to elaborate. She knew better. Robert may have been an emotionless, socially detached genius, but he had one human failing—he hated being wrong. He wouldn't share anything until he was certain.

Robert stood up and walked toward Buffy. "Mrs. Minington, I would like to look in the Dumpster where the discarded books are deposited. May I assume it's out this side door?"

Buffy looked at him. "Yes. It's the trash Dumpster. We don't discard enough recycling for a separate Dumpster."

"Thank you." Robert headed for the delivery entrance.

EZ watched him go and turned to me. "Tommy, go help him."

"Excuse me?" I was still hoping to get back to my movie script, where dead people were just non-union extras of the minimum wage variety. One quick look from EZ and I decided to help Robert.

I heard Buffy asking EZ as I headed out to catch Robert. "Why is he looking in my Dumpster?"

EZ shrugged. "I don't know, Buffy. But I've learned to trust Robert's instincts."

I pushed the panic bar and we were in the back of the building. The delivery door slammed shut harder and louder than I expected. I turned. The exterior of the door was featureless—no locks, or handles. No wonder everyone used the front door—once you went out, you were committed to your plan.

The Dumpster looked like every Dumpster I had ever seen. You'd think that being Florida that they'd at least be in tropic colors. Nope, it was standard grime-covered dark green with a lid of black. At least it was smaller than I expected.

I stood next to my brother. "Robert, before I start Dumpster diving, what the hell am I looking for?"

Robert studied the Dumpster. "We are looking for a book."

I looked at him and then the Dumpster. "A book? In a Dumpster? A Dumpster where a library tosses discarded books?"

Robert nodded. "We can limit ourselves to the top layers. We want to focus on the discards from Saturday."

I sighed and climbed in. Somehow, I was pretty sure this was not how David O. Selznick spent his spare time. I wordlessly started pulling out books and handing them to Robert. He soon had a stack of out of date textbooks, mildewed paperbacks, and a couple of discarded library books. I didn't know what Robert was looking, but his brow furrowed as I handed him the last book, a badly mutilated science book that looked like it had been out of date since the Eisenhower presidency.

I climbed out. "Why did I climb in there and you didn't?" At least the Dumpster lid was watertight, or I'd be even less happy.

Robert thoughtfully examined each book, then tossed them back in the Dumpster. "I didn't ask you to climb in. I was just going to look inside. Like I said, the top layer is all that we needed to focus on—they were all visible from out here."

I suddenly had a dull throbbing pain in my temples, which I normally get when talking to Robert. That was the missing piece to make my day complete.

We walked back to the door. There was no way to open it from the outside. Robert kept staring at it.

"Thomas, would you walk to the front door and then open this door?"

I just left. I was still a little annoyed about the whole Dumpster thing. I tapped on the front door, and Del let me in.

"Where's your brother?" Del asked.

"He's out back, staring at the fire exit like he's never seen a door before." It may have sounded a tad petulant, but I'd been playing in a Dumpster.

EZ was sitting with Buffy. I walked past and pushed the panic bar to open the back door. Robert poked his head in.

"Mrs. Minington, is it safe to assume this brick by the door is used to prop the door open when needed?"

Buffy nodded. "Yes. We block the door open to let delivery men back into the building."

Robert glanced at the door again then stepped inside the building. The door slammed shut behind him. It was louder than I would have expected in a library. Robert walked over to the bookshelves and started browsing.

"Robert, do you have insights you'd like to share, or can Buffy help you find a book?" EZ still hadn't figured out my brother had no grasp of sarcasm.

He pulled a book off the shelf, thumbed through it, and carried it back to the table. He handed it to EZ and started checking his phone.

She looked at it. "*Physics Fun for Little Scientists*? Dare I ask why you're giving me this?"

He just stood there, casually reading his phone. "This is why Bowie was killed."

EZ looked at it. "Robert, it's an old book, but I don't see why it's worth killing over."

Robert was used to walking people through his thought process. "Those 'old spy books' on the donation table are all first edition, first impressions of Ian Fleming's James Bond books. They're worth hundreds of dollars each to a collector."

EZ looked at him. "So you think one of the volunteers recognized the value? If they're valuable enough to kill Bowie over, why did she leave without them?"

I remembered what Buffy told us. "The false alarm." They all looked at me. "The alarm went off and the killer panicked."

Robert shook his head. "Not quite. One of the Fleming titles is not with the rest. If the original collector was meticulous enough to collect all first editions, the fact one is missing is odd. When the alarm went off, the killer panicked. Without knowing how long before the firemen arrived, the killer took the most valuable one and headed for the delivery door. But it was raining too hard to risk getting the book wet. So she hid it and went out before the fire truck arrived."

Buffy looked confused "Hid it? There are thousands of books in here."

Robert nodded, "Correct. Fortunately, we know exactly where it is."

"We do?" EZ was looking across the expanse of shelves.

Robert tapped the book in her hands. "You have it in your hands." Turning to Buffy, he continued. "The book was not properly placed on the shelf. Admittedly we're discussing a murderer trying to escape the building, but sloppy shelf work may indicate the volunteers need to be retrained.

"Robert." Even my brother knew EZ's 'shut up and focus' voice. She looked at the book. "Robert, it's an old science book, not an Ian Fleming novel. I don't see why it's worth killing over."

Robert just stood there. "Open it, Eothalia." Only Robert called her by her first name. At least he was the only one who did and had survived. She opened the cover. Inside was another cover. "What the—It has two covers?"

"No, the killer ripped the covers off the physics book and used it to camouflage the book. Any of the library volunteers would know the old science books don't get checked out."

EZ pulled the physics cover off. "Okay, it's another James Bond book—an old copy of *Casino Royale*. I assume you mean this is the missing one from set in the book drop room. So why hide this one?"

If Robert actually had emotions, I'd say he was enjoying this. "Again, open it."

EZ slowly opened the book and froze. "Is this what I think it is?"

Robert nodded. "It is an author-signed presentation copy of the first edition, first printing of Ian Fleming's first James Bond book, which completes the set of first editions on the donation table. I just checked online. A first edition presentation copy signed by Fleming recently sold at auction for $140,000. This is your motive."

Buffy gasped. "That's enough for a new roof and doors with enough left to have a real book budget!"

EZ looked at the book. "I don't suppose you also know who killed Bowie?"

Robert looked uncomfortable, which meant he didn't know. "There are only six people who knew those books arrived Saturday. We can eliminate the late Mr. Richards for obvious reasons. The anonymous donor was obviously unaware of the value, or Mrs. Minington would have heard from him by now. That leaves the four volunteer who sorted the books. I have no way to further narrow down the list."

I had an idea. "How about we just let the killer confess?" Everyone looked at me blankly. Now I knew what Robert felt like most of the time. "Haven't any of you ever watched a Charlie Chan movie? We set a trap."

"As much as I hate to admit it, Tommy may be on to something." EZ was thinking out loud. "We're the only one who knows where that book was hidden—except for the killer."

She glanced at the door to the book drop room. "Okay Tommy, walk me through a Charlie Chan trap."

Three hours later, Holly Enger, Allie Cathaway, Carol Wiggins, and Cat Commings were seated around a library table with Buffy and EZ. Del was set dressing, standing by the front doors, now draped with crime scene tape. Robert and I were sitting in Buffy's office, where we could watch without being noticed.

EZ started. "Thank you all for coming on such short notice. I'm sure word has already started spreading around town. There was an attempted robbery at the library Saturday after closing. Unfortunately, Bowie Richards apparently walked in on the burglar and was killed."

She paused as the four volunteers all started asking questions. EZ let them go on for a few minutes.

"Ladies, I can't tell you any details because it's still an active crime. We are pursuing several leads, but I need your help. You were the last people to see Bowie on Saturday, so I need to ask if you if you saw anything when you left Saturday night—strangers, unfamiliar cars in the parking lot, anything that struck you as odd?"

The four volunteers looked at each other blankly. No one had seen anything.

Robert leaned in and whispered. "Shouldn't she be interviewing them separately?"

"Probably," I whispered back. "But we're not looking for information. We're planting it."

"I don't understand, Thomas."

"You will, Robert. Give it time."

EZ opened up her notebook. "Oh well, it was a long shot. So, when did you all leave Saturday?"

Allie looked at the others. "I came in around 3:30 and left at 4:00—there really wasn't any need for me to stay."

EZ nodded. "And when did the rest of you leave?"

Cat stopped fiddling with her handbag. "You make it sound like we're suspects."

EZ smiled. "Nobody's a suspect. I'm just trying to build a timeline as to who was in the library when, so we can narrow down when Bowie was attacked."

Cat dropped her bag into her lap. "I left at five. I know because I slipped out as Buffy was locking the door."

Holly glanced at the crime scene tape festooning the entrance door. "Carol and I stayed until about six, maybe six thirty. We held the delivery door open so Bowie could take a box of books to the Dumpster and then we left."

Carol glanced at Holly. "I think it was closer to seven. You ran back in for your umbrella and I waited by the door. I saw the time on my phone when I was checking the weather report."

Holly looked uncomfortable. "That's right. I forgot my umbrella."

EZ closed her notebook. She hadn't written anything. "So nobody saw anything odd?"

They looked at each other and then shook their heads.

"Well, it was worth a shot. Thank you, ladies."

Buffy stood up. "Girls, the library is going to stay closed until the county crime scene technicians arrive. Hopefully, they'll be here tomorrow. Holly, can you contact the rest of the volunteers and let them know?" Holly nodded.

Buffy stood up. "I'll call Holly when we can open again. The sheriff tells me it could be a few days, depending on what they find. I'll have to be here to lock up after them, so it'll give me a chance to go through the collection. In fact, Dr. van der Grimmen has agreed to help—starting tomorrow, he and I will start weeding the collection. He'll start in the 500s and 600s while I work on fiction and biography. It'll be nice to have a scientist examining the science collection to remove out-of-date books."

EZ thanked them and Buffy walked with them to the delivery door. When I heard that familiar metal door slam, Robert and I came out of the office. EZ motioned for Del to come over.

She turned to Buffy. "Thank you, Buffy, you did fine."

She looked at the sheriff. "Now what?"

EZ looked more grim than usual. "Now, we see if Charlie Chan was really that good at catching bad guys."

The plan was simple. In case our killer was watching, Buffy would shut down the lights and let EZ, and Del out the front door, lock it and then head out the delivery door. Robert and I would stay behind since none of the suspects knew we were in the building. Everybody would drive away, leaving the library empty for the night. EZ would wait a few minutes and then double back and we'd let her in the delivery door. Robert and I could go home while she'd wait in the library to catch the murderer trying to recover the book.

We sat there. It gets dark fast in Florida, and just to make it creepier, the library was dead silent. We sat there in near darkness, the only light coming from a handful of ceiling lights scattered across the ceiling and the bright red light of the exit signs. Robert's glasses were reflecting the exit lights, making him look like a demonic owl. Then it struck me. Buffy had said there were three exits.

"Uh-oh." I suddenly had a bad feeling.

Robert looked at me. I stood up and went deeper into the library.

"Thomas?" Robert got up and followed me.

"Robert, I may have made a bad mistake. Buffy said there were three exits."

Robert looked around. "The main entrance, the delivery door—where's the third one?"

A shadow stepped out of the gloom. I heard the unforgettable sound of a gun being cocked. A woman's voice rang out in the darkness.

"That would be the one in the children's room. Everyone forgets that one is there. It's been unlocked for weeks."

I was torn between bolting for the exit or soiling myself. If I survived, I'd applaud myself for doing neither.

Robert did not look surprised. "Mrs. Cathaway, I presume?" Seriously, nothing bothered my brother.

Allie Cathaway stepped forward with an impressively large revolver pointed at me, which seemed inherently unfair, since Robert was the one talking, not me.

She looked at me. "Where is it?"

I shrugged. "I'm not sure what you mean, Allie."

Robert looked at me. "She means the Ian Fleming presentation copy of *Casino Royal* that she killed Bowie Richards to obtain. You really should pay attention when there is a weapon aimed at you."

Allie shifted the gun toward Robert. "I didn't mean to kill him. I just wanted him unconscious. He was looking at the books. If he spotted that autograph, he'd tell Buffy."

Robert glanced at the gun. "Mrs. Cathaway, that wasn't just an autographed book. It's a very valuable first edition. You may be underestimating the value by thousands of dollars."

It dawned on me—Robert wasn't being obtuse, well, at least no more than usual—he was stalling for EZ to return. Problem is, even if EZ showed up, she was locked out. She could probably catch Allie on the way out, but by then, we both could be suffering a fatal allergic reaction to bullet holes.

"Good to know. Again, where is my book?" The gun was pointed back at me.

"I don't know," I said truthfully. I hadn't noticed where Buffy put it for safekeeping.

"It is where you left it," Robert finally said. "As terrible of a trap as this turned out to be, we still needed the bait to be where you could find it."

Robert was a convincing liar. I'd have to remember that.

Allie led us at gunpoint toward the 500s. She snatched *Physics Fun for Little Scientists* off the shelf. Now, as long as she didn't open it to see we stuck a replacement inside the cover, we might get out of this alive.

She opened the book. She looked at and then slowly pointed the gun at my head. She turned to Robert. "Very funny. Where is it? I will shoot your brother if you don't tell me."

From behind her, a voice rang out. "Even if you do us a favor and shoot Tommy, I'm still going to shoot you." EZ stepped into the light from behind Allie. Her gun was even bigger.

Allie raised her hands and EZ quickly took the gun and uncocked it. As EZ handcuffed her, I looked at Robert.

"How did EZ get into the building?"

Robert watched as EZ led Allie out the door. It slammed shut with its usual noise. We walked toward the door. He pushed the door and it swung open.

I watched. "You didn't touch the panic bar. How do you unlocked it?"

Robert caught the door before it slammed shut again. "The panic bar is the only lock. Everybody hears the door and assumes it closed properly. However, there are small stones outside the door that showed impact damage. Apparently, Mr. Richards, if his hands were full, kicked a stone into the door jam. The door still slammed with all the noise, but the stone kept the door from closing snugly."

"Which meant the lock didn't engage."

Robert nodded. "I placed a stone in the doorway. Buffy heard the door slam and made the conclusion the door was locked. I had not anticipated how useful the experiment might be."

EZ came up to the door. "Allie confessed all the way to the patrol car. She's already trying to cut a deal. She says she and her husband are underwater on that fancy new house they own right before the last real estate bubble burst. Tough luck, but she's going to have time to rethink the matter—about 30 years, with possible time off for good behavior. And that's not including charges for threatening a law officer. Robert is technically a deputy."

"Excuse me, but she was pointing the gun at me too." I really didn't care , but EZ seemed a little nonchalant about my near-death encounter.

She looked at me and smiled. It was not a reassuring smile. "There's no statue for performing a public service."

She opened the door and kicked out the stone. "Gentlemen, I'll take your statements in the morning. I'm going to go lock that other door and introduce Allie to the Lockhaven jail cell."

It was a cool night as Robert and I started the 15-minute walk back to the house. I just wanted to get home and get on with my script. Robert was silent, but his head was tilted. That meant he was thinking—never a good sign.

Finally, he turned to me. "Thomas, exactly why were you at the library this morning in the first place?"

"I needed to look up that railroad route you wanted me to checked for *Dinosaur Women of Lake Erie.*" I knew what was coming, and I couldn't stop it.

"Thomas, that material is available in my library. All you needed to do is find the shelf with books about upstate New York—F129.B8 is the LOC number. This is why you need to learn Library of Congress classification system. Admittedly Dewey works for a public library, but still."

It was going to be a long walk home.

Inspector Cosgrove investigates a murder in his favorite local library in our next story, where the author deftly applies a gentle wash of humor over the grim realities of death.

Richard Lau is an award-winning writer with articles and stories published in newspapers, magazines, and anthologies, along with several plays produced. He also loves libraries so much that he married a librarian.

The Day the Librarian Checked Out

by Richard Lau

Inspector Cosgrove extended a trench-coated arm toward the tray of brownies on the bake sale table.

"Sir, don't eat those!" cried Sergeant Burell, his orthopedic shoes clattering across the tiled floor of the library's lobby.

"I was going to pay for it," growled the fifty-something Cosgrove, perhaps a bit too defensively, his face an angry, red tomato.

The much younger police sergeant leaned close, so that the two men's cheeks almost touched.

"Mrs. Tuttle, sir," he whispered, nodding toward the uneven squares of chocolate.

Cosgrove immediately understood and felt grateful toward his subordinate. Around the small town of Forestville, it was well-known that Mrs. Tuttle was not the best of cooks and an even worse baker. "Ah, I should have recognized them."

Trying to transition to the matter at hand, the police inspector continued. "Are we dealing with a poisoning case, by any chance, Sergeant?"

"No such luck, sir. A stabbing. With scissors. Mrs. Wilson."

"Emily Wilson? The librarian?" Cosgrove remembered the tall, thin, bespectacled woman from when he was knee-high with a mouthful of gum, constantly being shushed and told to use his "inside voice."

The young Cosgrove thought the scarecrow of shush would live forever. She probably would have if someone hadn't prematurely taken her out of circulation.

"Oh, Inspector!" A shrill voice echoed off the floor and walls, announcing the arrival of Mrs. Tuttle, a flying fireball in floral print. "Please help yourself to one of my brownies. My treat!"

"Sorry, ma'am," Cosgrove replied officiously. "I'd love to, but I'm on duty."

A patrolman rushed up. "Sorry, sir. She got around me."

"Please escort Mrs. Tuttle back to the room where we're holding the other suspects," ordered Sergeant Burell.

"Suspects? Suspects?" repeated Mrs. Tuttle, windmilling her baseball bat arms hysterically. "We're suspects?"

The patrolman led her away as Cosgrove asked, "So, who are we looking at?"

Burell pulled out his notebook. "Fortunately, the incident appears to have occurred before the library opened. So, only five people were here. The victim, Garrison the janitor, the assistant librarian Sheila Harris, and two volunteers who were going to run the bake sale table."

"And no one else could have gotten on or off the premises?"

"There's only this main entrance, which was locked, and the employee entrance in the back, which was also locked. Only Mrs. Wilson and Garrison the janitor had keys to them."

"We'll check to see if they still have their sets, starting with Mrs. Wilson."

With a final longing look at the other goodies on the bake sale table, Cosgrove followed his sergeant to where the head librarian had been permanently shelved. She was dutifully still at her desk, her white-haloed head slouched forward, as if uncharacteristically dozing on the job, the handles of a pair of scissors protruding from her chest. It was not a pretty sight, but corpses rarely were.

"Who did this to you?" asked Cosgrove, examining the wound and the rest of the body. She had always been able to answer his questions in the past, but this time he was on his own. Cosgrove felt a bit of his childhood had passed with the old librarian.

Her wool-sweatered arms hung loosely by her side. No dying clue scribbled on the informational papers and brochures on the desk. No accusing message had been typed on the desktop computer, whose monitor only showed the start-up page for the library's online catalog. At her age, death was probably almost instantaneous.

He pulled open the top desk drawer. Inside were pens, pencils, pads of paper, unactivated library cards, and various rubber stamps and ink pads. For young patrons, the drawer also contained pages to color, bookmarks, and stickers.

In the bottom drawer of the desk, he discovered Wilson's purse. A quick check revealed there was still money inside it. He glanced at her identification, not very flattering but better than the way she looked now. He also dug out a ring of three keys marked "Library Front," "Library Back," and "Desk."

Under the purse was a single book, a hardback of a classic, in very good condition. A slip of paper between the pages told Cosgrove the book had been purchased recently at a local used bookstore.

The book's back cover caused him to smile. Cosgrove turned to the computer and a few clicks and keystrokes later, his smile grew wider.

"I believe I have our motive," he told the sergeant. "Now let's go confront the killer."

Along with the patrol officer and the infamous Mrs. Tuttle, there were three other people in the library's largest conference room. Inspector Cosgrove introduced himself and flashed his badge.

"What's this I hear about us being considered suspects?" blurted a burly, heavily mustached man in a gray jumpsuit.

"Please, Mr. Garrison," began Burell.

"Mr. Garrison?" cut in Cosgrove. "You're the janitor who has the only other set of keys to the library?"

Garrison pulled out a ring with two keys on it.

"So, both sets of keys have been accounted for, and both doors were locked. Would you mind telling me what you were doing this morning?"

Garrison looked like he minded very much, but still he answered. "After setting up the table and chairs for Mrs. Tuttle and Miss Gramercy, I went to clean the bathrooms."

Cosgrove thought about the library's floor plan. "The bathrooms are off of the lobby. So, Mrs. Tuttle and Miss Gramercy, who were setting up the items for the bake sale would have seen you if you left the bathrooms?"

"And they did," said Garrison. "After I was done cleaning, I passed them on my way to report the inventory to Mrs. Wilson." He paused, for the first time, looking uncertain. "I was the one who found her body." Then the fire flashed back. "I didn't touch anything, and I didn't do it!"

"Who called the police?"

"I did," replied a woman in her mid-thirties. Her manner of dress and hair style was more in line with a political convention than Saturday at the library. "I'm Sheila Harris, the assistant librarian. I was going to ask Emily a question when I saw Mr. Garrison standing in front of the desk. As soon as I saw what happened to poor Emily, I called the police from my cell phone."

"Not from your desk?"

"Emily and I shared a desk," she explained. "There was really no need for two, as one of us was always roving and shelving, and the other was seated to help patrons with anything else."

"I don't recall seeing any of your personal items in the desk, Ms. Harris," Cosgrove said.

"I keep my things in the back room." Ms. Harris replied.

"Do you feel that they're safe there?" Cosgrove asked pointedly.

Ms. Harris blushed. "What do you mean, Inspector?"

Cosgrove narrowed his steely blue eyes. "Does the library have a theft problem?"

The assistant librarian shook her head vigorously. "Of course not!"

"Then why the bake sale?" asked Cosgrove. Burell wondered why his superior was pursuing this line.

It was Mrs. Tuttle who answered. "A little extra funding is always helpful, sir. I keep the records on donations; I can verify that there's no money missing."

The expression on the volunteer's face dared the police to challenge her accounting and her word.

"Do you really think one of us could have killed poor Mrs. Wilson?" asked a wide-eyed, tanned young woman, pulling worriedly at her long, dark hair.

"And you are?" asked Cosgrove, merely for formality.

"Heather Gramercy. I volunteer for library book sales and bake sales. Look, we obviously care a lot about this library, or we wouldn't be here. And Emily Wilson was certainly a large part of this library. I would say that she cared the most."

"Perhaps she cared too much," said Cosgrove, holding up the book that had been in the librarian's desk. "Mrs. Wilson recently purchased this book from a local used bookstore."

"So?" challenged Garrison. "Maybe she wanted to add to the library's collection!"

"Or check on a theory of what was happening with the library's collection." Cosgrove looked at the puzzled faces around him. He had to admit one of them was a really good actor.

"Can you see what's on the back of this book?" He held it toward his audience as they leaned forward. "You may notice it has a barcode sticker with the words 'Property of Forestville Library' printed on it."

"The sticker also has the word 'Discard' stamped across it." Gramercy pointed out.

"That's the interesting part," said Cosgrove. "A quick check with the library computer system shows that this book is still part of the library's collection and should be sitting on the shelf right now. Yet, Emily Wilson was able to purchase it from a used bookstore a week ago."

There was silence in the room.

"Do you have anything to say…" Cosgrove paused dramatically and suddenly narrowed his attention to a single person. "…Ms. Harris?"

"Me?" snapped the assistant librarian with a shocked expression.

"Yes." He decided to put on the pressure. "Who else besides Mrs. Wilson would have easy access to the Discard rubber stamp in the desk drawer?"

"Everyone here!" insisted Harris, her voice rising a couple of octaves.

Cosgrove nodded. "But wouldn't it look strange if the janitor or a volunteer was going through the librarian's desk? And when would they do it, if either you or Mrs. Wilson was always at the desk?"

"Garrison has the keys to the library!" Harris charged. "He's always here after hours and could stamp as many books as he wanted to!"

"True, but Garrison doesn't have the key to the desk, do you, Mr. Garrison?" asked Cosgrove.

"No, of course not!" said Garrison. "Why would I need to?"

"But someone who had access to the desk after Mrs. Wilson unlocked it in the morning, someone who belonged behind the desk and was expected to be there would have all the time in the world to stamp a book as discarded without attracting any unwanted attention."

He moved closer toward the assistant librarian, who sat trembling slightly in her chair. "I'm willing to bet the bookstore owner will remember who's been selling them 'discarded' library books. Or at the very least, remember Mrs. Wilson asking them about it."

Cosgrove's accusing finger came up like a drawn gun.

"What happened this morning? Did she confront you about the discarded book? Had she figured the whole thing out? She did, didn't she? And in an act of haste and panic, you grabbed the scissors off the desk and stabbed her!"

Sheila Harris turned paler than a page intentionally left blank, and her guilt was twice as clear.

"I would even guess you didn't have enough time to clean the scissors adequately before you heard Mr. Garrison approaching. You ditched around some shelves and came up behind him, to put him on the spot for discovering the body."

"Why you…" began Garrison, half-rising from his seat. A stern look from Burell changed his mind.

"Mrs. Wilson knew this library like the back of her hand. I'm sure when she spotted this book in the store, she knew it didn't belong there. And checking the back cover, she knew it hadn't been officially discarded. How many books did you steal and sell, Ms. Harris?"

The assistant librarian shifted her gaze to the floor, as if she could lose herself in the swirling carpet pattern. "I want to speak to a lawyer," she said, barely above a whisper.

As the patrol officer handcuffed her and read her her rights, Burell said to his superior, "That librarian's got a due date with the death penalty."

"Or Mrs. Tuttle's brownies," replied the inspector, growling along with his empty, but sorely tempted stomach.

Next, we jump back in time to Home Front America in 1943, where librarian Emily Applegate, fan of crime fiction, is about to stumble into a very real sinister, and murderous plot.

Janet Raye Stevens writes short stories and novels in the mystery, young adult, and science fiction, and contemporary romance genres that so enthralled her as a child. She is a two-time RWA Golden Heart finalist, and four-time Daphne finalist, and the recipient of that award in 2014.

The Vanishing Volume

by Janet Raye Stevens

January, 1943

"Good morning, Miss Applegate," Sgt. Duffy said, coming up to Emily at the library's front desk.

Emily placed a just-returned book on the cart with the other books needing to be shelved and turned to him with a welcoming smile. "Sergeant! I didn't see you come in."

"Snuck in when you weren't looking." He unwound the wool scarf from around his neck. "Mighty brisk out there today."

"More than brisk, I'd guess, the way you're bundled up." Emily ran a glance over his policeman's coat, buttoned snugly over his tall, portly frame. His hands were red from the cold, and so were his cheeks.

"True," he said. "The temperature hasn't inched above ten degrees all morning. But, I suppose that's to be expected in Massachusetts."

The weather report complete, an awkward silence fell. Emily straightened some papers, her belly fluttering. She'd met the sergeant when he'd attended the launch of the library's *Victory Book Campaign*, a drive to collect new and gently used books to send to servicemen here and overseas. That was nearly two weeks ago and Sgt. Duffy had been dropping by each morning around ten o'clock, with a variety of reasons for coming in--a visit to Periodicals to skim the newspapers for the war news, to check on the library's evacuation plans in case of an emergency, to pick up or drop off a book.

But the way he looked at her, puffing out his cheeks and shuffling from foot to foot, Emily wondered if there was something else that drew him to the library each day.

"How's the campaign going?" he asked, breaking the conversational logjam. He pointed to a wooden box across the wood-paneled room near the door. A sign, *Drop Books for the Boys Here,* was taped to the bin. "Has business been steady since the launch?"

"Yes, I'm delighted to say." Emily flushed with pride. She'd volunteered to run the city-wide campaign, as a way of doing her part for the war effort. "So many people are donating, the bin's full at closing time each day. And our back room's overflowing with the other books brought in from collection points all over the city. Preston's going all-out to support our servicemen."

He nodded. "I know the boys will appreciate it. A book is like a piece of home."

There was a catch in his voice and Emily wondered if he thought of himself, a young soldier far from home during the last war, the one that was supposed to end all wars.

He cleared his throat. "Miss Applegate..." He paused, his cheeks turning a darker shade of red. "I'm wondering... Ah, I mean, would you... Would you recommend a detective novel for me to read?"

Emily felt a sting of disappointment. She'd been anticipating an entirely different sort of question.

She led him to a bookshelf near the windows, stuffed with crime and detective fiction. After a spirited debate on the merits of men versus women authors, he gave in and chose one written by the latter--Agatha Christie's *Evil Under the Sun*.

Back at the desk, Emily stamped the due date on the borrowing card and slipped it into the pocket on the inside back cover.

"It's a clever story, and Hercule Poirot is a clever man," she said, handing him the book. "I'm sure you'll enjoy it."

"With your recommendation, I'm sure I will."

He dropped the book into one of his coat's wide pockets and Emily watched him leave, frustrated. It seemed as if the good sergeant was going to ask her for a date. It had seemed that way every day he'd come in, and though she was a short, skinny, forty-year-old spinster librarian who had no business going on dates, if he asked, she would say yes. But he never seemed to get up the gumption to ask.

"That policeman, here again?" the library director Mr. Purdy said, bustling up. A spare man of fifty, not much taller than she, he had a beak-like nose, a balding pate, and a fondness for sober black suits. "One would think there wasn't a crime or juvenile delinquent in the whole city to attend to with him haunting the library every day." He sniffed. "I wish you'd discourage him, Miss Applegate, instead of flirting. It's most unbecoming of a lady of your age and station."

A sharp retort sprang to her lips. It was none of his business. She would encourage Sgt. Duffy, and flirt with him, too, as much as she liked. She was eligible and so was he. He was a widower with no children, only a few years older than Emily, and they had much in common, including a fondness for hiking, love of Humphrey Bogart pictures, and a passion for detective fiction.

Fortunately, Mr. Purdy rushed off to admonish someone else before Emily could speak her mind. It'd do her no good to rile her boss. He could make her life difficult if he felt like it, and she didn't want to give him a reason to feel like it.

She went back to work. The clock ticked the minutes away and soon it was time for lunch. She left Marian in charge of the desk and went over to check the donations box before heading for the back room and a liverwurst sandwich.

There were already a dozen books in the bin, including several dog-eared Zane Grey westerns, the books servicemen clamored for most. One larger, hardbound book caught Emily's eye, John Steinbeck's *The Moon is Down*. There was a tiny tear at the top left of the dust jacket and a slight discoloration in the *O* in the word *Down*, but otherwise it was like new.

Emily hadn't read the book yet, but knew the story was about a people conquered by a totalitarian enemy. Perhaps that was why she hadn't read it--the fictional plot echoed her doubts and fears about this very real war. She preferred to escape in the pages of her detective books, and she gobbled up several chapters of Chandler's *Farewell, My Lovely* as she ate her lunch.

At closing time at six, she helped Marian tidy up the desk, ushered several lingering patrons out the front door and turned the lock. Then, as her last task of the day, she scooped twenty-three books out of the bin and lined them up on a wheeled wooden cart to bring to the back room.

Something was odd. She scanned the books' spines and their titles and quickly figured it out. *The Moon is Down* was gone. Did the book's donor have a change of heart and come back to retrieve it? Or had someone pilfered it? The library was always busy, and the bin was near the door, it would be easy for someone to swipe the book without being noticed.

Puzzled, Emily rolled the cart across the main room, the wheels bumping on the floorboards, to the back, where Mr. Purdy was waiting to escort her out the rear exit.

"You'll have to clear these books out soon," he said, watching her with a sour expression as she rolled the cart next to the towering stacks of books near the wall. "They're becoming a hazard, and a nuisance."

"A truck will collect them next week and take them to campaign headquarters in Boston," she said, omitting the fact that she'd simply begin all over again as donated books were dropped off from the city's churches, movie theaters, and businesses. "Mr. Purdy, I would think you'd be proud our library's spearheading such an important project for the war effort."

"Yes, of course," he said quickly. "It's just so untidy."

Emily put on her coat and Mr. Purdy tapped his foot while she went through the detailed process of fitting her rubbers over her shoes. He could stew all he'd like, she was *not* going out into this winter slush in her Oxfords, with shoe rationing meaning she only got one new pair a year.

They left together and parted ways at the end of the walkway, Mr. Purdy to his fine home and fat wife on the west side, Emily to her rooms at Mrs. Miller's Home for Ladies. Mrs. Miller was an old battleaxe, but she kept a tidy establishment and meals were provided, so Emily wouldn't complain.

Tonight was beef stew, light on the beef, due to rationing, but heavy on the potatoes, so Emily ate her fill. After supper, she kept the other ladies company in the parlor, listening to one of her favorite detective shows on the radio, *Boston Blackie*. After, she retired to her bed, determined to finish *Farewell, My Lovely* that night, though she had a hundred pages to go.

In the morning, she met Mr. Purdy on the rear steps of the library at five minutes to nine, but he scowled as if she was as late as an overdue book. She opened the front door and greeted their first customers of the day. She was at the desk an hour later when she saw Sgt. Duffy, standing by the book donation bin, then she lost track of him, as a patron claimed her attention.

"You were right about Agatha Christie," the sergeant said, coming up to her as she was shelving books in the children's corner, near the door. "I'm already halfway through the book. Very tense, despicable characters, a real humdinger."

"I'll resist the urge to say I told you so," she said, slipping a new book, *The Poky Little Puppy*, between two others.

Another awkward silence fell. Emily was tempted to tap her foot with as much impatience as Mr. Purdy. Would Sgt. Duffy ever get his tongue untied long enough to say what was on his mind?

"Well, put me down for Miss Christie's next one, when it comes out," he said, then, touching the brim of his policeman's cap, he left. Emily frowned at his retreating back. Perhaps she'd been wrong, and there was another reason for the sergeant's daily visits than an interest in an old hen like her.

Feeling blue, she finished shelving and headed back to the desk, glancing into the donation box as she passed. She jerked to a stop. *The Moon is Down* was at the top of the pile. One of 1942's best-selling books, there were a lot of copies in print, but this was the same copy, Emily was sure of it. There was the same rip in the dust jacket, the same discoloration on the word *Down*. Curious. Had the person who'd snatched it from the bin yesterday returned it in a fit of remorse?

Mr. Purdy was hovering nearby, his beady eyes on her, so Emily didn't take the time to puzzle it out. She returned to work, and kept busy locating books for patrons, helping Marian at the desk, tidying up in Periodicals, and shelving more books.

Things got even busier after school, when the high school students flooded in, girls in bobby sox and saddle shoes, boys in high-waist trousers and those silly beanies with crown points. They were as loud and rambunctious as teens could be, and Emily was exhausted by the time she closed the door on the last of them at six o'clock.

She retrieved the cart and went to collect the donations, stiffening in surprise--*The Moon is Down* was nowhere to be found.

Was this a joke at her expense? Emily looked around, half expecting to see Marian or Mr. Purdy peeking out from behind a bookshelf, snickering, but no one was there. If not a joke, then what? Who had dropped the book in the bin in the morning, and removed it in the afternoon, two days in a row? Why?

Emily pushed the cart to the back, trying to shake off her uneasiness. She'd been reading too much detective fiction. There was a perfectly logical explanation for the book's disappearing and reappearing act.

The next day, she tried to keep watch on the bin, but that was difficult, what with trying to avoid Mr. Purdy's censuring eye, Sgt. Duffy's daily visit--to read the newspaper headlines today--and much work to do.

She had a moment around noon and peeked in the box. She gasped. *The Moon is Down* was back. She picked it up, flicked a finger over the small tear, then opened the book and fanned through the pages, looking for some clue as to what made this particularly tome special, what made it keep vanishing and coming back again. Finding nothing out of the ordinary, she placed it back in the bin, vowing to keep an eye on it the rest of the day.

Emily's thoughts rocketed back and forth between thinking herself silly for her suspicions and fear that something was amiss. She was at the desk a few minutes before closing, only half-listening to Marian's lengthy story of her fruitless quest to find silk stockings for her cousin's wedding, when she spotted a thin man in a wool coat sidle up to the bin.

Emily held her breath, stunned, as she watched him, quick as a sneak thief, pluck the book from the bin and slip it into his coat's wide pocket. Before she could holler, he was gone. Before she could think, Emily ran after him.

Cold slapped her as she burst through the door and raced down the steps. The thin man turned up the sidewalk, walking at a brisk pace. Emily hurried after him, her Oxfords tapping a rapid tempo on the slushy pavement. It was still light, thanks to wartime daylight savings, and she could see him clearly, weaving between pedestrians as he moved up the hill. He was tall, she was not, and he soon outpaced her. He turned at the corner and she lost him.

She'd caught her breath by the time she got back to the library, but it took a lot longer to warm up. Mr. Purdy hadn't noticed her absence, since he'd been attending to some important loafing in his office all afternoon, and he didn't seem to notice the way she was shaking when they closed up for the day. For that, she was glad. She was so frightened by the wild thoughts that swirled around her mind, one sideways word from him would probably make her snap.

Emily ate supper then went straight to bed, but sleep evaded her. It *wasn't* her imagination, there was something nefarious going on with the book, but the devil only knew what. She fluffed up her feather pillow. She had to tell someone, and the most logical person to tell was Sgt. Duffy. But what would she say? That a man came in twice a day, leaving a book in the morning and retrieving it in the afternoon? Well, maybe not just one man, the thin man could have an accomplice.

Emily sat up straight. Icy pinpricks danced down her spine. No, it couldn't be. He was a policeman, for pity's sake. And yet... She couldn't recall seeing Sgt. Duffy at the library before the *Victory Book Campaign* launched. The book seemed to appear after the sergeant made his daily visit. And she'd seen him by the bin several times.

What was she thinking? She had to have bats in her brain to think he was somehow involved. Only one thing to do--she'd flat out ask him, that would solve everything.

Emily woke Friday morning, feeling sluggish from worry and lack of sleep. She dragged her feet from the trolley stop to the library's rear entrance, so late Mr. Purdy was already inside.

She planted herself at the desk, watching the front door like a hungry hawk, silently cursing any patron who interrupted her surveillance. She watched the clock, too. Ten o'clock arrived, and so did ten-ten, then ten-twenty and still no Sgt. Duffy. Emily chewed on a fingernail. Where was he?

She was so focused on watching the door, she almost missed the man hovering by the book bin. No, not Sgt. Duffy, she was insanely happy to see, but another man, different from the book thief she'd chased yesterday. This man was younger, with a beak-like nose, and wearing a brown overcoat and a ragged fedora. Emily watched as he dipped his hand into his coat pocket, pulled out a book, and *plop*, dropped it into the box. Then he scrammed so fast he nearly left smoke in his tracks.

Emily thought to give chase but knew she'd never catch him. The book was the important thing. She hurried over, snatched it from the top of the pile, and brought it back to the desk, determined to figure out what was so important about the darned thing.

She placed the volume under the desk lamp and peeled off the dust jacket. She examined the pages, looking for something inserted, or notes in the margins, or letters circled in some sort of code, as was the key to solving the case on last week's *I Love a Mystery* radio program.

Finding nothing suspicious on the pages, Emily ran her fingers down the spine and over the covers, inside and out. She went still. Something was there, inside the back cover, a slight bump under the linen lining. Looking closer, she saw a slit in the cloth about two inches long.

She yanked open the junk drawer and dug around inside. Patrons left behind all manner of things at the library, eyeglasses, fountain pens, baby rattles, even a pair of false teeth. Emily knew one of the forgotten items in the drawer was a pair of tweezers.

She paused a moment, thinking she should wait for Sgt. Duffy to arrive. This was a matter for the police, after all. But her curiosity got the best of her. She slid the point of the tweezers into the tiny opening, her hand trembling as she latched onto whatever was under the lining. She drew it through the slit as carefully as pulling a needle through lace.

It was a sheet of paper, small and thin as a V-Mail. She unfolded it and squinted at the tiny, penciled print. Emily's breath stopped--it was a list of scheduled shipments from H&G Firearms, a factory downtown.

Emily stared at the paper, her heart hammering. She needed Sgt. Duffy to get here, *this instant.*

"What *are* you doing, Miss Applegate?"

She jumped in alarm. Mr. Purdy. Why must he continually creep up on her like that? He eyed her intensely, and, for once, his gaze wasn't annoyed, it was curious. That encouraged her.

"Mr. Purdy, a strange thing… I believe spies are using our library to pass messages."

His upper lip curled and her shoulders sagged--he didn't believe her.

"My dear, I believe your friendship with that policeman is making you see crime where it doesn't exist."

She ground her teeth, frustrated. "It's true! Spies are passing information on shipments of arms, and who knows what else, from the firearms factory. They are using this." She held up the book and the paper. "The message is slipped into the lining and someone drops it in the donation box in the morning. His accomplice picks it up later in the day. I've seen both men with my own eyes."

His own eyes went wide. "You have?"

She nodded. Perhaps he was beginning to believe her. "Mr. Purdy, we *must* alert the police."

He eyed her a moment, his expression indecisive. Then his posture snapped up straight. "You're right. Forgive me for doubting you. We *should* alert the police." His voice took on an urgent note as he added, "Come with me."

He crooked a finger and she followed him toward the back, hugging the book--with the paper tucked safely inside--to her chest. The idea of spies using her library for such a nefarious plot made her head spin.

He let her precede him through the door to the back room, closing it behind him.

"Get your coat," he said, sticking his arms into his own over-coat, then digging into his pockets as if searching for his gloves.

Emily shifted the book from hand to hand as she dutifully donned her coat. A thought struck her. "Wait, why don't we simply *call* the police? I'm sure they'll want to come here and inspect the scene for clues--"

She turned to him and froze right down to her toes. He held a gun--pointed at her.

"Mr. Purdy," she breathed, her voice wreathed in disappoint-ment. "You? Mixed up with spies?"

"I prefer to call them business associates. My *wealthy* business associates."

He backed up to the door, his gaze, and the gun, trained on her. He felt for the lock, and Emily's heart sank when she heard it click into place--cutting off an escape route. That left only one avenue of escape, the rear exit. Should she risk getting shot and make a run for it?

"You betrayed your country for money?" she said. "You used our library to pass on guarded secrets?" Though she quaked in fear, she gave him her best librarian scolding look. "*Shame* on you."

He gave a smug snort. "Shame on *you*. You insisted the library get involved in this cockamamie campaign, I simply took advantage of it. My nephew's been stealing plans and passing secrets for months, but it's risky for him to meet his contact in dark alleys. We saw this project as the perfect way to exchange information. The bin's in a public place, where people come and go, easier not to be noticed. The plan worked perfectly until you stuck your nose into it. Now you're a problem."

His expression hardened. He was no longer the officious, prudish, and sorely underpaid library director. He was a traitor with a hard heart. Emily's fear intensified.

"What are you going to do?" she breathed.

He stepped toward her. "You've seen their faces, you figured out the scheme, what do you think I'm going to do?" The gun shook in his hand as he gestured toward the rear exit. "Come on, let's go."

"No!" Emily backed up, bumping into a wall of books. "Mr. Purdy, you can't--"

She flung *The Moon is Down* at him. He shrieked in surprise and ducked. Emily spun, hooked her arms behind as many of the teetering stacks she could reach for and gave them a shove. The towers toppled, knocking Mr. Purdy off balance. He crashed to the floor, buried under a pile of books. The pistol jumped from his grip as he fell, going off with a resounding bang that nearly deafened Emily.

Shaking, she gaped at Mr. Purdy in horror and disbelief, until roused by the sound of pounding and someone shouting, "Emily! Emily!" Sgt Duffy. Emily sprang to the door, flipped the lock and he burst inside, his expression contorted in fear and alarm.

His gaze bounced from Emily, to Mr. Purdy, groaning under a treasure trove of tomes, to the still-smoking gun on the floor, then back to Emily, and his questions poured out in a heated rush. "*Are you all right? What happened? Are you all right? What the hell happened?*"

He didn't wait for an answer, he snatched her to his broad chest and enfolded her in his arms.

"And that's the whole story," Emily said, her voice still some-what shaky. Sgt. Duffy scribbled down every word, while one of his colleagues slapped a pair of handcuffs onto Mr. Purdy's wrists and another cop gathered up *The Moon is Down*.

"It was a plot worthy of Mr. Hammett," the sergeant said, watching the cops wrestle the prisoner out the door. He turned to her. "You've had quite the adventure, Emily."

Indeed she had, and if she was tempted to forget, her still-trembling legs would remind her. She looked at the donated books, strewn all over the floor. "I have another adventure ahead of me, cleaning up this mess."

"I'll help if you'll let me. But later." He gave her a soft, almost shy smile. "Right now, I think you need a break. Will you allow me to buy you a cup of coffee? "

"Really, Sergeant, coffee? With rationing and all? I'm shocked," she teased.

"We'll make it tea then," he said, laughing. "And, you know, my name's Seamus. I'm sergeant to the boys down at the precinct. Seamus to my friends. I hope that's what we can be."

He offered Emily his arm and she fit her hand in the crook of his elbow. "Why, Seamus, I think this is the beginning of a beautiful friendship."

She stepped over a pile of books and let him lead her out the door.

"There is no such thing as a harmless librarian," states a character in our next story, a tale that reveals a little-known truth about librarians, that they make notorious—but we are getting ahead of our story.

Michael Brandon lives in the UK with his wife and children. His work with RealDeal Theatre, which performs experimental sitcoms in libraries, provided him the impetus for this story.

Where Agents Go to Die

by Michael Brandon

Tom Ellis, junior intelligence officer, glanced at his wristwatch and wrote his latest observations in a small notebook. 3.30 pm. No activity.

There was in fact plenty of activity; a steady stream of people coming and going through the library doors. But the only thing that mattered today was her, the target of their surveillance. When she arrived, when she left to buy a sandwich, when she returned, and when she went home

Of special interest were her inconsistencies. Did she leave alone or with a colleague? With or without the purse she had arrived with? Pastrami? On a Tuesday? And when there were inconsistencies it was Ellis who raised a telescopic camera and took a series of snaps.

Ellis drummed his fingers on the steering wheel even though he knew, or because he knew, it would annoy his partner. A rebuke from a senior agent would at least break the monotony.

It had an immediate effect. Agent Joseph Strickland lowered the binoculars.

"Stop that."

"Stop what?"

Never one to take his eye off the ball, Strickland raised the binoculars and scanned the front of the library. A red brick municipal building circa 1970. Squat, ugly, and brutalist. It reminded him of his wife. "This is hopeless," said Ellis. "A sixty year old librarian? Our intelligence must be faulty."

Without lowering the binoculars, Strickland sighed wearily and imparted a gem of wisdom to the rookie pup.

"Ellis, a helpful word of advice. If the best place to hide a tree is in a forest, then the best place to hide a terrorist is inside a library."

Ellis stopped drumming and pondered for a moment.

"That makes no sense."

"Doesn't it, Ellis? Doesn't it?"

Strickland felt a surge of pity for his naïve protégé. With only six weeks in the field it was hardly the kid's fault. He had much to learn. And with retirement less than a year away for Strickland, he rather enjoyed being the tough-to-be-kind father figure. Ellis had the makings of a half decent NSA surveillance officer. In time his youthful, positive idealism would go the way of an overused pencil. Through regular operation it would be worn down to a tiny, annoying little stub, blunted and incapable of being sharpened ever again. His idealism would be placed in a tin and the tin in its turn would lie forgotten at the back of a drawer.

"It's the best place to hide a book," replied Ellis. "Or a librarian. But a terrorist? Wouldn't they want to keep away from public places?"

Strickland lowered the binoculars and tapped his nose for emphasis.

"Experience, Ellis. Experience tells me this; of all the professions, which is the most ordinary? The most…" He searched for the word. "To be blunt, Ellis, what is the most boring job you can think of?"

"You mean, apart from ours?

Ellis could see the logic and conceded a shrug.

"Maybe. But why can't you just say that? Why do you have to talk about trees?"

Strickland scanned the library again.

"Trying to see the good in people will get you killed. Take it from me; there is no such thing as a harmless librarian. They're evil, twisted people. Libraries are a breeding ground of bitterness and disaffection. Why? Because you spend your whole working day stamping dusty old books in and out. In and out. In and out. You work in silence. You can't hold a proper conversation with your colleagues or the readers. At parties people shun you when they hear you work with books. It's a lonely life for sure. That's what makes them susceptible to radicalization. I'm not saying all librarians are, or will become, terrorists. But they must be watched. All of them. All of the time."

Ellis placed his hands on the steering wheel but decided not to drum. He yawned and flexed his shoulders.

"Isn't everything automated these days?" Ellis asked.

"What?"

"They don't stamp books anymore. You scan them yourself or you order online before you visit. I'm surprised we still have librarians. They'll be replaced by robots soon enough, you mark my words."

Strickland considered this for a moment and was amused. An uncharacteristic smile caused his cheeks to dimple. Ellis was aware of the change and felt uneasy. He had never seen Strickland smile before.

"You think that's funny?"

Strickland shrugged.

"You wouldn't say it was funny if it was you being replaced by a machine."

"Me? Replace me with a machine? Impossible. Machines don't feel emotion."

"You don't feel emotion."

"A machine," he continued as if Ellis had not spoken, "can never understand the nuance of body language. The cultural relativity of a half-smile. The significance of a nervous twitch. Let me give you an example. Say it's a cold winters day and a bum walks into that library smelling of liquor. He's creeping around between the Thrillers and Romances looking for somewhere to sleep. A human shows him the door. But a robot? A robot recommends the latest Dan Brown novel and tells him to have a nice day. Meanwhile the bum instructs the robot to turn the heating up and the robot obeys. You see? A world with robot librarians would be a world in chaos. Anarchy."

A hard rapping of knuckles on the window startled the agents. Aware he had taken his eye off the ball for just a moment, Strickland cursed and reached for his gun. By the time he found it Agent Kathy Browning was already opening the back door and getting in the car. Strickland relaxed. Browning welcomed their discomfort. Having spent six hours inside the library pretending to read a reference book on Oriental Porcelain, it was their turn to suffer.

"Damn it guys, wake up!" She yelled as soon as the door was closed. Let's try and be professional."

"I am awake!" Strickland growled. "What's wrong? Why aren't you inside?"

As the senior officer, Strickland had decided Browning should go inside and observe the target at close quarter. She was, he said, best qualified on account of wearing glasses and having a wallflower personality. She would easily pass for an amateur enthusiast of say, Oriental porcelain. Browning promised herself there and then that he was not going to reach retirement. Her gun was going to misfire the next time they drove over a speed bump. It would be an accident. A good agent has to be ready for anything, and that includes having your safety catch off.

"What were you two beating your gums about?" She asked.

Ellis could feel himself flush hot with embarrassment. He did not care what Strickland thought of him, but he quite admired Browning. She retained a residue of idealism that he could relate to. She was not one of Strickland's blunt pencil stubs. Not yet anyway.

"Never mind us, Browning." Strickland said. "What's going on?"

"She's dead. She's been poisoned."

Strickland scratched his stubble and pondered. Even he had not expected that one. For the second time that day he smiled.

"Agent Browning?" Ellis said. "Would you mind telling me what the hell just happened in there?"

"You got your report book, Ellis? Take this down."

Ellis took up his notebook and pen. Strickland made a call on his cellphone, sticking a finger in his ear to block out Browning's narrative.

"At 3.15 the target took her final coffee break. She sat at her desk reading a book. Her coffee remained untouched. The book was titled The Name of the Rose."

"Name of the Rose," Ellis repeated, scribbling frantically. It was hard to concentrate with Strickland talking at the same time.

"3.25. I saw she had not turned a page. Not one. She hadn't even blinked. From this I deduced three possibilities. One; she was an extremely slow reader. I discounted this. Two; it was a difficult text. A plethora of literary grandiloquence."

"How are you spelling that?"

"Just write difficult."

"Difficult."

"Three; and the most likely explanation. She was dead. As I left the library I stopped by her desk, pretending to ask if she had anything on the Ming dynasty. I observed some of the pages of her book were dog-eared and stained with a blue dye."

"Slow down. Blue dye."

"Also, her right index finger was stained blue. And finally her tongue, which was protruding ever-so slightly, was stained blue. She had been poisoned."

Strickland ended his call. His face was a grotesque mask fixed somewhere between joy and disgust. Ellis recognized it at once. He was wearing a mask of extreme smugness and vindication.

"I told you, Ellis! Didn't I tell you? A library is the perfect place for a terrorist to lie low. She's been assassinated. Now who would do a thing like that to a simple, sweet old lady? Maybe she was slurping her coffee a bit too loud, huh?"

"Forget that Strickland," Browning said. "What do we do now?"

"Now? Now we do what agents do best. We wait. Remember, the killer might still be inside. We watch the doors."

The agents remained in the car for several more hours. No ambulance came. No cops were called. As it grew dark the last of the readers and staff had left the building and the janitor locked the doors.

"What the hell?" Ellis asked no one in particular.

"Occam's Razor." Strickland replied. "When presented with competing hypothetical answers to a problem, you should select the one that makes the fewest assumptions. In other words, no one knows she's dead."

Ellis was disgusted. In his short time with the NSA he had witnessed some unspeakable acts of cruelty. Preventing them or bringing the perpetrators to justice was his prime motivation for joining the agency. But no act of depravity could compare to an elderly librarian dying at her desk and going unnoticed by her by colleagues. She was in there now, in the dark, alone and undiscovered in an alcove with an open book and cup of cold coffee. But wasn't that Strickland's point all along? She was invisible.

A long silence descended as the agents pondered their next move. Ellis assumed they could all go home and file a report in the morning. But Strickland and Browning were considering other options.

They could break in and examine the old lady in more detail. Could there be something of interest in her desk or purse? Should they take a sample of the poison for analysis? It might indicate who had killed her and why. But they would need blueprints of the alarm system and that could take hours.

Strickland wondered how long it would take before the librarian's colleagues realized she was dead. When she decomposed? When someone asked for the book back? When it was her turn to fetch coffee?

At last they decided to call it a day. Not for any particular operational reason, but because Strickland needed a pee and his pee-bottle was full. Out of respect for the senior agent, Ellis offered him his own bottle that was only half full. Strickland declined.

"I'm good. Browning? You go back inside tomorrow morning and pretend to discover her. I'll alert the local P.D and tell them to treat it as natural causes. Then we wait for the toxicology report."

Ellis drove them home. He dropped Strickland outside his apartment in Upper Manhattan, which is where Browning changed seats. She handed him his pee-bottle.

"Don't forget this, boss."

As they drove away Ellis observed him in the rear view mirror. He was standing forlorn on the sidewalk holding two liters of pee in a milk carton and a lit cigarette. He saw him glance up at the apartment block and continue walking. Ellis knew he would go to a bar before he went home.

Heading for Brooklyn they were met by roadwork. Ellis was glad the mission had ended abruptly. He was heartily sick of the car interior. Browning on the other hand was relieved to be out of the library. The car seats were heated and she was enjoying the noise and bustle of the streets. Neither had much to say. After several minutes in front of a red light, Ellis thumped the steering wheel.

"God damn it! I hate it when he's right!"

Browning unwrapped a piece of gum and neglected to offer him a piece.

"I thought it was faulty intelligence. A case of mistaken identity. But what do you know? Assassinated right under our noses."

He looked at her plaintively but her attention was fixed on the red light.

" Maybe he was right about me too?"

Browning ignored him. She tried to blow a bubble but it was premature. The gum required more chewing.

"I try to see the good in all people, see? But that's not who we're looking for is it? The good guys? Browning? Are you even listening to me?"

"I'm listening. What do you want me to say? There's plenty of good people out there. More good than bad. But it's like…"

She drifted away, trying to think of an analogy. She succeeded in blowing a bubble. A blue membrane split and stuck to her bottom lip.

"It's like what?"

"Say I release a tiger in Central Park. You wouldn't go around telling people to chill because we outnumber tigers in this city eight million to one. Tigers are cute. But tigers are lethal."

Ellis considered this for a moment. "Yeah. I suppose."

"You get a rifle and you deal with it, cute or not."

"Yeah. With tranquilizers."

Browning sighed and shook her head.

"You see!" Said Ellis. "I want to tranquilize the tiger. I'm not cut out for this job."

"Green."

The lights had changed. The line of cars crawled forward.

"Listen Ellis, you want me to tell you you're a good agent. I don't know you well enough to say that. Maybe. Maybe not. You have to decide that for yourself. But don't let Strickland decide that for you. You sure you don't want gum? It helps you think."

"No thanks."

"The thing about Strickland is he thinks he's on top when really he's way behind. He's a dinosaur."

"You don't like him then?"

"I didn't say that. It's not a question of like or dislike. Times change. Methods change. He's not best placed to judge whether or not you're a good agent. You get me?"

They pulled over outside Browning's apartment. She unbuckled her belt and gathered her belongings. Taking hold of the door handle she hesitated.

"Strickland is full of wisdom," Browning said. "But he reminds me of Aesop. Have you heard of Aesop's fables, Ellis?"

"Aesop? Sure."

"He was sent on a special mission by his king. His mission was to win the people of Delphi over to his king's line of thinking. But he made the people of Delphi real mad. And do you know what they did?"

"No."

"They took hold of Aesop and threw him over a cliff. True story. And do you know what the moral of this tale is?

"No."

She climbed out of the car and closed the door, looking back in through an open window.

"Nobody likes a smart ass."

Assuming she was talking about Strickland and not himself, he smiled.

"Only you can decide, Ellis."

Somewhere between Brooklyn and Queens, tired and hungry, Ellis found a place to pull over. In the time it took to drop Browning and find a place to park he had made an important decision, the most important decision since joining the NSA. He was going to quit. In the morning he would give notice. And when, as they surely would, they asked him what he was going to do next, he would tell them.

"I'm going to be a librarian."

After all, he knew they had a vacancy.

Our next story delves into a deeper mystery than do the other stories in this collection. It is indeed, a mystery that has bedeviled our kind throughout our brief existence in this mortal coil.

Author Ed Ahern returned to writing after decades of working in foreign intelligence and commerce. He has well over two hundred stories and poem published and three books. He also serves on the review board of Bewildering Stories. This story was previously published in Sacred City (2015) and Fast Forward (2016)

The Fortune Teller

by Edward Ahern

The Crusader's Latin was crudely scribed, with many misspellings, but Brother Willman read along quickly, absorbing the narrator's pride in the pillage and destruction of Constantinople. Christians off handedly killing Christians. The writer had felt no need for apology.

Brother Willman sighed. The victors always wrote from moral superiority. He turned off the light above the vellum book and took a step over to an adjacent table, where loose parchment sheets were arranged. These sheets, also written in Latin, were an account of the same events by a Byzantine priest. He claimed moral superiority as well, but in defeat, and cited the atrocities of the Crusaders as evidence of their demonic nature.

Willman's thoughts wallowed in ancient gore. He typed his Latin notes into a computer and left, unlocking and relocking the door. A Vatican guard let him out of the library wing housing among other sections the *Liborum Prohibitorum*, the works condemned by the church.

Niles was waiting for him in the vestibule. Both men were Dominican brothers, sworn to vows of poverty and chastity. Both had the stooped posture of scholars who hunched over documents for weeks on end.

"So, Willman, did you obsess about the winners or about the losers today?"

"Both. It's incredible how much material was retrieved from the losing sides, given that the winners wrote the histories and burnt the libraries of the losers. Squads of friars must have searched through the rubble for heretical scraps."

They walked to their customary cafe. The waiter brought them each a bottle of Moretti beer.

"Well, learned associate, any revelations?"

"No. Same daily grind, atrocities and sins, sins and atrocities."

"I envy your exploration of churchly shortcomings. My hagiography is almost too uplifting. The saints are all so *good.*"

"Don't be sarcastic Niles. We can't all be virgins and martyrs."

"It's just ironic that I, sardonic if not cynical, am assigned to study the blessed and you, who could have written Pollyanna's autobiography, study the church's shortcomings."

"Blame it on the cardinal."

Willman had been tucked away in a Catholic university in Connecticut, presenting dead languages to uncaring undergraduates. One evening, while flickering his attention between computer chess and television, he received a telephone call from his bishop. He muted President Obama's assurances about troop withdrawal from Iraq and picked up the telephone.

The bishop was almost brusque. "Brother Willman, your aptitude in languages and analysis has come to the attention of the Vatican."

"Excellency?"

"We're sending you to Rome for evaluation. If you pass their scrutiny they'll have some sort of long term assignment for you."

Willman's thoughts churned. "Your Excellency, did they indicate the nature of the task?"

"No. They're being coy and won't tell me what it is."

Once in Rome, Willman was tested in medieval German and French, as well as Latin. His arcane capabilities impressed both his evaluators and Cardinal Benetelli, who summoned Brother Willman to his private quarters.

"Brother Willman we want you to study the church's defects."

"Your Eminence, Holy Mother Church is not considered fallible."

"Yes, yes, like our holy father in pronouncements on matters of faith. But our history has been…deviled by a series of horrific transgressions. We don't want you to look at individual failings, although the Lord knows we've had enough of those. No, we want you to study our systemic aberrations-the murders committed by early Christian sects, simony and indulgence selling in the Middle Ages, papal wars, the crusades, the persecution of Jews and trials of witches, down to pederasty in our own days. We've never had a century without some sort of collective travesty.

"We want you to study two millennia of our defects. You'll need to set aside the random violence- the wars, pillage and rape engaged in by the laity for which we were spectators. Focus on church instigated atrocities.

Willman opened his mouth, shut it, and opened again." Eminence, I have no background in doctrinal verification…"

The bishop gently waved his hand. "Precisely. A fresh outlook. And you should know that your many homilies have not gone unnoticed. We need your independence of thought. Then, assuming you've been able to digest what I've described,, we want you to try and project what our future transgressions could be."

"I don't think I'm capable of accomplishing that, your Eminence."

"We have no one better suited. You'll have access to the entire Vatican library, including the books that are condemned and restricted. This is a labor of years, so you should plan on becoming a Roman."

"Yes Eminence."

Willman burrowed into his research, so deeply buried during the day that his thoughts were in the Latin vulgate. His evening reversions into English and Italian required several minutes. The church had no index of aberrations, and Willman had to speed read through stacks of documents and pick out the blemishes. He identified scores of monstrous jigsaw pieces but couldn't fit the abnormalities into a meaningful pattern.

His fertile imagination let Willman stare at the horror underneath the dry and self-praising descriptions- the unrecorded torture and rape, looting, disease and starvation. The souls wrenched from their bodies for no sin other than being in the way. He was amazed that the church repeatedly held together and healed, a spiritual amoeba able to absorb and neutralize the poisons of persecutions and internal rots.

Willman's mind spun without traction, his thinking soggy. He felt trapped in a confessional with a series of boastful transgressors. He prayed daily to see a structure behind the vicious acts, to accept that these evil deeds were balanced by great good, but could only painfully absorb the egregious sins.

Months passed without progress. He began to imagine that he heard the cackles of demons rejoicing in his failure, that the butchered dead stood nearby in silent recrimination to his futile efforts. Brother Willman, by nature upbeat, succumbed to depression.

"Niles, tell me about a saint, I need something to counteract the day's readings."

"Well, I'm working on St. Jerome, doctor of the church, translator of the bible into the Latin vulgate. He often used a quotation from Vergil to describe hell, 'The horror and the silences terrified their souls.' At one point, in Rome, he was accused of having an improper relationship with the widow Paula, but that may have been because he was exposing the wrong doing of many priests. He died in a hermit's cell near Bethlehem. His head was revered posthumously in two different locations at the same time."

"'The horror and the silences terrified their souls.' That's maybe also true outside of hell."

"Don't get morose on me. God has given us ample reading material and Moretti beer."

"Amen."

Willman's summaries to the cardinal read like a child's book report, describing actions with no clue about motivation. Cardinal Benetelli wrote back that he knew the hours and intellect that Willman devoted to his labor, and felt guilty about being unable to offer further guidance.

It was while studying the persecution of Spanish witches and heretics that Willman sensed a faint outline, a skeleton with a few bones protruding from the graveyard dirt. And something else. The hint of infernal will that impelled clergy into violators of Christ's teachings.

Willman circled through the library like a dervish, not just comparing aberrations but interweaving them, creating tapestries in his mind's eye that blanketed the walls of the rooms. His cringed as he climbed inside the minds of the perpetrators, but delighted as he drew closer to the underlying pattern.

He lived within the scriptorium, and left Niles to drink his daily beer alone. His thoughts rode the collective failings like dragons, and he saw the violence and killings in the present tense, with identifiable faces, through the eyes of the perpetrators. As his reality lurched he intensified his prayers.

Then, like the unfolding of a particularly ugly flower, he saw the pattern, a suppurating tableaux of wounds barely healed before being reopened. The eagle that each day ate away at bound Prometheus' liver.

Willman felt afraid to put his thoughts into the computer, and wrote them down in Latin. Had he vellum and a quill pen he might have used them. Willman carefully arranged the religious riots and deaths in first century Alexandria, the slaughter of French Huguenots in the sixteenth century, the machinations of often unholy Popes.

He paused several days to let his findings settle into the belly of his mind and then made an about face—staring into the future and discerning with great fear the shapes of atrocities to come. The wars driven by religious hatreds. The slaughter of hundreds of thousands of innocents.

Long hours and wracking tension had ground down his health. Willman wrote a guarded note to the cardinal suggesting that he might have a hypothesis and allowed himself three days of bed rest and meditation.

On the fourth day, needing a human voice, he called Niles. They met at the café.

"Niles, I think I've detected a pattern."

"Little Brother, at the pace you were working I assumed you would either have a stroke of genius or just a stroke."

"I need to think it through a bit more, but I have my hands around it."

"Willman, just be prudent in your presentation. We sometimes treat new ideas with hostility. Look what happened to Galileo."

They finished their one beer and parted. Willman was too excited to return to his small apartment and walked back to the Vatican library. He stood in the center of his scriptorium and viewed his many work tables covered with books and scrolls. Like music stands in an orchestra, he thought, and wondered that evil could create such terrifying harmony and melody.

The thought further saddened him, and he turned to leave. After the watchman had let him out and he was pacing down the corridor there was a bell like noise behind him. Willman turned and saw a very large man, backlit in the corridor lighting. His frayed nerves tore inwards from his skin.

"You're…you're not allowed in here."

Willman had blurted this out in third century vulgate. The person before him responded in kind.

"Brother Willman I came to offer consul."

"Do I know you?"

"Not in the sense you mean. We have observed your work."

"I work alone, without observation."

"And yet we are aware of what you surmise. Come with me."

It was a command and not an invitation. Brother Willman crossed himself and followed the figure through basket weave passageways to a dead end alcove. In the dimness the figure appeared faintly self-illuminated.

"You know your way here."

The figure smiled, "I have visited often."

"Who are you?"

"Your names for me are vague and tongue distorted, but two you would recognize are Malach and Raziel."

"Those are angelic."

The visitor shrugged. "Perhaps. Lucifer is also an angel. Brother Willman, I must show you the impact of revealing what you think you know."

"I won't talk of private church matters."

"There is no need. Our only wish is to illuminate the consequences of your deductions becoming known to others. You see a pattern through a billowing veil. What you infer approaches truth, but your telling of this partial truth will set no one free."

"But I'm charged with reporting my findings to the church."

"And would be sinless in so doing, Brother Willman. Most of what is unfortunate is not evil."

"But these two thousand years of outrages are surely inspired by the devil!"

"Are you so sure? Is not Asmodeus in his efforts selfish, working for the ruin of individual souls rather than whole churches? Are not calamities and group transgressions rife outside of religious contexts? Do we not accept that life consists largely of pains and disappointments?

"Think in terms of the chess games that you love Brother Willman. What do you do if your opponent makes a move that is unexpected?"

"I would think through the new variables."

"And have you considered the consequences of your revealing this partial truth? Or have you just assumed that your pearls of wisdom would somehow eliminate the inequities for which the church is the stage? Do not answer immediately- devote at least as much thought to it as you would to a chess game."

Willman noticed that the presence in front of him did not seem to breathe, but also discovered that he had lost his fear.

"You're saying that the future would be worse than what I now see?"

"Beloved Brother, do you remember the quotation used by St. Jerome to describe hell?"

"The horror and the silences terrify their souls."

"If you reveal your findings, you will have discharged your duty. You'll be spared much personal anguish. But by acting to diminish or eliminate your visions of future evil the church will create even worse alternatives. Your silence spares others painful and useless foreknowledge. But you must abide in self inflicted anguish. You would be uniquely burdened and tormented. You have free will. It is your choice."

Willman found himself alone in the alcove. He stood motionless for several minutes, then turned and found his way back to the scriptorium. The guard seemed unsurprised by his reappearance. He walked into the center of the prohibited wing and rehung the mental tapestries that illustrated his solution. Willman impelled his thoughts forward in time, racing through almost endless chains of if-then, if-then. After two hours of motionless thought his shoulders slumped.

Willman had a farewell beer with Niles two weeks later.

"So you're going back to teaching dead languages to over privileged children?"

"Yes."

"How badly did Cardinal Benetelli beat you up?"

"Not so badly, considering all the time and money involved. When I told him that my note was in error, and that I'd been unable to make any sense of the church's missteps, he seemed unsurprised. He thanked me for my efforts and asked for my research. I've provided him with all the computerized files. He assured me that I have an academic position to return to.

"May real peace be with you Brother."

"Thanks, Niles. You remind me of someone I met recently. I think that's a compliment."

As Willman walked slowly back to his apartment he thought of what he hadn't told Niles. About carefully burning his handwritten notes and stirring the ashes. About the Cardinal's final comment to him.

"Brother Willman, I should tell you that you were not the first to be given this task, nor the first to admit defeat. Two hundred years ago we assigned the project to a Franciscan priest. After lengthy study and prayer he acknowledged his failure to resolve this issue. He was thanked for his strenuous efforts and assigned to a quiet parish here in Italy. But the work had a malignant effect on him, and he drank himself to death a few years later. We sincerely hope that if you become troubled you will rely on us for help."

Brother Willman's apartment, sparse as a monk's cell, was not welcoming. He sat down in the only chair in the room and opened his breviary. But his vision refused to shift focus from dark images of the future. He knew that sleep would come grudgingly, and would be infested with unshared dread.

Let us now return to the world of the small-town library, where everyone knows the other, and secrets are difficult to keep hidden. Emma, our librarian protagonist, is out to solve a murder with the help of her canine companion, the ever-drooling Billy.

Amy Ballard is a high school English teacher and freelance writer. This story was partly inspired by life in her tiny Idaho town. Ms. Ballard wants readers to know that any resemblance between the dog Billy in the story and her real-life rescue pooch, Max, is not coincidence.

Bookish Dreams

by Amy Ballard

When Theodora announced she was going over to the old library building in the city park, I offered to go with her in case she needed help.

Theo waved a dismissive hand. "You mind the desk. I'm only hauling the last of the donation boxes for the book sale. It won't take twenty minutes."

She was back in five, her face white as printer paper. "Emma. Someone is living in the old building," she hissed in her best library whisper.

The old library was a one-room, one-story edifice that had served our tiny community for fifty years. Then grants and donations allowed the library board to renovate a larger building on Main Street. The water and power in the old place must have been turned off long ago.

Theo eyed me suspiciously.

"What?" I asked.

"There was a perfumey smell in the air over there. Bookish Dreams. I'd know it anywhere."

"What about it?"

"That's your scent, isn't it?"

Theodora had complained about my wearing perfume to work until finally I gave it up. "Are you implying that I have been secretly living in the old library?"

"Well, have you? You mentioned just this morning that you need a new apartment."

"That's because my current place doesn't allow pets!"

On cue, my English bulldog rescue pet barked in the alley where I had tied him.

Theo was still looking at me funny.

"It's not me!" I squealed.

"*Shh!*" she reminded me, looking over at the patrons at the computers nearby.

"Sorry. I'd better reshelve these books."

"I'll call the police. That building is not a boarding house for tramps."

I wondered if Theo was still referring to me. I was wearing red lipstick, after all. That might not be appropriate for work.

<hr>

"The lock hasn't been tampered with," Sheriff Dan Hector said, leaning on the metal railing of the porch at the old library later that day. Since the town was too small to afford its own police force, the county sheriff's office was contracted to enforce the law within city limits. "Who has a key to the building?"

Theodora glanced at me.

"I've never had a key," I assured them.

My boss almost looked disappointed. "The city office has at least one," she said, "and I have two. That's it, as far as I know."

"And your keys are accounted for?"

Theo produced a key ring from her purse and a second from her work tote. She had closed the library at noon so we could meet with the sheriff. As it turned out, the only evidence the building had been occupied was a sleeping bag unrolled on the carpet. That and, as Theo had mentioned, perfume in the air. She was right, too—it was Bookish Dreams.

The sheriff didn't put much stock in smells as evidence. "I can't say that any crime has been committed, but I'll see if the city wants to put up cameras"

"No crime?" Theo twisted her mouth into a kidney shape. "What about trespassing?"

"I didn't see any 'No Trespassing' signs. I'll mention that to the mayor, too. The city owns the building, they need to maintain it. Now let me help you haul these boxes."

Conversation over.

When all the boxes had been loaded into the back of Theo's pickup, the sheriff pointed to the stacks of *National Geographic* magazines on a tall bookshelf in one corner of the now-bare room. "What about those? Should I load them up, too?"

Here we go, I thought.

If you ever want to distract Theodora Gray, just mention that heap of bright yellow magazines. Sure enough, she started in on a tirade.

"There they sit taking up space, yet I can't sell them, give them away, or throw them away. Why, you may ask?"

He hadn't.

"Because as redundant as they are in the Internet Age, they were donated by a well-meaning member of the library board. A generous member. We may have a new building with eight times the square footage, but that doesn't mean there's shelf space for sixty years of *National Geographic!* I appreciate the thought—"

"Bless her heart," I supplied.

"—but our space is not infinite."

The sheriff looked sorry he had asked.

Theodora ranted on, and I became aware of a presence outside the door. Billy, my dog, had gotten free and tailed us. Grabbing the leash that dragged from his collar, I brought him inside. He took an interest in the sleeping bag, and I let him sniff around. When he tried to settle in for a nap, I checked the time on my phone.

Theo was showing no signs of winding down. Someone should reopen the library.

"Let's go, Billy," I said.

Billy frowned as only a bulldog can, but got to his feet.

Apparently, Theodora had given up on my being the squatter, since she sent me to the city office to ask about the key.

"Does that dog have a license?" the clerk, Allison, greeted me.

"I'm fine, thanks, how are you?"

I shelled out for a dog tag. "Does the city have any keys to the old library?"

"There's one here, and Lee has one for maintenance purposes. He's the city engineer."

Billy sniffed around, tail wagging. Did he smell Bookish Dreams? I sniffed, too.

Allison was taking out the contents of the drawer. "It should be in here! Probably the mayor borrowed it and didn't put it back. She's absent-minded."

I leaned in to get a better whiff. Nothing.

"I'm sorry," Allison said. "I'll let you know if it turns up."

Billy went to the door, having exhausted the sniffing opportunities in the room.

"Thanks, Allison," I said.

"Any time."

On the way back to work, I splurged and bought lattes for Theo and myself.

"How thoughtful," my boss said, leaning back in her chair to enjoy her drink. "Did you turn anything up?"

I liked feeling like a detective on a case. "We struck out."

"We?"

"Billy and me. I got him a license, though."

"Ah. I'd been meaning to ask…"

After coffee, we propped open the back door and carried in the boxes for the sale. The back room was bursting with paperbacks, hardcovers, children's books, and even VHS tapes, which I doubted anyone would buy.

"Some people still have VCRs," Theo insisted.

A lanky woman with brown hair in a ponytail poked her head in the back door. "Cute dog," she said. "Who owns him?"

"That would be me."

"Well, lucky you! He's a honey."

"Have you met Lily Gilman?" Theo asked me.

We shook hands. "Pleased to meet you," I said.

Lily gestured to the back door. "I have some paperbacks in my car. For the sale. Is this a good time to bring them in?"

"It's the perfect time," Theo said.

We unloaded the donations and the woman left after another cuddle session with Billy.

I opened one of the boxes Lily had brought. "Huh. They're all Asian-themed romance novels. That's a very specific sub-genre! Will they sell?"

Theo flipped through the floral-covered paperback I handed her. "You never know what somebody will buy."

The sheriff came by later, a stack of overdue library books under his arm. "Thought I'd have my kids round up whatever they could find," he explained sheepishly. "What do I owe you?"

Time to use my privileges as a librarian's assistant. "You're in luck. It's fine-forgiveness week."

Looking relieved, he picked up a storytime flyer, folded it, and tucked it into his pocket. "Is Theodora in?"

I waved him into her office. He left the door open, so I listened in.

"The mayor had a copy of the key at one time, but she's mislaid it," Dan began. "The city engineer has his copy. It's on the nail where it belongs."

Theo sounded frustrated. "Could someone have had a copy made?"

"Not likely. If you look at your key, you'll see it has 'Do not duplicate' stamped on it. No licensed keysmith will disregard that.

We're working on getting a security camera or two, but the city council will have to sign off on it."

"How long will that take?" Theo asked.

"The earliest we can get it on the agenda is two weeks."

"Should I attend?"

"Not unless you want to. The mayor seems to think it won't be a problem."

When the sheriff left, I popped into Theo's office. "Dan doesn't sound too worried."

"Not as worried as he should be. We can't have vagrants in the old building. Just because nothing was vandalized doesn't mean it's not a crime."

———•◦•———

The next day, Theodora and I had bigger fish to fry. The city was flushing the fire hydrants, a routine procedure, and the library's tap water was swimming with silt.

"I'll call Allison," I volunteered.

"No, I'll handle it. You go read shelves."

As I checked the stacks for misshelved books, I thought about my need for new digs. Not only did Billy and I need a place that allowed dogs, but we also needed more room. It wouldn't be fair to keep a big dog like him cooped up while I was at work. Right now he spent every night at my mom's.

When I got bored, I recorded my progress in the computer, then checked the book drop. There were five books, all from one patron. Scanning them in, I paused. The books smelled like perfume—Bookish Dreams. I glanced at the patron's name on the screen: Marjorie Firth. Her address was just across from the old library. But Marjorie would not have a key. Her husband sold cars in the next town, and she didn't have to work because she had won a settlement after a drunk driver hit her car a few years ago. She still walked with what could only be called a lurch.

So Marjorie wore perfume and read pulp fiction? Who knew?

Billy barked in the alley, so I got him a bowl of water. He turned up his already puggish nose.

"Sorry it's full of dirt," I said. "Theo called the city. Apparently it's okay to drink."

He sniffed my hands.

"Do you smell perfume from the books?" Would Billy remember the scent from the old building yesterday?

When my shift ended, I grabbed Billy and swung by the city office to see if the key had turned up. I picked a bad time. Lee Xiang, the city engineer, was being shouted at over the phone. Some guy upset about the silt in the water, by the sound of it. Allison sat at her desk on her phone, also taking abuse, though her assailant was female, judging by the shrill squawks coming from the earpiece. Allison's eyes bored into me as I edged toward the door.

Billy wanted to stay. He'd picked up a scent, but the fragments of phone conversations were unnerving me.

"Come on," I insisted. "Time for a run."

Before I could let Billy off the leash at the park minutes later, a voice from the house nearest the old library startled me. Cade Firth, husband of Marjorie, stood in his yard declaiming into a bluetooth headset. "What kind of a water system are you running?" He followed it with a paragraph of expletives.

"Cover your ears, Billy," I muttered.

I poked around the old library with my sniffer dog. While I peeked through the windows and checked for footprints, Billy investigated aromas. He did seemed interested, but didn't turn up anything meaningful. It was time to let him have his run and then head home. I had to find an apartment so Billy could stay with me. Billy might be cute and my mom loved me dearly, but even a mother's love has its limits.

The next morning, I checked my messages and found four texts from Theodora, who rarely texted. I wasn't supposed to go in today—what was the deal?

The first: *Murder at the old library. Emma, call me!*

The next: *Meeting police there now. Call!*

Then: *It's Marjorie Firth. She's DEAD!*

And: *I knew something was wrong!*

After throwing on some clothes, I drove straight to the old library, where an ambulance and two sheriff's vehicles lined the street. Theo was talking to the county's only deputy, a heavy-set guy named Luis whom I had been crushing on for a year. Ignoring the caution tape, I walked up to Theo and gave her a big hug. We didn't have a hugging relationship, but this was an emergency.

Theo's husband Darren and a few neighbors hung around the caution tape. To my relief, Luis didn't try to make me join them.

"What happened?" I asked.

"They're not sure." Theo glanced at the deputy. "It looks like murder."

Luis provided, "The south window was shot in, and the victim has a bullet in her head." Not one of those tight-lipped law enforcement types.

"That's awful!" Even though Theo's texts had warned me, I was stunned. "Who found the body?"

"Several people heard a shot. Cade Firth called it in. He's terribly shaken up."

"Where is he?"

"Talking to the sheriff."

Luis broke in. "We'll need a statement from you, too, Emma."

"Me?"

"You were on the premises on the morning of the eleventh, right?"

"I guess so. We went over to show the sheriff what Theo found. The sleeping bag and the perfume."

"Perfume?" Luis flipped through a notebook. "I don't know anything about that."

Theo went to stand with her husband, and Luis drew me aside to where a marked SUV shielded us from onlookers and from the glare of the rising sun. "What's this about perfume?"

I explained that Theo and I had both smelled Bookish Dreams inside the old library.

"How do you know which scent you were smelling?"

"I used to wear it and Theo used to sell it when she was a Devon Products rep."

He nodded. "You say you *used to* wear it?"

"Yeah, I stopped because Theo said it was unprofessional to wear fragrance to work."

"And she never wears it?"

"Never."

"Who else do you know who might wear… what was it?"

"Bookish Dreams. It smells like leather book covers, perfect for bibliophiles. Er, book lovers."

"I'm a bibliophile myself," Luis said. He flashed a white-toothed grin that I returned.

"Marjorie Firth may have worn it. Some books she returned to the library were drenched in it. You know, the sheriff didn't seem to think the perfume was important. Do you think it could help identify the killer?"

"No telling. But you're right about Marjorie Firth. She was found wearing perfume and not much else."

<hr>

The murder was all over the news. Apparently, a witness had been in the old library with the victim at the time of the murder. I puzzled over who the witness could be, not like anyone was asking my help solving this murder.

If only the city had moved faster getting security cameras. Maybe this never would have happened. One good thing had come of the tragedy, though: Theo's *Nat. Geo*s had been spattered with blood. Now she could dispose of them with a clear conscience as soon as the sheriff's office cleared the scene.

I returned to work the following day, leaving Billy at my mom's. If the criminal element had come to roost in our little town, I didn't want anything happening to my dog. As I assisted patrons, scanned books, and ran virus checks on computers, I mentally picked at the murder of Marjorie Firth.

Marjorie didn't have a key to the old library, but her body was found inside the unlocked building. Her companion had probably unlocked the door. The murderer had not needed a key, since he or she had shot Marjorie from outside.

Knowing full well it was unethical, I pulled up Marjorie's account on the computer. For the past six months, she had checked out romance novels, five or six at a time. She returned them promptly, and there were no outstanding fines.

"Look at these titles, Emma!"

I jumped. Theo had sneaked up behind me. I glanced at the printout she handed me. Marjorie Firth's account history. Great minds think alike.

"Should we take it to the sheriff?" Theo asked.

Luis's cute smile flashed before my eyes. "Let me run it by."

The sheriff wasn't in, so I buttonholed my favorite deputy.

"Look," I urged Luis, pointing out a few of the more salient titles: *The Love He Could Not Give*, *The Other Man*, and *Her Husband's Rival*. "Marjorie *may* have been unhappy in her marriage."

"Lots of people read to escape reality. It's like binge-watching TV shows or taking a drug. It might not mean anything," Luis said.

"True."

"Still, it helps give a more rounded understanding of the victim."

"Do you have a rounded understanding of who she was with that night and why?"

Luis leaned against the counter where the dispatcher, Greta, was going through files. "I'm not at liberty to say. Sorry."

I gathered up my purse and sunglasses. "Oh. Well, good luck."

Before I could leave, Luis cleared his throat softly. "Maybe we should have lunch sometime. We could talk about books. If you like."

Greta's nose emerged from behind her files.

I giggled nervously. Stupid habit. "I do! I mean… I like."

Driving away, I wondered, was anyone at the sheriff's office taking our clues seriously? Marjorie had been using the old library as a trysting place with someone known to the sheriff's office—

someone who had access to a key. It could be anyone from the city payroll—the engineer, a council person, the guy who helped plow snow in the winter. Even Evelyn Marquis, the mayor, or Allison, the city clerk. And if people with keys were possible love interests of the victim, Theo's husband Darren must be on the list. He would know where his wife kept her keys.

But Darren and Theodora Gray had a great relationship. He brought her flowers at work and chauffeured her to library meetings all around the region. She never had an unpleasant word to say about him.

There must be a way to narrow down the suspects. Suddenly, I knew that Billy's role in this charade was not over. I pulled a U-turn and headed to my mom's.

"Why is that dog in the library?" Theo asked, her lips doing that kidney shape thing. Bringing Billy inside must rank as a more heinous crime than sporting red lipstick, plucking one's eyebrows, or smelling good in the workplace.

I held Billy's leash firmly and tried to make my voice as firm as my fist. "I'm going to need the morning off."

Why did I feel the need to investigate Marjorie Firth's murder? Maybe it was because Theo had once imagined me capable of camping out in the old library to save on rent. Or maybe I wanted to impress a certain deputy with dimples in his swarthy cheeks. Whatever the reason, my dog and I were on the case. We were going to solve our community's Crime of the Century.

Stop One: The coffee shop

Person of Interest: Darren Gray, retired; husband of librarian Theodora Gray

I allowed Billy free rein, but he showed no interest in Darren other than to pilfer his macadamia nut cookie. I replaced the cookie and bought a mocha for me, and Billy and I left.

Stop Two: Random fire hydrant

Person of Interest: Mayor Evelyn Marquis

I stopped the car when I spotted the mayor inspecting a fire hydrant at the edge of the park. The mayor and I made small talk about flushing hydrants while Billy approached Evelyn. She let him sniff her, but he soon lost interest, turned his attention to the hydrant, and did what doggies do.

Stop Three: City work shed

Person of Interest: Lee Xiang, City Engineer

Billy and I approached the bay where Lee was tinkering with a riding lawn tractor. Lee asked if I was having trouble with silt in my water. No, I said, I was not. Lee went back to work. Billy, meanwhile, freaked out. *Sniff, sniff, wag, wag.*

I had one more stop to make, but it was in Hoxton, thirty miles away. Before that, Billy and I went back to the library.

"I need the afternoon, too. I've got to find out who was in the library with Marjorie Firth."

"Emma, the whole town knows who was in the library with Marjorie Firth."

"What?"

"I thought you knew. Everyone who's come in the library today knows all about it."

"Well, who was it?"

"Lee Xiang. Apparently he started sleeping there to get away from his irritable mother. Marjorie followed him there one night, and the rest is history."

"Why does everyone know about this but me?"

"Small town gossip. You were out with Billy all morning, when it looks like you would have gotten what you were looking for just by showing up to work."

I winced. "Billy and I still have to make one more stop. Can you spare me for the afternoon? If there's any more juicy gossip, you can tell me when I get back."

Theo rolled her eyes. "Go on then, Nancy Drew. Go get your man."

Stop Four: Jimison Auto Ranch, Hoxton
Person of Interest: Cade Firth, Sales and Leasing Consultant
I chewed the fat with Cade, who, for a guy who just lost his wife, tried doggedly to interest me in a Jeep Renegade. Billy sniffed the garbage can near Cade's desk, stirring up chip bags and beer bottles like a gourmand but showing no interest in Cade. I treated Billy to a dog biscuit from a jar, then headed home.

It was nearly five when I pulled into town. I stopped at the cafe for carryout before driving to the sheriff's office. Billy whined the whole way. "Not for doggies," I scolded. "I'll give you a big supper at Mom's."

There was plenty of food, so the sheriff, Luis, and I gathered in the back room to enjoy. Greta, the dispatcher, had to stay at her desk, but we made sure she got plenty of eats. As we stuffed ourselves on battered shrimp and onion rings, I outlined my day's adventures.

"You've interviewed Cade Firth," I said. "Were he and Marjorie unhappy?"

"He made it sound like they were an average couple," Sheriff Dan said.

"They weren't. His trash can at work is full of beer bottles. Most people don't drink at work, so he must drink a lot. Marjorie can't have liked that. She was injured seriously by a drunk driver not long ago. Cade's drinking must have bothered her. Maybe he drank more because of the way the accident..."

"Messed her up?" Greta offered from the other room.

"Sure. And she read novels about finding passion with another man. Their marriage was not 'average,' not in my book."

Dan nodded. "What else have you got?"

"Lee Xiang. He met Marjorie for a tryst at least once before the night of the murder. You've interviewed him, too."

"Of course."

"And he admits to being with her, maybe even how serious they were. But did he mention he has enemies who might have aimed for him and hit her instead?"

The sheriff and Luis exchanged glances. "Enemies? In this town?"

The onion rings were gone, so I nibbled a shrimp while collecting my thoughts. "Some of our residents get pretty upset when anything turns up in the water. There are nasty phone calls every time Lee flushes the hydrants. People blame Lee for specks of sand in the tap water, even though the specks go away in twenty-four hours. People blame Lee if the snow doesn't get plowed, if the bathrooms in the park aren't open, or if the weeds in the city right of way get too tall. The town's too small to be able to pay a full maintenance staff. Most of the year, city maintenance is a one-man operation. That means Lee is everybody's scapegoat."

The room had gotten quiet. Had I said too much? "I'd better check on my dog."

I brought Billy in from the car and watched as he sniffed around for leftovers. "Feast later at Mom's, remember?"

My audience still sat waiting. "So who's Lee Xiang's arch-enemy?" Dan asked.

"Cade Firth."

Dan didn't look sympatico. "Cade called us when he heard the gunshot, and he doesn't act guilty. He's never owned a gun, at least not that's registered to him, and even if he and his wife had marital problems, does that make him a killer?"

"If he looked in the library window and saw his wife with Lee, he might kill her in a fit of passion. Or, he might aim for Lee and hit her by mistake. He made an angry phone call to the city over the water issue. He had more than one reason to hate Lee Xiang."

"Cade is a suspect, but what you're saying is conjecture."

"Not the beer bottles. Not the call to the city. Also, Cade doesn't seem to be grieving. He tried to sell me a car today! I'd like Billy to sniff around a little more. See what he can turn up at Marjorie's memorial. If the killer attends, maybe Billy will know."

"How? He hasn't had a chance to get the killer's scent."

"Maybe he has. I took him to the old library to sniff around."

The sheriff was starting to sound patronizing. "Your research generally lines up with ours," he said. "There's just one problem."

"What's that?"

"Billy's not a police dog."

I tilted my head. He might be. He was a rescue. I had no idea what Billy had been in his past life. "Couldn't we try? No one would suspect because he's not a cliché German shepherd. He's a bulldog. He's like—undercover!"

Luis laughed, putting me at ease.

Dan scratched his head, but he was smiling, too. "Well, it couldn't hurt. Keep him on a leash, and if there's any trouble, remove him from the premises."

"Of course." I scruffed Billy's big cheeks fondly.

"Cade Firth has no idea who wanted his wife dead," the sheriff mused, "and neither do we. Maybe that dog can tell us."

The memorial was at the high school gym, the only venue large enough to hold a community of mourners and other people who wanted more juicy details about the murder. No arrests had been made, so the whole town had a sense of unfinished business.

I went with my mom, Theo, Darren, and of course Billy. We sat in the bleachers near the doors instead of in folding chairs on the gym floor. That way Billy would be less conspicuous.

The service began with a reading of an obituary that somehow omitted the fact that Marjorie had been murdered. Next, a church soloist relative of the deceased sang a passable rendition of "In the Sweet Bye and Bye," to many tears from the assembled. A few words by the local pastor and the service was over. People streamed by the lotus-strewn casket paying respects and embracing Cade, who clearly would rather be anywhere else.

Billy and I posted ourselves by the doors. *Sniff, sniff, squirrel!* Billy wanted to go outside and play.

Luis came by in the stream of people leaving the gymnasium and offered a commiserating look. "Any luck?"

"I'm afraid everyone just smells like human to him today."

"It was worth a try. And there are lots more people leaving." He patted Billy on the head. "I'll call you later, Emma."

As frustrated as I was with my dog, I was thrilled that Luis was going to call.

A moment later, Theo rushed over, bumping hips with a black-clad woman and not stopping to apologize. "Emma! Emma, I have it! We've been blind!"

Theo, Billy, and I ducked outside and away from the crowd. As the dog strained his leash to sniff a tree trunk for territorial markings, Theo caught her breath enough to explain. "Did those lotus flowers on the casket remind you of anything?"

I racked my brain, but couldn't connect the dots.

Theo went on feverishly. "We were so caught up in Marjorie's library withdrawals. We should have considered who else had unconventional reading tastes."

I labored to think of surprising book/patron pairings. "I can't remember any suspicious check-outs," I said.

"Not check-outs. Donations."

"The *National Geographics?*"

"No!" Theo looked like she wanted to slap me for my stupidity. "Who in this town has eyes for Lee Xiang besides poor Marjorie Firth?"

I snapped my fingers. "Someone who reads a lot of Asian lit!"

"Well, 'lit' is stretching it. But I think we've found our woman."

Billy had found his squirrel. He woofed from the depths of his enormous lungs, causing mourners to stare our way in disapproval. "Come on, Billy," I said, tugging the leash. "You had your chance to be a hero."

"Do you think Billy was a police dog in his past life?" I asked.

"Not a chance."

"He's a cute mascot."

"True. Have you found an apartment that will let you have pets?"

Luis and I had just ordered chop suey and fried rice at the cafe. Of course Luis had eaten there before, since it was one of just a handful of eateries in town, but I planned to introduce him to all its delicacies. Maybe it would become "our spot."

"As it turns out, Lily Gilman's house came open when she was arrested for murder, so I spoke to the landlord this morning."

"You won't mind living in a murderer's house?"

"Not as much as I'll mind having Cade Firth for a neighbor."

"Just lead him to believe you're in the market for a car."

Our food arrived and we put our chopsticks skills to the test. As Luis chatted about his family and work, I listened with the enthusiasm of the enamored.

"So is it official?" I asked as we spooned our leftovers into a Styrofoam box. "Did she really do it? Was Theo's hunch right?"

"Lily Gilman owns the gun that fired the bullet that killed Marjorie Firth. And—" He whispered, "she confessed."

"No."

"She feels terrible for what she did. Especially since she intended to kill Lee. She loved him from afar, followed him to the library that night in hopes of making him love her, and saw him in the arms of her rival."

"But the gun! Did she have it with her?"

"Lily Gilman is a paranoiac. She believes her neighbor, Cade, has lusted after her ever since his wife's accident. Whenever she leaves the house after dark, she packs heat."

We headed out to my car, where Billy was asleep in the back seat. As I looked closer, I realized his head was on an open book and he was drooling. "Oh, no! Billy…" I slid the book out from under his head. "And it's a library book, too."

"Which one?" Luis asked.

"*Chiefs* by Stuart Woods."

Luis turned to glare at the dog. "Billy, you are off the force. Let's have your gun and badge."

"At least he's discriminating." I plopped the soggy book in Luis's lap and started the car.

A stolen statue of Hiawatha and Minnehaha is at the heart of our next story, by Baraba Schlichting. It's a fast-moving tale as Annie, our intrepid PI, tackles a decades old mystery.

Ms. Schlichting is the author of the popular First Ladies Dollhouse mystery series, also set in Minneapolis. In addition to crime fiction, she writes historical fiction, picture books and poetry.

Havoc in the Library

by Barbara Schlichting

The early morning phone call from my boss, Pam Sterno, did little to ease my digestion, nor help me wake up. I was out of my morning pills and the date last night—well—I should've known better. He was my ex and still able to get me where I didn't want him to—right into the sack. Fortunately, he left when the phone rang at six.

I did smell fresh coffee, so that gave me a happy lift, and after a shower the day looked brighter. I also made an oath to myself never go to bed with Ted again. I poured myself a cup of fresh coffee and fried an egg. I knew it would be a long day. When finished, I dumped the dirty dishes in the sink, and headed out into the bright, spring morning. Fresh air! It made my heart sing. Fresh smells from a nearby bakery and diner, plus all the loud sirens, indicated a normal day in downtown Minneapolis.

My old Chevy van, better known as the Hippie, popped into gear on the first try and we chugged away from the curb, heading to Pam's. I didn't know what to expect. She hadn't called me for a few weeks to run an investigation, so I figured this had to be important.

The drive to south Minneapolis, Mill City as locals called it thanks to Gold Medal and Pillsbury and their flour mills, was uneventful. I crossed under the old Burlington Northern viaduct and headed straight through the bottleneck of seven corners, which was near the University of Minnesota. The area became known as seven corners because of the crazy number of inter-secting streets, but was better known for its even more numerous liquor establishments. I sailed through the lights of Cedar and Lake, passing by the old cemetery and soon turned onto Hiawatha Avenue. South Minneapolis was originally inhabited by Native Americans, and the first European settlers were Scandinavians. The many Swedish, and Norwegian Lutheran churches attest to the history of the area. Pam lived near the Longfellow Library and Minnehaha Falls. A special spot was always saved for me out front of her house. It was her personal, reserved parking space, but she'd loaned me her extra sticker. I was the only person who had permission to use it other than her few short friends, and yes, she was a midget. A midget who carried a big stick, metaphorically speaking. She also didn't drive. Pam relied on her cook and butler who were one in the same, Hector. She also had a seamstress. The outdoors gave her the heebie-jeebies, so she always stayed indoors. For company, she raised goldfish and sold them to a retailer. I like to believe that she was paid well since it looked like she furnished her house with all new furnishings every time I came over. My bank account wasn't anything to laugh at, either. I just returned from traveling on the Orient Express through Turkey and had money left in my account.

I parked the Hippie and looked up toward the front window of Pam's place and hoped that she was in a good mood. When Pam was crabby, watch out. She set the former police detective's ears on fire one day because he didn't catch the burglar before her best friend's jewelry was stolen. I'm glad that I wasn't on the end of that tongue lashing. My ears burn from the memory.

I climbed from the van and walked up to the door, pressed on the doorbell and waited for Hector. He reminded me of Lurch from the Addams Family. He knew that and enjoyed playing the part for me. We also shared a slight fear of the boss.

"You rang?" Hector asked upon opening the door.

"May I enter?" The door opened wider so I could enter the foyer. "Where is she?"

"She, who?"

"You know bloody well who I'm talking about. Her ladyship," I glanced around him to peer into Pam's study and found it empty. "I'll wait in there."

"Coffee?" Hector asked.

"A beer, please." I gave him a cheesy grin. "It brightens my day and gets me ready for the boss lady."

"You know better, Annie. Not allowed this time of the day." He walked from the room shaking his head. "It's too early for this nonsense!"

"Hector! I'm thirsty!"

"No!"

Now back to the matter at hand. The desk paper piles of her ladyship;s looked semi-neat, per usual. The chair was slightly askew and needed straightening. I fixed it and made sure that the telephone books were stacked perfectly on the chair for her to sit upon and the stool which she climbed onto was strategically placed. I gave the chair and stool a once over and liked their position. A shiver raced through me, which was a normal sign that she would soon enter the study. Unfortunately, there wasn't time for me to peruse the papers before going to my seat.

"Hector will bring a tray of coffee with muffins," her ladyship pronounced. The top of her dyed black hair was neatly coiffed into a tight bun on the top of her head. The navy pantsuit she wore was quite dapper looking. Her bright red lipstick gave color to her stark white complexion. "I specifically told him no beer."

"Yes ma'am." I smiled back at her, keeping my thoughts to myself. "Sounds good."

"I would hope."

I watched as she climbed up to sit. I was able to see her from the chest up. Without the aid of the stool and books, just her head was visible.

"What's this all about?" I asked. Hector entered the room at the same moment, pushing a cart loaded with two coffee cups, saucers, small plates, spoons and butter knife, milk, cream (in the appropriate dishes) a basket covered with a tea cloth and a butter dish. Presumably the muffins were warm inside the basket. "Looks good."

"Thank you Hector," her ladyship said. When he'd cleared the room and shut the door, she looked me square in the eye. "Well?"

"Well what?" When her eyes fixed on the cart, I said, "Sure." I poured us each a cup, fixing hers the way she likes it, and placed her food and drink before her on the desk. After tending to myself, I sat down and took a sip of coffee and looked over to her. "Why am I here?"

"Besides to see your bright, shiny face, you mean?" Her ladyship sipped her coffee and waited for me to shift in my seat. "It's like this. I'm afraid that there might be mayhem tomorrow at the Longfellow library. Remember the stolen statue?"

"I sure do." I set my muffin bite down and stared at her. "That library is named after Henry Wadsworth Longfellow." My eyes opened wider and it occurred to me what the case was all about. "The statue was donated by a Longfellow descendant and stolen on the same date in 1955. The fake statue stands in the back corner under lock and key if I remember correctly." I took a sip of coffee and thought for a moment. "It's a beautiful statue of Hiawatha carrying Minnehaha across the Minnehaha Creek and matches the larger version near the falls. It means an awful lot to the people around here."

"The original was never found. It's listed as an open case with the police. An up to date version will be presented tomorrow. I want you to be there and make sure that it doesn't get stolen from under our nose." Her ladyship reached for a yellowed newspaper clipping and showed it.

"Let me read it." I reached for it. "It's a hundred years after the Song of Hiawatha was first published." I handed the article back. "We must have a good plan."

"Yes. And, I agree, but eating is more important. You can't work on an empty stomach. You can't think, either," she said. Her ladyship took another sip of coffee and bite of the muffin. "All we can do now is figure out a strategy."

"We had to memorize the Hiawatha poem in school when I was a kid." I sipped the coffee and thought about the poem. "It depicts an Ojibwe man, Hiawatha and the tragic love for his Dakota woman, Minnehaha."

"I'm surprised at your knowledge of the poem."

"I can still recite it. I did learn a thing or two in school." I finished my food and drink. "I'll look into the situation and so on. I promise the new statue won't have the same fate as the old one."

"Good! I'll hold you to your promise." Her ladyship finished her coffee and set the cup down. "You must figure out where to be when the sculpter presents it to the Head Librarian."

"Like when he comes into the library?"

"She's a she." Her ladyship eyed me closely. "Her name is Beatrice Adams and is driving from Madison, Wisconsin. Keep close watch from beginning to end."

"Is there a picture of her?"

At the very moment, Hector arrived, carrying an envelope.

"Ma'am?" Hector cleared his throat, it echoed in the room.

"One for each."

"Thank you, Hector." I took the offered picture. He groaned, which is his normal manner of acknowledgement.

"Pretty good looking for an older woman. I wonder if she's also a wordsmith?"

"Look it up." Her ladyship shrugged. "The policeman in charge of the case retired long ago., but is still around here." She handed over a slip of paper. "Here is his name and contact info."

"Archie Hitchcock."

"Be careful tomorrow. We can't let it happen again," she said. "Now if you'll excuse me but I have work to be done. Meet me back here at five o'clock with news of your a plan of action."

"You didn't say what time the event is tomorrow," I said.

"Eleven."

"Okay, I'll get right on it."

As protocol, I left the room before she did. I figure it's because she doesn't want me to see her either falling off the chair or rolling down to the ground and pushing herself back up to standing. She generally slides off the chair and onto the stool via her belly. I know because I peek every so often.

The Hippie started on the first crank and I turned the wheels toward Minnehaha Avenue. Once I came to the lights on the Minnehaha Parkway, I headed toward the library. The two-story replica of Longfellow's house in Cambridge, Massachusetts, was built by a Mr. Robert Jones. Eventually, the house fell into the hands of the Minneapolis Park Board which gave it to the library system. The final move for the old house was to the Minnehaha Falls area and put on the Minnehaha Park Historic District. A newer library was built near where the old one once stood.

I found a nearby space and parked.

Once inside, I went right up to the librarian. She glanced up at me over a pair of eyeglasses.

"I'm a private investigator and plan to set up a surveillance for when the Longfellow descendant Beatrice Adams, donates the new statue."

"Really? You don't look like a detective," she said. This time, her eyebrows sort of twitched. "Why on earth do we need a detective?

"Someone stole the first statue," and reminded her that the statue on display was a replica. I didn't care to have a verbal match with her so I said, "Do you mind if I look around?" I gave her a polite smile.

"Go right ahead, but don't plan on staying all day and stalking the library. I'll call the police," she huffed. "The nerve of some people."

"Here is my card." I dug out from an inside pocket of my bag and handed it to her. "My employer is Pam Sterno."

"The Pam Sterno who discovered the stolen art objects in St. Paul?"

"The one and only," I said. "Which room will it be presented in?"

"Downstairs. There's a large room for gatherings."

"Mind if I look around and get a feel for the building?"

"Go right ahead." She turned her eyes back to her work. As I started walking away, she said, "Keep me informed of your plans."

"Will do, ma'am." I almost called her Marian.

I walked away and proceeded into the main room. While circling the interior and casually walking the aisles, I kept an eye peeled for any untoward books or placement of odd objects. Nothing seemed out of place. A set of stairs was off from the main desk and I descended down them. The bottom of the stairs presented two doors, one labeled 'Janitor'. I chose the other door and found a large meeting room. In a back corner was a glass case that stood waist high and displayed the fake statue. Next to the podium was a table with a picture of Minnehaha Falls balanced on an easel. The picture shown the larger statue on the creek bed before the water reaches the falls. My guess is that Beatrice would set the new statue beside it.

It seemed a shame that the original was never found. At that moment, I knew it was my mission to find it because it was only right. The library and Minnesotan's in general needed closure.

A man entered the room as I was about to leave.

"Are you the janitor?"

"Yes, ma'am. How can I help you?" He stood tall, wearing a black and red plaid shirt. He reminded me of a Swedish lumberjack, red hair and straight from the north woods of Minnesota.

"Are you the person that gets the room ready for meetings?"

"Yes, ma'am. I'll be setting up the chairs here pretty soon. I've got a few things to take care of first."

"I'd like to know how far back from the podium the audience sits?"

"A few feet." He went over to the spot and showed me how the rows of chairs would be set up. "Satisfied?"

"You betcha!"

I went back upstairs, called 'goodbye' to the librarian, and left the building.

My next stop was to call on Archie Hitchcock. I sort of knew him because he once assisted her ladyship on a job. If I remembered correctly, he was a liability.

Archie answered on the first knock.

"Whatcha want?" he asked. His voice was gruff.

"You Archie Hitchcock?"

"Yeah? So what?"

"You worked on the case of the stolen Hiawatha statue, didn't you?"

"So?"

"Another one's being donated tomorrow. Big ceremony at the library."

"I'm busy."

He slammed the door in my face. Fortunately, one of my qualities is persistence. I knocked again. When he answered, I slipped my foot between the door and frame so it couldn't shut.

"Go away, I'm busy." He tried to squeeze the door shut.

"Ouch!" Persistence sometimes hurts.

"I don't want anything to do with it. Leave me alone."

"Not possible." I stared at him. "One more thing. Any idea who stole the first?"

"Nope." He tried to slam the door shut. "Go on with you! I'm not a cop anymore!"

Nothing about this guy seemed right and my gut instinct told me to pursue the matter.

"You cookin' something? I smell burning bacon." I pushed the door open as Archie turned around, which caused him to move his foot. "Gotcha!"

"Oh no you don't!" Archie raced to the kitchen and went straight out the back door.

"Hey!" I hollered. "Stop!"

As I passed through the kitchen, I grabbed two cans of soda from the countertop and threw one at him. It hit him square in the back. "Stop!" I shouted but he kept running into the garage. I rounded the corner of the building as a car door slammed shut. Fortunately, Archie liked to tinker. I picked up a heavy hammer and smashed his driver's window. When he reached for me, glass chards fell on top of him. I knocked him alongside of the head with the other can of soda. As I held the hammer ready to bang him in the head, I punched two emergency numbers. I gave the dispatcher the address and where to find us.

"Where'd you hide the statue?"

"Not on your life."

"Why'd you take it?"

"My grandparents were some of the first settlers in the area. Grandpa was a Native American and believed he was related to Hiawatha. I deserve the statue."

"Everyone deserves it. It belongs to us all. You can go to the falls and sit and commune with him whenever you want but the statue belongs to the library. You're a thief. Where is it?"

When Archie was about to speak, sirens blared in the distance and became louder with each passing minute.

"Cough it up Archie. You know I'll find it."

"Ahh, what the hell." He nodded up toward the house. "It's on top of the bedroom dresser."

The police parked in the driveway. It wasn't long before Archie wore handcuffs and was escorted to the back of the squad car. I gave them the lowdown about what caused the ruckus and had to go the precinct to make my statement. Afterwards, I phoned her ladyship.

"Instructions?"

"Tell them where it's located, then get back here."

"Will do."

We disconnected.

Thirty minutes later I was in her office eating, drinking, and celebrating our good fortune of locating the missing statue. Hector even supplied me with two beers.

I slept better than usual that night.

In the morning, I was at the Longfellow Library early. I escorted Beatrice from her car into the building and down to the meeting room. It felt like my toes twinkled when she said, "The statue is still just as gorgeous as it always was, but isn't it only a replica?"

"Not today." I smiled. "That's the original."

The room filled with observers. Once she'd presented the new statue to the library, the room thundered from all the clapping. For the remainder the day, I kept my eye on the magnificent statue and thought of Minnehaha within in the strong arms of Hiawatha.

Up next, another present-day story rooted in the past, in this case, the infamous Lawrence, Kansas Massacre committed by Quantrill and his raiders during the American Civil War. A young librarian working in the Lawrence Public Library is about to receive a first-hand education in adventure.

Ms Elmendorf is a teacher of history and literature in Hawaii, by way of Tennessee.

The Lawrence Library Liquidation

by M. M. Elmendorf

"Are you coming for Sunday brunch this weekend, dear?"

I crossed my arms over my chest, taking care not to jostle the cellphone under my chin, and withheld my sigh. Though my mother wasn't here to see my defense move, I nevertheless felt the need to protect myself against the follow-up punch that always shadowed my answer. Even when I seemingly pleased her with my answers, that follow-up happened, and I instinctively knew she was winding up for said punch.

"I'm scheduled for Sunday afternoon, Mom," I heard her suck in her breath and knew to speak quickly before she had a chance to launch a verbal barrage, "but I'll stop by for a bit before I come in to work." Speaking of work, I glanced at my watch and winced. Conversations with my mother always ate into my break and rarely left me feeling relaxed. "Do you want me to bring anything with me? Drinks? Scones?"

"Why not bring a nice young lady with you this time?" There it was. The follow-up punch. *"You know, Miles, your Great-aunt May just this*

week asked me if your door swung on different hinges. You know what that means don't you?"

I closed my eyes and shook my head, "That Great-aunt May has little understanding of the physics of door hinges?" Opening my eyes again, I looked skyward and held up my free hand, palm suppliant to the powers that be. Why? Why did we always have to have this conversation?

"Miles, this isn't funny. You know she's very concerned about you. Your father and I, we are all very-"

"Concerned about me, I know." I couldn't sit still any longer and took to my feet, pacing up and down the little garden area that sat adjacent to the employee lounge. "I'm glad to have a family that loves me so much that ever since I first told you that I wanted to become a librarian the lot of you began to watch me as if wings would sprout from my back and horns from my head." My mother took another telling breath, but I continued as if I hadn't heard. "I know dad would've preferred his son to follow in his footsteps into his prescribed understanding of what it means to be a man and to embrace his form of masculinity." I was surprising myself even as the words kept coming despite my usual filter; never had I managed to admit these feelings aloud to either of my parents. "And I know Ethan gives vague answers whenever people ask him what his older brother does for a living; unless he's taken to the route he threatened he would and has since claimed I was damaged by some kind of chemical like a superhero only, unlike the cool powers of superheroes, I became 'just a librarian.'"

Ethan was the most verbal about how "lame" my job was and how embarrassing it was with a librarian for an older brother. Having a younger brother by sixteen years had its pros and cons, but I found I preferred my brother's upfront aggression against my chosen profession to the rest of my family's subversive attitudes of latent dismay. It seemed that the world's judgement against male librarians extended into my own family and though I'd been successfully working at the Lawrence Public Library for nigh unto two years, and making a decent living to boot, they were still holding their breath for when I'd "wake up" to my real profession.

The chiming of the library clock and the increasing pitch of my mother's pleaded justifications for her behavior sounded at once, signaling to me that I'd gone too far in the conversation and I'd spent too much time on the phone. If I wasn't back to the desk in exactly five minutes, Mrs. Fischner would have my hide as the library welcome mat. I'd been fooled by her five-feet, three-inches, thin-as-a-rail stature once: when I'd first met her. I now knew that she hid wolf's teeth and serpent's cunning behind old-world politeness and could make a grown man doubt not only his sanity but his very existence with a simple sentence, leaving him near tears as he walked away (I'd seen this happen more than once). I found that I feared Mrs. Fischner's wrath more than I feared the repercussions of cutting off my mother, so I interrupted.

"Mom, I really have to go now. No, I'm not just saying that as an excuse. I know we need to finish this conversation, and we will, but later." I added further salve to her pride, "I'm sorry to have spoken so sardonically. I should never have broached this topic on the phone."

I heard her sniff before she replied, *"It's okay, Miles. Just... well just..."* I imagined her opening and closing her mouth as she sought for the right things to say. *"We'll see you Sunday. And we'll be happy to see you even if you don't bring anyone. We just want to spend time with you, Miles."*

"Will do, bye." I hung up the phone and bolted back into the employee lounge.

I didn't slow my sprinting steps until the library common area came into view. Mrs. Fischner had eyes everywhere, it felt, and she had a particular distaste for running and loud talking in the library. I was not about to heap burning coals upon my head with such "improper decorum." When I rounded the corner, I saw her finishing up with a college student and I took advantage of her distraction by sliding into my seat with approximately one minute to spare. I felt my heart relax its vice grip on my lungs only after I set my hands to typing, entering the data Mrs. Fischner had tasked me with earlier in the day.

"You must be feeling particularly bricky today, Mr. Watson." She spoke to me in the same humorlessly polite tone of voice that she used with everyone (I'd once given myself nightmares wondering if she used the same tone of voice with her husband).

I offered her as dazzling a smile as I could muster, "Whatever do you mean, Mrs. Fischner?"

"I'll have none of your podsnappery, Mr. Watson, and I also won't have you falling back into your duties at this desk like a bright-eyed toddler, fit for nothing yet demanding everything." She swiveled in her chair until she faced me. She lacked the glasses most librarians were "supposed" to have, having had eye surgery not long ago, but I found myself wishing for at least that miniscule barrier against her scrutiny. "Your generation is always demanding more of this and that; namely entertainment. You lack imagination. You lack the initiative to create your own desired 'more' and instead passively wait for it to land in your lap like a gift-wrapped present."

I realized then that her lecture had less to do with my near tardiness and more to do with the student she'd just helped. Mrs. Fischner had little respect for college youth, often saying they were educated enough to know better but had yet to develop the gumption to act on that knowledge. Though she could be accused of being overly harsh, I knew her to adore the younger ones. Whenever an elementary school came through, she would personally give them a tour and always returned to the desk with an air of hope around her shoulders, declaring that so long as a mind remained in the throes of curiosity that the future didn't look so bleak after all.

"Mr. Watson." I blinked Mrs. Fischner's pinched face back into focus. "I asked if you'd taken that cart of resource books back down to vault." She did NOT like repeating herself and the expression on her face reminded me of that fact.

It seemed I would not escape her wrath after all: I had forgotten to do that very task. My conversation with my mother had caused the lapse in judgement, but I was NOT about to blame my mother to someone like Mrs. Fischner. I picked up the pieces of my smashed pride after the hammering of Mrs. Fischner's glare and hurried to finish off the only other thing she'd asked me to do today. For all her eccentricities, she was fair-minded, and I would be hard-pressed to find a better mentor than the Lawrence library's oldest and longest serving librarian.

The path to the vault was a long and lonely one. Though I'd never met another soul on my way in the two years I'd worked here, I had heard stories of past librarians finding college students in clandestine postures hidden away in the darkened corridors that were the norm of the lower levels of the library. Maybe that was why the older generation was so judgmental on the younger: they were incredulous that the younger generation was too worried about college debt to be bothered with sneaking away for a snog session. Youth was being wasted on the youth. I chuckled at the momentary attempt of my imagination to picture Mrs. Fischner pulling her doting husband, then beau, down this very corridor to one of the small alcoves that my squeaky cart and I passed.

So caught up in my own thoughts, I never heard her approach. I was just coming around the corner at the top of the ramp that led the rest of the way down into the vault when I felt something hard press between my shoulder blades moments before a husky voice whispered into my ear, "Don't move."

The hair on my arms stood up and I gave an involuntary shiver. I'd like to say both reactions were purely out of fear, but I'd be lying. This woman, as it was indeed a woman who now stood behind me with a weapon pressing into my back, had the sultry voice of the likes of Lauren Bacall and other femme fatales of old. I didn't even have to see her to know that this woman, whoever she might be, would have knockout looks to go along with her knockout voice. What in the world had I just walked into?

"What do you want?" Gripping the cart, I wished I'd used the newer cart; this old one didn't have a brake lever I could kick down and then be able to let go of the cart without worrying of it running away from me. As it was, with this cart, I had no choice but to keep a firm hold otherwise it'd go careening down the ramp and through the drywall at the bottom. "Who are you?"

"I want you to take me to the vault." She continued to whisper. I didn't bother telling her that she had no need of speaking so quietly. No one would hear us all the way down here. At this level, we were underground and, besides that, we were at the end of the library people rarely frequented without either guide or strict authorization. "I need you to take me there right now."

I mentally assessed the worth of the rare books inside the vault and raised my eyebrows. Unless she had quite a few henchmen to help her out, and a big truck hidden away inconspicuously to cart them off, it was unreasonable to think that she'd come all the way down here for those. Yes, we had quite a few worth a pretty penny, but again it just didn't seem feasible. Chancing uncomfortable consequences, I glanced over my shoulder at the woman and gulped. My earliest assumptions were spot-on: she was every literary and Hollywood femme fatale come to life. Her auburn hair, thick and wavy, was loosely knotted at her neck and she wore a pill box hat with a black veil drawn across her features. The veil did nothing to hide her almond-shaped blue eyes, pixie nose, and heart-shaped lips from my view; if anything, it enhanced their allure.

When she noticed my assessing look, her eyes widened, and her lips parted on a silent gasp. She then reminded me of my place by pressing the weapon against my back again and I dutifully averted my eyes. However, I'd had just enough of a look to see that she was conflicted with her current course of action. I could work with that.

"I know library fees can be at times ridiculous," I looked down at the resource books as I spoke, "but we can work with you on a finance-based system more suited to your needs. I could even work my magic with the head librarian and get you a discounted library card."

I heard her snort, "Magic." She leaned close again and spoke in a louder voice, "I'm not here to check out a book."

"Why else would you come to a library?" I must indeed be feeling particularly "bricky" today as I again looked over my shoulder to gaze at her directly.

Before she answered I saw her eyes widen, this time in blatant fear, as her gaze moved to rest on something over my shoulder. I followed her stare down the length of the ramp to see two dark-suited men standing in the murky light there. They looked official, though for what sort of organization I couldn't tell, and they did not look friendly in the slightest. When this was all done, whatever this was, I was going to have to talk to Mrs. Fischner about increasing our security in the rare books section of the library.

"I see you've met our little jay bird." The taller of the two men spoke first. "Has she sung the tale to you about her father already?"

"I, er, um," I lost my voice when I felt her step close, until the warmth of her body mingled with my own. I gulped.

"She's lying." The shorter, more muscled man pulled out a billfold and flashed a badge, though I couldn't tell what it was: it was out and back inside the folds of his jacket too quickly. "We didn't kill her father. We work for a reputable collector and have no need to resort to such violence."

The taller man spoke again. "We need you to cooperate with us, mister…"

I answered without thinking, "Watson," and I felt her put a warning hand upon my elbow. Though thoroughly confused by this entire episode, I found I quite enjoyed her proximity now that the air current had shifted and I could smell her perfume: jasmine and vanilla.

"Mr. Watson, the woman at your back is the daughter of a notorious thief. She would have you believe that her father was killed by his most recent benefactor, our employer, but that is just not the case. While it is true that her father recently met with a car accident, this is not surprising considering he was a known drunk." Even at this distance I saw the taller man's lips twitch as if resisting a smile. "The river bottoms are full of drunk drivers."

I heard her gasp and the hand on my elbow tightened. The object that had been pressed between my shoulder blades disappeared, but I doubted I'd be able to run away from all of them without coming to some harm. Besides, call me masochistic, but my curiosity refused my retreat. I would see this through to the end.

"They're lying." Her husky voice was back against my ear. "Be careful." In pressing closer to talk, her lips grazed my skin and I shivered, "Don't trust them."

"What is she saying now, Mr. Watson?" The shorter man had started up the ramp in my brief distraction and there was something about the way he walked, almost as if something weighed down his left side, that seemed to confirm the woman's words. "Is she telling you not to trust us?" He smiled and shook his head. "That we're dangerous and will kill you now that you've seen us?" With each step this man took, the woman found a way to come closer, now flush up against me, holding onto me as if to both protect me as well as seek protection through me.

I shook my head and kept myself from looking down at the only available defense weapon I had, "No, she was wondering how she could check out a book without a library card."

The man's right hand began to move across his torso then under his suit-jacket, "And what did you tell her?"

"I told her there are no exceptions made; that everyone needs a library card." I tipped my head to the side in feigned innocence, "Where's yours?"

"Right here."

I saw the glint of light upon metal in his hand and knew then that she'd been in truth. A surge of fear immobilized my reasoning but not my reflexes. In my terror, I not only let go of the heavy, book-laden cart, but gave it a push for extra measure. *BANG!* The light above us exploded, showering us with glass particles. Her cry in my ear and her grip loosening from my elbow had me pivoting on my heel and wrapping my arms around her. We continued our twirl until we hit the carpeted floor of the ramp, my body under hers.

Her hat lay on the floor beside my head and her hair had come loose in the shuffle. My arms were tight around her body, my hands covering the sensitive skin of her neck from threat of glass, but when I felt her begin to push against me, I loosened my hold. Bits of her hair framed her face when she raised herself up enough to stare down at me. Her expression was one of confused gratitude and I was certain my expression belied my own smugness at having been able to rescue a damsel in distress.

We both stiffened and turned as one towards the sound of a gun clicking. The taller man stood alone with a murderous expression on his face, "That wasn't very smart of you Mr. Watson. I was told that librarians were some of the smartest people on the planet." He gestured with his gun for both myself and the woman to stand to our feet, slowly, with our hands in sight. "I seem to have met the one dumb one."

"My parents aren't too thrilled with my profession either."

"Shut up." The man again used his gun to wave us forward. "Now, you're going to take us to the vault and you're going to open it without any more funny business."

We stepped over the unconscious body of the shorter man, bloodied and semi-broken after his abrupt meeting with printed knowledge. I couldn't be certain, but it looked as if I'd killed him. I swallowed the ball of panic that rose in my throat. Once I calmed down, I would be a wreck crumpled in the corner rocking back and forth in shock. That was only if I didn't end up with a bullet in my head. The latter was most likely to happen.

My predictions for my future were cut short when I felt the woman shyly press a warm hand against my own. Looking down, I marveled at how easy it was to intertwine our fingers though we'd just met; how much it already felt like a habit of ours to hold hands while we walked into an uncertain future. I brought my eyes back to hers and her ambiguous visage had me gulping back my own fears and straightening my shoulders. I gave her hand a reassuring squeeze just before we reached the vault door.

"Open it." I looked over my shoulder and saw a triumphant gleam about his eyes. "Now."

I let go of the woman's hand and stepped up to the code box. There was an intercom system just beside the code box but I'd be dead before I could manage to call Mrs. Fischner. I quickly entered in my code then stepped back to the woman's side as the locks recoiled and the door swung open. We preceded the man into the vault without prompting. Nothing looked out of the ordinary. In all the hubbub prior, I'd almost expected something spectacular to have apparated into the room in my absence. Everything looked exactly as it always had before: shelves and shelves of old books all delicately filed in protective coverings. There were metal drawers along the bottom edges of the circular room, but I already knew them to contain old, loose leaf documents. There were no diamonds or treasures in here, aside from the treasure of knowledge. Nothing worth the effort it seemed these three individuals had gone through.

"Where is it?" After having eyed the parameters of the room from his stance at the doorway, the man shifted his gun until it pointed directly at my chest.

I shook my head, "Where is what?"

"Don't play coy with me, librarian. Everyone knows that the James brothers left the Massacre loot behind when they fled with Quantrill back into Missouri. When they tried to take it back from the city later, it had already been hidden away in the library vault."

I looked over to the woman for confirmation, but her face gave away nothing but beauty. It took me a few moments of mental sorting before I pieced together what I could of history and reconciled it with what this man had said.

"This library was built in 2014." The man merely blinked so I continued. "The Lawrence Massacre was in 1863. There's no way William Quantrill or Frank and Jesse James could possibly have left plundered goods here." Besides, I was certain Mrs. Fischner would have taken great pride in telling me of such valuables being stored away inside our library vault.

"But of course, that's what most people would think." The man smiled and waved at the woman by my side. "That's where her father came in handy. You see he wasn't just a thief but also a historian. He unearthed evidence that the plunder had been found around the time that the city had secured funding from Carnegie for the new library. But instead of turning it over to the authorities, the men who'd found it decided to keep it for themselves. Only the curse of the plunder befell them, isn't that what your father liked to say, and they died before they could spend all of it."

The woman stiffened, "Stop talking about him."

"Why should I? He was so fond of talking about himself. Perhaps that's why he never mentioned you. Why, we didn't know existed until you'd already run off with the documents he found." The man chuckled. "Too bad too. You were a great secretary."

"Assistant." She spoke through gritted teeth. It appeared to me that she suffered as much from gender stereotypes in her profession as I did in mine.

"So," I brought his attention back to myself, "you're trying to tell me that these men in the nineteenth century found a stash of plundered items leftover from the Lawrence Massacre, kept it away from the James brothers when they came back for it, and then tried to spend it for themselves only to die before they could?"

The man sighed, "You already know all that, librarian, why are you insisting upon making your inevitable death more painful by stalling?"

"Humor me and let's pretend I don't know. Please explain where the library vault comes into play. Were any of these men librarians?"

"No, but the son of one of them was. He decided that the stash was cursed and so locked it away from everyone, not wanting to risk harm to the survivors. And it remained locked away in the library vault, guarded diligently by secretive librarians, until this day." The man's mouth turned upward into a Cheshire grin. "Now I will happily relieve you of both the burden of the cursed treasure as well as the burden of living."

I edged closer to the woman, "I find living not exactly burdensome and would like to do more of it."

"Enough!" His voice painfully echoed in the vault but didn't carry beyond it.

The woman's hand shot out and grabbed hold of mine. What a pity. I finally found a woman interesting enough to ask for her number, only I'd die before I could take a chance at the asking. At least I could find comfort in knowing that she wanted to hold my hand as much as I wanted to hold hers, even if it was out of sheer desperation for human comfort prior to death.

"Tell me where it is now or else-" A sickening thud sounded right before the man fell to the floor in a daze.

I felt the woman's shock mirror my own when we both took in the image of our savior: Mrs. Fischner. She held in her hand one of the encyclopedias I'd been sent to refile and I marveled at both her ability to heave the thing around without falling over and also that she'd managed to hit the man hard enough to daze him.

"Do not just stand there like an almighty biddy, Mr. Watson." She stepped forward and dropped the reference book on the man's hand when he started to reach for his gun. His whimper echoed in the room. "Exfluncticate this ruffian and inform the authorities with do haste."

The woman beside me leaned close, "What did she say?"

"She wants us to disarm him and call the cops."

In the whirlwind that was the following few hours of my life, I discovered quite a few things that were both alarming and thrilling. Prior to the arrival of said "authorities," Mrs. Fischner interrogated the woman with such alacrity that I was certain the coming detectives wouldn't get as good of answers from her. Alma Lee Jones was indeed a managerial assistant and her historian/thief father had used her position within an antique dealer's company to gain access to her employer, a connoisseur of all things regarding the infamous James brothers. What her father had not anticipated was the ruthlessness of Alma Lee's employer and when he'd tried to blackmail a higher payment out of the man, he and his car had found their way to the bottom of a river.

Alma Lee had gotten it into her head that if she could find the stash first she could take it to the authorities to use as evidence against her employer, proving his hand in her father's murder. The men who'd attacked us, and thankfully neither of them had died either by my hand or Mrs. Fischner's or else I'd have a lot more to explain to my mother on Sunday, had been trailing Alma Lee for weeks and had nearly killed her at least twice and had also killed three other people who'd tried to help her. I would've been the fourth had it not been for my new friends: reference books.

To find out that this alluring woman was not a lying murderess (and her confession to having used the end of her hairbrush as the "weapon" at my back had only further endeared her to me) was what was thrilling. When the police arrived and everyone else was distracted by them, the alarming bit of information had come from Mrs. Fishner.

"You know the truth now." Was all she'd said, in her by-the-by tone of voice and no-nonsense gaze.

My stomach plummeted and then picked itself back up again. It seemed my days as a librarian would resemble a superhero's after all, in that I'd never be able to tell my family the truth about my newly acquired duties as part of being a librarian at the Lawrence Public Library.

I took my life into my hands for a third time that day when I told Mrs. Fischner to wait when she'd begun to explain what it was I'd now be doing. Instead of glaring at me I thought I saw a knowing smirk grace her lips when she saw my eyes follow Alma Lee's path through the library common room towards the doors, escorted by two detectives. When I looked back to Mrs. Fischner she nodded her approval.

"Excuse me," the detectives eyed my approach with curious apprehension whereas Alma Lee looked genuinely pleased, "may I speak to Ms. Jones for a moment?"

The detectives looked to Alma Lee for instruction and she nodded. After their retreat to a respectable distance, she gave me a reassuring smile. I found myself forgetting why it was I'd approached her in the first place. She saved my mental floundering when she leaned forward and plucked out the pen I kept tucked into my shirt pocket. She gestured to my hand and I mutely gave it to her. The feeling of my pen against my skin, deftly curving this way and that by her fingers, tickled and delighted. When she was done, she let go of my hand, put the pen back in my pocket, and stepped close. Her kiss against my cheek was both soft and swift, as were her words, "See you later Mr. Watson,"

She turned on her heel and carried on through the library doors with the detectives and I stood stupefied. Mrs. Fischner brought me out of my stupor with a sharp snap of her fingers by my ear.

"What did she write there on your hand?"

I looked down then over to Mrs. Fischner, "Her number."

"Cheeky girl." Mrs. Fischner smiled. "I like her."

"Me too."

As I followed Mrs. Fischner back towards the desk and more mind-boggling revelations, I pulled out my phone and typed in the number. I managed to send off a quick text before I mindfully put away my phone and gave my mentor my full attention.

Miles: So what's your opinion on Sunday brunch?

. . .

. . .

Alma Lee: I love it.

When a librarian's neighbor is murdered, she is must confront the possibility that there is a killer living in her quiet neighborhood, before she becomes the next target.

Modern day crime is far afield from Nupur Tustin's usual beat, the world of Austria in the Eighteenth Century, and composer Joseph Haydn, who serves as her detective in a series of popular novels. This story was previously published in 2016, in Heater Magazine.

The Christmas Stalker

by Nupur Tustin

A hammering on the front door startled Elsa out of her light doze. Her eyes flew open. She sat upright, heart thundering, when the pounding on the door began again.

What the—

Cursing, she hauled herself out of the comfy red armchair before her fireplace, and marched out of the living room. Was that Taylor, her new neighbor? She'd made the mistake of offering to help the dratted woman and…

The hard rat-a-tat-tat continued, and a face beneath a dark blue peaked cap showed itself through the frosted panes of the hallway window. Elsa slowed down, worried.

What were the police doing at her door? Running her sweaty palms down her sweatshirt, she took a deep breath, and then twisted the doorknob open.

A tall uniformed officer and a husky man in a dark suit stood on the second step of the stoop. Both flashed badges at her as soon as she opened the door. Over their shoulders, she saw yellow crime scene tape cordoning off the house opposite.

"What's going on?" she asked, her voice coming out faint and hoarse.

The husky man stepped up before her. "May we come in, Ma'am?" He pushed the door in, giving Elsa no choice but to step back.

"Yes, of course." She led them down the short hallway into the living room, mind awhirl, and gestured toward the plaid couch next to the red armchair.

The next few minutes were a blur. Jared, her new neighbor's fiancé, had come home to find the beautiful Taylor dead, her head in a bucket of water, her hands tied behind her back.

"The body is still warm, Ma'am, meaning—"

To Elsa's relief, the flow of gruesome details skidded to a halt, brought to an abrupt end by Detective Shephard's sharply barked: "Cooper!"

She saw how Cooper wilted under the hard stare the Detective directed at him. Then the stare, a little softer now, was directed at her.

"Whatever took place next door, happened within the past hour, Ma'am. Can you remember seeing or hearing anything—anything at all—in that time?"

She tried to gather her thoughts.

"They had just moved in," she said, and took a deep breath. How could such a thing happen in her quiet neighborhood? On a sunny Friday afternoon, just a week before Christmas? "I was helping Taylor unpack. Just this morning. It's my day off…"

"Yes, we know," Detective Shephard said gently. "Jared mentioned it. Did you see anyone suspicious hanging around the house?"

Elsa stared. "You think someone broke into their house?" That was even worse than the other possibility, that Jared, the man who had found his fiancée and reported the crime, was responsible. That had been her first thought, and knowing Taylor, who could blame him? The woman could try the patience of a saint.

But Jared obviously wasn't a suspect if Detective Shephard wanted to know if she'd noticed anything untoward that morning.

"There are signs of a break-in, yes," he conceded. "Did you see anyone while you were with her?"

Elsa shook her head. There was the moving van with the two burly men helping to unload Taylor's furniture. But other than that...

"I thought I heard a light knock on my door. I was tired, dozing off, so I ignored it." *What if it had been Taylor, looking for help?*

Elsa actually had thought it was Taylor. That was why she'd ignored the knocking, tired of her voluptuous neighbor's prima donna personality; the way she'd subtly manipulated Elsa into doing all the heavy work, gently criticizing the whole while.

Now Taylor was dead. Elsa's guilt-ridden feelings must have revealed themselves in her face. Detective Shephard leaned forward and, touching her lightly on the hand, said: "From the little we can tell, she was in no position to call for help."

The deep sympathy in his voice, and the steady gaze from his dark brown eyes did much to calm Elsa down.

"It was most likely her killer at the door," Officer Cooper added, oblivious to his superior's disapproving gaze. "You weren't expecting anybody, were you, Ma'am?"

Elsa shook her head, chilled by the thought of a killer knocking on her door. "Only the community gardener, Neal. But he never comes in. He has a key to the garage where all my gardening tools are."

Both men rose. "Please be very careful," Detective Shephard said as he gave her his card. "If there's anything you remember, anything at all pertinent, please call."

The murder cast a pall on Greendale Village. It was front-page news in the local paper every day, replete with gruesome details and rife with speculation. After a week, the police were no closer to finding the mystery man who had tried to rape Taylor, and then brutally killed her when she resisted his advances.

There was no doubt now the killer had been an intruder, and Taylor the unfortunate victim of a random attack. The thought made Elsa shiver as she locked the doors of the Greendale Elementary School Library where she worked. It was drizzling outside, but for once she was glad the school parking lot was in an open-air area adjacent to the school building.

There was something depressing about the overcast day. Even the brightly lit stores on Main Street seemed cheerless. There were few shoppers about, and Elsa was sure it had less to do with the gloomy day than the murder

Mike, the locksmith whose house was to the left of hers, was sitting on his porch when she pulled into her driveway. But the young men, college students, who shared the house on the right, were still out. Elsa shivered again. She was the only woman on the street. Other than old Mrs. Perez and her daughter, Diane, who lived with her.

Diane Perez worked in the Emergency Room in the next town, and was rarely home. That meant, if the killer decided to strike again, Elsa would probably be next on his list.

For the first time, she found herself wondering whether either Mike or the college students tried to rape Taylor last Friday. She'd seen the students sitting on their porch. They'd been smoking pot—openly ogling Taylor's rounded breasts and her tight butt in those skimpy shorts of hers.

And as for Mike…

"She's a tasty little thing, isn't she?" he'd remarked to Elsa, angling his chin at Taylor arranging potted plants in her garden that awful morning. Elsa, feeling oddly jealous, had buried the remark deep in the recesses of her brain. Now she remembered it.

That had been before the moving van had arrived. Before Taylor had enlisted Elsa's help with an angelic smile on her doll-like face.

Mike had been called to a job just before the movers arrived, but Elsa thought she'd seen him in his kitchen when she returned, exhausted from her exertions.

Now as she watched him push himself out of his porch swing, and stride down toward the fence that divided their houses, Elsa pulled the edges of her baggy flannel jacket closer together. She gave him a curt wave as she got out of her car, and then turned her head resolutely away.

She didn't want Mike trying to engage her in conversation. There'd been a time when the dazzling smile that lit up his lean, handsome features had made her pulse race. She'd actually looked forward to their flirtatious banter, convinced he was attracted to her. But that had been before Taylor's cameo appearance on their street. Before he'd commented on her body. Before…

"Don't be silly, Elsa," she scolded herself. She'd no real reason, after all, to believe that he'd killed Taylor.

"Hey there, stranger!"

Mike's cheerful holler startled her into dropping the keys she'd been fumbling with. She retrieved them, and turned around with a lackluster smile.

"Hi."

"Bad day?" he asked, mouth turning down sympathetically.

"Not at all. I'm just tired."

"And worried, I guess." Mike jerked his head toward the crime scene tape that still festooned the white fences of the house opposite. He hoisted himself over the fence. "I've been thinking about that, and something doesn't quite add up."

"No." Elsa pushed herself back against her car, although that probably wasn't the best move under the circumstances.

"Why don't we go inside?" Mike glanced up at the still overcast sky. "It might start drizzling again, and I don't want to keep you outside."

"What doesn't add up?" Elsa asked, once they were inside her house. She brought two steaming mugs of coffee over to the kitchen table. The windows faced the street, and somehow it felt safer. As though there'd be witnesses if anything were to happen. But other than old Mrs. Perez, who was there to watch?

Mike wrapped his large, calloused hands around the green-and-red Christmas mug she'd handed him. "I don't see how anyone could have broken into that house. All the locks were custom-made. I designed them myself."

"People do it all the time. No lock is foolproof. The damage—"

"Looks like it was made after the fact. And the alarm—"

"Wait. How do you know this? About the locks, I mean?"

"I inspected the doors."

"When?"

"Oh, naturally after all the hubbub had died down, and the police and the crime lab techies had gone."

Elsa stared. "But there's crime scene tape around the house."

Mike shrugged. "So?"

Elsa looked out the window, careful to keep her expression guarded. She had read somewhere that killers liked to insert themselves into an investigation. Was that what Mike was doing now?

She turned back to him. "So, you could get into trouble for doing something like that. Not to mention that you have no way of letting the detective on the case know what you found out without admitting to breaking in."

His face fell. "No, I guess not." He pushed himself to his feet. "I'm inclined to think she let her killer in.

"Be careful, okay?" he said as he left.

She was wondering whether Mike was right—which would mean that Taylor knew her killer—when another thought occurred to her.

Mike had designed the locks on every house on this street. And he had a master key to every one of them. Including hers.

———————

Her house had come wired with a security alarm, but Elsa had never bothered with it. Greendale Village was one of the quieter and safer neighborhoods in Los Angeles, and her street, until last Friday, had been more secure than most.

She watched Mike sprint up his driveway and slam the door shut against the fine spray of rain that had started up again. Then she went to the keypad near the door. There was a way of testing it, but the numerous icons on the grey buttons made about as much sense as the Chinese instructions in the multi-language manual for her television remote.

She poked her finger into one of the soft buttons. A soft, incessant beeping started, and the screen above the keypad prompted her to enter a code. *Damn!*

What code? She couldn't remember ever having set one. The beeping continued, drilling into her brain. She vaguely recalled being given an instruction booklet. Had she kept it? She rummaged around in the drawers of the small cabinet near the door, but only found some kitchen twine, tiny scented candles, a few stale pieces of candy, and a dusty instruction manual for a blender she no longer possessed.

Damn!

Desperate to stop the beeping, she punched a couple of other keys at random. That worked, but she was no closer to knowing how to set the alarm.

Before Taylor's murder, she would simply have walked over to Mike's house and asked for his help. But she didn't want him fiddling with her alarm system now. Detective Shephard might not have her handsome neighbor on his radar, but he sure was on hers. Especially after all that talk about crawling around the crime scene.

She wondered if the alarm company, Atlantic Security Systems, was open today. She doubted it. It was nearly four o' clock for one thing. And the day before Christmas Eve for another. Still, she went back into the kitchen, and looked the number up on her iPhone.

"It's almost Christmas, Ma'am," a voice curtly informed her when she made her request. "We can't send anyone out until next week. Would you like to schedule an appointment?"

Great!

She made the appointment and hung up.

Back at the front door now, Elsa drummed her fingers on the top of the waist-high cabinet. A week was a long way off. She wouldn't be able to sleep in peace tonight unless she sorted this thing out. The pistol she kept under her pillow—it had been left by an ex, and she'd never bothered to return it—would be no good if the intruder—in all likelihood, Mike—managed to make his way into her home while she slept. Would she even have time to grab it before he began his assault?

She glanced out the hallway window. He was in his kitchen now, rinsing dishes. The college students who lived next door were just pulling up. A faint memory stirred. The guy they rented from owned a security company, didn't he? Or worked at one. Elsa couldn't remember which.

On an impulse, she dashed out of her house, running over to their porch.

"Hey!" she panted.

The taller of the two young men—she'd never noticed before how large and muscular they both were—turned around. "Anything we can do for you?"

His eyes dropped to her cleavage, pushed up to the neckline thanks to the sports bra she was wearing.

Lovely! She'd forgotten her flannel at home. At twenty-eight, she was nearly a decade older than this overgrown, over-sexed boy. But with that single unabashed stare at her breasts, he'd managed to diminish her. Feeling naked and irritable, she pushed her hair out of her eyes.

"I'm having trouble with my alarm," she said. "I wanted to call…" She couldn't for the life of her recall the guy's name, although she remembered vividly his tubby, bearded figure.

"Prentiss?" the shorter guy asked.

"Yeah! " Elsa nodded. "But I've lost his card." A small lie, but all in a good cause, she thought. And maybe Prentiss wouldn't mind doing the neighborly thing.

Prentiss was willing to come over. "Sure thing," he said after she'd explained her problem over the phone. "I'm just finishing up at a client's. I'll be there in an hour."

Excellent! That would give her plenty of time for a bath. It had been a long day, and a nice, hot soak followed by a cup of chamomile tea was just what she needed to de-stress.

But she'd barely finished washing and conditioning her hair when she heard a loud knocking. Could Prentiss be here already? She wrapped a towel around her wet tresses, and pulled on her bathrobe, cinching the belt tight as she padded barefoot toward the door. Her shower would have to wait.

Elsa thrust open the door.

"Neal!"

Irritation flared as she stared up at the lanky figure and greasy hair of the community gardener.

"The tools are in the garage"—she flung a hand out toward it—"as always."

Neal's gaze—had it always been so shifty and sly?—traveled down her bare neck. Elsa clutched the door, irritation giving way to fear. Neal had been expected in to work about the time Taylor had been attacked. If he'd been out in her garden, right opposite the crime scene, how could he *not* have seen a thing?

That's what he'd told the cops. And her.

Unless...

"What do you want?" Fear made her speak more brusquely than usual. She resisted the urge to pull her robe closer together. He was still looking down her front.

He raised his head slowly at the sound of her voice, and reached into the front pocket of his gray overalls.

"I'm off until January, remember?" He gave her a damp, crumpled piece of paper. His bill for the month of December.

"Oh, that's right! I'd forgotten. Wait here. I'll get your money for you."

She was about to close the door when he pushed it back against her. "Hey, it's cold and damp outside. Can I come in?"

Elsa sighed, not wanting to be rude. But at the same time...

"I won't be but a minute," she said firmly. "And I'm expecting guests."

She supposed Prentiss could be called that. After all, he didn't have to come out to help her. He worked for a different alarm company. One that had the sense to be available through the holidays.

Fortunately, Neal didn't protest. When he left, Elsa locked the door behind him, and returned to her shower.

She'd just finished when Prentiss arrived. Still clad in her bathrobe, she let him in, and was pleasantly surprised to see him avert his eyes. The first male she'd encountered today who wasn't interested in sneaking a free look!

"If you'd like to finish dressing, I can wait outside while you…"

"There's no need to wait outside, Prentiss. There's a pot of coffee in the kitchen. Why don't you pour yourself a cup?"

By the time she'd put on a sweatshirt and a pair of jeans, Prentiss had already taken the alarm control panel apart, and was examining its interior.

He looked up when she came out into the hallway. "The batteries are still good, fortunately. But a couple of wires need to be connected before you can start using this thing."

"Oh," she said, not quite understanding. "What wires might those be? I don't know if I have any…" She looked around helplessly.

"They'll be in the attic. Do you know where your attic entrance is?"

"Oh yes!" she said, embarrassed that he'd even had to ask. He'd probably never encountered a homeowner so clueless about her own security system. "In the bedroom, right by my nightstand." Elsa led him down the hallway.

In her room, she pointed toward the long dangling hook above her nightstand. "Would you like me to bring you a stepladder?"

She glanced over her shoulder. Prentiss didn't look much taller than she. He was probably only four or five inches over five feet.

She doubted he'd be able to reach up to the hook, even standing on tiptoe.

He nodded, and she ran out to the kitchen. When she returned, dragging the ladder behind her, she found him waiting patiently near the window, eyes still on the trapdoor that led into the attic.

Elsa was amused. She'd always considered herself socially awkward, but Prentiss seemed even more awkward than she. He'd barely looked at her, and seemed careful not to let his eyes rest on any of her belongings either.

It took him a half hour of scrambling about before he finally emerged. "You're all set," he informed her with a smile.

"Thanks." Elsa reached for her purse. "How much do I…?"

Prentiss smiled again, seeming a little more comfortable in her presence now. "There's no charge. I'm always happy to help out a neighbor. You'll need to select a number code, and I'll show you how to set the alarm, and turn it off."

She took down his instructions on a small yellow legal pad, and saw him off.

"Here's my card. Give me a call, if you have any trouble with your alarm. Although it should work just fine."

<hr>

It did work just fine. Elsa set the alarm that night, carefully reading through Prentiss's instructions on engaging the door and window protection and setting the motion sensors near each entry point. She didn't think she needed the smoke and fire detectors or the carbon monoxide gauge.

For the first time since the murder, Elsa slept well, falling into a deep and dreamless slumber from which she awoke at eight the next morning. She re-set the alarm just before heading out to Mrs. Perez's cottage opposite the college students' rented house. Diane Perez had pulled a double shift at the Emergency Room on Christmas Eve, so Elsa had volunteered to take her mother to St. Thomas's on Ridge Lane for their afternoon mass.

"I'm too old for Midnight Mass," Mrs. Perez sighed as she hobbled into the dimly lit, heated nave, leaning heavily on Elsa's arm. "When old Perez was still alive, we never missed it. Diane would sleep over at her grandmother's house. But he's been gone these twenty years…" She sighed again.

Elsa murmured sympathetically as they walked down the aisle looking for Mrs. Perez's favorite pew.

She kept the old lady company after the service until the evening, glad to be able to forget the horrific incident that had shaken their lives.

"That nice young man who lives next door to you came by and changed our locks for us," Mrs. Perez confided, opening the door to let Elsa leave for home. "You should have him take a look at your locks, too. It's just not safe here anymore. To tell you the truth, I'm glad Diane's going to be at the Emergency Room tonight. They have twenty-four hour security down there."

Elsa didn't say anything, although privately she thought that letting Mike tamper with the locks was far from a good idea.

He was on his porch when she returned home. Elsa had the uncomfortable feeling he had been waiting for her. He got up, heading toward her, as soon as she opened the white gate into her front yard.

"I noticed you had Prentiss over to take a look at your alarm system yesterday," he began. "That was good thinking."

She shrugged, hemming a vague response. His eyes, she noticed, were riveted on her house.

"So, eh-m… would you like me to inspect your door and window locks? Make sure they're tamper-proof?"

"I—" she was about to say no, but changed her mind. What harm could it do? If he tried to break in, her alarm would go off. And if that happened 9-1-1 would be alerted immediately, Prentiss had explained. "Sure. That would be nice."

That night as she once again tested and set her alarm, Elsa tried to let go of her misgivings. She wasn't sure letting Mike into her house had been such a good idea. But she had followed him from room to room as he checked each window and door.

She sighed. Next week when businesses re-opened, she'd contact another locksmith, and have her locks changed. For now, the alarm and its instantaneous link to 9-1-1 would have to do.

Elsa opened her eyes, making the journey back to consciousness instantly. She lay still in her darkened room, not sure what had interrupted her sleep. Or, what it was making the skin on her nape prickle.

Was someone in the house? She thought she heard a faint scuffle on the rug by the window. *In her bedroom?*

She pushed her right arm up, reaching for the Glock under her pillow.

A slight breeze caused the drapes at the window to flutter. The faint light that came in illuminated a dark, bulky figure. For a single stunned moment, she lay paralyzed. Then, she saw the intruder stealthily approaching her bed.

Bang!

Before she could even think about it, the pistol fired, and it was only now that she noticed its cold touch against her palm.

"You bitch! " came a low growl in the dark. It sounded oddly familiar, Elsa thought, as she watched the intruder trip on the edge of the rug, and thud down onto the hardwood. The pounding on the door started at the same time.

"Open up!"

Great! The cops were here. How was she going to explain having a gun she didn't actually own? Or her intruder's injury? His bulky form reared up in the darkness.

She decided to ignore whoever it was ramming at the door, concentrating on her intruder instead.

"I will shoot you up if you come any closer," she warned as the man stumbled to his feet, and with an angry snarl, lumbered toward her.

He toppled clumsily across her bed just as she leapt out—ears still reverberating from the incessant battering— and headed for the light switch near the bedroom door. CRA-aa-CK!

What was that?

She reached for the switch, fingers desperately groping through the darkness when a large, warm, calloused palm closed over them. She stiffened, recognizing the touch.

Mike!

The light came on just as she swung her right arm around, intending to hit him with the pistol butt. Temporarily blinded by the glare, she turned her face aside, simultaneously fending him off with her left arm. She felt his hard grasp on the gun, felt it slipping out of her clammy fingers.

"No-o-o." A high-pitched shriek echoed through the rooms. It was her voice.

"Elsa. Elsa, stop." Mike was yelling at her.

Elsa opened her eyes, still clawing at Mike's neck. Then she saw the man sprawled unconscious on her bed, a red wetness fanning out around him.

"Prentiss?"

———————

"I still can't believe it was Prentiss who killed Taylor." Elsa shuddered and huddled closer to Mike, enjoying his warmth.

He's just providing contact comfort, she told herself. She wasn't counting on it to last very long, but she was determined to enjoy every blissful moment of it. She deserved it, after last night.

Detective Shephard had confiscated her pistol. Since she'd only used it in self-defense, he was turning a blind eye to her "illegal possession" of it. Not without a long-winded lecture on gun safety, though.

Elsa's shot had narrowly missed Prentiss' chest, embedding itself just below his shoulder blade. The injury had caused him to lose consciousness, but he would still live. *If she'd killed him...*

Elsa shivered again, and Mike drew her closer into his arms.

"It's okay. You're all right. I'm just glad I was still awake last night. I saw someone sneak into your house, but your alarm never went off. That got me worried. I decided to head over. Then I heard the gunshot. That got me really worried. I put in a call to

Detective Shephard and—" He looked sheepish. "Well, under the circumstances, I felt justified in using my master key to let myself in. I'm sorry."

"No." Elsa shook her head. "Don't be." She huddled closer to him, glad he'd been there for her.

"But what I don't understand," she said a few minutes later, "is why Prentiss came after me. Or why he attacked Taylor." She glanced up at Mike. "I mean, why now?"

"I doubt we'll ever know," Mike replied, stroking her hair. "But I had heard stories about him. Didn't think anything of it. I just assumed he was inept around women."

"I should never have let him into the house."

When he'd taken apart the control panel for her alarm, Prentiss had re-routed Elsa's security system to his home server. That had enabled him to remotely disable her alarm before he attempted to break in.

Left unspoken was the thought that she ought to have trusted Mike instead. But his open admiration of their stunning new neighbor, and the sharp pang of jealousy it had caused Elsa, had prejudiced her against him.

"How could you have known?" Mike asked lightly. "You called in someone you thought would be the best person to help. Although"—with a finger under her chin, he gently swiveled her head around to face him—"just so you know, we locksmiths know a thing or two about alarms, too. Next time you need help, come to me, okay?"

His eyes—gray flecked with iridescent streaks of green—bore into hers, so intense, she could barely stand to look at him.

Her own eyes dropped. "Okay," she began to murmur, but her response died on her lips as his mouth closed over hers.

"I hope you don't have any plans for the day," he whispered, his lips warm against hers. "I want you to have Christmas dinner with my parents." He pulled back, and grinned. "I've been trying to ask you for nearly a week now. But every time we met, I'd get nervous and start babbling about other things. "

"Really?" Elsa drew back to gaze into his eyes. She couldn't believe it. Mike—tall, gorgeous Mike, who could have any woman he wanted—was asking her to meet his parents!

"Really," he confessed. "You seemed so cold and distant these past few days, I'd given up hope of getting you interested in me."

Elsa smiled, and laid her head on his chest. "Then, I guess I'm glad I was stupid enough to become Prentiss's target."

Our second-to-the-last story is by Albert Tucher, another name familiar to readers of Darkhouse Books volumes, and crime fiction in general. Set shortly before Prohibition was enacted, this story takes place at the Newark, New Jersey Public Library, and features Beatrice Winser, the real-life librarian who ruled that institution for decades.

If our author appears to know that library well, it is with good cause. Albert Tucher has worked as a cataloger at the Newark Public Library since the mid nineteen-eighties. Mr. Tucher is the author of numerous novels and short stories.

The Patience of the Dead

by Albert Tucher

"*Unmoeglich!*"

With those three syllables Beatrice Winser shed her burden of frustration. In English, the task would have taken time that she could not afford.

"Impossible."

"Outrageous."

"Unacceptable."

"Out of the question."

That single word encompassed them all. Closing the Newark Public Library in middle of the afternoon certainly called for a protest in the language of her diplomatic childhood in Germany.

Belatedly, she looked around to make sure no one had heard. The war that everyone had feared, and that President Wilson had promised to avoid, had become a reality, and overnight the language of Goethe had acquired a tinge of treason. Fortunately, the stairway was deserted.

She continued down to the basement of the library and found the man she sought in his tiny office.

"Please start securing the building, Mr. Bradshaw."

Her head of security glanced at the clock on the wall. Normally, the criticism implicit in his gesture would have called for a frosty look instead of an explanation, but nothing was normal about today.

"I have received a telegram from Trenton," she said.

She paused to let him consider the implication. The state government did not interfere lightly in the affairs of the city.

"The Department of Health has decreed an emergency. All public places where the citizens congregate must close to prevent the spread of the influenza. I have determined that the order covers the library."

"Has the mayor said so?"

His question bordered on insubordination, but it was also treacherous ground for her. At the first opportunity Mr. Bradshaw would head for his favorite saloon, wherever that was. She had never made an effort to find out where he cultivated his puffy, reddened aspect. Anything he told the proprietor would travel straight to the office of Mayor Gillen. It was well known that the city's drinking establishments served as the mayor's eyes and ears.

"Not to my knowledge," she said.

As he waited for her to say more, his expression grew bolder and more insolent. He expected her to add that the New Jersey state authorities outranked the mayor of Newark. The mayor frequently made it clear that he disagreed.

It took a subtler trap than that to catch her. She went on.

"Mayor Gillen has decreed that drinking establishments may make 'side door' sales, because of his contention that alcohol prevents the spread of the influenza. I make no judgment as to the scientific validity of his theory, but the Newark Public Library does not purvey alcoholic beverages. We are defenseless against contagion and must be prudent."

Her flanking attack left Mr. Bradshaw looked confused.

"Perhaps," she said, "you know of a physician who will pre-scribe Aristotle instead of alcohol."

The addendum was probably unwise, but she could not resist. She also felt confident that her words would be garbled beyond understanding by the time they reached the mayor.

"Please go search the book stacks for straggling patrons."

Mr. Bradshaw decided to drop his challenge for now. He left his office and headed for the stairs. Miss Winser followed him up to the lobby. From there she climbed the main stairway, which culminated at the doors to the reading room.

Let the grand stairways of the Old World serve royalty, Miss Winser always thought as she made the climb. In the New World the educated citizen was king.

Of course she knew the reality was more complicated. The mayor, for instance, regarded the Library as nothing more than a financial drain.

She passed through the double doors with their polished glass panes. Inside, at the urging of the library staff, patrons were gathering their belongings. None looked pleased, but all appeared resigned.

The epidemic was now a week old in Newark, and news to no one.

After the reading room had emptied, she descended the stairs to the lobby. Miss Winser's knees produced one of the twinges that had been coming regularly for several years. In less than six months she would turn fifty. The contrast between mind and body was growing every day.

She scolded herself for wasting mental energy on something she could not change, and continued past the Charge Desk in the lobby to the door that led to the Lending Department.

"All is in order," reported Miss Treuernicht, the head of the department.

"Very well. We shall gather in the lobby."

More than a hundred men and woman were clustered there. At least half had pulled on sanitary masks. Miss Winser doubted the efficacy of the measure, but said nothing. She preferred prudence to drunkenness, especially the officially sanctioned kind. She looked upward for inspiration but found nothing to help her. The sight of the magnificent stained glass skylight normally lifted her spirits. That it did not do so now told her how the events of the day had affected her.

"Good afternoon," she said, in her public speaking voice. "This is the first time I have ever found it necessary to close the library before the appointed hour. I hope it will be the last, but for now, we do what we must. Please go home safely, do your utmost to stay well, and wait for further instructions. That is all."

The departing staff filed out through the main entrance in sober silence. Last to leave was the newest custodian. The man had changed from his uniform into his suit, which had an eastern European cut. He always wore the same one. Even when she saw him in his uniform, his origin was apparent. He had the lined and wizened look of privation.

"Good day, Mr. Vladic."

She pronounced the Serbian name correctly, as "Vlah-ditch," which always made him smile with appreciation.

"Good day, Miss Winser." He, in turn, pronounced her name as "Vinser".

He pulled a sanitary mask over his face and followed the other assistants.

Miss Winser corrected herself. Mr. Vladic was not the last assistant to leave. She had not seen Mr. Bradshaw since sending him on his rounds. She started toward the main stairway, which would take her to the reading room, and from there to the Library's book stacks.

She paused for a moment to take in the deserted reading room with its wooden paneling and matching tables and chairs. All seemed ready for the return of the Library's patrons, but she had no way to know when that would be. The thought was ominous and unprecedented.

Still no Mr. Bradshaw. She had sent him to the book stacks, and so that was where she must look for him.

The stacks were almost a building within the building. Two stack levels occupied the same vertical space as each floor in the main building, meaning that six stacks corresponded to three floors. From the second floor she entered the third stack and started down to the first.

She did not find him there, nor in the second stack, nor the third. Miss Winser suppressed a grimace of sympathy for her knees and soldiered upward.

Stacks four and five were also deserted, which left stack six, where the history and travel books were shelved. She proceeded down the center aisle, looking left and counting off the subdivisions of European history: 942, Great Britain; 943, Germany; 944, France; 945, Italy; 946, Spain; 947, Russia; 948, Scandinavia.

And in 949, which encompassed a miscellany of the trouble spots of Europe, she found a dead man.

"How fitting."

The words hovered in the air. Miss Winser looked around, as if she might have spoken the words aloud. She decided she had not, but she blushed nonetheless and resolved never to share the thought with anyone. But the fact remained that 949 included the Balkans. Wasn't a dead man in Serbia the cause of the terrible war?

So it was fitting, if also horrifying.

It never occurred to her to wonder whether the man might still possess a hint of life. His profound and utter surrender to gravity left no doubt.

The silence deep in the book stacks was total. The design of the stacks isolated them from the already muted activities in the rest of the Library, and those activities had ceased on her order to evacuate the premises. Miss Winser found the stillness weighing on her ability to think. She admonished herself that passivity was unacceptable, and after a moment her mind began to work.

First, she decided, she must observe and remember as much as possible. The man lay face up on the floor, which showed signs of only moderately successful recent sweeping. This area, she recalled, was Mr. Vladic's responsibility.

The dead man's suit looked of Central European origin, and its familiarity nudged her like a rude elbow. Did she know the man? A sanitary mask covered the lower half of his face, and worse, the half that showed above the mask had already donned the anonymity of death.

The mask reminded her of the chaos in the city. Everywhere, people in their prime were dying where they lay. Could this be a case of contagion? It seemed unlikely that a desperately ill man had dragged himself to the Library, but the influenza sometimes came on like a surprise attack.

Her second task was to search the remainder of the 900's: Asia, Africa, North America, South America, and finally Australia and the Pacific. No further surprises awaited her, nor did Mr. Bradshaw. He must have taken one look at the dead man and run for his saloon, using an exit from the Library other than the front door.

And she knew who would soon be hearing about the dead man.

Her responsibility now was to call the police. She thought of her friend Captain Redmond, who commanded the local police precinct, and the thought of his support calmed her.

Her office was on the third floor, corresponding to stack six, which spared her more stairs. But when she reached her desk and lifted the telephone, the line was dead. Of course. The operators must be overwhelmed with emergency calls, and so were the police.

She could see no alternative. She would have to go to the local precinct house in person. The trip back down the stairs would be only the beginning of her ordeal.

At the front door she made sure lock up. No one but a dead man kept watch in the Newark Public Library today.

Around the corner on Orange Street she hesitated at her normal streetcar stop. She continued past it on foot, but she noted that other regular passengers had lined up as usual. Behind her she heard the trolley approaching. She frowned. The mayor should have stopped the streetcars, in which possibly infected people would press dangerously close to their fellow citizens. He had apparently decided to defy the state government on this matter as well.

Miss Winser refused to succumb to irresponsibility, nor could she afford to become ill. She trudged onward, grateful for her topcoat. The early October weather had become brisk.

Another two blocks brought her even with a saloon on the other side of the street. She had passed it a thousand times. When she rode the street car, such establishments barely impinged on her awareness, but today she could not ignore the disreputable men lining up at the side door, heedless of the broad daylight that exposed them to public scrutiny. She thought it might be her imagination, but the unclean odors of the alley seemed to reach across the street and importune her like a beggar. As she watched, the first man in the line handed something to someone inside the establishment. It must have been currency, because the man received a bottle in return.

Miss Winser turned her head away, but then she forced herself to look again. Her distaste would not make the unpleasant reality disappear. While most of the men in the alley looked ragged, some would have made an acceptable appearance behind a desk in any bank in the city. After only a week of the emergency ordinances, some citizens were abandoning civilized restraint.

These individuals obviously did not care how they complicated the efforts of Miss Winser and other citizens who opposed the looming prohibition of alcoholic beverages on the grounds of personal responsibility.

But that was an issue for another time. She continued toward the precinct station. Her legs were losing their resilience, and her feet hurt, but she pushed onward.

In the police station another eerie silence greeted her. The desk sergeant, a man named Fitzpatrick, seemed alone in the building. He listened to her report.

"The problem is, ma'am, there's no one to send."

"No one?"

"No, Ma'am. We're out picking up bodies all over the city. We've had to send coppers down to the South Ward. Things are even worse there."

"Can nothing be done for the poor man?"

"He'll have to wait his turn."

He anticipated her next question.

"Captain Redmond put his uniform on and went with every-body else."

That brought the emergency home to her as nothing else. She had never seen her friend in anything but a civilian suit. It was also awkward. With Captain Redmond she was sometimes able to smooth the jagged edges of official policy.

"Please send help when you can."

"Of course."

She could think of nothing else to do but return to the Library. She expected to spend the night there. It could be done. She kept a change of clothes and some imperishable, if unpalatable, food-stuffs in her office, and the staff lunchroom had a sofa. No one would be on hand to witness her undignified sprawl.

The impending night of solitude did not distress her. In fact, she felt a twinge of guilt. It was unseemly to take pleasure in any aspect of the emergency, but she could not deny her anticipation.

But the trip on foot back to Washington Street sapped her last of her endurance and removed any trace of a smile on her face. As she walked, the October twilight descended, and the half-light made the scene around the saloon resemble a circle of hell.

When she reached the Library she saw a group of four men standing at the main entrance. Three of them looked familiar, which made her suspect she had seen them loitering at City Hall. The fourth was never a welcome sight.

"Good evening, Miss Winser."

"Mr. Dwyer, how may I help you?"

Roscoe Dwyer called himself a lawyer. He had an office down-town on Commerce Street, but he had never represented a client that Miss Winser was aware of. He made his living doing things that Mayor Gillen could not be seen doing.

Such as taping a large sign to the Library's front door. Actually, one of his underlings was performing the chore.

"Quarantine," she read.

Dwyer watched for her reaction, which was why she resolved to give him nothing. He broke first.

"We have received a report that leads us to believe the Library is a hazard to the public health. Why did the report not come from you?"

She knew how to translate his words. The Library was really a hazard to the mayor's freedom to spend the Library's budget appropriation on other matters. The mayor was not above making the influenza do his work for him. With the Library closed, he might find it easier to make it stay closed.

"I have just come from reporting the dead man to the police," she said. "As any citizen should."

"You are closed until the mayor decides otherwise. Not the state. I emphasize that point."

Arguing with Dwyer would be futile. Despite his words, her proper appeal would be to the state authorities, and that would have to wait.

So would her decision about Mr. Bradshaw, who had obviously carried the news of the dead man to his saloon.

"How will you undertake to remove the poor man?" she asked Dwyer. "Since you have made him your responsibility."

"I will inform the health authorities. The city health authorities. They will come when they can."

Again she understood. Mr. Dwyer cared not about the poor man in the stacks, but about making difficulties for her.

Dwyer strode away with his henchmen. The all climbed into a Ford automobile parked at the curb. The vehicle swerved heedlessly into the path of a horse-drawn milk wagon. The milkman shook his fist and shouted his outrage.

That was increasingly the modern way of things. Even in the absence of a deadly epidemic she sometimes failed to recognize her city.

Miss Winser turned toward the front door. If Dwyer expected her to obey his quarantine herself, he was mistaken. She used her key and reentered her domain.

But once inside, she wondered what she could accomplish. She could think of nothing to do beyond returning to the poor dead man in stack six. She decided to spare her knees more wear and tear by using the elevator. It was one of her responsibilities, and she had learned to run it. Fortunately, the operators always left the car on the main floor when the Library was closed.

As she made for elevator, a sound failed at first to penetrate her awareness. In fact, she could not be sure she had heard anything. Was it an echo of her own movements, or was someone else walking about in the Library? She held still and listened, but the stealthy movements did not repeat themselves.

She stepped into the elevator car and grasped the operating lever. As the machinery hummed, and the indicator swept past each floor, Miss Winser caught herself hoping the dead man had somehow revived himself and departed.

But of course he had not solved her problem for her. He lay where he had fallen. Again, a feeling of familiarity nagged at her. She knew this man. If only she dared removed his mask, she could satisfy her curiosity, but the risk of contagion was too severe.

She looked away, and her eyes fell on the spine of a book on the nearest shelf.

949 G35. *The Balkan War,* by Gibbs.

The history section was large. Why had the dead man chosen this aisle?

And when she surveyed the shelves, she saw large gaps, as if the entire reading population of Newark had taken an interest in the Balkans. It was possible. The region had never loomed large in the awareness of most Americans, but now library patrons had good reasons to seek to understand the origins of the war in Europe.

That was the optimistic explanation, but she could think of another, darker possibility. And she could think of a way to test her suspicion. It would be arduous and time-consuming, but the mayor and his henchmen had left her with time.

With no one else to serve, the elevator was waiting for her. Miss Winser piloted it down to the main floor and crossed the lobby to the Lending Department. She went to the row of boxes of charge slips in the office behind the circulation desk. They were filed by the date the books had been borrowed. She took the first box and rested it on Miss Treuernicht's desk.

Miss Winser settled herself in the wooden swivel chair. Not for the first time she wished her budget would allow more comfort for the assistants. Library work would always be a Spartan business, but there should be limits.

She could do nothing about that now. Her task was to go methodically through the slips and look for 949 call numbers.

Several hours later an ungenteel growl from her stomach reminded her that her usual sandwich and fruit cup had become a distant memory. Her hunger would have to wait. She went on to the next box.

She found a few charge slips for books about Serbia, and the Balkans in general, but not enough to explain the large gaps on the shelf.

So where had the books gone?

She had left the door to the Lending office ajar, which enabled her to hear a pounding on the main entrance. Miss Winser stood. She paused to let a moment of light-headedness pass, along with a painful twinge in her lower back. Then she hastened to the door and opened it.

A man in uniform faced her. His military bearing made him look formidable and dangerous enough that she squelched a flare of alarm.

"Captain," she said after a moment. "I did not recognize you in uniform."

The two men in masks who stood behind Captain Redmond also loomed in their anonymity. They held something between them that had become too familiar to every Newark resident—a stretcher.

"Thank you for coming," she said. "I need you."

"I'm here by way of apology for not being available earlier."

The familiar voice reassured her, but a closer look told her what this visit was costing him. Captain Redmond looked beyond exhausted.

"There are certainly extenuating circumstances," she said. "And if this were another case of the influenza, I would beg you to go home and rest."

Normally he followed her thoughts as quickly as she formed them. But he could barely stand, and his mind was also working slowly.

"Wait," he said. "You did report a case of influenza."

"So I thought. I think I have a homicide here in the Library. I also believe I have the culprit when you need him. Come."

Today of all days she would not inflict the stairs on the Captain. She led him and his two men to the elevator. In stack six she pointed down at the man who waited with the patience of the dead.

In these times the living could use some of it as well.

"From the first moment I felt I should recognize him. And once I understood what happened here, I did. His name is Boris Kalman."

"How do you know him?"

"Professionally. He is, or was, a difficult man. I did not personally suffer much contact with him. In fact, I can recall seeing him only once, when he insisted on making some ridiculous complaint. But my assistants could tell you stories. Public libraries attract a certain number of persons with too much time and too little to do. Some entertain themselves with contention and disruption. And if they are shrewd, they can avoid crossing the threshold of what we will not tolerate."

"Kalman," said the Captain. "The name is familiar. We may have met him also. The police, I mean."

"I am unaware of what factors in his life brought him to Newark, but he was an Austrian, and he was not thriving here. That much is obvious from the amount of time he had to spend in the library."

Miss Winser pointed at the book shelves.

"I draw your attention to where we find him. 949, Balkan history."

"An ironic coincidence."

"Oh, there is no coincidence. I believe that when you examine the body, you will find that he died violently. Perhaps he was killed in a way that produced little visible evidence."

"That is possible, but why do you think so?"

"I will have to show you. But before we go, please note the empty shelves. Someone has taken a disproportionate interest in this part of the Library's collection."

Over the years of their acquaintance Captain Redmond had learned to follow where she led. He signaled his two men to wait with the body.

They rode the elevator down in silence, until it opened into a part of the Library that patrons never saw. Nothing about the basement implied learning or scholarship. It could as easily have represented the seams and sinews of a hospital, a military installation or a prison. Miss Winser kept lighting to a minimum, because the taxpayers should not be asked to carry an impossible burden. More lightbulbs would be more money spent to no purpose.

The effect was ominous, especially today. Miss Winser led the way to the custodians' quarters.

She pushed the door open.

The cot in the corner was definitely not Library issue, and the man who raised himself to one elbow should not have been there.

"Mr. Vladic," she said, "I trust those books are properly charged."

She pointed to a half dozen books stacked on the table.

The man got to his feet. He wore the trousers to his suit but only an undershirt above the waist.

"Not all of them, Miss Winser."

"Normally that would be cause for dismissal. But I believe there are extenuating circumstances. Am I correct?"

She waited, but the man had practiced his silences under tougher questioning than hers.

"I heard you moving about earlier. You have been living here in the basement. With your keys to the building you return with your cot after we close."

"This country is expensive," he said.

"And I assume you have to send money home."

It would be a rare refugee who did not.

"You are a war veteran?"

"I fought for Serbia."

"Tell me."

"I fought from the beginning. We repelled the Austrians twice. Then we could hold out no longer. We were forced to retreat. I nearly died of cholera in Albania while we were waiting for evacuation."

Miss Winser knew the history of war was the history of disease.

"And you came here."

She did not mean the words as a reproach, but he took them that way, probably because they echoed the reproaches in his own mind. Somehow the opportunity had arisen for him to escape, and he had taken it for the sake of his family. He could do more for them here, but she could barely imagine the agonies that abandoning kin and country must have caused him.

"I had no strength for more."

"We all have limits."

"But then I was called upon again. I had to save the books. From him."

"The books on Serbia."

"Yes."

"Because you thought Mr. Kalman was removing them from the shelves."

"I know he was. Austrian swine. The sufferings of the Serbs were there in the books for people to learn about. He claimed it was all lies."

"Did he know you were aware of his thefts?"

"I think he suspected. We argued many times about the war."

"When you should have been doing your work."

She exchanged glances with Captain Redmond and saw that he understood the implications of her remark. Vladic had not come to her with his suspicions, because Kalman had extorted silence from him.

The same silence grew, until Miss Winser asked, "What happened today?"

"I caught him putting books under his coat. To steal them. To hide the truth."

"And what did you do?"

"I used this."

An ice pick appeared in his right hand. It was not there, and then it was. Miss Winser took a step backward.

Even as she cringed at her own futility, she marveled at Captain Redmond's reaction. While she paused and analyzed, he surged forward, using his superior bulk to overwhelm the other man. He twisted Vladic's arm behind him.

The ice pick landed on the floor. With the knees and lower back of a youngster, Miss Winser stooped to remove the weapon from the fray. For a moment she felt like a woman of action. She decided not to examine the feeling too closely, or the silliness of it would become too plain.

Mr. Vladic seemed unperturbed.

"You were in no danger," he said. "I am done."

But Captain Redmond watched the other man carefully. Miss Winser found this glimpse of their reality as fascinating as it was unwelcome. She would not wish to live in a world devoid of trust or restraint.

But perhaps she already did. She found she was looking forward to informing Mr. Dwyer that the Library was free of contagion, and that she would reopen her domain at her discretion.

And she would await the next round of their contest, and deal with it when it came.

We close our anthology with a story featuring a brace of larcenous librarians named Hammer, Doom, and Carter. Although author Michael Guillebeau set out to write a short story, and did, he didn't stop there. Mad Librarian, a novel based on this story, recently won the 2017 Foreword Reviews Indie Award for Humor Book of the Year.

Mr. Guillebeau a mystery/humor writer whose story, Male Leary Comes Home, was published in the Darkhouse Books anthology, The Anthology of Cozy-Noir. He is the author of the novels, Josh Whoever, Shark's Tooth, A Study in Detail, and numerous short stories.

Keeping the Books

by Michael Guillebeau

The Maddington Public Library was the eminently normal center of an eminently normal small Southern city. Children sat at tables, reading politely. People smiled, politely. It was America at it's best.

At the center of the library, tucked between racks of books on CDs for people too lazy to actually read, and DVDs for people too lazy to even listen, was a door with a small sign that read, "Librarian Serenity Hammer. PRIVATE." Behind the closed door, Amanda Doom and Joy Carter sat in front of Serenity's desk while Serenity slumped behind the desk. All three of them stared at the desk, horrified.

The library rat was peeing in Serenity's coffee cup again. The big, brown-and-gray-and-dirt colored Alabama Roof Rat (Rattus Alexandrinus Geoffroy—you could find his picture in 598.097, *Peterson Field Guide to Mammals of North America*, on shelf 37) had climbed up on the desk while they were talking. Now he was balanced on Serenity's chipped "Books are Power" cup adding his input to the cup without giving his audience a second thought.

Doom—nobody called her Amanda—jumped up and snatched a book from the nearest stack and hurled herself straight up in the air, the book poised over her head like a sword of vengeance from the graphic novels she lived for. She screamed at the top of her arc and crashed down and smashed the cup on the rat, the cup shattering into shards, the rat motionless on his back with his feet sticking up in the air. Brown liquid and rat pee flew all over the messy stacks of papers, cards, books, CDs, pink message forms, invoices, yellow post-its and leftover food on Serenity's desk.

"Jesus Christ, Doom." Serenity dug a handful of paper napkins from her half-eaten Wendy's lunch and wiped down a now-stained book. She held it up and shook it at Doom. "Look at this. Look at this. That's a review copy from a local author. What am I supposed to tell Mike?"

Joy sat coiled into a chair in the corner looking like a fugitive from an Addams Family cartoon. Skinny white arms covered with tattoos poked out of the black Bocephus tank top the seventy-year-old woman was wearing. She glanced up sideways from studying her bare feet and said, "Tell him the rat gave him his first honest review."

Serenity glared and sopped up liquid.

"Ms. Hammer, he was peeing in your coffee," said Doom.

"I don't care. We protect things around here." She poked the dead rat in the middle of the mess.

The rat flipped over, hissed at her, and ran back into the clutter.

"Thank God Faulkner's all right," Serenity said. "He's good luck, and we need all the luck we can get."

Doom sat down. "Sorry, Ms. Hammer. I just don't think…" She paused and added, "No disrespect intended, Ms. Hammer. I know you're in charge here, but this is supposed to be the city library, not a zoo."

"What it is, is a dump," said Joy. "Broke toilets, a headless tin man in the playground from where kids were throwing rocks at him. And slow WiFi." She studied a fresh blue tattoo on her pale arm.

Serenity stuffed the wet towels in the trash and sat down. "What it is, is the best we can do with what we've got. This city needs us and our books, whether it knows it or not."

She pulled up a coffee-and-rat-pee-stained sheet and squinted at it. "Let's get back to budgets."

"Rat should have peed on the budgets," said Joy.

Serenity shook liquid off the paper. "Thanks to Doom, he did. Like everybody else."

"How bad?" asked Doom.

"Bad. The council is divided between our backers, who think that, since we're already one of the best small libraries in the South,"—Joy snorted and Serenity glared at her— "we don't need more money."

"And then the Evil One," said Doom.

"Councilman Bentley's not evil," said Serenity. "He just wants to zero out the library budget and give everyone in the city Amazon discounts."

"Evil."

Serenity stared at the numbers floating on the brown-stained paper. "Maybe. In any case, we've got to live with this. I don't see a way out—either we cut back on buying books or we cut salaries. Or close. And that's a real possibility if we don't do something."

Doom jumped up and clenched her fist in the air. "We don't cut books. Books are our power."

Serenity said, "Well, look around you. We're the only three full-time paid employees left. We're each doing two jobs. We are barely keeping up with getting books to people as it is. And it's getting worse: because we're so short-handed, we're receiving more complaints. If we can't do something soon, we won't have time to do anything but handle complaints."

Doom stood up and stabbed a set of dog-eared blueprints that covered one wall. "That's why we've got to push harder for a better future. What does your precious budget say about the library expansion we all know this city needs?"

Serenity closed her eyes. "Not happening this year."

Doom slapped the blueprints. "No tutoring area for kids and teachers?"

"No."

Doom slapped them harder. "No incubator for writers and entrepreneurs, small creators who can use the library to form the creative core of the city?"

"No."

Joy mumbled. "Not even the coffee shop?"

Serenity opened her eyes but couldn't look at them. "Maybe next year."

Doom uttered an un-library-like expletive and dropped herself back into her chair. "We're not giving up books. Cut my salary."

"Not mine," said Joy. "Got a spot on my stomach just itching for skin art of the Last Supper with the masters of rock and roll as disciples."

"I'm not cutting anybody's salary, Doom. Not again." Serenity sighed. "I don't know what I'm going to do, but we've all got more work than we can get done as it is. Let's get back to it. This is my problem, not yours. I don't know why I called a meeting just to bitch."

The two women rose and made for the door. Serenity stood staring at the blueprint until they left. Eyes watering, she turned her back and picked up a spare coffee cup. She opened a drawer and took out a bottle of Myers rum and filled the cup half-full. Stared at it and wondered what she was doing here. Then she added the other half. She put the bottle back and turned around. Doom was standing there looking at her with a great sadness.

"That's not coffee," she said.

Serenity took a long sip and the smooth, sweet burn took her away to a Florida panhandle beach with white sands and gentle waves.

"Ain't rat pee either," she said.

Councilman Bentley was a pediatrician popular with every parent who wanted someone tough on their kids. Which left him plenty of time to be a city councilman, and be tough on the money-wasting bureaucrats who worked for the city.

"Lie-brarian." He waved a finger at Serenity's face. She had come to his office to discuss library funding. He had her sitting on an examining table in his office, making her sit there in her blue business suit on the crackling sanitary paper like she was a child faking a sore throat to get out of school.

"You're just a lie-brarian, tell any lie to keep your feather-bedding government job."

Serenity thought about telling him what he could do with her job. Thought for the millionth time about giving up and going South to the beach. At forty-five, she still had the legs to get a cocktail waitress job on the Panhandle and fight off old men at night and bake her troubles away on the hot sand during the day. Probably pay more, and be a hell of a lot more fun.

She had just the right comment for Bentley on the tip of her tongue. She opened her mouth, ready to let the words fly like cannonballs. Then she thought about how quickly Bentley would find a TV news camera. On screen, he would turn into a kindly grandfather shocked at what the librarian had said to him. He would use her comment to tear down the library. She could run away to the beach, but her books could not.

"No sir," she said. "You'll see that the budget I'm submitting complies with everything the council has directed me to—"

"Lies! Lies! Serenity girl, you sat there in the council chambers and promised that this expansion was cancelled."

"No, sir. The council suspended expansion funding for this year. You'll see that the only token funding the expansion has is just from our Special Projects fund, which comes from donations. No taxpayer money involved—"

"Lies. And who do you think makes those donations? Taxpayers." He waved the finger in her face again and Serenity wanted to reach out and break it off. "We are going to reduce your government-boondoggle library until it's small enough to drown in a bathtub."

He scrawled his name at the bottom of a form and shoved it at her.

"Pay your deductible on the way out."

Serenity scanned the paper and looked up at him. "You're billing this as an office visit?"

"Only way I can get paid for your visit."

Serenity opened her mouth to object but he talked over her.

"What? You want me to take your temperature?"

<hr>

Serenity had Doom in her office.

Doom waved her finger at Serenity. "Ms. Hammer, I worship you and I know you're my boss."

Serenity took a sip of the mug. "Why do I always know that, when you start like that, I'm about to catch righteous bloody hell?"

Doom was standing with her feet apart. One hand was on her hip, on top of her tight red Superman shirt worn with skinny designer jeans. She dropped the hand that had been pointing at Serenity like a loaded gun.

She said. "It's still not right. We work for books and readers. You told me so when you hired me."

"I know I told you that, but Bentley's right," Serenity said. "He's an asshole, but he's right. That's what the council voted."

"Any man that's trying to imprison books is wrong," said Doom, with both hands on her hips. She threw her head back and yelled. "Freeee-doom."

Serenity ignored that. "Doom, he's right: We're city employees. And the city wants you in the computer room—"

"You mean the children's reading room."

"—Which the city has made us convert to hold the city's computer servers. As long as the severs are here—and as long as you bragged about having a computer science minor—Bentley has cancelled the contract for maintaining that software, and wants you to do the maintenance in-house. In your spare time."

"And you're just going to give in to him?"

Serenity picked up her coffee mug and took a long sip that was dark and mind-clouding. "I work for them. You work for me."

Doom waved her arm at the closed door. "Look, I had other job offers. You promised me that we were going to turn Maddington into Book City."

Serenity took an even longer pull of the rum. "I made a lot of promises. Turns out I'm just a lie-brarian. Get your ass out to the computer room."

Doom drew herself up into her full superhero pose, fists clenched and skinny arms tense at her side like she was going to destroy a small building with her hands. Then she slumped and dragged herself out the door.

Thirty minutes later, Serenity followed Doom into the computer room.

"Children's reading room," corrected Doom when Serenity called it the computer room.

"Yeah." Serenity looked at the tiny children's desks and chairs piled up in the corner like discarded toys to make room for the servers. She felt old and tired and beaten. "Look, Doom."

"Amanda. I want to be called Amanda if I'm just a computer jockey instead of goddess of the books."

"Amanda. I wanted to apologize to you for snapping at you back there."

Doom was slumped over the one desk in the middle of the room, her hands on the keyboard and red-rimmed eyes locked on the monitor. "No need, Mistress Hammer. I am your slave. I get it."

"Oh, for crying out loud. You're nobody's slave. It's just a job, not a mission from God. Look, keeping up the city's software is important, too. The city bills all the utilities and cable TV and internet services through this."

Doom stabbed the screen. "You think this is important? Look at what I'm working on now: A fraction of a cent. You've taken me away from Jane Austen and put me to work justifying pennies. Less than pennies. See, this person owes the city one hundred seventy-five dollars and thirty-four cents for their electricity last month. Actually, they owe 34.12 cents. So the city bills them for thirty-five cents. At the end of the day, those fractions get swept into a fund called 'Residuals' and that account has to have a justification written at the end of the month explaining where this money came from, since it really isn't owed to the city."

Serenity started to take another drink, looked at the screen, and then set her cup down. "So this is money—the fractions of a cent, anyway—that the city is legally charging, but not really entitled to?"

"Yeah. Instead of teaching children to read the book 'Robin Hood,' you've got me robbing from the rich and the poor and giving the money to the Bentleys of the world. I don't even want to be called a librarian anymore, just put 'faceless bureaucratic thief' on my paycheck."

"Yeah," Serenity said. Then she stood up straighter. "No. Wait. Yeah."

She pulled one of the children's seats off the stack and sat on it with her knees up around her face. Stared at the screen and mumbled.

"Yeah," she said. "Yeah. Yeah. Yeah."

"Go sing somewhere else."

"No, listen to me, Doom."

"Amanda."

"Whatever. Listen, I read a book once."

"Is this supposed to be like a line from a movie? 'Mister, I read a book once.' By the end of the story we're all inspired and accept our roles as little cogs in the great wheel of life?"

"Hell, no. Listen: In this book, a guy who worked at a bank took all the fractions of a cent, and rolled them into his account."

"Good for him." Amanda stopped her typing and turned to look at Serenity. "Oh."

"Let me get Joy in here."

Serenity ran out into the main room. Joy was checking out a stack of books to a woman with five kids. Serenity scooped up the books and dumped them on the woman.

"Free book day," she said. "Take what you need, bring them back when you're done." She looked at the line of nice people waiting politely to check out books. "Free book day. Take anything."

She snatched Joy up by one elbow and dragged her, complaining, into the computer room and closed the door.

"Joy, you used to be a cop, right?"

"Yeah, till they fired me for accidentally setting a body on fire. Was a blessing in disguise, though. Washington PD had a no-tattoos policy. I could never have found my true calling as God's canvas if—"

"Yeah, yeah," said Serenity. "I really want to hear that story—again—sometime. Right now, we need legal advice. The city is billing customers for fractions of cents that they don't owe. If that money went to a different city account, like to the library Special Projects Fund, it wouldn't be embezzling?"

"No, I guess—"

Doom said, "It would be like un-embezzling."

"Yeah," said Serenity. "That's it."

Joy shrugged. "No crime against un-embezzling that I know of."

Serenity turned back to Doom. "You think you could do that, Amanda?"

"Oh, hell yeah. And it's Doom."

Serenity and Joy peeked over Doom's shoulder while she worked and chanted, "Free-Doom, Free-Doom." When she was finished, she said, "There. Go to your office and check the Special Projects fund.

They marched out in a line like three excited ducks. Marched through the main room and ignored the chaos as the nice people of Maddington fought over books like they were designer dresses at a penny-a-dress sale. Serenity patted a little girl running with a stack of Seuss books as tall as her head.

"Read them all, dear," she said.

Serenity reached over and separated the garden club president and the Baptist minister's wife who were fighting over a DVD of *Scareface*.

"Dear, this is too violent for either of you. You want…" she rummaged through a pile of books now on the floor and came up with one of Debra Webb's steamiest romance books and handed it to the garden club president… "this." She dove into the pile again. "And you, dearie, you really need this." And handed the Baptist minister's wife a copy of *The Electric Kool-Aid Acid Test*.

They marched into Serenity's office and clustered around her computer. The budget was still up on the screen. All three heads leaned in.

"Jesus," said Serenity without taking her eyes off of the screen.

"Christ," said Doom.

Joy said something considerably stronger. The other two looked at her and she shrugged. "I'm not religious."

Serenity clicked the refresh button and the Special Projects Fund grew. A lot. They pulled their heads back and looked at each other.

Serenity said, "In the words of our immortal president Richard Nixon, we could do this, but it would be wrong."

They paused, and then all three of them laughed harder than they had laughed in a long time.

The rat crawled out of his hole and sat on a copy of *All the King's Men* and studied them.

———

Bentley stood in the doorway to Serenity's office with his hat in his hand, looking uncomfortable.

"Councilman," said Serenity.

She wore a big fake smile. "So nice to see you." She pushed her designer sunglasses back and waved at a chair. "We haven't visited in a while."

Bentley took in Serenity's new office, with a big mahogany desk set up on a platform so visitors had to look up to Serenity. A signed photograph of Serenity with the governor hung on the wall behind her desk. Bentley kept an eye on her as he sat down.

"It's been a long time since I've been here," he said. "Your office is different than it used to be. And you don't come to my office anymore."

"My temperature's been fine. And I've been busy."

"Yeah," he looked around, still trying to regain his balance. He remembered why he came here. "I haven't authorized a lot of what's going on here. Those uniforms, for one thing."

"Uniforms?" Serenity laughed. "Oh, you mean the 'MAD' shirts? Those are just sort of a joke. Back before our upgrades, we only had one stamp for books. 'MAD,' the abbreviation for the Maddington library. The 'D' was faded, but we couldn't afford a new stamp. Doom thought it would be funny to make up some tee shirts with the old stamp on them."

Bentley pointed a finger. "They're not just cheap tee shirts. Your assistant out there is wearing one that probably cost a hundred dollars, looks like something for a superhero or a model from Paris, France."

"Probably more than a hundred. You can buy one yourself in the new gift shop. Better yet, I'll buy you your own shirt. It'll match the one your wife bought last week. Everybody in the city is buying them."

He looked out the window at the construction crew. "There's a lot of stuff here I haven't authorized."

He looked past Serenity, horrified. "There's a big rat behind you."

"That's just Faulkner."

Bentley leaned forward and squinted. "The rat has his own tiny pool and exercise wheel. He's sitting in a lounge chair, staring at me."

Serenity waved Bentley away. "We take care of our own. Now tell me all about your problems." She put her fingertips together and leaned her head toward him, staring at him through the dark glasses and giving him the same look she'd seen from politicians and mob godfathers on TV.

"The gift shop expansion," he said. "The new children's wing. Free tutoring for all students. GED training. I didn't authorize any of this."

"You left out the co-working space for entrepreneurs, service centers for in-house venture capitalists." She gave a small nod to the wall with an architect's sketch of a multi-story building. "Once we get the new expansion finished, every major bank is going to relocate here and take advantage of our free computer services." She pointed to a framed cover of Forbes on another wall. "Really, councilman, you aren't keeping up. Maddington is the hottest city in the South. Read the headline: 'A City Built on Books.' And every dime of it paid for by contributions. If you have a complaint, take it up with the mayor. Or the governor."

Bentley sat up straight and started to say something, but the door opened and Joy came in and sat a long box on the desk. She grabbed her shirt.

"Hey, Serenity, I have to show you this."

She started to pull up her MAD tee shirt and Bentley screamed a little-girl scream.

"Oh, for crying out loud," Joy said. "You've seen old-woman flesh before. I know your wife."

Joy turned so they both could both see her naked stomach and the fresh, multi-color tattoo of The Last Supper on it.

Serenity took off her sunglasses. "That's Shakespeare where Christ's supposed to be." She squinted. "Faulkner. Chandler. Hemingway. Jane Austen. Wait, who's that one?"

"Pat McGroin. He wrote a very sexy book that I discovered at thirteen that changed my life. Really just cheap porn. Nothing we'd have in here."

Serenity shrugged. "If it changed a girl's life, who knows? Maybe we'll get a copy." She turned back to Bentley and smiled a dazzling smile. "You never know what we might do next."

Joy left and Bentley eyed the box. "What's that?"

"Present for you." Serenity smiled, took it out of the box and handed it to him. "Horse thermometer."

He dropped it like it was a snake. Then he waved a finger at her.

"There is something going on down here and I'm going to get to the bottom of it. Serenity girl, you better—"

Serenity leaned over and stared coldly down at Bentley.

"Call me Hammer."

They were gathered in Serenity's office: Doom in her haute-couture superhero costume, Joy in a crop-top MAD tee shirt to show off her tattoo, Serenity in a power suit with a small, tasteful MAD broach on the lapel.

Joy had taken to wearing an accountant's green eyeshade at work. She said, "So that's the report," and looked up from her papers. "We've got all the money we need for what we've got planned."

Serenity nodded curtly. "Then let's plan more. Grow or die."

Doom said, "We've got a couple of growth opportunities. A genetics firm approached me about adding a wing for their headquarters here. When I told them I wasn't sure, they offered a ten percent kickback."

Joy said, "If anyone wants to hear me say this anymore, like I've said it a hundred times lately, that one's clearly illegal."

Serenity said, "Not if we own the police. Make it twenty percent."

"We may own the police," said Joy. "But Bentley's hired an ex-FBI agent to look into us."

Serenity drummed her fingers on the desk. "Ideas?"

Doom said, "Maybe. We've got all the cable TV records. Saturday nights, when his wife has her bridge game, he rents movies."

"So?"

"Movies like, 'Debbie Does Decatur', something called, 'Meat with Feet.'" Doom shuddered.

"OK," said Serenity. "We can blackmail him if we need to. What if that doesn't scare him off? What we are doing here is too important to let one man stop it."

Doom's eyes were bright and excited. "I've got some ideas I'm working on. Something to use the power of books to take care of anyone—permanently—who tries to stop us."

Joy looked at Doom, horrified. Serenity folded her hands back into a church steeple and pursed her lips. "Ladies, we are going to have to draw a line." She paused and studied the wall while Doom and Joy waited.

"Somewhere," she said.

The rat scampered out and climbed into the big rhine-stone-encrusted wheel behind Serenity and started running, faster and faster until the stones blurred into one big sparkle.

About This Book

The typeface in this book is 11.5 Garamond and Helvetica (for the headings). It was laid out using Adobe InDesign software and converted to PDF for uploading to the printing facility.

About Darkhouse Books

Darkhouse Books is dedicated to publishing entertaining fiction, primarily in the mystery and science fiction field. Darkhouse Books is located in Niles, California, an inadvertently-preserved, 120 year old, one-sided railtown, forty miles from San Francisco. Further information may be obtained by visiting our website at www.darkhousebooks.com.

Sanctuary
A Collection of Poetry and Prose
Edited by Susannah Carlson & Peter Bradbury

Also Available from Darkhouse Books

Black
Coffee
Stories from the
Noir Side of Town
Edited by
Andrew MacRae

Duck Lessons
James M. LeCuyer

www.ingramcontent.com/pod-product-compliance
Lightning Source LLC
Chambersburg PA
CBHW030610170726
48283CB00002B/538